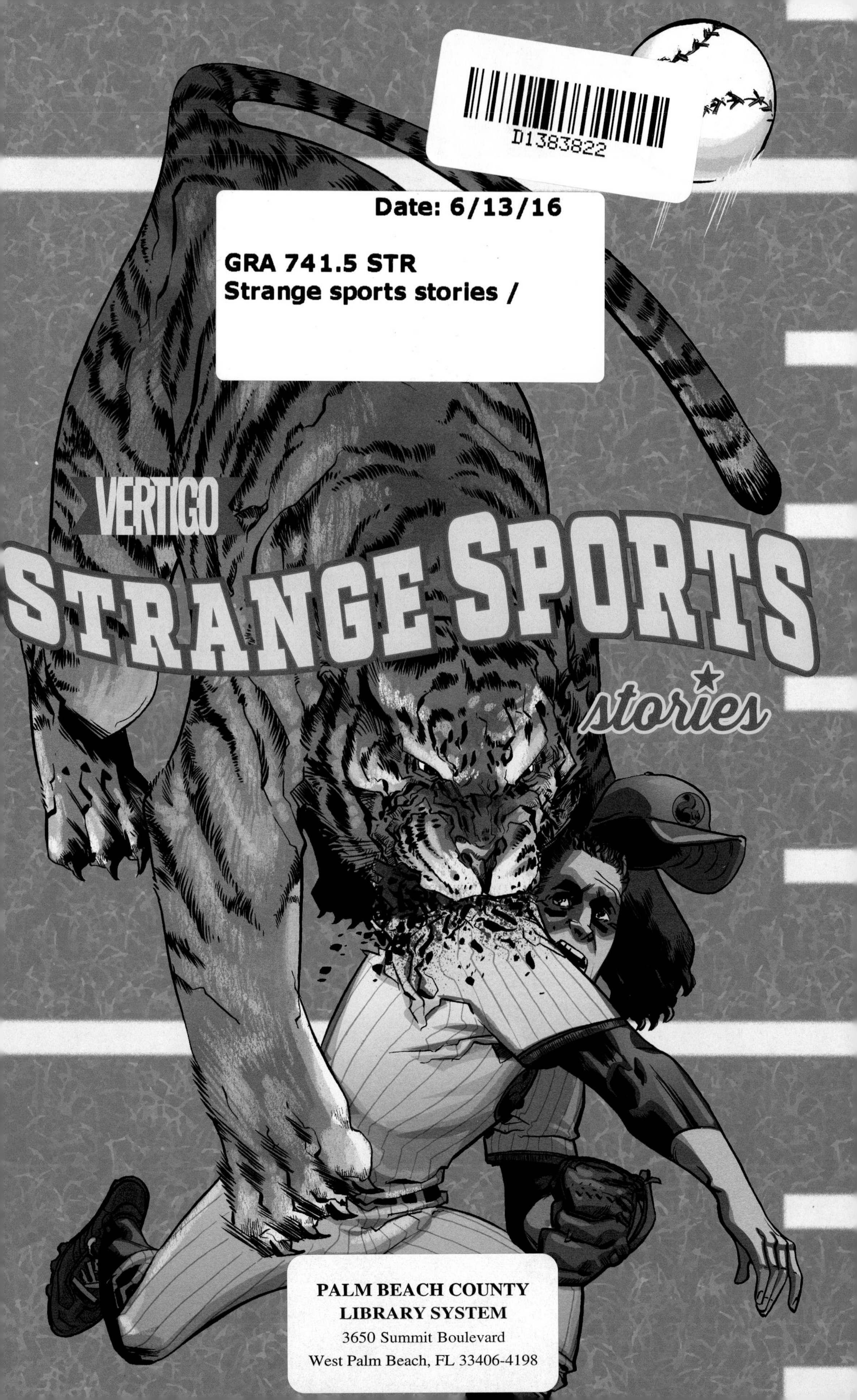
VERTIGO
STRANGE SPORTS
stories

VERTIGO

STRANGE

WRITERS

Lauren **Beukes** Ivan **Brandon**
Brian **Buccellato** Amy **Chu**
Nick **Dragotta** Mark **Finn**
Tim **Fish** Monica **Gallagher**
Dale **Halvorsen** Gilbert **Hernandez**
Chris **Hunt** Ben **McCool**
Brandon **Montclare** Paul **Pope**
CM **Punk** Aubrey **Sitterson**
Gabe **Soria** Genevieve **Valentine**

ARTISTS

Natacha **Bustos** Rich **Clark**
Michael J. **DiMotta** Nick **Dragotta**
Max **Dunbar** Tim **Fish**
Tana **Ford** Gilbert **Hernandez**
Joseba **Larratxe** Megan **Levens**
John **Lucas** Andy **MacDonald**
Christopher **Mitten** Ande **Parks**
Paul **Pope** Darick **Robertson**
Ronald **Wimberly** Amei **Zhao**

SPORTS ★ stories

COLORISTS

Giulia **Brusco** Natacha **Bustos**
Eva **de la Cruz** Michael J. **DiMotta**
Nick **Filardi** Joseba **Larratxe**
Lee **Loughridge** Patricia **Mulvihill**
Shay **Plummer** Amei **Zhao**

LETTERERS

Wes **Abbott** Corey **Breen**
Pat **Brosseau** Sal **Cipriano**
Jared K. **Fletcher** John J. **Hill**
Carlos M. **Mangual** Tom **Napolitano**
Clem **Robins** Dezi **Sienty**
Saida **Temofonte** Steve **Wands**

COVER ARTIST

Mike **Mitchell**

ORIGINAL SERIES COVERS

Paul **Pope** (Issue #1) Dave **Johnson** (Issue #2)
Wes **Craig** (Issue #3) Celia **Calle** (Issue #4)

WILL DENNIS GREG LOCKARD MOLLY MAHAN JAMIE S. RICH ROWENA YOW Editors – Original Series
JEB WOODARD Group Editor – Collected Editions
SCOTT NYBAKKEN Editor – Collected Edition
DAMIAN RYLAND Publication Design

SHELLY BOND VP & Executive Editor – Vertigo

DIANE NELSON President
DAN DIDIO and **JIM LEE** Co-Publishers
GEOFF JOHNS Chief Creative Officer
AMIT DESAI Senior VP – Marketing & Global Franchise Management
NAIRI GARDINER Senior VP – Finance
SAM ADES VP – Digital Marketing
BOBBIE CHASE VP – Talent Development
MARK CHIARELLO Senior VP – Art, Design & Collected Editions
JOHN CUNNINGHAM VP – Content Strategy
ANNE DEPIES VP – Strategy Planning & Reporting
DON FALLETTI VP – Manufacturing Operations
LAWRENCE GANEM VP – Editorial Administration & Talent Relations
ALISON GILL Senior VP – Manufacturing & Operations
HANK KANALZ Senior VP – Editorial Strategy & Administration
JAY KOGAN VP – Legal Affairs
DEREK MADDALENA Senior VP – Sales & Business Development
JACK MAHAN VP – Business Affairs
DAN MIRON VP – Sales Planning & Trade Development
NICK NAPOLITANO VP – Manufacturing Administration
CAROL ROEDER VP – Marketing
EDDIE SCANNELL VP – Mass Account & Digital Sales
COURTNEY SIMMONS Senior VP – Publicity & Communications
JIM (SKI) SOKOLOWSKI VP – Comic Book Specialty & Newsstand Sales
SANDY YI Senior VP – Global Franchise Management

Logo design by **JARED K. FLETCHER**

STRANGE SPORTS STORIES

Published by DC Comics. Compilation Copyright © 2015 DC Comics. All Rights Reserved.

Originally published in single magazine form as STRANGE SPORTS STORIES 1-4. Copyright © 2015 DC Comics.
All Rights Reserved. VERTIGO and all characters, their distinctive likenesses and related elements featured in
this publication are trademarks of DC Comics. The stories, characters and incidents featured in this publication
are entirely fictional. DC Comics does not read or accept unsolicited submissions of ideas, stories or artwork.

DC Comics 2900 West Alameda Avenue, Burbank, CA 91505. Printed in the USA.
First Printing. ISBN: 978-1-4012-5864-1.

Library of Congress Cataloging-in-Publication Data

Strange sports stories /Buccellato, Brian. Paul Pope.
pages cm
ISBN 978-1-4012-5864-1 [paperback]
1. Sports—Comic books, strips, etc. I. Buccellato, Brian. II. Pope, Paul.
PN6720.S76 2015
741.5'973—dc23
2015031190

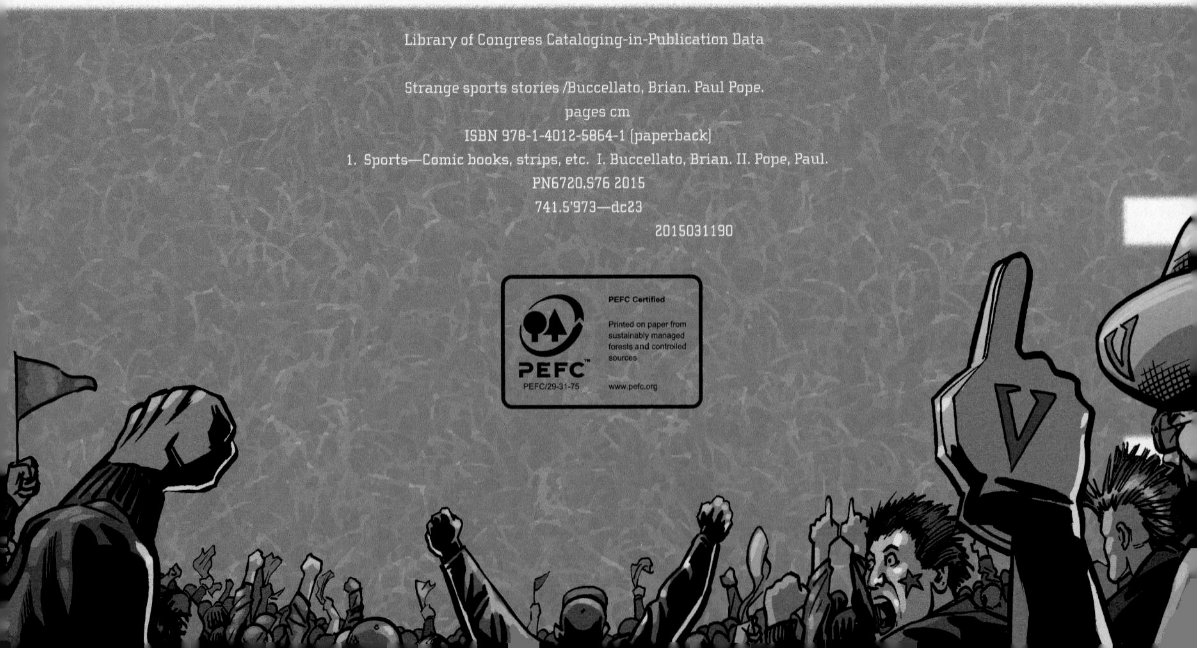

VERTIGO

STRANGE SPORTS stories™

FOURTH DOWN AND DEATH!

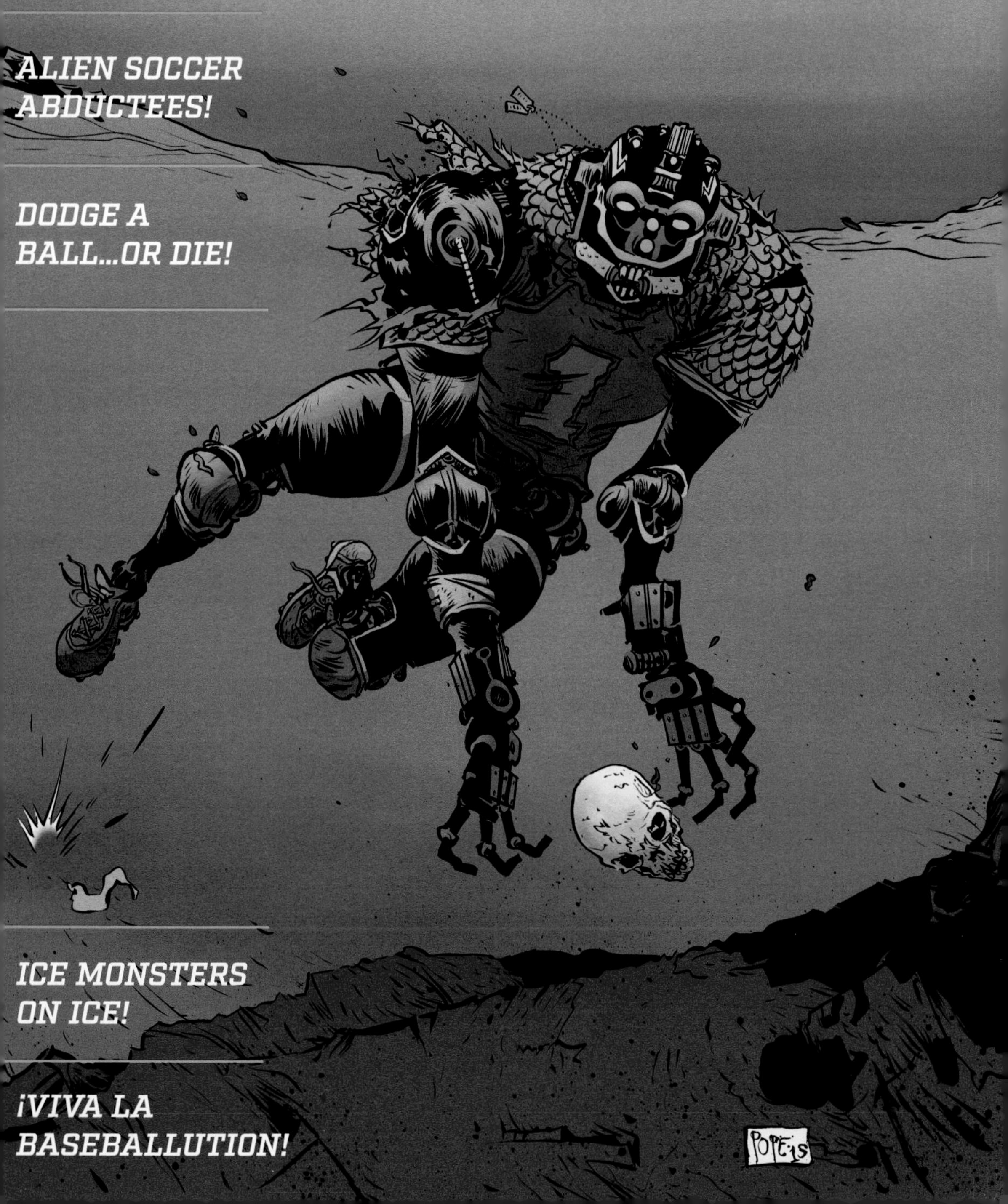

ALIEN SOCCER ABDUCTEES!
DODGE A BALL...OR DIE!
ICE MONSTERS ON ICE!
¡VIVA LA BASEBALLUTION!
POPE '15

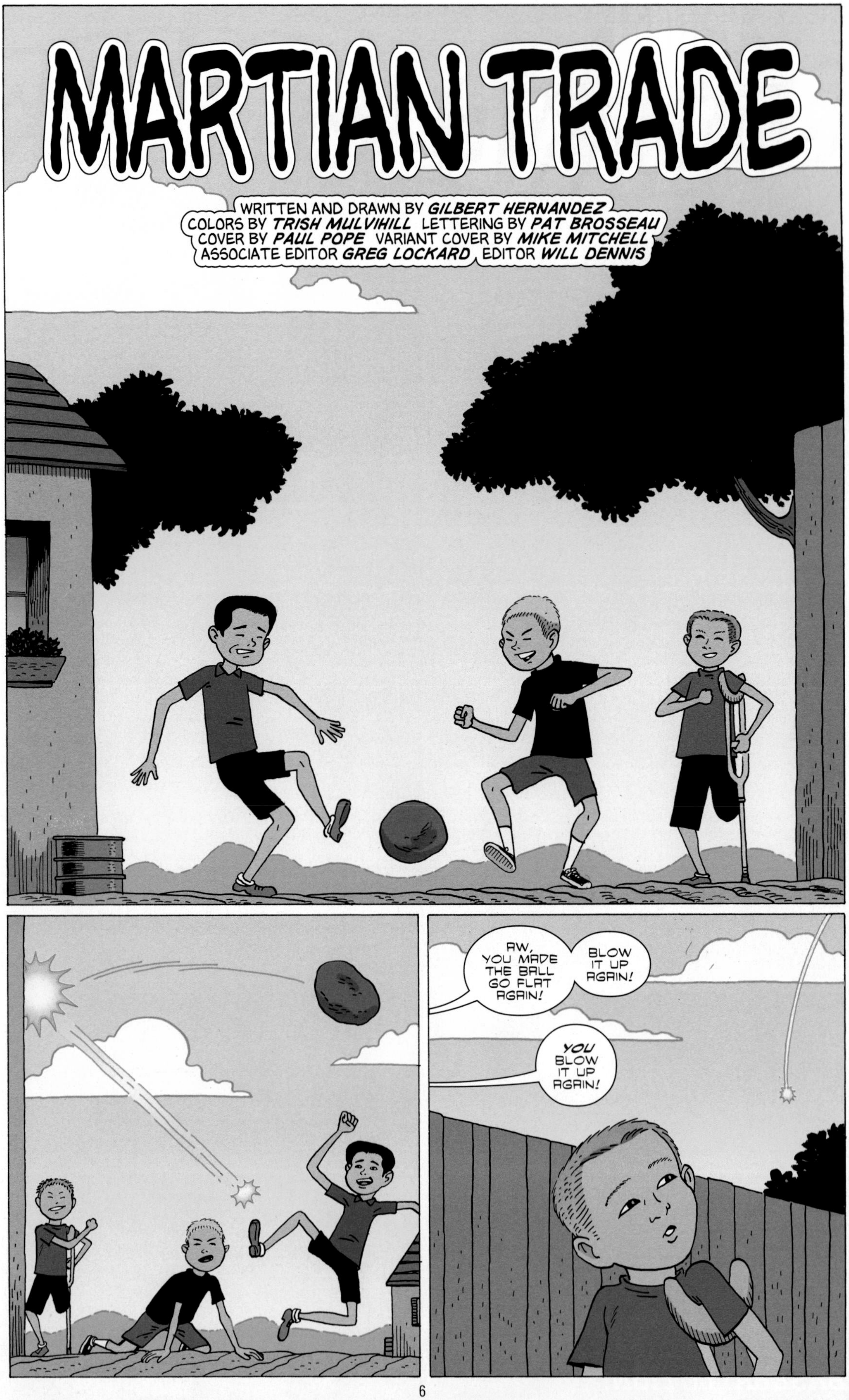
MARTIAN TRADE
WRITTEN AND DRAWN BY GILBERT HERNANDEZ
COLORS BY TRISH MULVIHILL LETTERING BY PAT BROSSEAU
COVER BY PAUL POPE VARIANT COVER BY MIKE MITCHELL
ASSOCIATE EDITOR GREG LOCKARD EDITOR WILL DENNIS
AW, YOU MADE THE BALL GO FLAT AGAIN!
BLOW IT UP AGAIN!
YOU BLOW IT UP AGAIN!

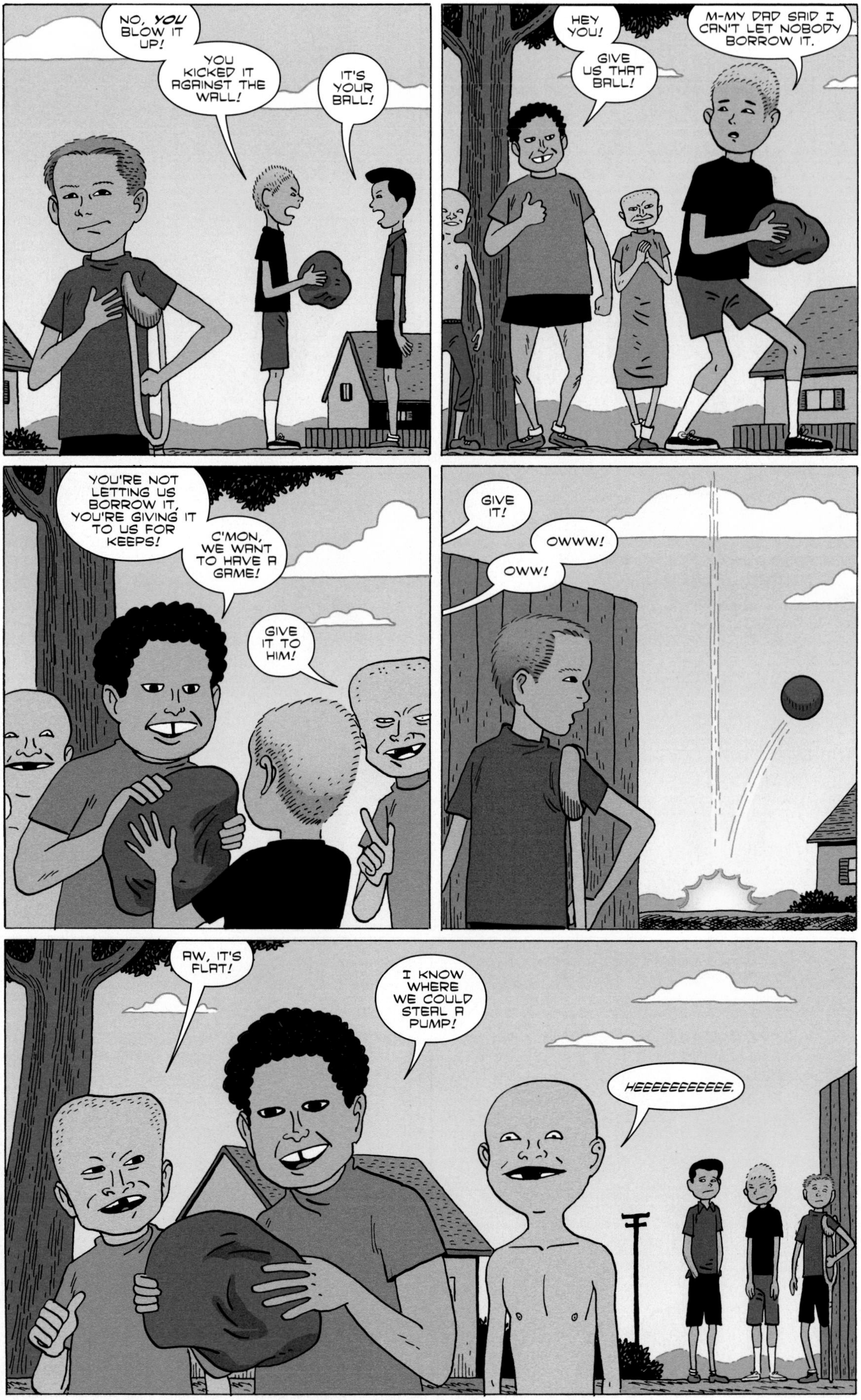
NO, YOU BLOW IT UP!
YOU KICKED IT AGAINST THE WALL!
IT'S YOUR BALL!
HEY YOU!
GIVE US THAT BALL!
M-MY DAD SAID I CAN'T LET NOBODY BORROW IT.
YOU'RE NOT LETTING US BORROW IT, YOU'RE GIVING IT TO US FOR KEEPS!
C'MON, WE WANT TO HAVE A GAME!
GIVE IT TO HIM!
GIVE IT!
OWWW!
OWW!
AW, IT'S FLAT!
I KNOW WHERE WE COULD STEAL A PUMP!
HEEEEEEEEEEE.

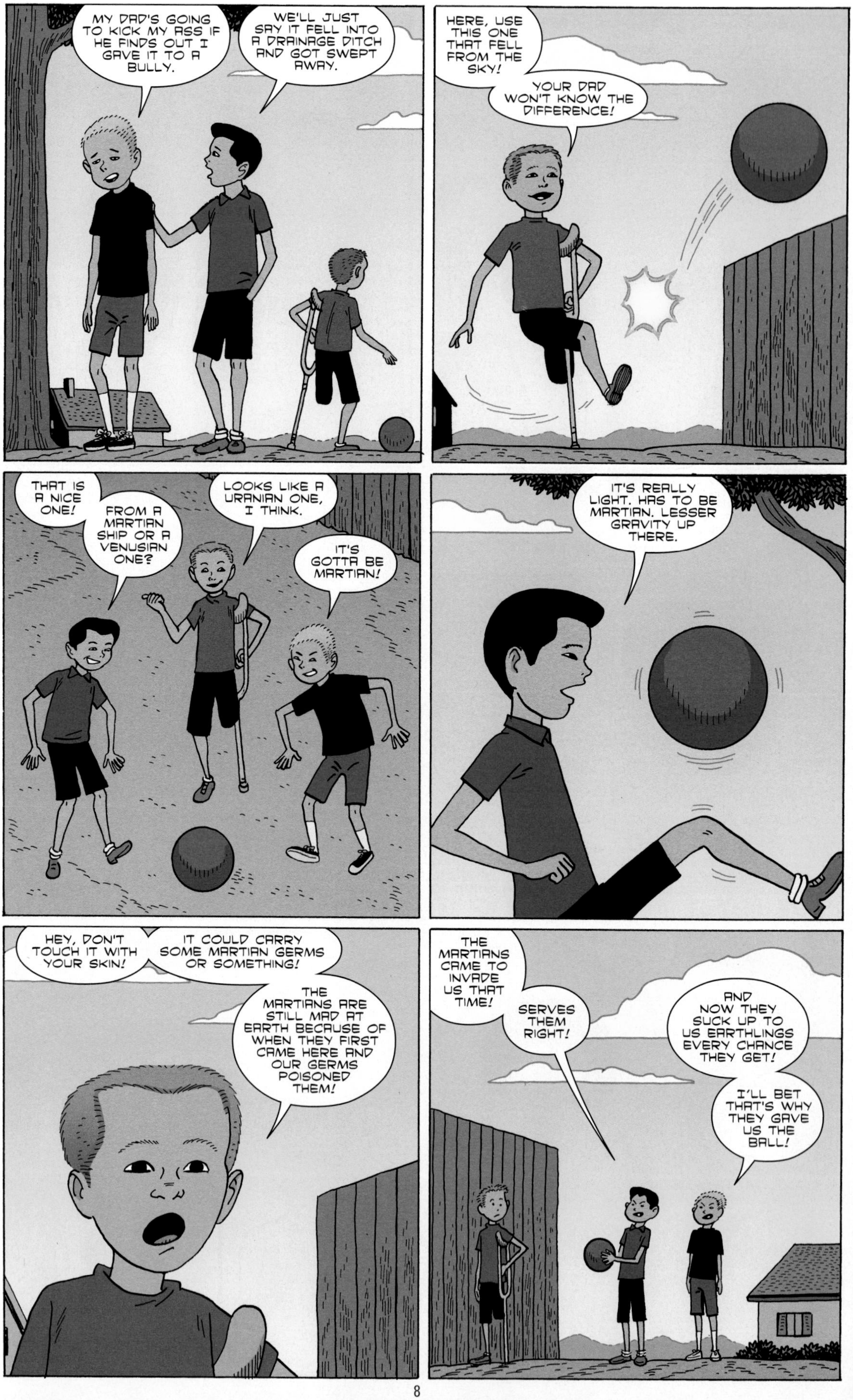
MY DAD'S GOING TO KICK MY ASS IF HE FINDS OUT I GAVE IT TO A BULLY.
WE'LL JUST SAY IT FELL INTO A DRAINAGE DITCH AND GOT SWEPT AWAY.
HERE, USE THIS ONE THAT FELL FROM THE SKY!
YOUR DAD WON'T KNOW THE DIFFERENCE!
THAT IS A NICE ONE!
FROM A MARTIAN SHIP OR A VENUSIAN ONE?
LOOKS LIKE A URANIAN ONE, I THINK.
IT'S GOTTA BE MARTIAN!
IT'S REALLY LIGHT. HAS TO BE MARTIAN. LESSER GRAVITY UP THERE.
HEY, DON'T TOUCH IT WITH YOUR SKIN!
IT COULD CARRY SOME MARTIAN GERMS OR SOMETHING!
THE MARTIANS ARE STILL MAD AT EARTH BECAUSE OF WHEN THEY FIRST CAME HERE AND OUR GERMS POISONED THEM!
THE MARTIANS CAME TO INVADE US THAT TIME!
SERVES THEM RIGHT!
AND NOW THEY SUCK UP TO US EARTHLINGS EVERY CHANCE THEY GET!
I'LL BET THAT'S WHY THEY GAVE US THE BALL!

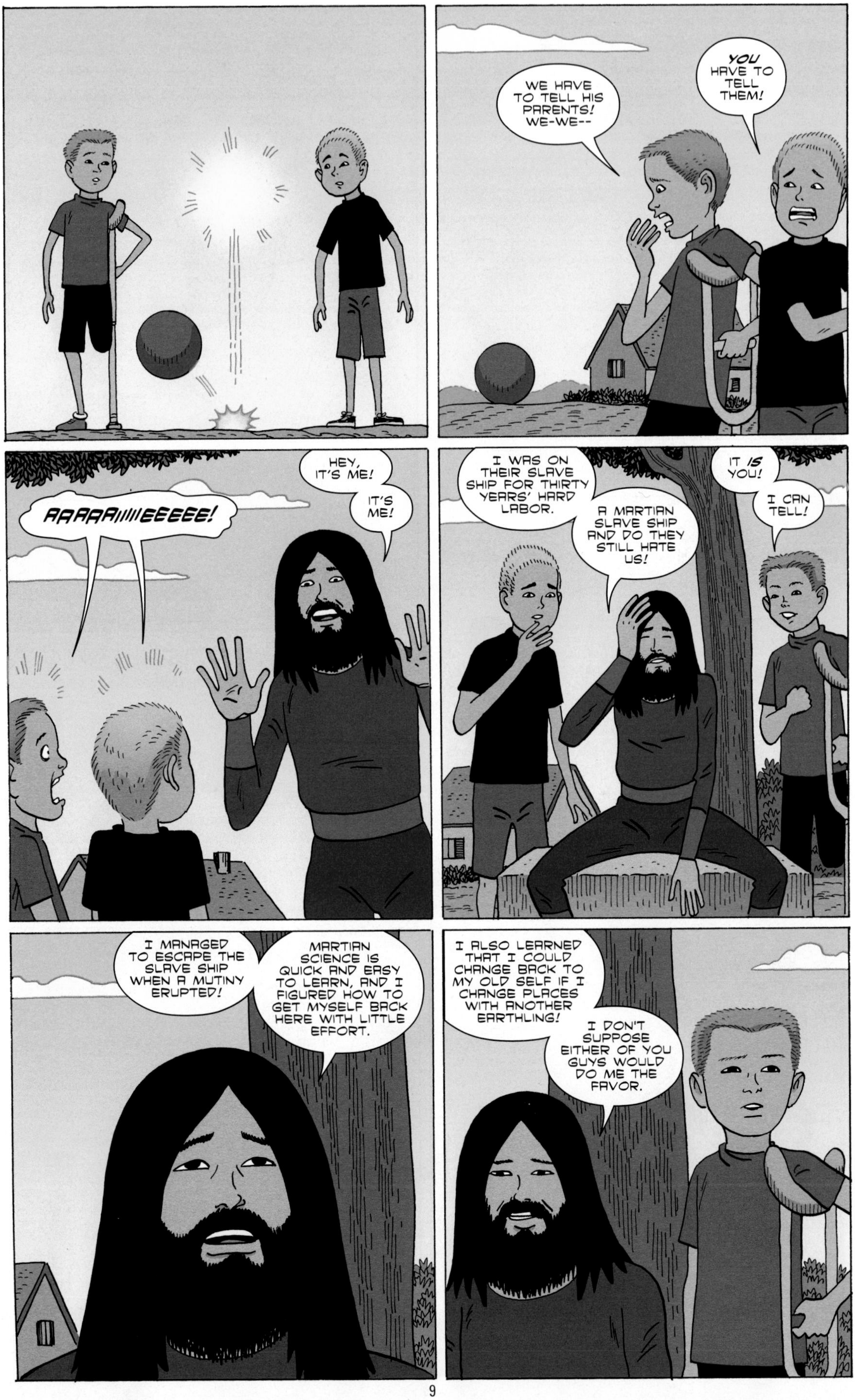
WE HAVE TO TELL HIS PARENTS! WE-WE--
YOU HAVE TO TELL THEM!
AAAAAIIIIIEEEEE!
HEY, IT'S ME!
IT'S ME!
I WAS ON THEIR SLAVE SHIP FOR THIRTY YEARS' HARD LABOR.
A MARTIAN SLAVE SHIP AND DO THEY STILL HATE US!
IT IS YOU!
I CAN TELL!
I MANAGED TO ESCAPE THE SLAVE SHIP WHEN A MUTINY ERUPTED!
MARTIAN SCIENCE IS QUICK AND EASY TO LEARN, AND I FIGURED HOW TO GET MYSELF BACK HERE WITH LITTLE EFFORT.
I ALSO LEARNED THAT I COULD CHANGE BACK TO MY OLD SELF IF I CHANGE PLACES WITH ANOTHER EARTHLING!
I DON'T SUPPOSE EITHER OF YOU GUYS WOULD DO ME THE FAVOR.

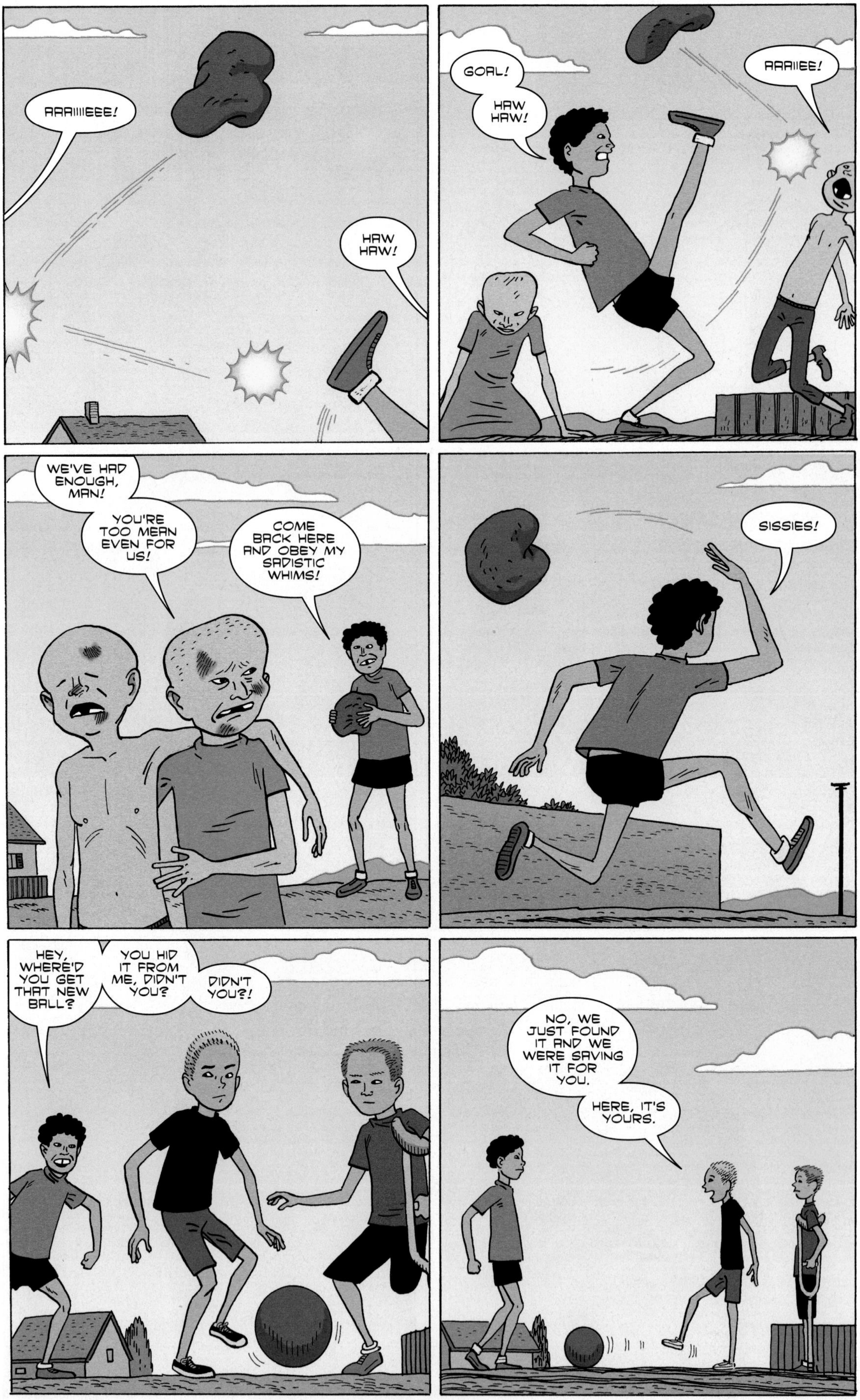
AAAIIIIEEE!
HAW HAW!
GOAL!
HAW HAW!
AAAIIEE!
WE'VE HAD ENOUGH, MAN!
YOU'RE TOO MEAN EVEN FOR US!
COME BACK HERE AND OBEY MY SADISTIC WHIMS!
SISSIES!
HEY, WHERE'D YOU GET THAT NEW BALL?
YOU HID IT FROM ME, DIDN'T YOU?
DIDN'T YOU?!
NO, WE JUST FOUND IT AND WE WERE SAVING IT FOR YOU.
HERE, IT'S YOURS.

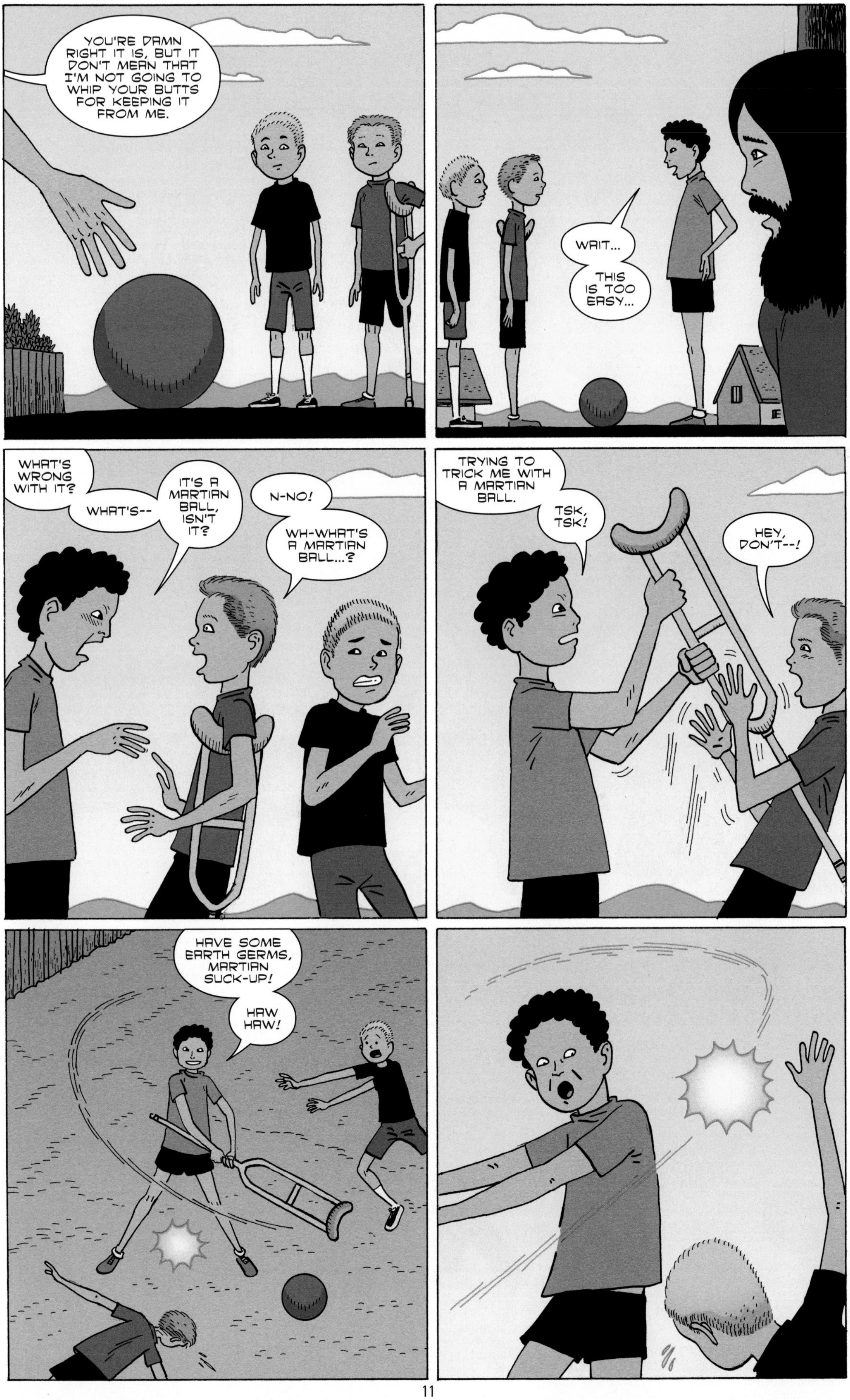
YOU'RE DAMN RIGHT IT IS, BUT IT DON'T MEAN THAT I'M NOT GOING TO WHIP YOUR BUTTS FOR KEEPING IT FROM ME.
WAIT...
THIS IS TOO EASY...
WHAT'S WRONG WITH IT?
WHAT'S--
IT'S A MARTIAN BALL, ISN'T IT?
N-NO!
WH-WHAT'S A MARTIAN BALL...?
TRYING TO TRICK ME WITH A MARTIAN BALL.
TSK, TSK!
HEY, DON'T--!
HAVE SOME EARTH GERMS, MARTIAN SUCK-UP!
HAW HAW!

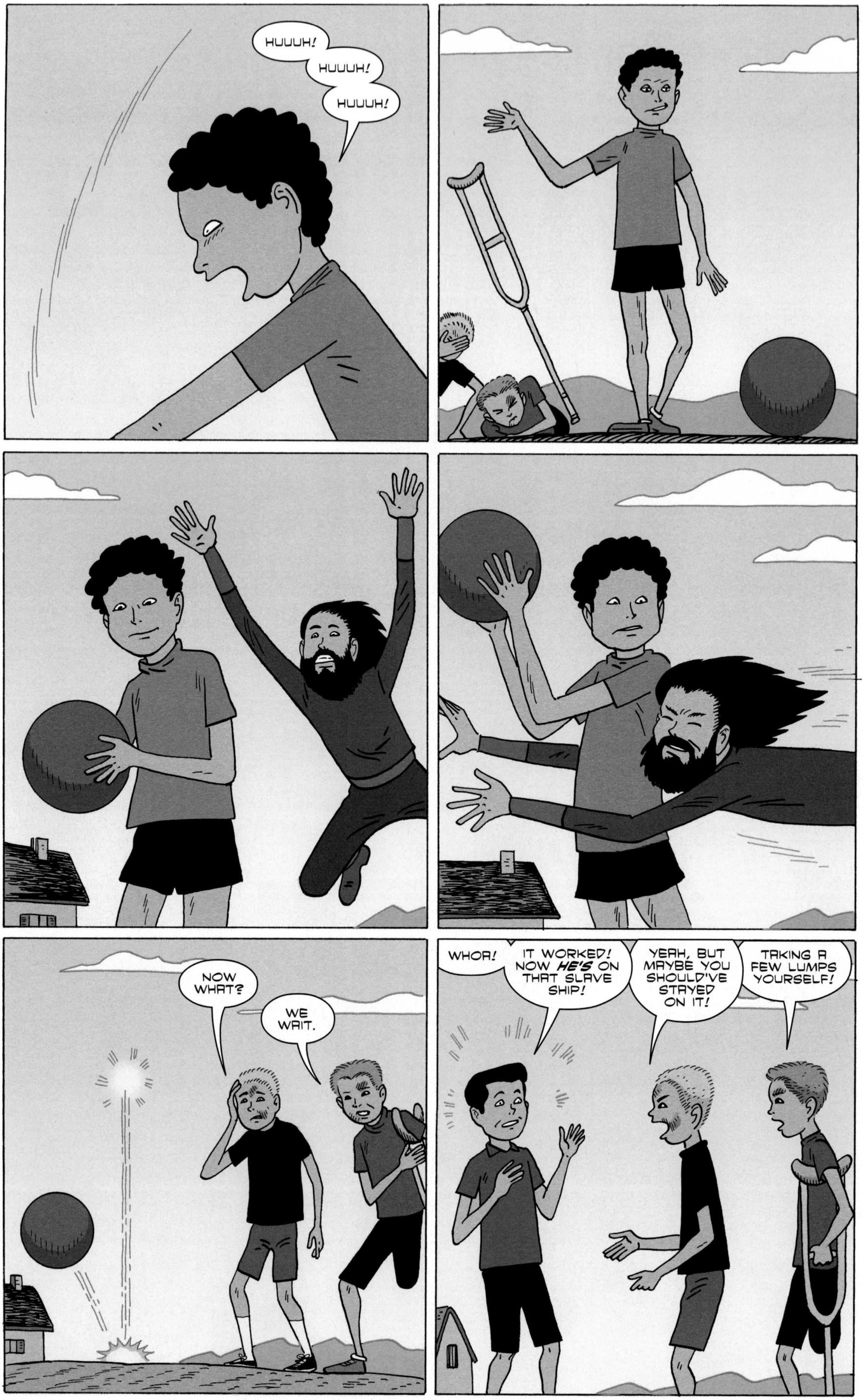
HUUUH!
HUUUH!
HUUUH!
NOW WHAT?
WE WAIT.
WHOA!
IT WORKED! NOW HE'S ON THAT SLAVE SHIP!
YEAH, BUT MAYBE YOU SHOULD'VE STAYED ON IT!
TAKING A FEW LUMPS YOURSELF!

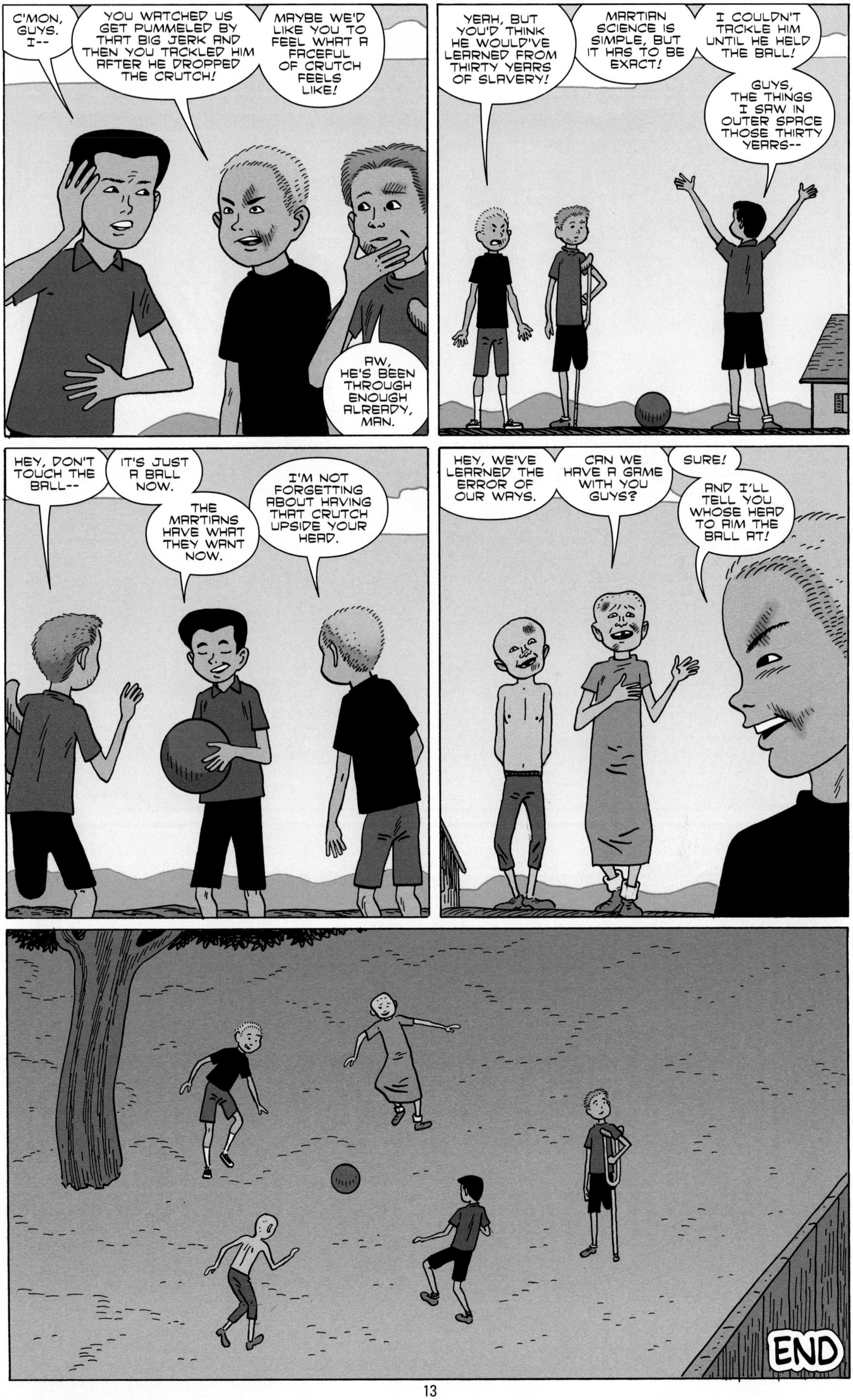
C'MON, GUYS. I--
YOU WATCHED US GET PUMMELED BY THAT BIG JERK AND THEN YOU TACKLED HIM AFTER HE DROPPED THE CRUTCH!
MAYBE WE'D LIKE YOU TO FEEL WHAT A FACEFUL OF CRUTCH FEELS LIKE!
AW, HE'S BEEN THROUGH ENOUGH ALREADY, MAN.
YEAH, BUT YOU'D THINK HE WOULD'VE LEARNED FROM THIRTY YEARS OF SLAVERY!
MARTIAN SCIENCE IS SIMPLE, BUT IT HAS TO BE EXACT!
I COULDN'T TACKLE HIM UNTIL HE HELD THE BALL!
GUYS, THE THINGS I SAW IN OUTER SPACE THOSE THIRTY YEARS--
HEY, DON'T TOUCH THE BALL--
IT'S JUST A BALL NOW.
THE MARTIANS HAVE WHAT THEY WANT NOW.
I'M NOT FORGETTING ABOUT HAVING THAT CRUTCH UPSIDE YOUR HEAD.
HEY, WE'VE LEARNED THE ERROR OF OUR WAYS.
CAN WE HAVE A GAME WITH YOU GUYS?
SURE!
AND I'LL TELL YOU WHOSE HEAD TO AIM THE BALL AT!
END

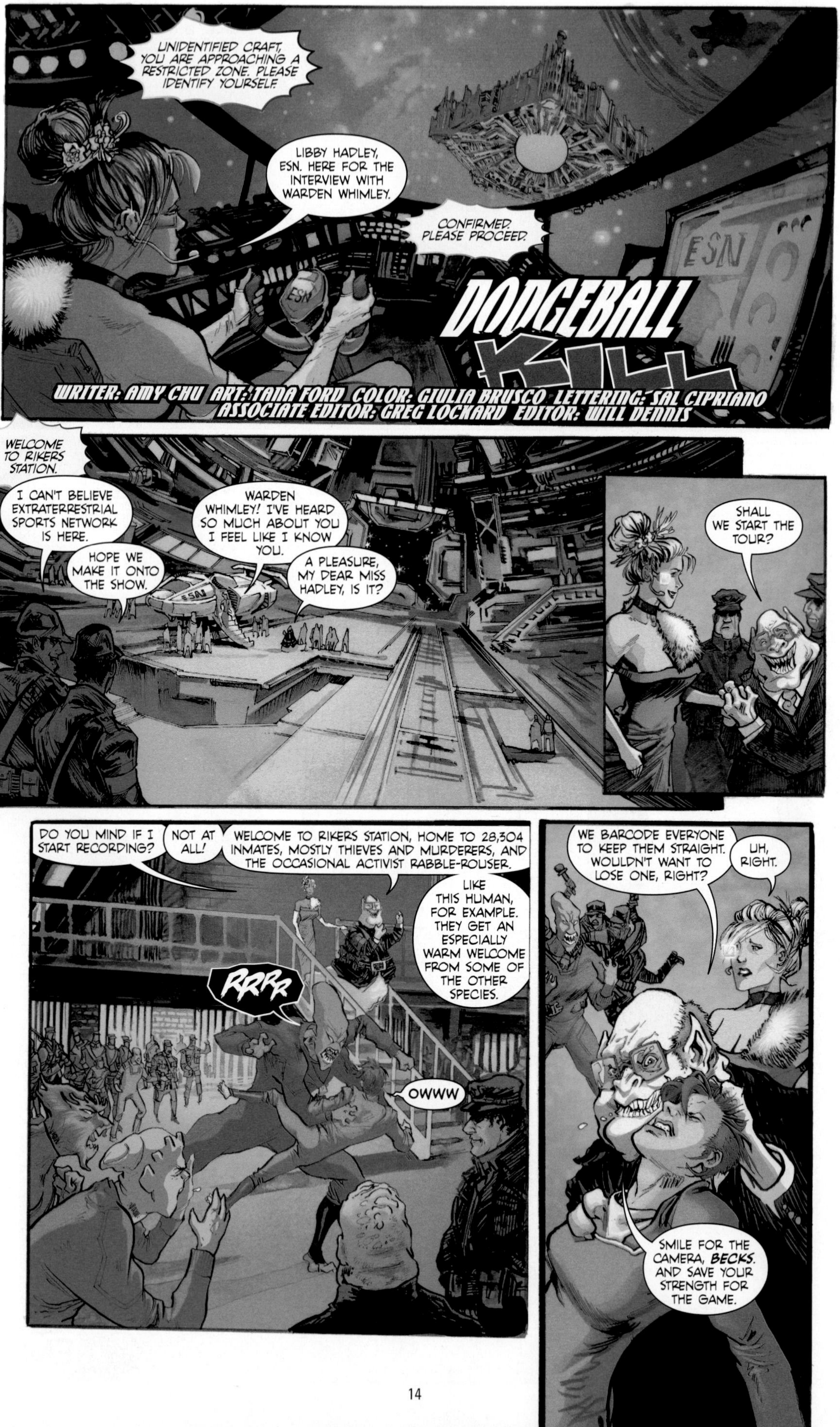
UNIDENTIFIED CRAFT, YOU ARE APPROACHING A RESTRICTED ZONE. PLEASE IDENTIFY YOURSELF.
LIBBY HADLEY, ESN. HERE FOR THE INTERVIEW WITH WARDEN WHIMLEY.
CONFIRMED. PLEASE PROCEED.
ESN
DODGEBALL KILL
WRITER: AMY CHU ART: TANA FORD COLOR: GIULIA BRUSCO LETTERING: SAL CIPRIANO
ASSOCIATE EDITOR: GREG LOCKARD EDITOR: WILL DENNIS
WELCOME TO RIKERS STATION.
I CAN'T BELIEVE EXTRATERRESTRIAL SPORTS NETWORK IS HERE.
HOPE WE MAKE IT ONTO THE SHOW.
WARDEN WHIMLEY! I'VE HEARD SO MUCH ABOUT YOU I FEEL LIKE I KNOW YOU.
A PLEASURE, MY DEAR MISS HADLEY, IS IT?
SHALL WE START THE TOUR?
DO YOU MIND IF I START RECORDING?
NOT AT ALL!
WELCOME TO RIKERS STATION, HOME TO 28,304 INMATES, MOSTLY THIEVES AND MURDERERS, AND THE OCCASIONAL ACTIVIST RABBLE-ROUSER.
LIKE THIS HUMAN, FOR EXAMPLE. THEY GET AN ESPECIALLY WARM WELCOME FROM SOME OF THE OTHER SPECIES.
RRRR
OWWW
WE BARCODE EVERYONE TO KEEP THEM STRAIGHT. WOULDN'T WANT TO LOSE ONE, RIGHT?
UH, RIGHT.
SMILE FOR THE CAMERA, BECKS. AND SAVE YOUR STRENGTH FOR THE GAME.

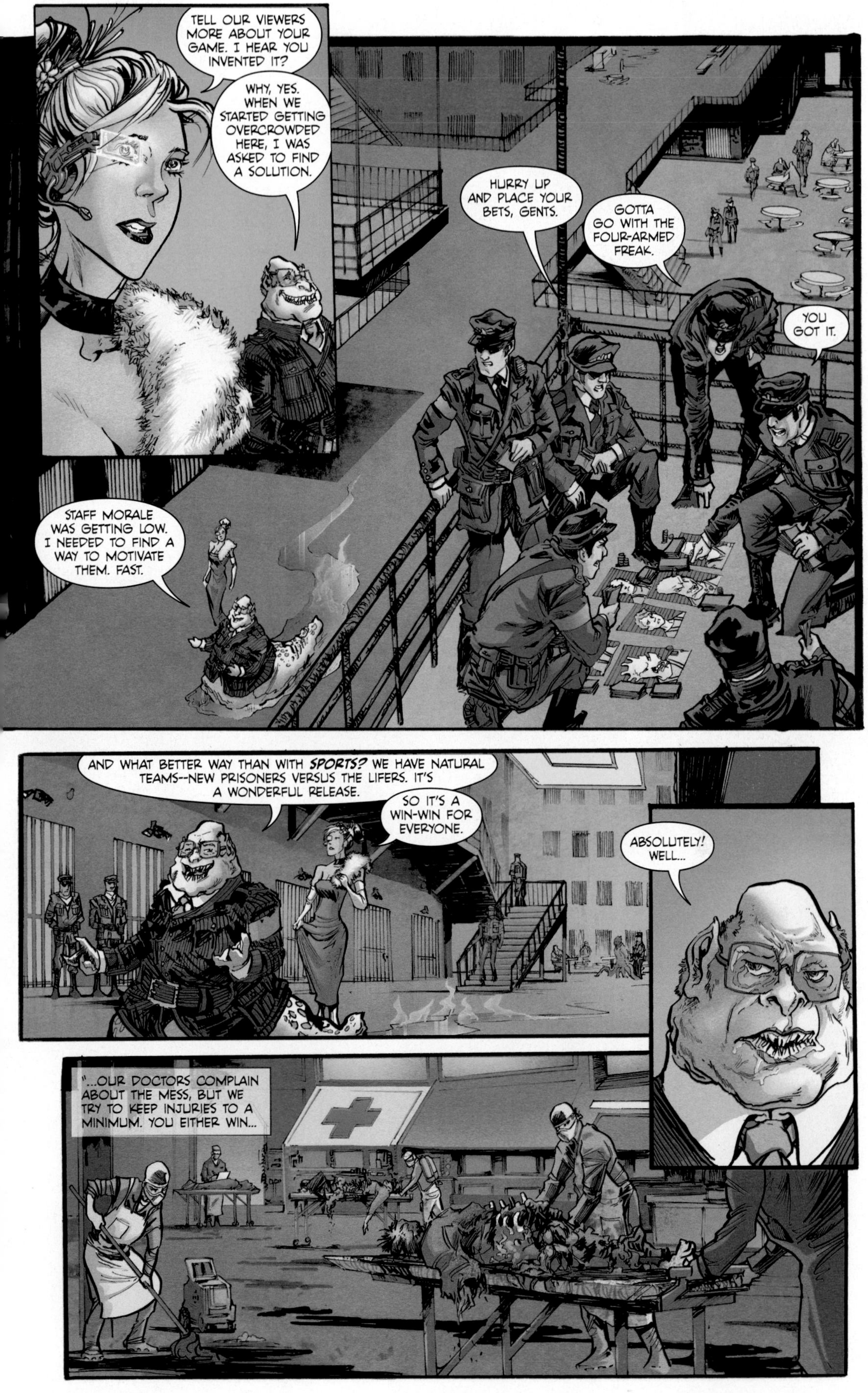
TELL OUR VIEWERS MORE ABOUT YOUR GAME. I HEAR YOU INVENTED IT?
WHY, YES. WHEN WE STARTED GETTING OVERCROWDED HERE, I WAS ASKED TO FIND A SOLUTION.
HURRY UP AND PLACE YOUR BETS, GENTS.
GOTTA GO WITH THE FOUR-ARMED FREAK.
YOU GOT IT.
STAFF MORALE WAS GETTING LOW. I NEEDED TO FIND A WAY TO MOTIVATE THEM. FAST.
AND WHAT BETTER WAY THAN WITH SPORTS? WE HAVE NATURAL TEAMS--NEW PRISONERS VERSUS THE LIFERS. IT'S A WONDERFUL RELEASE.
SO IT'S A WIN-WIN FOR EVERYONE.
ABSOLUTELY! WELL...
"...OUR DOCTORS COMPLAIN ABOUT THE MESS, BUT WE TRY TO KEEP INJURIES TO A MINIMUM. YOU EITHER WIN...

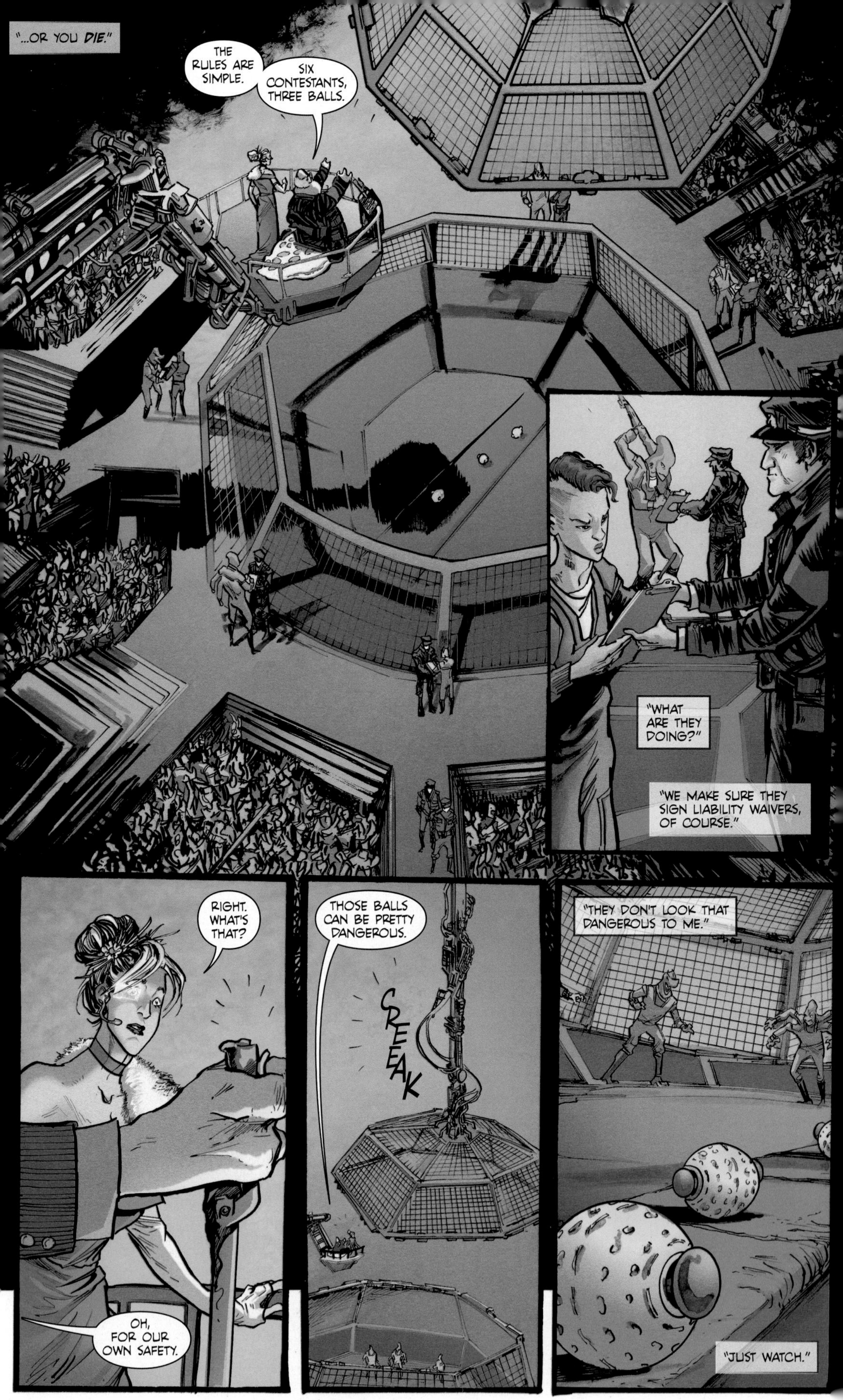
"...OR YOU DIE."
THE RULES ARE SIMPLE.
SIX CONTESTANTS, THREE BALLS.
"WHAT ARE THEY DOING?"
"WE MAKE SURE THEY SIGN LIABILITY WAIVERS, OF COURSE."
RIGHT. WHAT'S THAT?
OH, FOR OUR OWN SAFETY.
THOSE BALLS CAN BE PRETTY DANGEROUS.
CREEAK
"THEY DON'T LOOK THAT DANGEROUS TO ME."
"JUST WATCH."

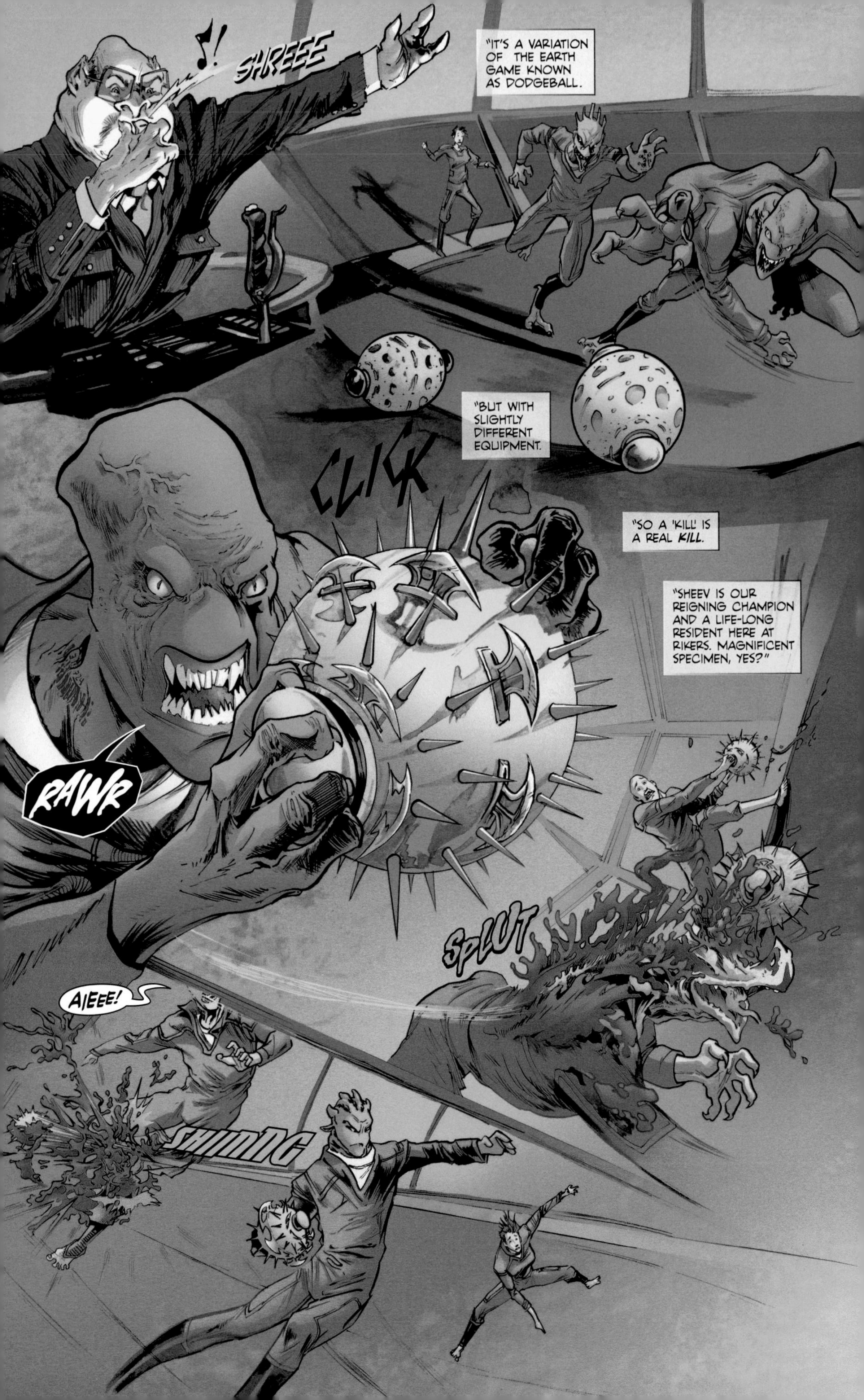
♪!
SHREEE
"IT'S A VARIATION OF THE EARTH GAME KNOWN AS DODGEBALL.
"BUT WITH SLIGHTLY DIFFERENT EQUIPMENT.
CLICK
"SO A 'KILL' IS A REAL KILL.
"SHEEV IS OUR REIGNING CHAMPION AND A LIFE-LONG RESIDENT HERE AT RIKERS. MAGNIFICENT SPECIMEN, YES?"
RAWR
SPLUT
AIEEE!
SHING

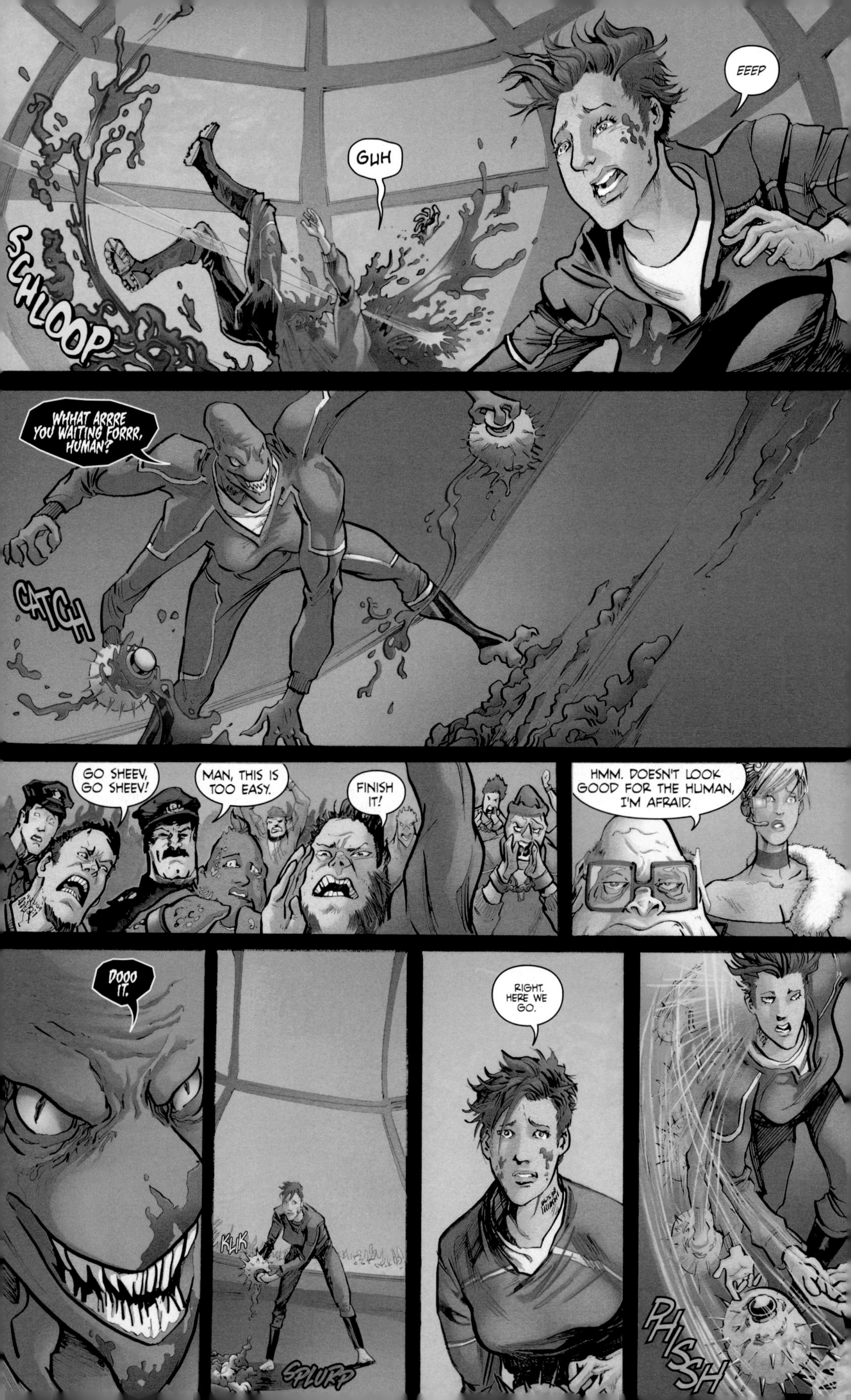
EEEP
GUH
SCHLOOP
WHHAT ARRRE YOU WAITING FORRR, HUMAN?
CATCH
GO SHEEV, GO SHEEV!
MAN, THIS IS TOO EASY.
FINISH IT!
HMM. DOESN'T LOOK GOOD FOR THE HUMAN, I'M AFRAID.
DOOO IT.
KLIK
SPLURP
RIGHT. HERE WE GO.
PHISH

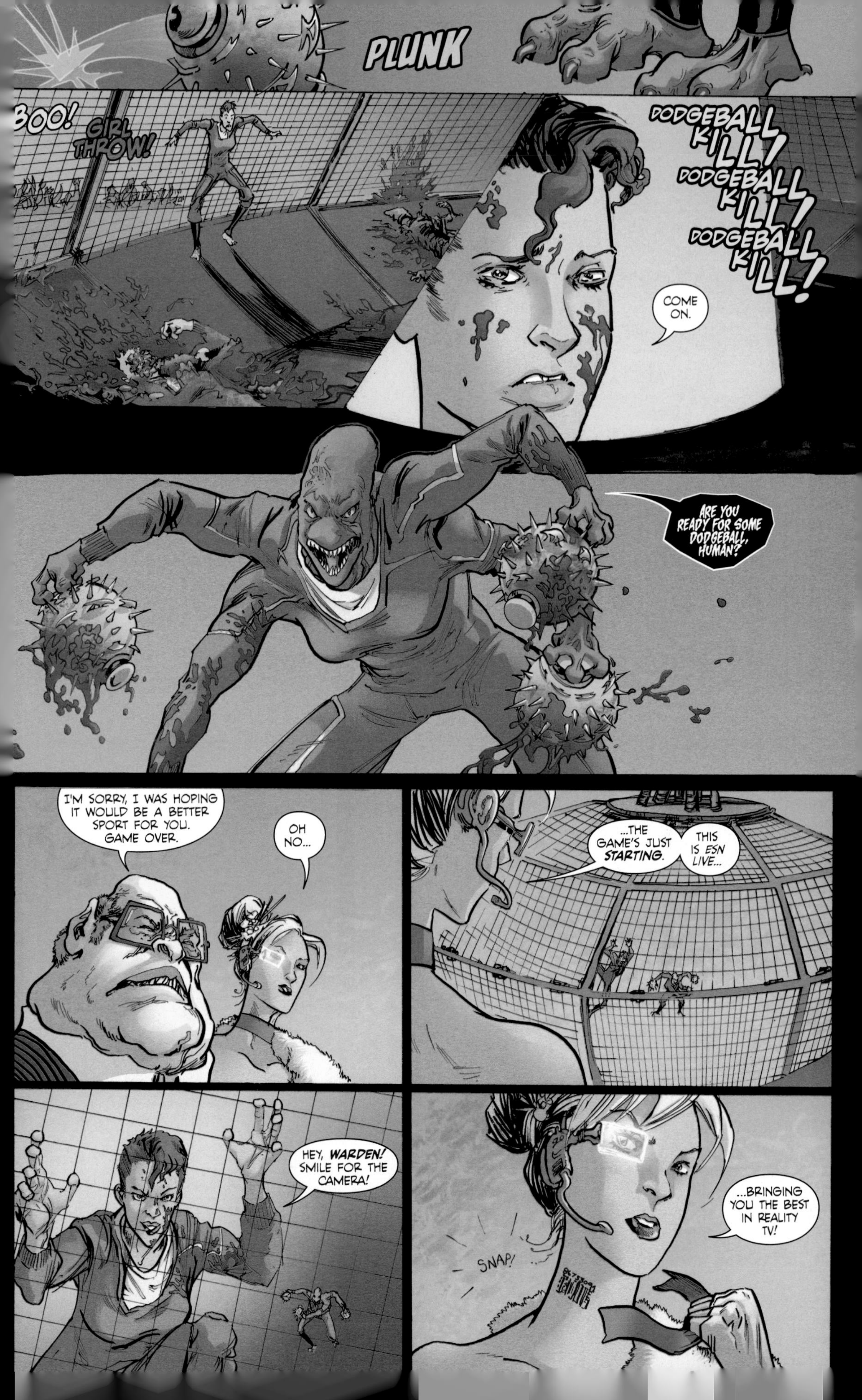
PLUNK
BOO!
GIRL THROW!
DODGEBALL KILL! DODGEBALL KILL! DODGEBALL KILL!
COME ON.
ARE YOU READY FOR SOME DODGEBALL, HUMAN?
I'M SORRY, I WAS HOPING IT WOULD BE A BETTER SPORT FOR YOU. GAME OVER.
OH NO...
...THE GAME'S JUST STARTING.
THIS IS ESN LIVE...
HEY, WARDEN! SMILE FOR THE CAMERA!
SNAP!
...BRINGING YOU THE BEST IN REALITY TV!

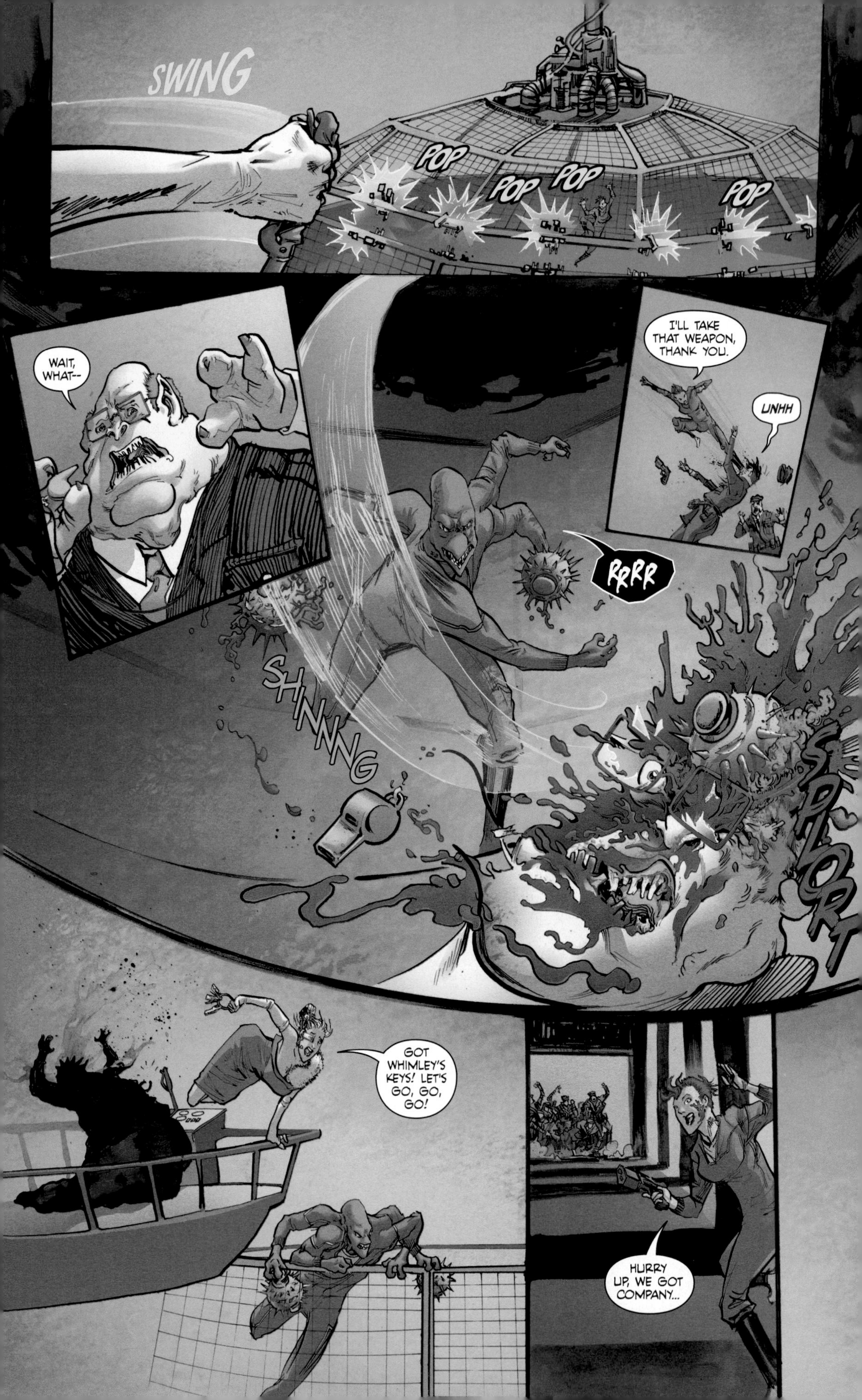
SWING
POP
POP
POP
POP
WAIT, WHAT--
I'LL TAKE THAT WEAPON, THANK YOU.
UNHH
RRRR
SHNNNG
SPLORT
GOT WHIMLEY'S KEYS! LET'S GO, GO, GO!
HURRY UP, WE GOT COMPANY...

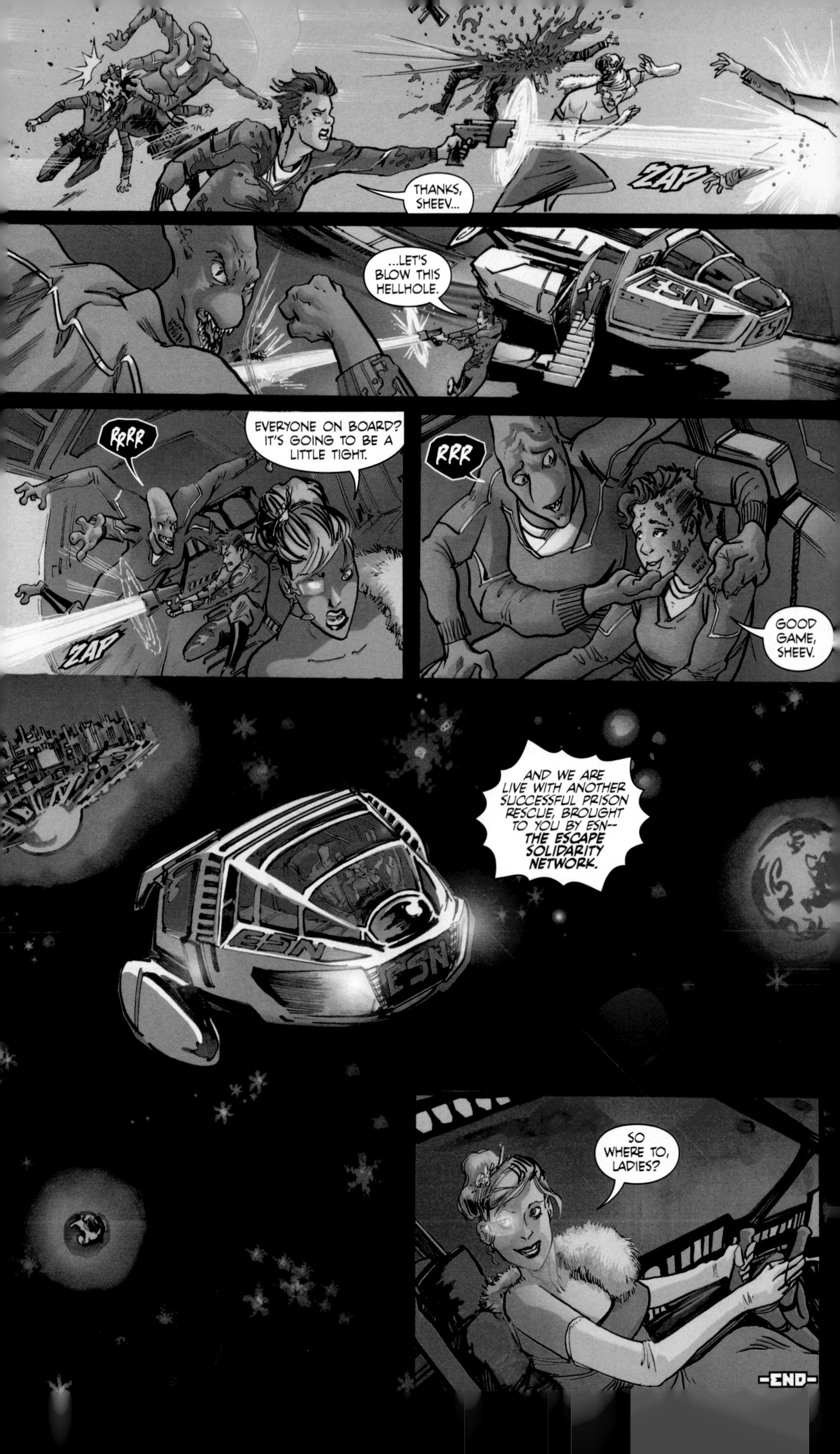
THANKS, SHEEV...
ZAP
...LET'S BLOW THIS HELLHOLE.
ESN
RRRR
EVERYONE ON BOARD? IT'S GOING TO BE A LITTLE TIGHT.
ZAP
RRR
GOOD GAME, SHEEV.
AND WE ARE LIVE WITH ANOTHER SUCCESSFUL PRISON RESCUE, BROUGHT TO YOU BY ESN-- THE ESCAPE SOLIDARITY NETWORK.
ESN
SO WHERE TO, LADIES?
-END-

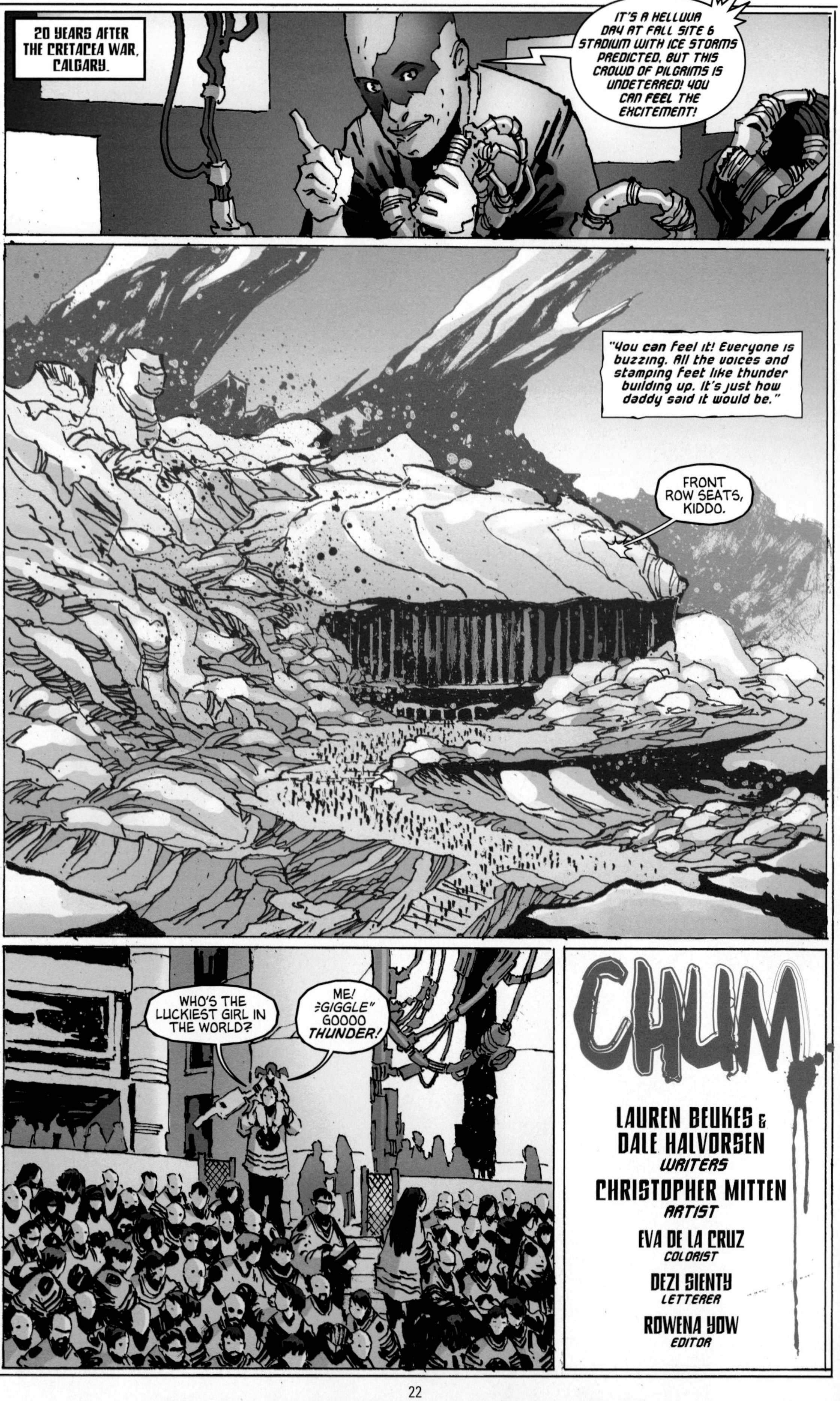
20 YEARS AFTER THE CRETACEA WAR, CALGARY.
IT'S A HELLUVA DAY AT FALL SITE 6 STADIUM WITH ICE STORMS PREDICTED, BUT THIS CROWD OF PILGRIMS IS UNDETERRED! YOU CAN FEEL THE EXCITEMENT!
"You can feel it! Everyone is buzzing. All the voices and stamping feet like thunder building up. It's just how daddy said it would be."
FRONT ROW SEATS, KIDDO.
WHO'S THE LUCKIEST GIRL IN THE WORLD?
ME! "GIGGLE" GOOOO THUNDER!
CHUM
LAUREN BEUKES & DALE HALVORSEN
WRITERS
CHRISTOPHER MITTEN
ARTIST
EVA DE LA CRUZ
COLORIST
DEZI SIENTY
LETTERER
ROWENA YOW
EDITOR

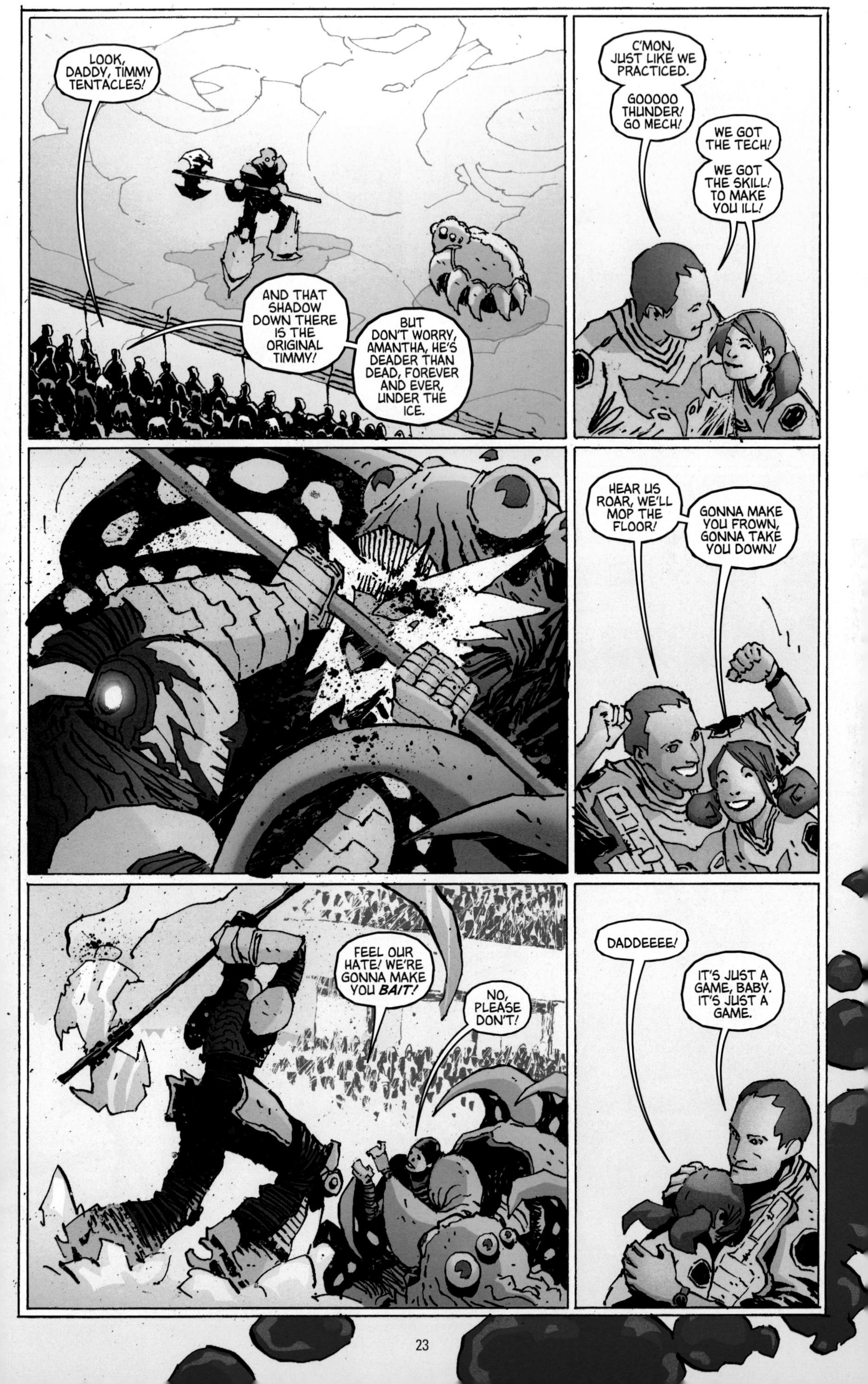
LOOK, DADDY, TIMMY TENTACLES!
AND THAT SHADOW DOWN THERE IS THE ORIGINAL TIMMY!
BUT DON'T WORRY, AMANTHA, HE'S DEADER THAN DEAD, FOREVER AND EVER, UNDER THE ICE.
C'MON, JUST LIKE WE PRACTICED.
GOOOOO THUNDER! GO MECH!
WE GOT THE TECH!
WE GOT THE SKILL! TO MAKE YOU ILL!
HEAR US ROAR, WE'LL MOP THE FLOOR!
GONNA MAKE YOU FROWN, GONNA TAKE YOU DOWN!
FEEL OUR HATE! WE'RE GONNA MAKE YOU *BAIT!*
NO, PLEASE DON'T!
DADDEEEE!
IT'S JUST A GAME, BABY. IT'S JUST A GAME.

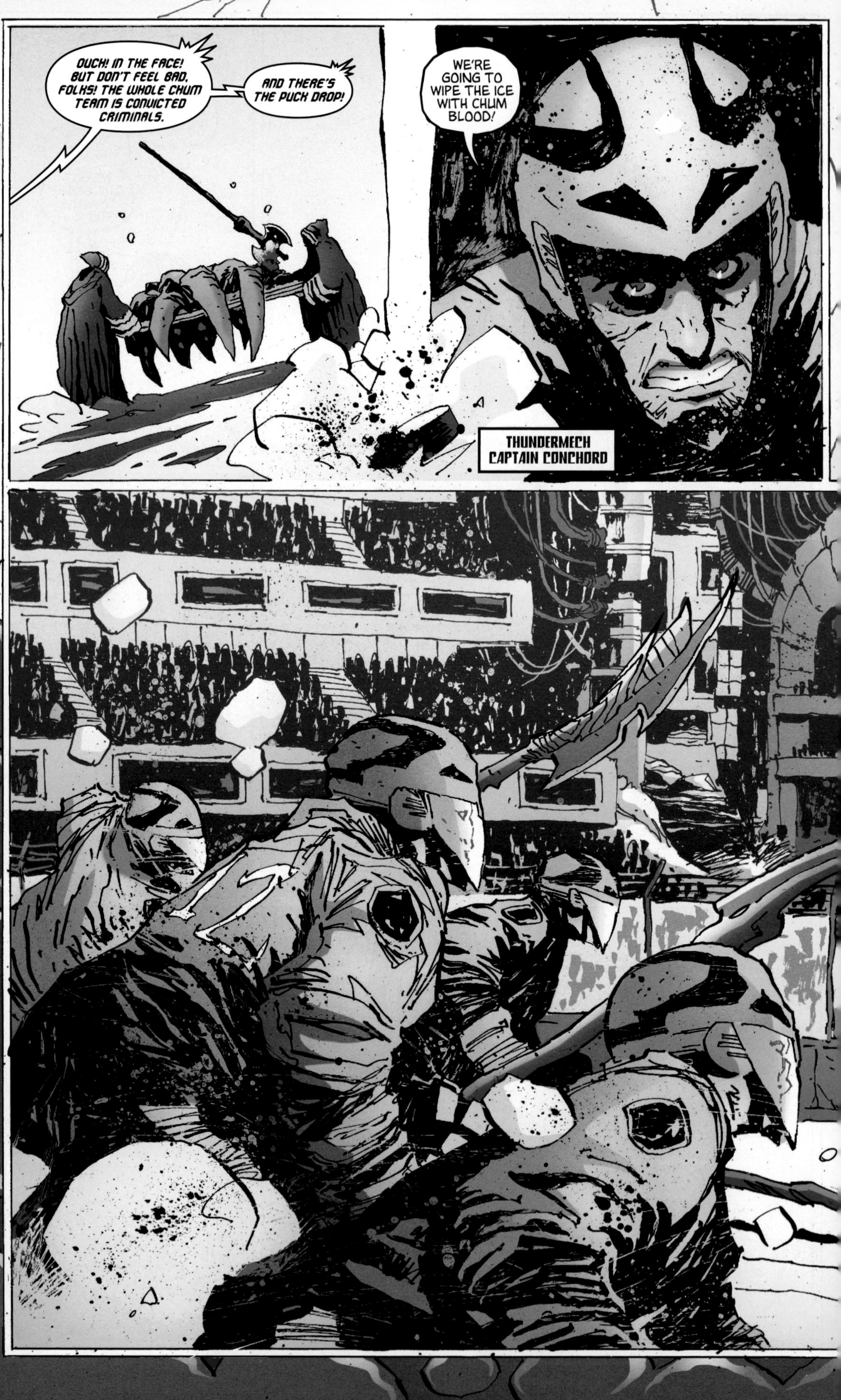
OUCH! IN THE FACE! BUT DON'T FEEL BAD, FOLKS! THE WHOLE CHUM TEAM IS CONVICTED CRIMINALS.
AND THERE'S THE PUCK DROP!
WE'RE GOING TO WIPE THE ICE WITH CHUM BLOOD!
THUNDERMECH CAPTAIN CONCHORD

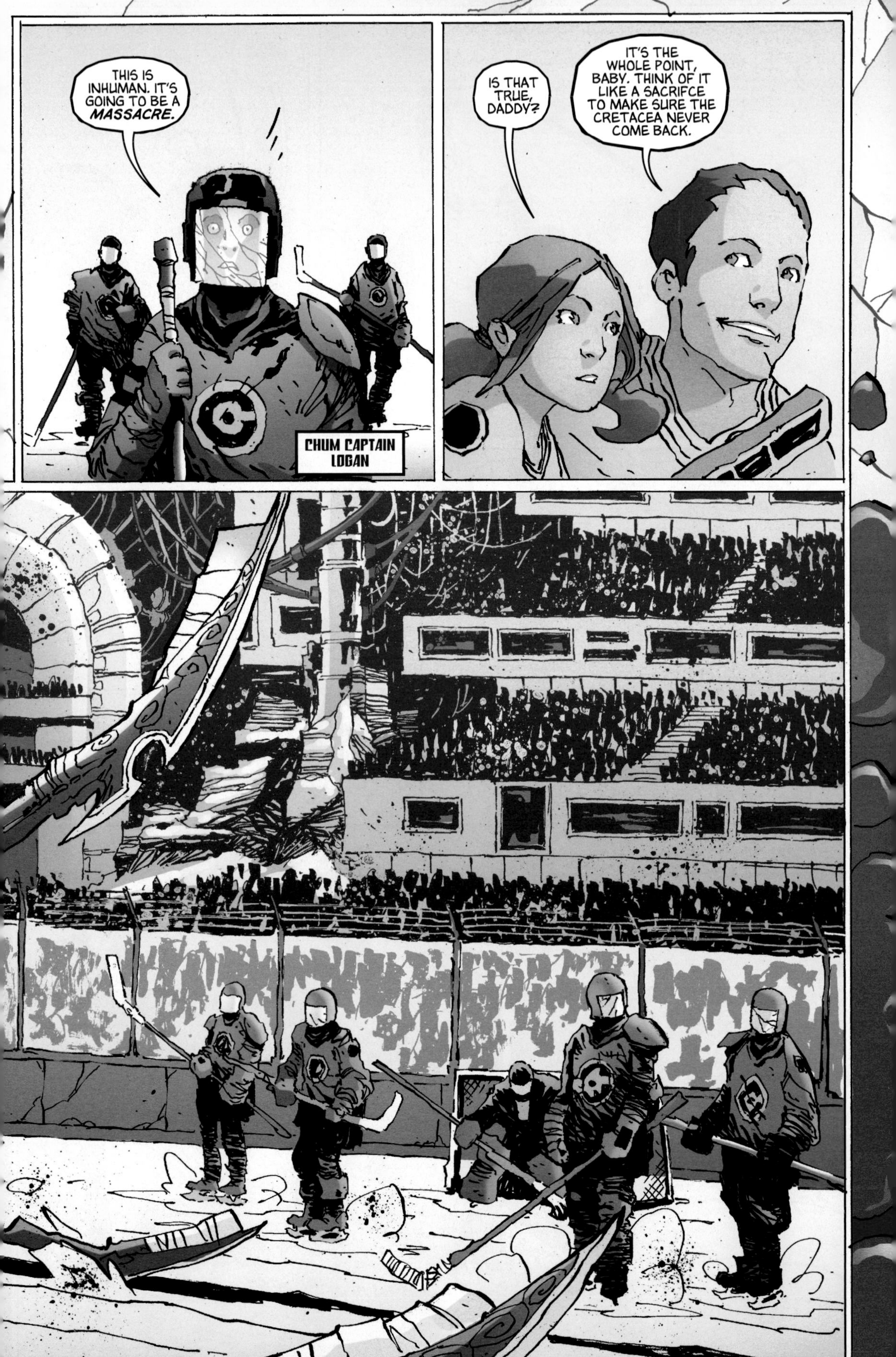
THIS IS INHUMAN. IT'S GOING TO BE A MASSACRE.
CHUM CAPTAIN LOGAN
IS THAT TRUE, DADDY?
IT'S THE WHOLE POINT, BABY. THINK OF IT LIKE A SACRIFCE TO MAKE SURE THE CRETACEA NEVER COME BACK.

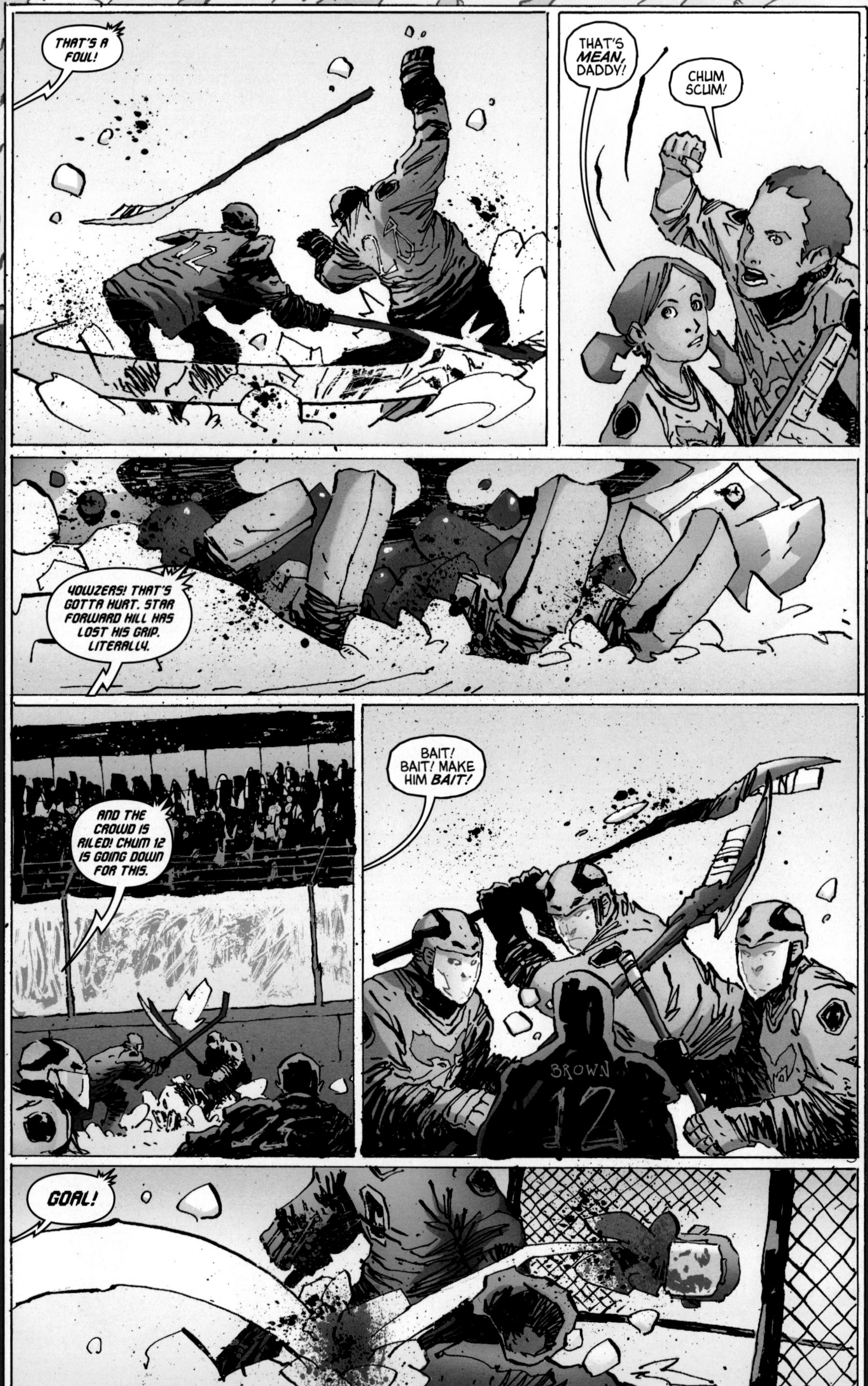
THAT'S A FOUL!
THAT'S MEAN, DADDY!
CHUM SCUM!
YOWZERS! THAT'S GOTTA HURT. STAR FORWARD HILL HAS LOST HIS GRIP. LITERALLY.
AND THE CROWD IS RILED! CHUM 12 IS GOING DOWN FOR THIS.
BAIT! BAIT! MAKE HIM BAIT!
BROWN 12
GOAL!

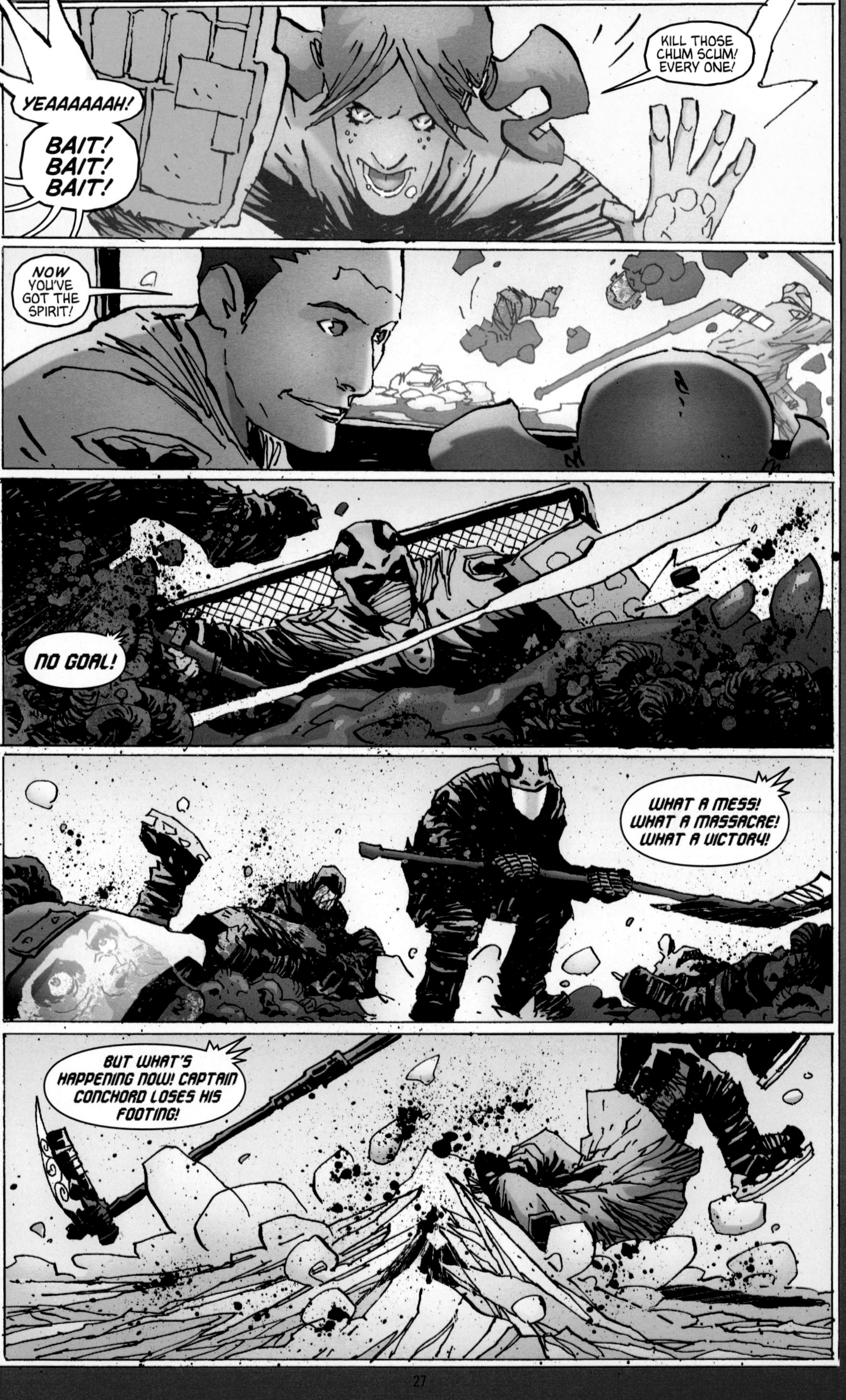
YEAAAAAAH!
BAIT! BAIT! BAIT!
KILL THOSE CHUM SCUM! EVERY ONE!
NOW YOU'VE GOT THE SPIRIT!
NO GOAL!
WHAT A MESS! WHAT A MASSACRE! WHAT A VICTORY!
BUT WHAT'S HAPPENING NOW! CAPTAIN CONCHORD LOSES HIS FOOTING!

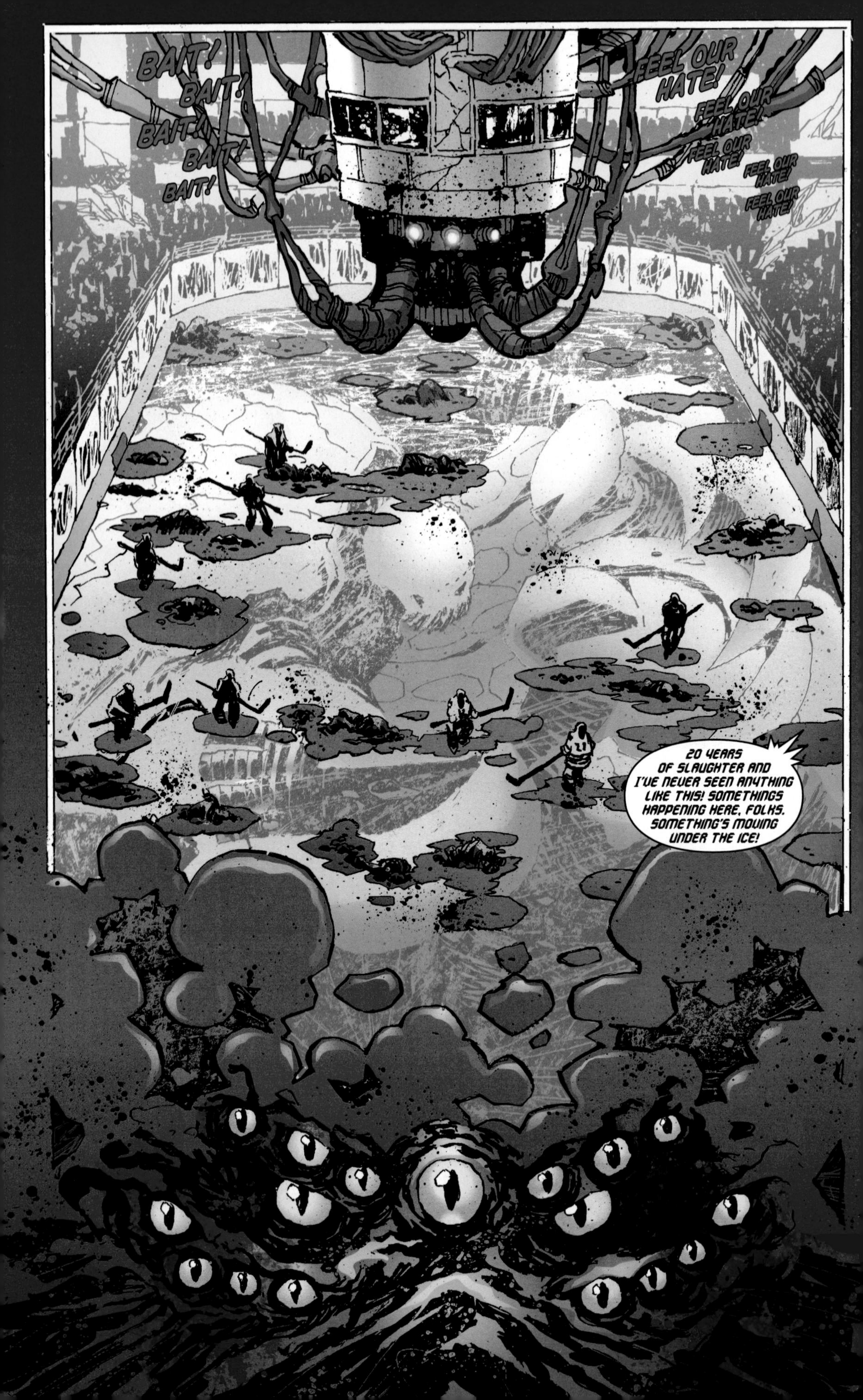

BAIT! BAIT! BAIT! BAIT! BAIT!
FEEL OUR HATE! FEEL OUR HATE! FEEL OUR HATE! FEEL OUR HATE! FEEL OUR HATE!
20 YEARS OF SLAUGHTER AND I'VE NEVER SEEN ANYTHING LIKE THIS! SOMETHINGS HAPPENING HERE, FOLKS. SOMETHING'S MOVING UNDER THE ICE!

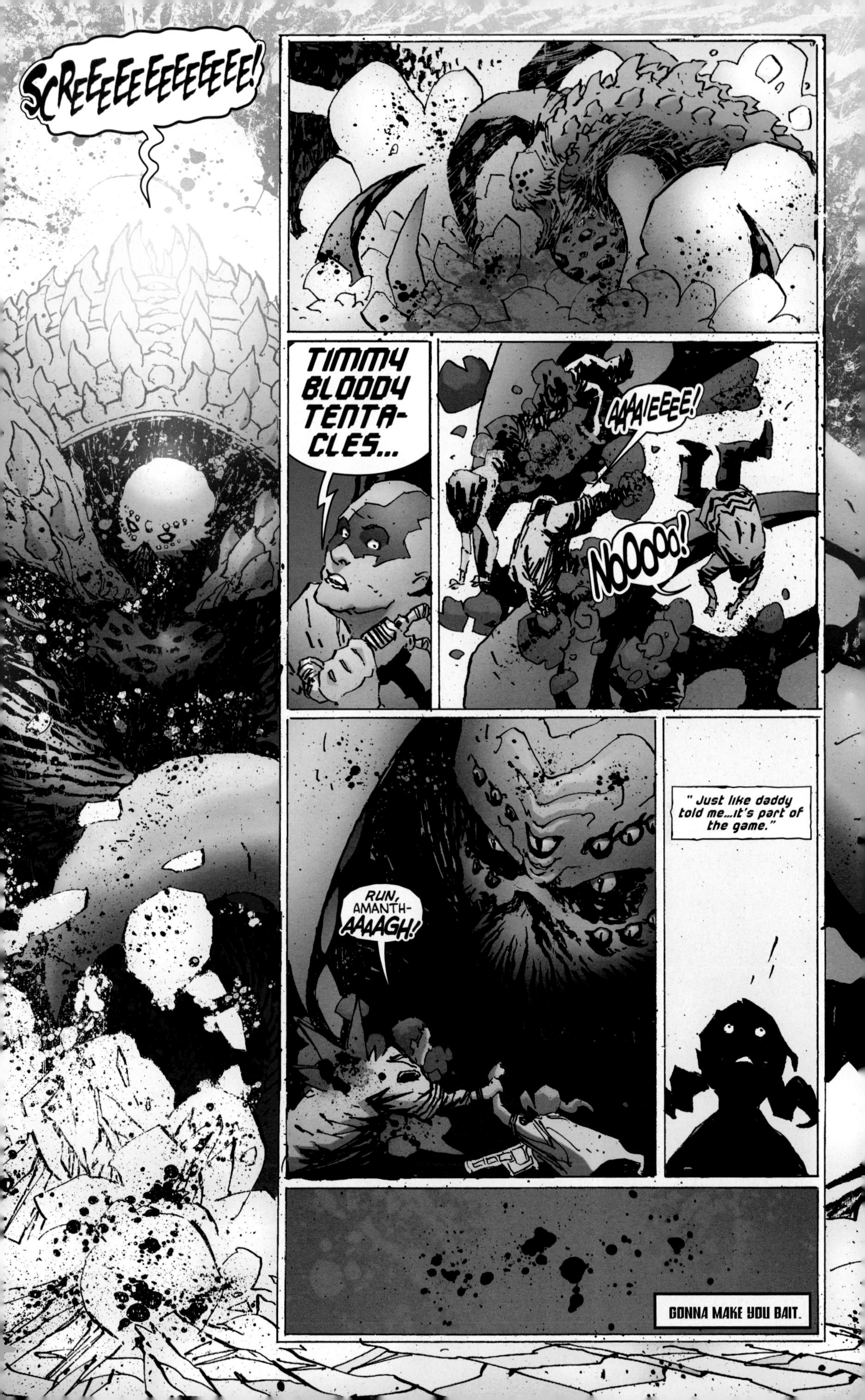
SCREEEEEEEEEEEEE!
TIMMY BLOODY TENTA-CLES...
AAAAIEEEE!
NOOOOO!
"Just like daddy told me...it's part of the game."
RUN, AMANTH-AAAAGH!
GONNA MAKE YOU BAIT.

DAYS PASSED SINCE THE LIGHTS WENT OUT, BUT WITHOUT THE LIGHT NOBODY KNEW HOW MANY.

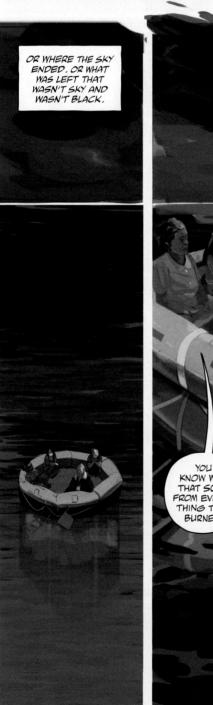

OR WHERE THE SKY ENDED. OR WHAT WAS LEFT THAT WASN'T SKY AND WASN'T BLACK.

WHY AIN'T THERE A SUN?

YOU KNOW WHY. THAT SOOT FROM EVERYTHING THAT BURNED.

FINALLY WENT AND BURNED THE WORLD DOWN.

AND MAYBE WE HAD.

EVERYTHING GONE EXCEPT THE NIGHT.

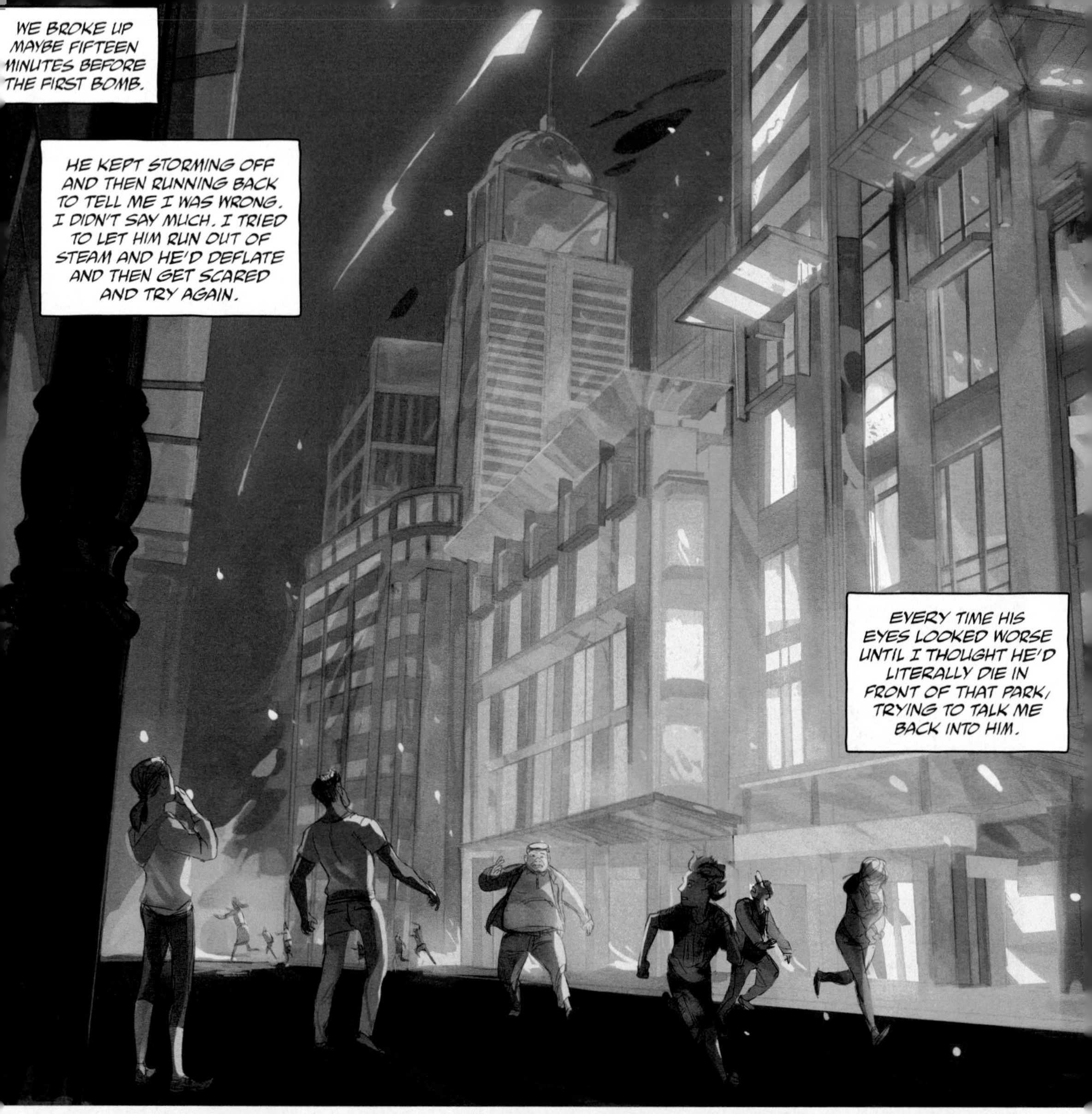
WE BROKE UP MAYBE FIFTEEN MINUTES BEFORE THE FIRST BOMB.
HE KEPT STORMING OFF AND THEN RUNNING BACK TO TELL ME I WAS WRONG. I DIDN'T SAY MUCH. I TRIED TO LET HIM RUN OUT OF STEAM AND HE'D DEFLATE AND THEN GET SCARED AND TRY AGAIN.
EVERY TIME HIS EYES LOOKED WORSE UNTIL I THOUGHT HE'D LITERALLY DIE IN FRONT OF THAT PARK, TRYING TO TALK ME BACK INTO HIM.

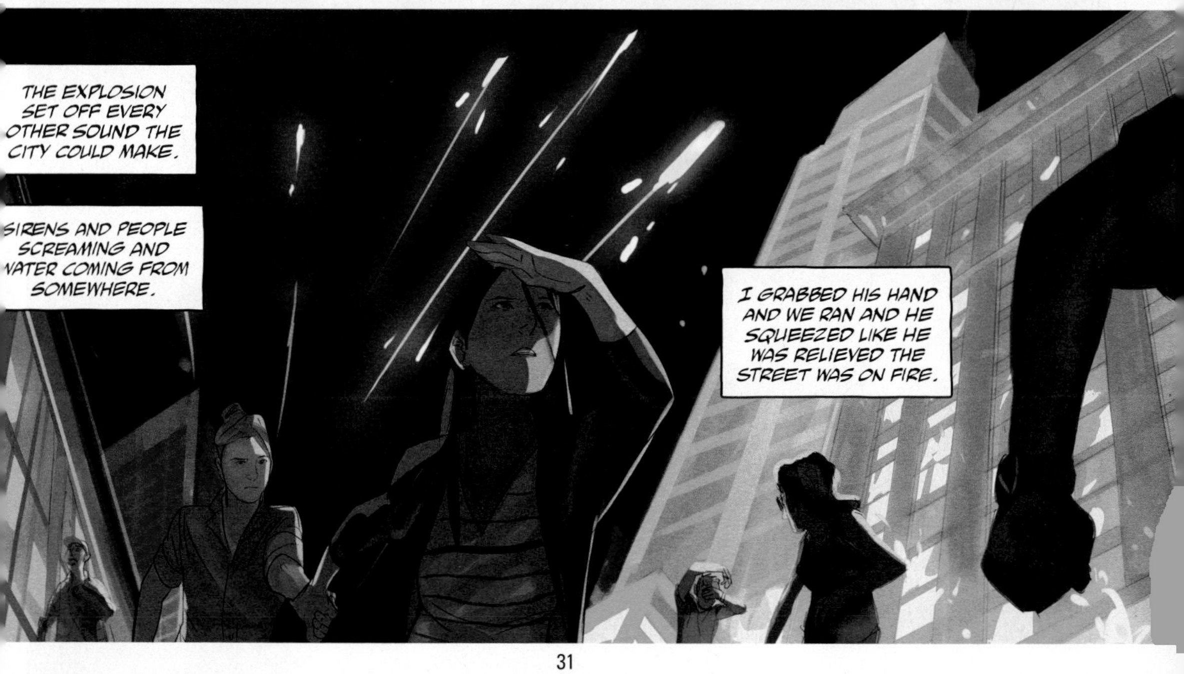
THE EXPLOSION SET OFF EVERY OTHER SOUND THE CITY COULD MAKE.
SIRENS AND PEOPLE SCREAMING AND WATER COMING FROM SOMEWHERE.
I GRABBED HIS HAND AND WE RAN AND HE SQUEEZED LIKE HE WAS RELIEVED THE STREET WAS ON FIRE.

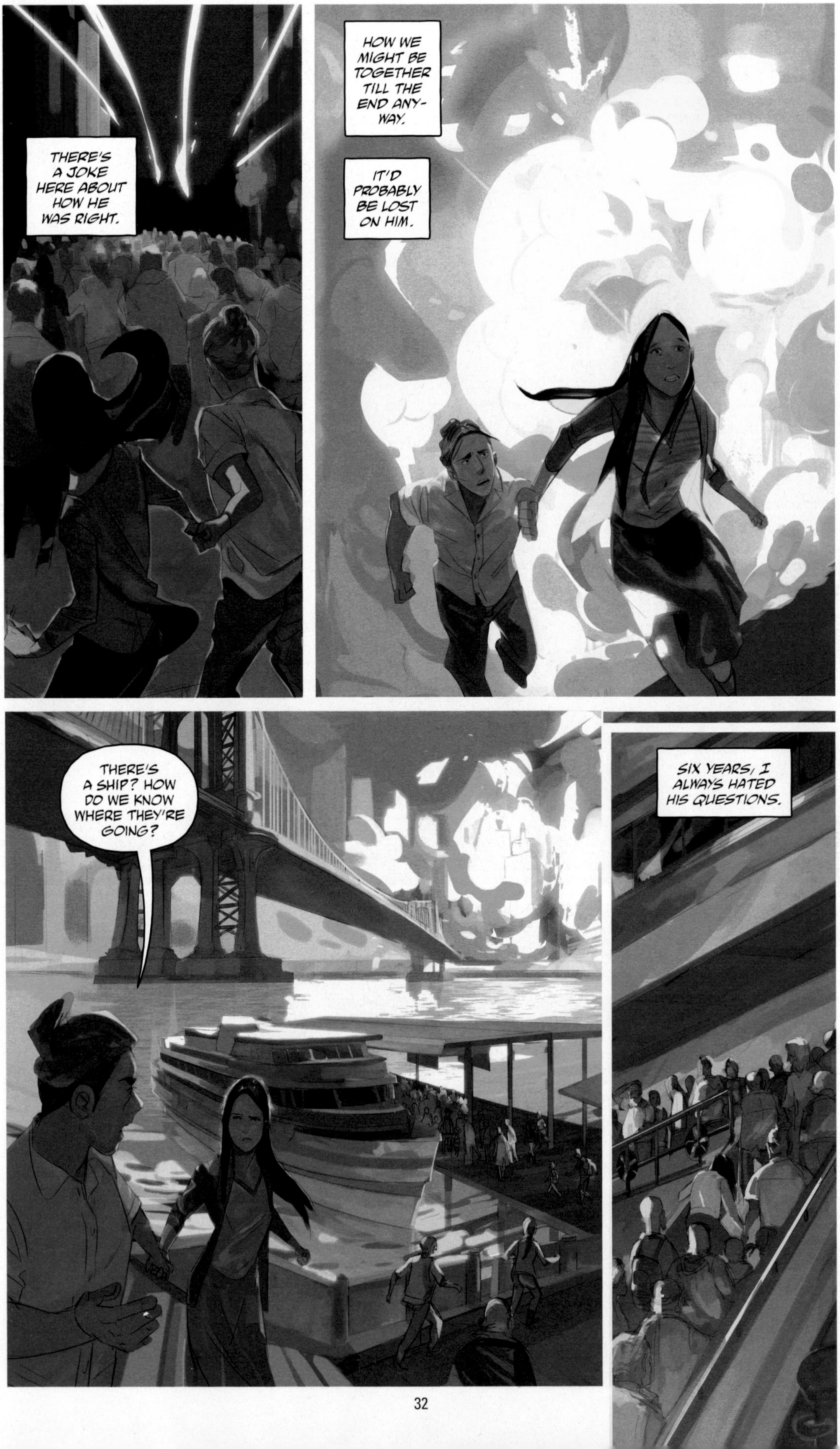
THERE'S A JOKE HERE ABOUT HOW HE WAS RIGHT.
HOW WE MIGHT BE TOGETHER TILL THE END ANY-WAY.
IT'D PROBABLY BE LOST ON HIM.
THERE'S A SHIP? HOW DO WE KNOW WHERE THEY'RE GOING?
SIX YEARS, I ALWAYS HATED HIS QUESTIONS.

PULLING AWAY FROM TEN YEARS IN THIS CITY, ALL I COULD THINK, EVEN LOOKING AT THE FIRE...

WAS THAT I'D WASTED HALF OF IT WITH ANDY.

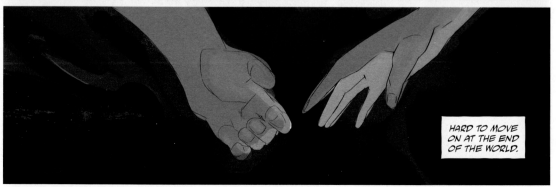

HARD TO MOVE ON AT THE END OF THE WORLD.

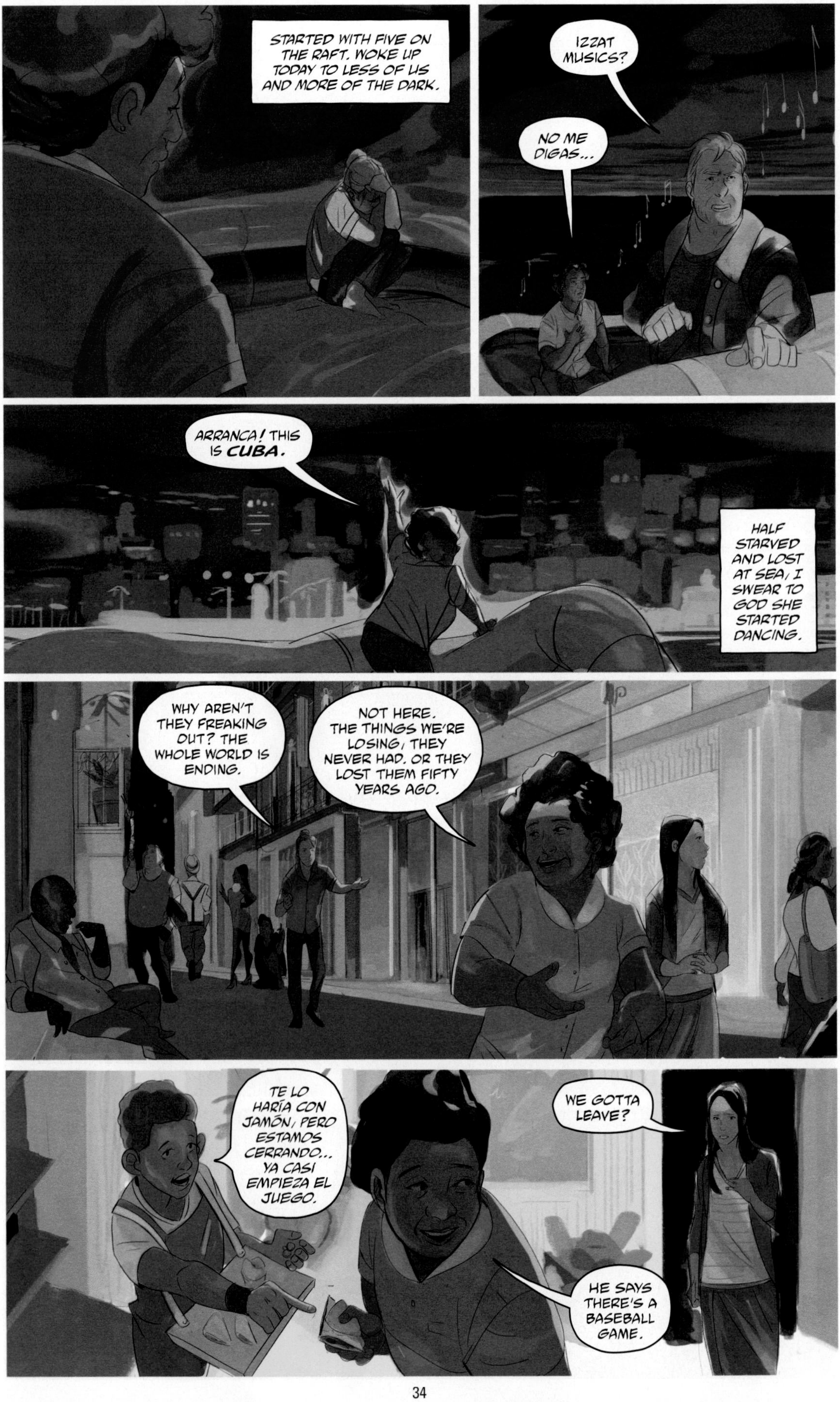
STARTED WITH FIVE ON THE RAFT. WOKE UP TODAY TO LESS OF US AND MORE OF THE DARK.
IZZAT MUSICS?
NO ME DIGAS...
ARRANCA! THIS IS CUBA.
HALF STARVED AND LOST AT SEA, I SWEAR TO GOD SHE STARTED DANCING.
WHY AREN'T THEY FREAKING OUT? THE WHOLE WORLD IS ENDING.
NOT HERE. THE THINGS WE'RE LOSING, THEY NEVER HAD. OR THEY LOST THEM FIFTY YEARS AGO.
TE LO HARÍA CON JAMÓN, PERO ESTAMOS CERRANDO... YA CASI EMPIEZA EL JUEGO.
WE GOTTA LEAVE?
HE SAYS THERE'S A BASEBALL GAME.

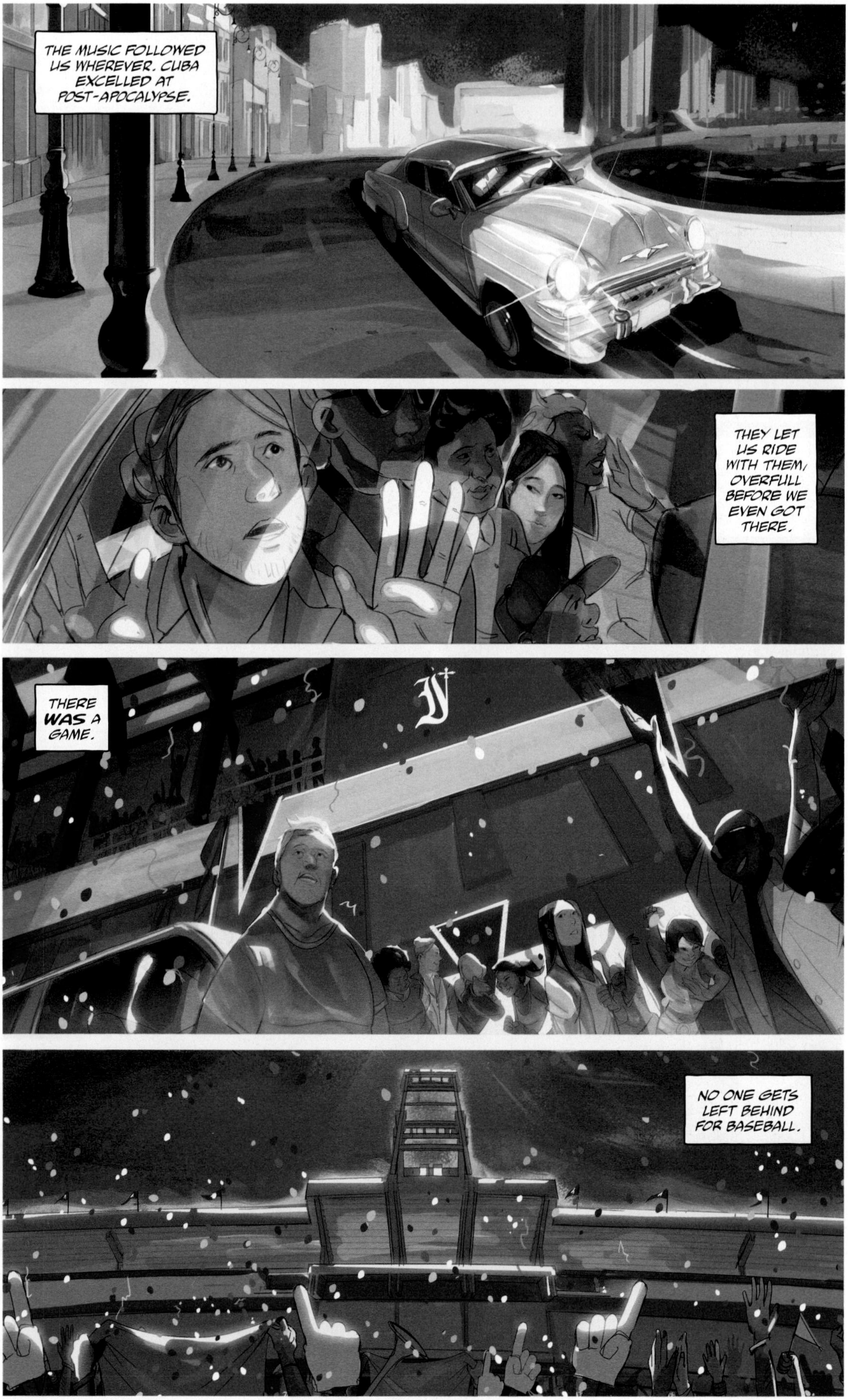
THE MUSIC FOLLOWED US WHEREVER. CUBA EXCELLED AT POST-APOCALYPSE.
THEY LET US RIDE WITH THEM, OVERFULL BEFORE WE EVEN GOT THERE.
THERE **WAS** A GAME.
NO ONE GETS LEFT BEHIND FOR BASEBALL.

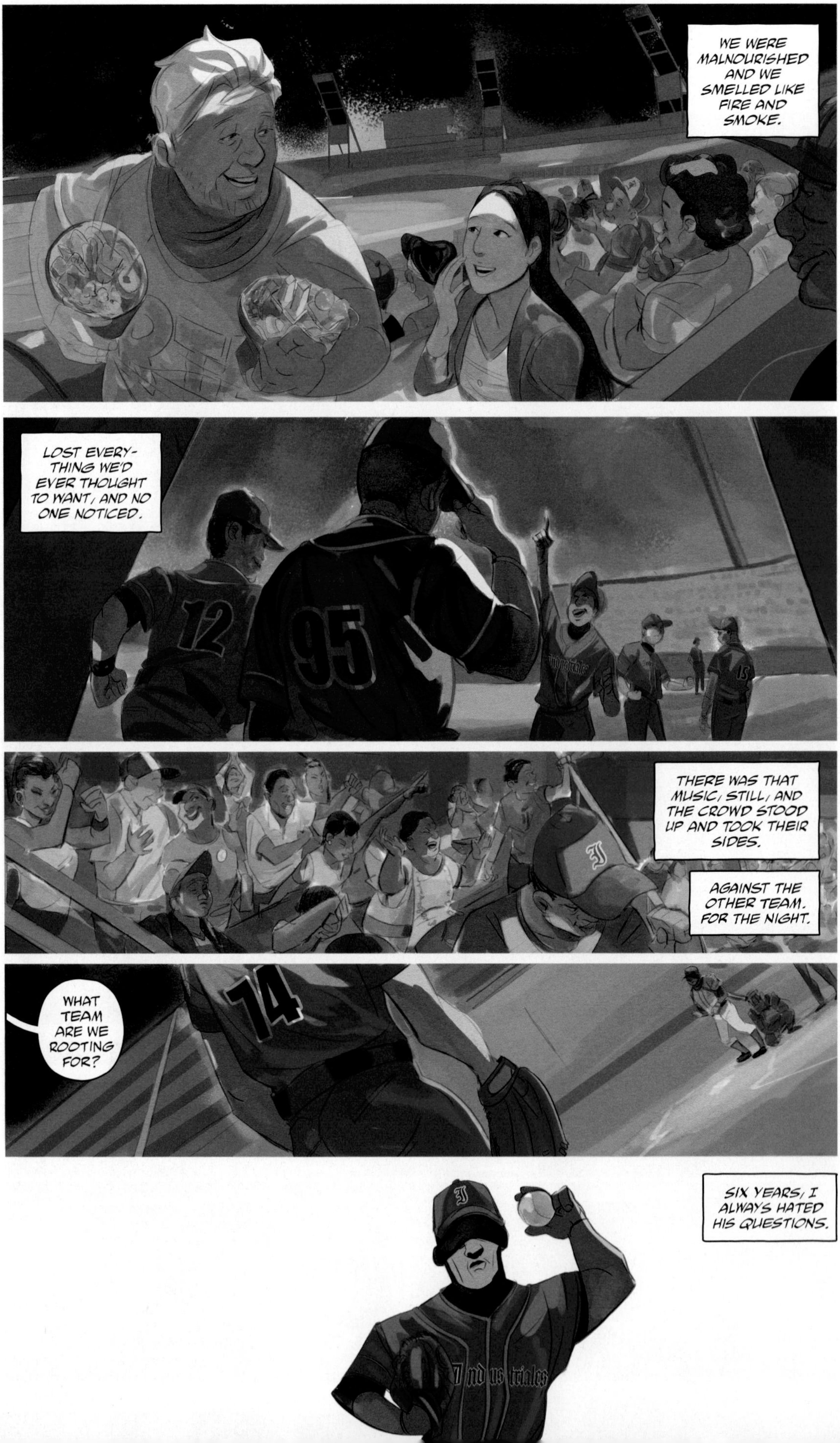
WE WERE MALNOURISHED AND WE SMELLED LIKE FIRE AND SMOKE.
LOST EVERY-THING WE'D EVER THOUGHT TO WANT, AND NO ONE NOTICED.
95
12
THERE WAS THAT MUSIC, STILL, AND THE CROWD STOOD UP AND TOOK THEIR SIDES.
AGAINST THE OTHER TEAM. FOR THE NIGHT.
74
WHAT TEAM ARE WE ROOTING FOR?
SIX YEARS, I ALWAYS HATED HIS QUESTIONS.
Industriales

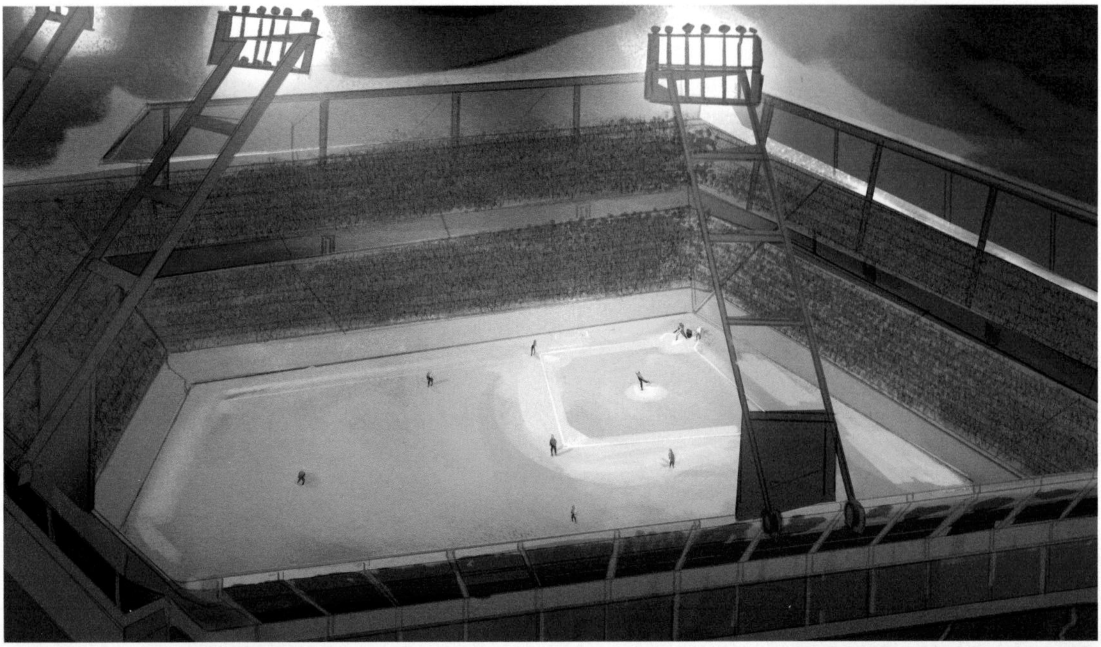

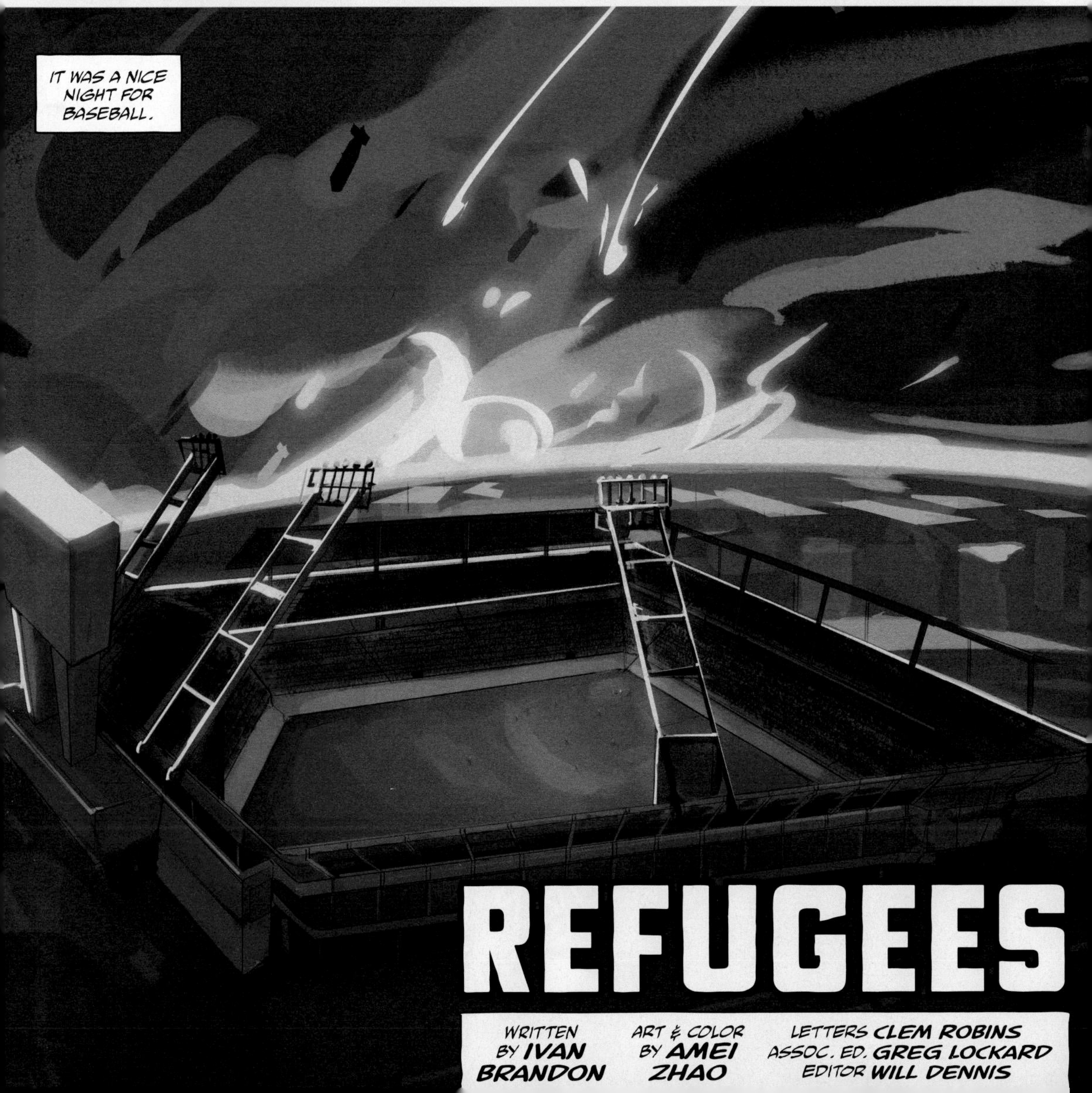

IT WAS A NICE NIGHT FOR BASEBALL.
REFUGEES
WRITTEN BY IVAN BRANDON
ART & COLOR BY AMEI ZHAO
LETTERS CLEM ROBINS
ASSOC. ED. GREG LOCKARD
EDITOR WILL DENNIS

Variant cover art for issue #1 by **Mike Mitchell**

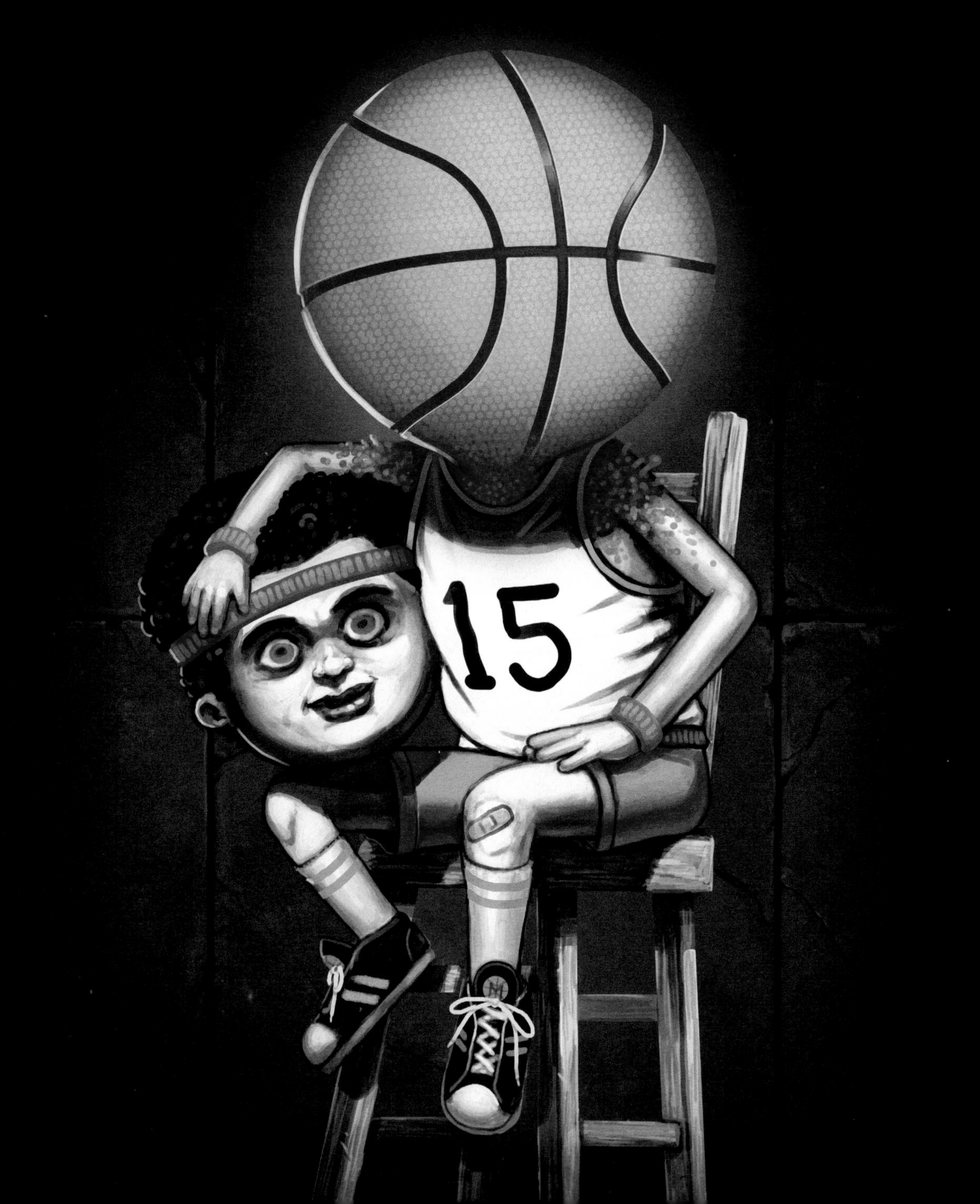
15

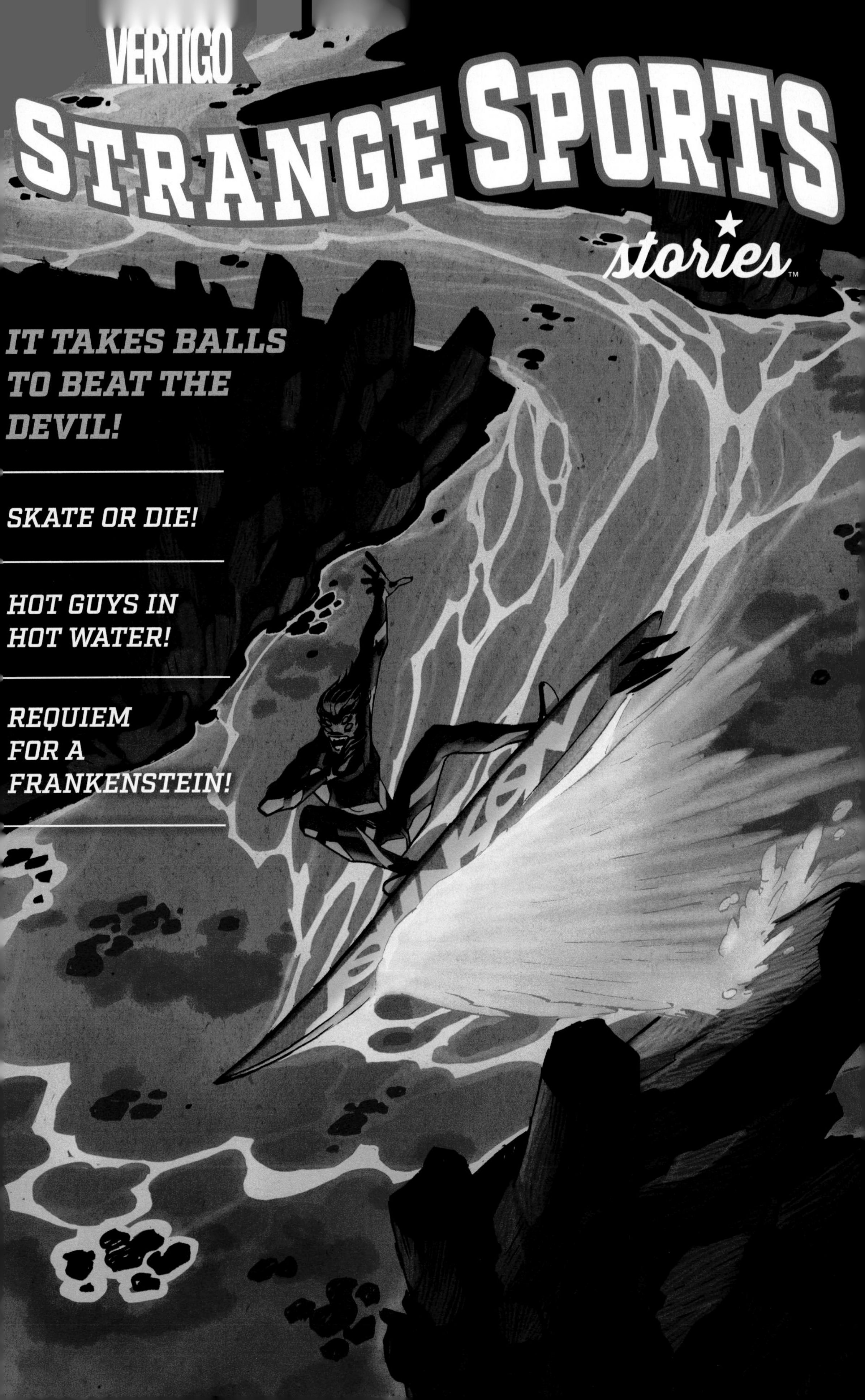
VERTIGO
STRANGE SPORTS
stories™
IT TAKES BALLS TO BEAT THE DEVIL!
SKATE OR DIE!
HOT GUYS IN HOT WATER!
REQUIEM FOR A FRANKENSTEIN!

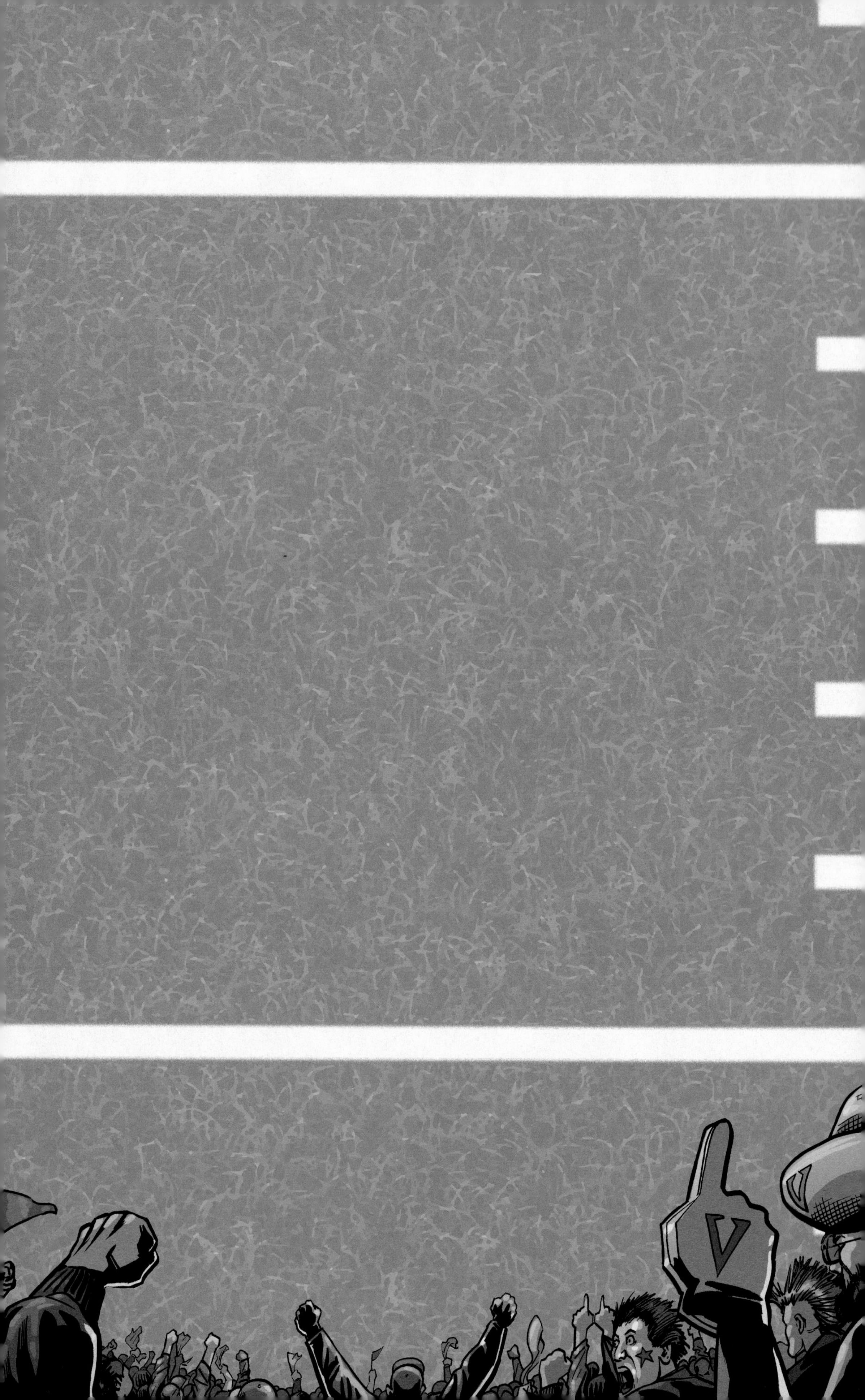

SKATE THE CYNIC

LOUGHRIDGE
DRAGOTTA
FLETCHER
LOCKARD + DENNIS

NOTE TO SELF: NEVER SEARCH THE WORD "DUKE" ONLINE.

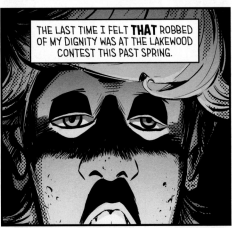

THE LAST TIME I FELT **THAT** ROBBED OF MY DIGNITY WAS AT THE LAKEWOOD CONTEST THIS PAST SPRING.

IDIOTS THERE HAD NO **FUCKING** IDEA WHAT I DO...

WHAT I DO IS **ART**... EXPRESSION ON A SKATEBOARD...

THEY JUST WANT SOME FUCKING ROBOT TO DO AS MANY TRICKS AS POSSIBLE...

NO FALLING OR YOU CAN KISS ADVANCING GOODBYE...

CONTEST GUYS ARE NEVER THE BEST GUYS...

NO STYLE OR INTEGRITY... KOOKS...

THAT'S THE BANGER!

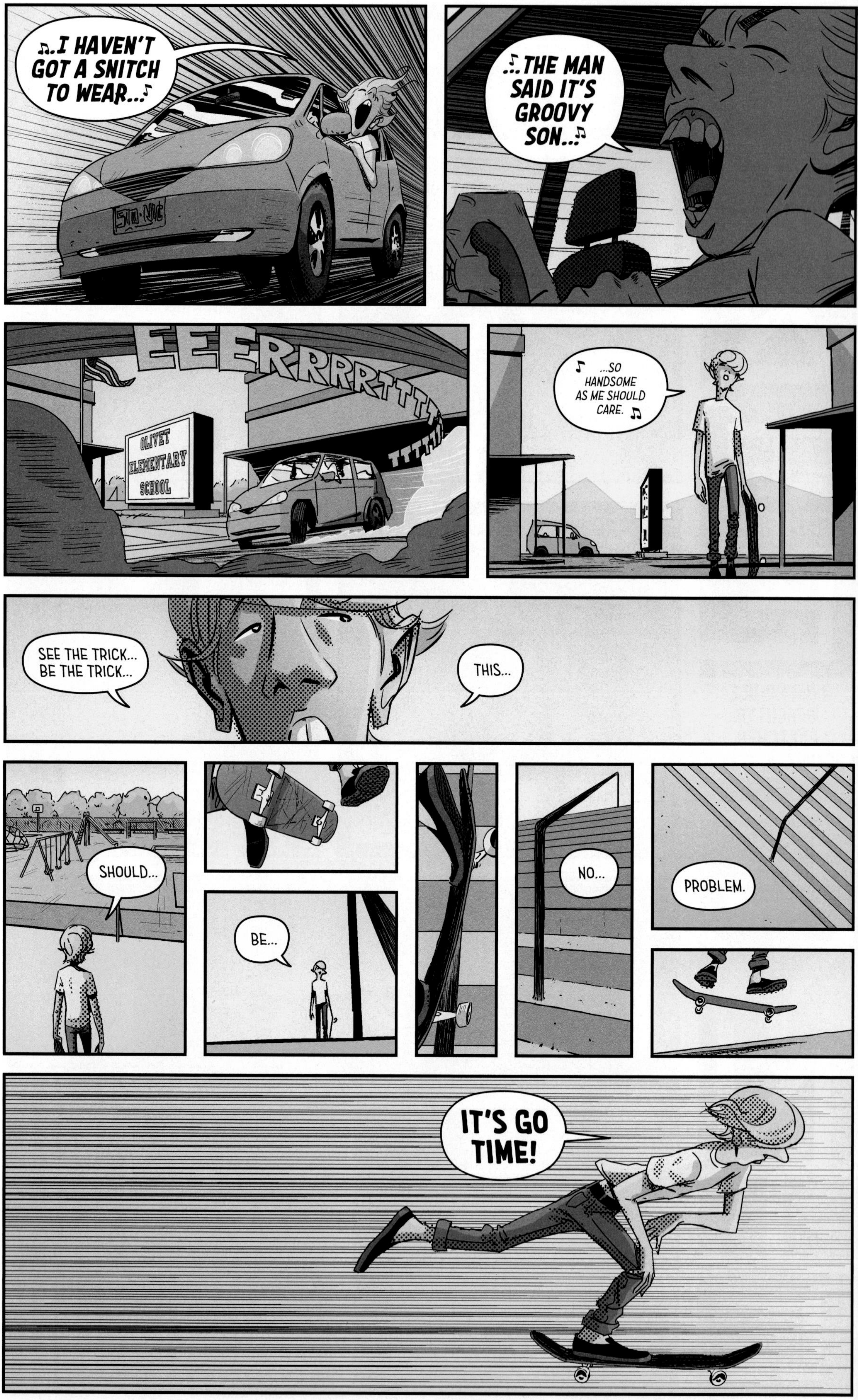
♫..I HAVEN'T GOT A SNITCH TO WEAR..♪
♫..THE MAN SAID IT'S GROOVY SON..♪
EEERRRRRTTTTTTTT
OLIVET ELEMENTARY SCHOOL
♪ ...SO HANDSOME AS ME SHOULD CARE. ♫
SEE THE TRICK... BE THE TRICK...
THIS...
SHOULD...
BE...
NO...
PROBLEM.
IT'S GO TIME!

KAK!
OH!
YARD SALE!
HOWP!
NO... KIDS
...BACK-WARDS!
THIS...
NONONO!
REALLY?!
ISN'T
ASSPP!
C'MON!
GOLF!
OOOMMMPPPHHH!
GOLDEN GOD!
BOING
IF NO ONE HEARS ANYTHING, BY DEFINITION THERE WAS NOT A SOUND.
...

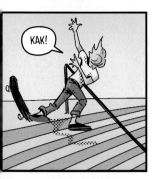

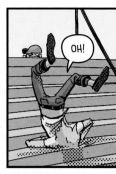

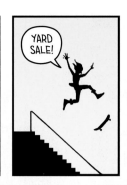

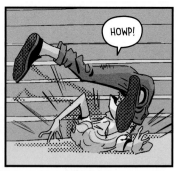

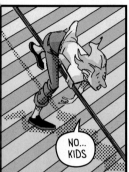

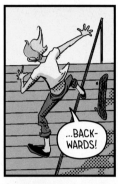

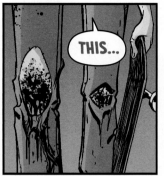

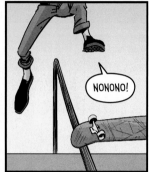

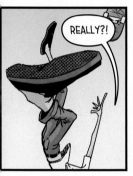

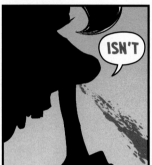

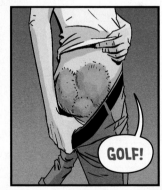

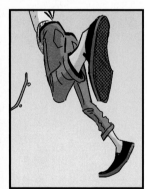

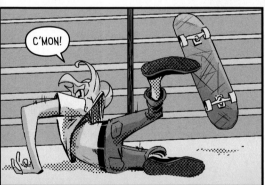

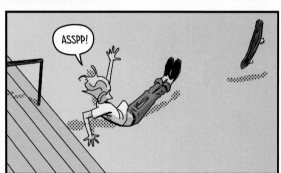

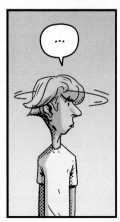

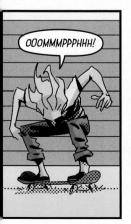

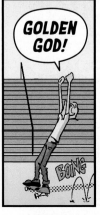

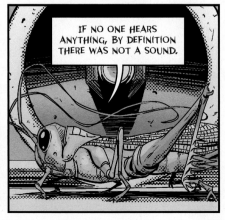

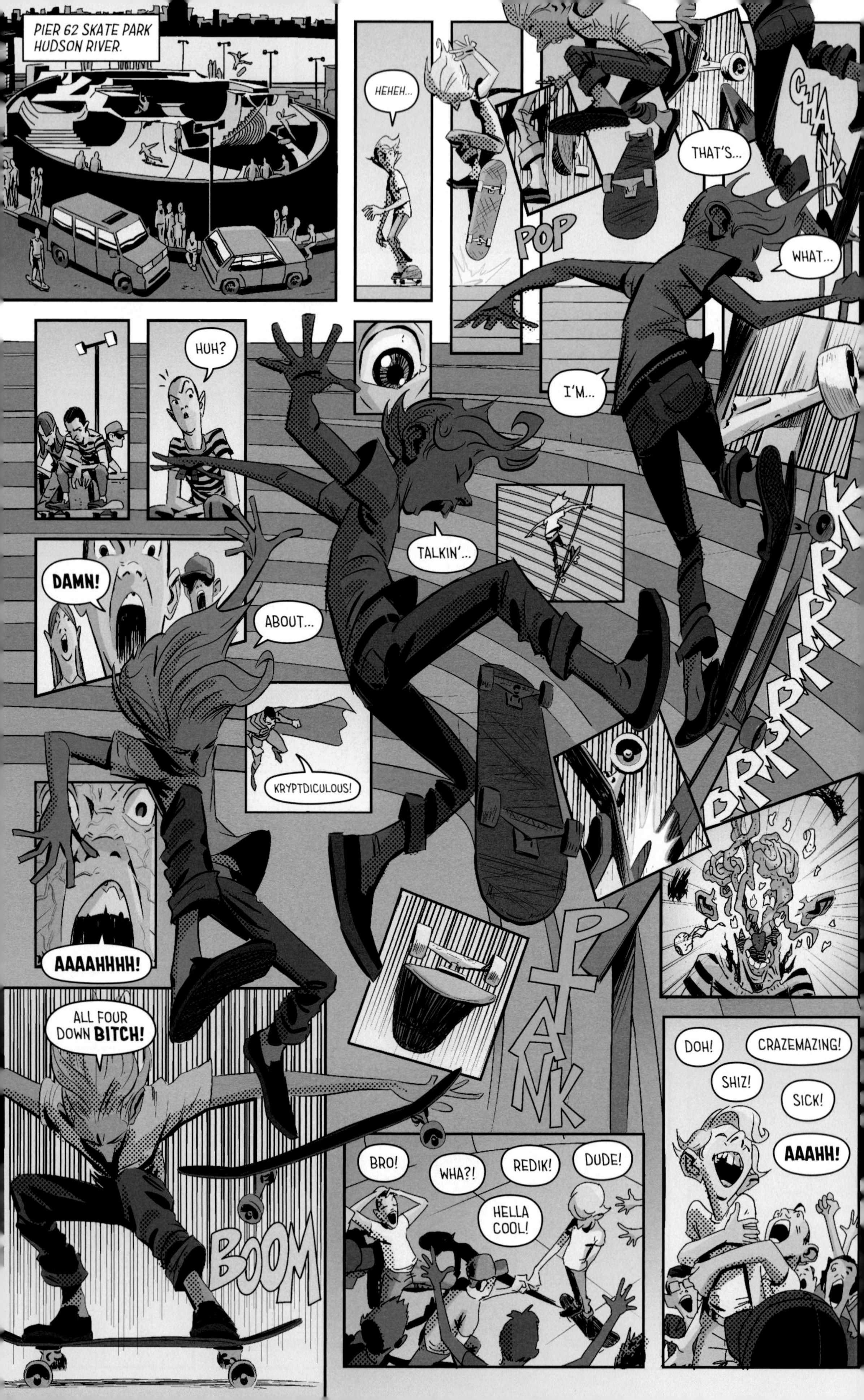
PIER 62 SKATE PARK
HUDSON RIVER.
HEHEH...
POP
THAT'S...
CHANK
WHAT...
I'M...
HUH?
TALKIN'...
DAMN!
ABOUT...
KRYPTDICULOUS!
KRRRRRRRB
AAAAHHHH!
PANK
ALL FOUR
DOWN BITCH!
BOOM
BRO!
WHA?!
REDIK!
DUDE!
HELLA
COOL!
DOH!
CRAZEMAZING!
SHIZ!
SICK!
AAAHH!

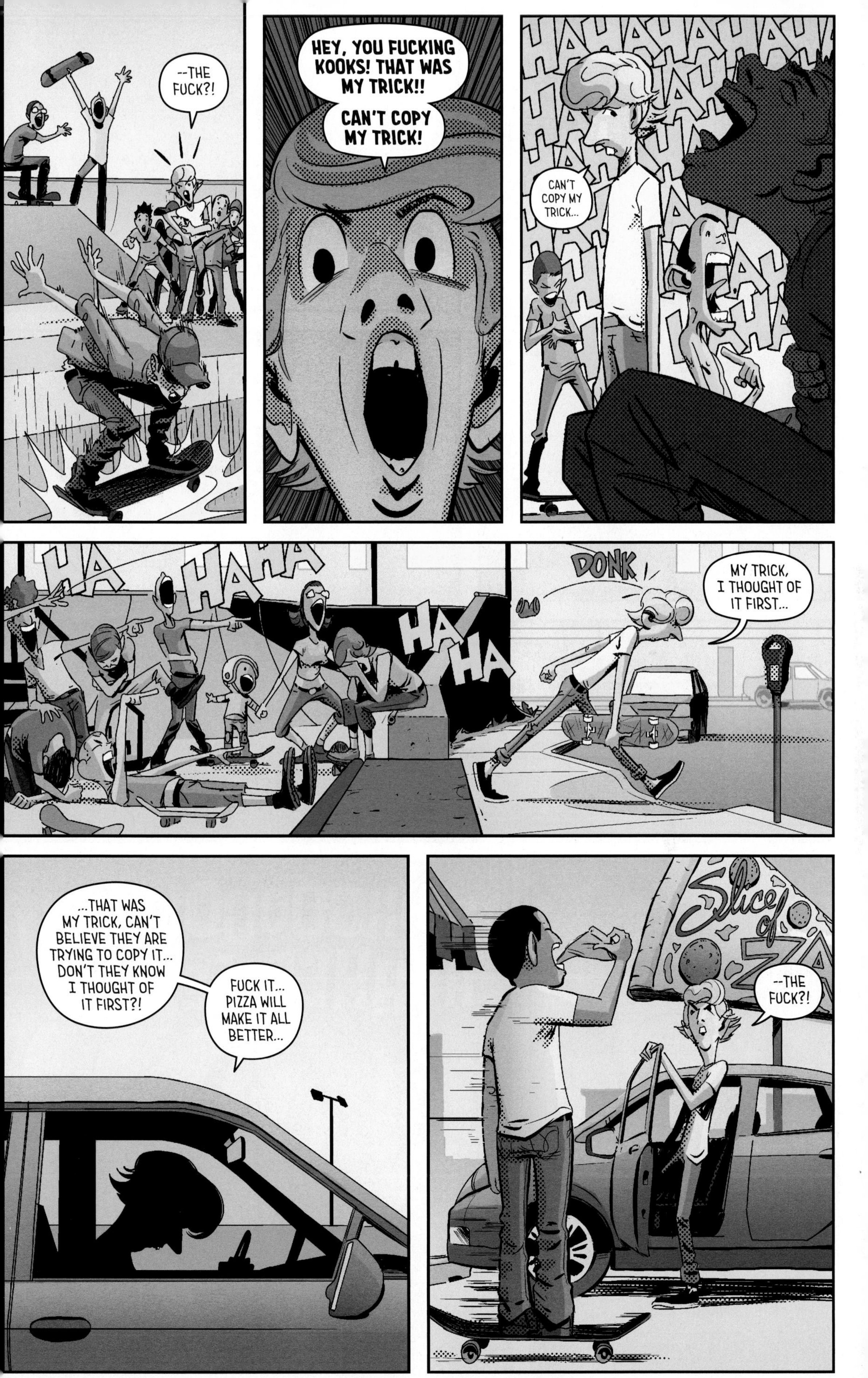
--THE FUCK?!
HEY, YOU FUCKING KOOKS! THAT WAS MY TRICK!!
CAN'T COPY MY TRICK!
CAN'T COPY MY TRICK...
HAHAHA
HA HAHAHA
HA HA
DONK
MY TRICK, I THOUGHT OF IT FIRST...
...THAT WAS MY TRICK, CAN'T BELIEVE THEY ARE TRYING TO COPY IT... DON'T THEY KNOW I THOUGHT OF IT FIRST?!
FUCK IT... PIZZA WILL MAKE IT ALL BETTER...
Slice of ZA
--THE FUCK?!

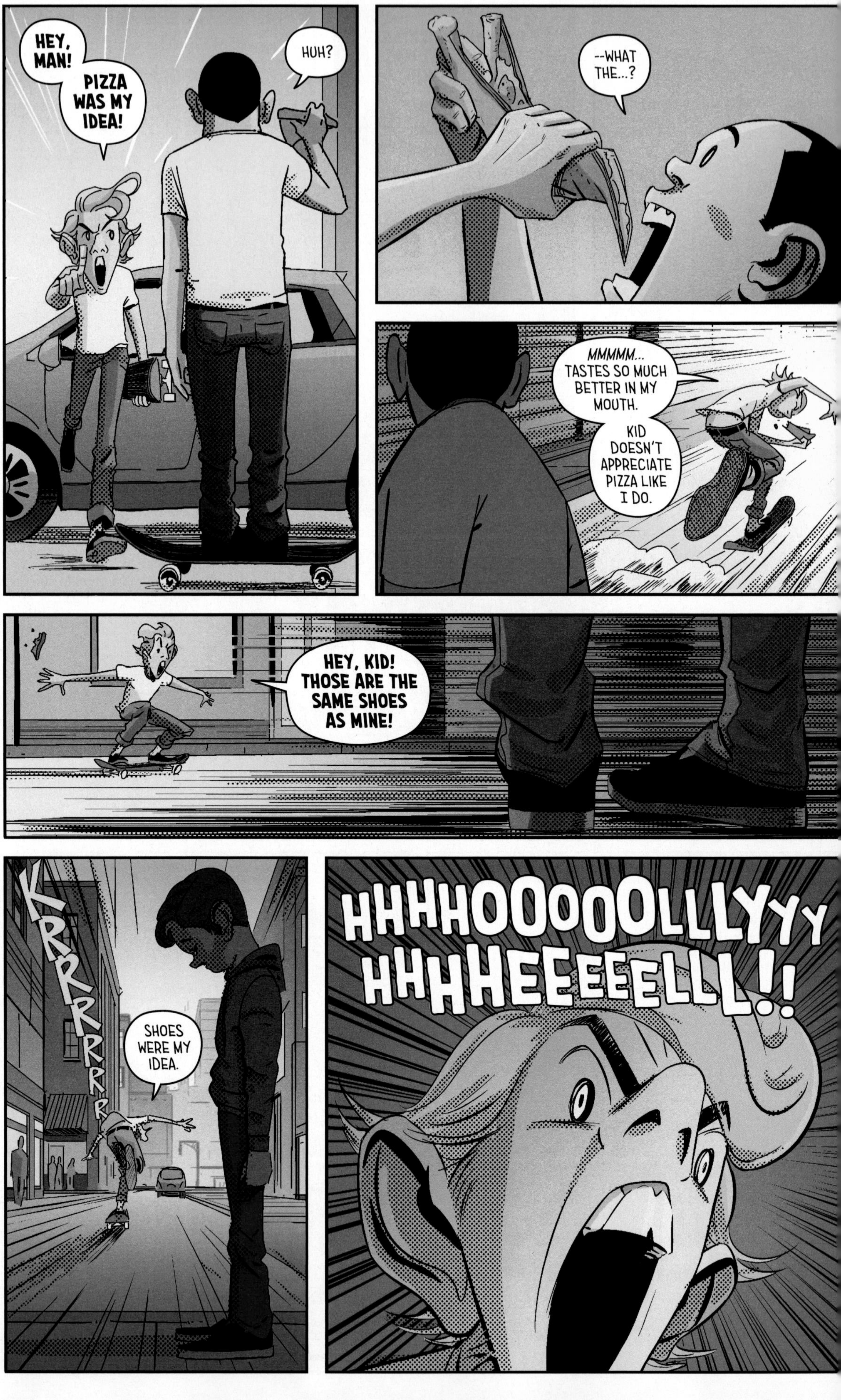
HEY, MAN!
PIZZA WAS MY IDEA!
HUH?
--WHAT THE...?
MMMMM... TASTES SO MUCH BETTER IN MY MOUTH.
KID DOESN'T APPRECIATE PIZZA LIKE I DO.
HEY, KID! THOSE ARE THE SAME SHOES AS MINE!
KRRRRRRR
SHOES WERE MY IDEA.
HHHHOOOOOLLLYYY HHHHEEEEELLL!!

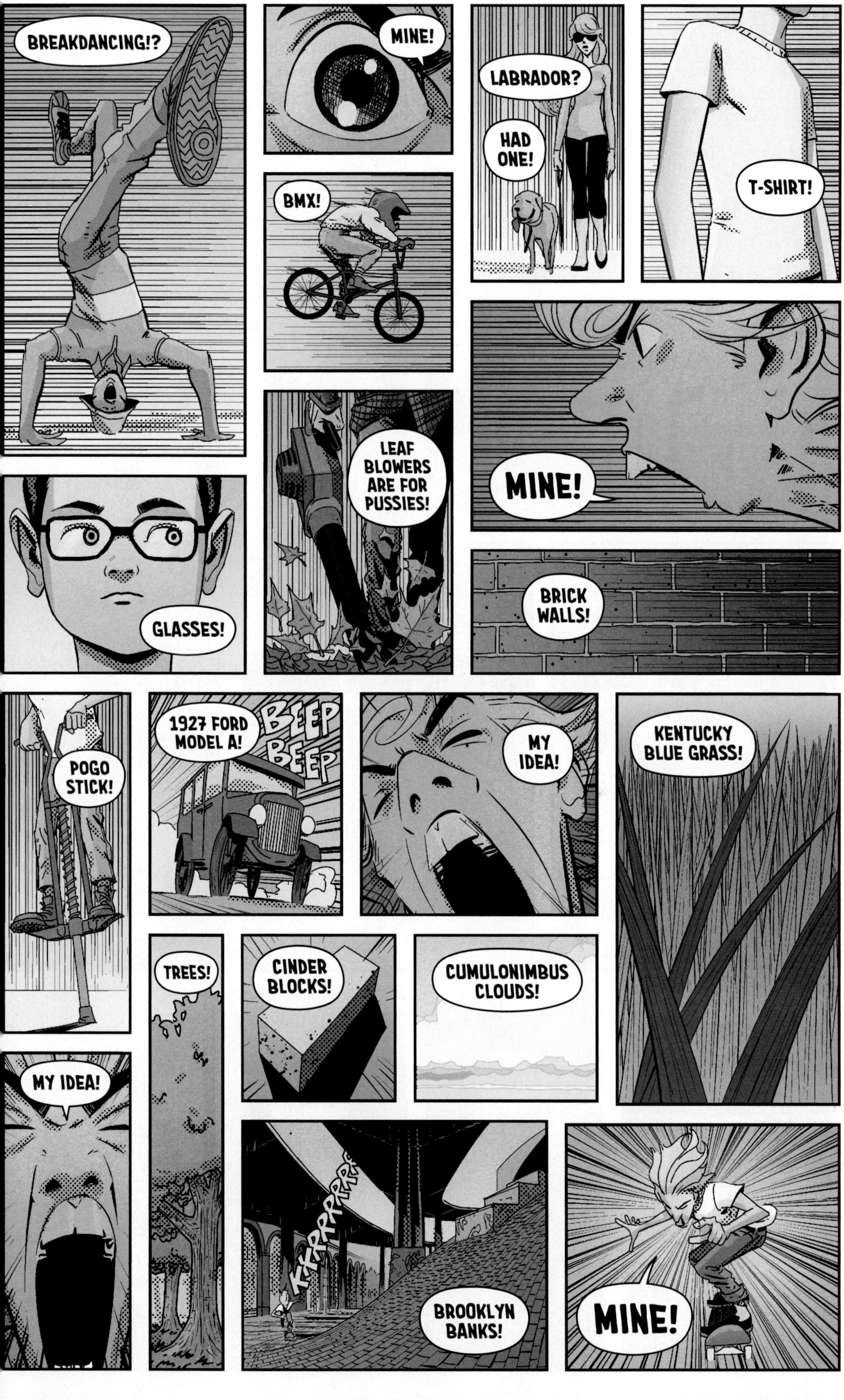
BREAKDANCING!?
MINE!
BMX!
LABRADOR?
HAD ONE!
T-SHIRT!
GLASSES!
LEAF BLOWERS ARE FOR PUSSIES!
MINE!
BRICK WALLS!
POGO STICK!
1927 FORD MODEL A!
BEEP BEEP
MY IDEA!
KENTUCKY BLUE GRASS!
TREES!
CINDER BLOCKS!
CUMULONIMBUS CLOUDS!
MY IDEA!
BROOKLYN BANKS!
MINE!

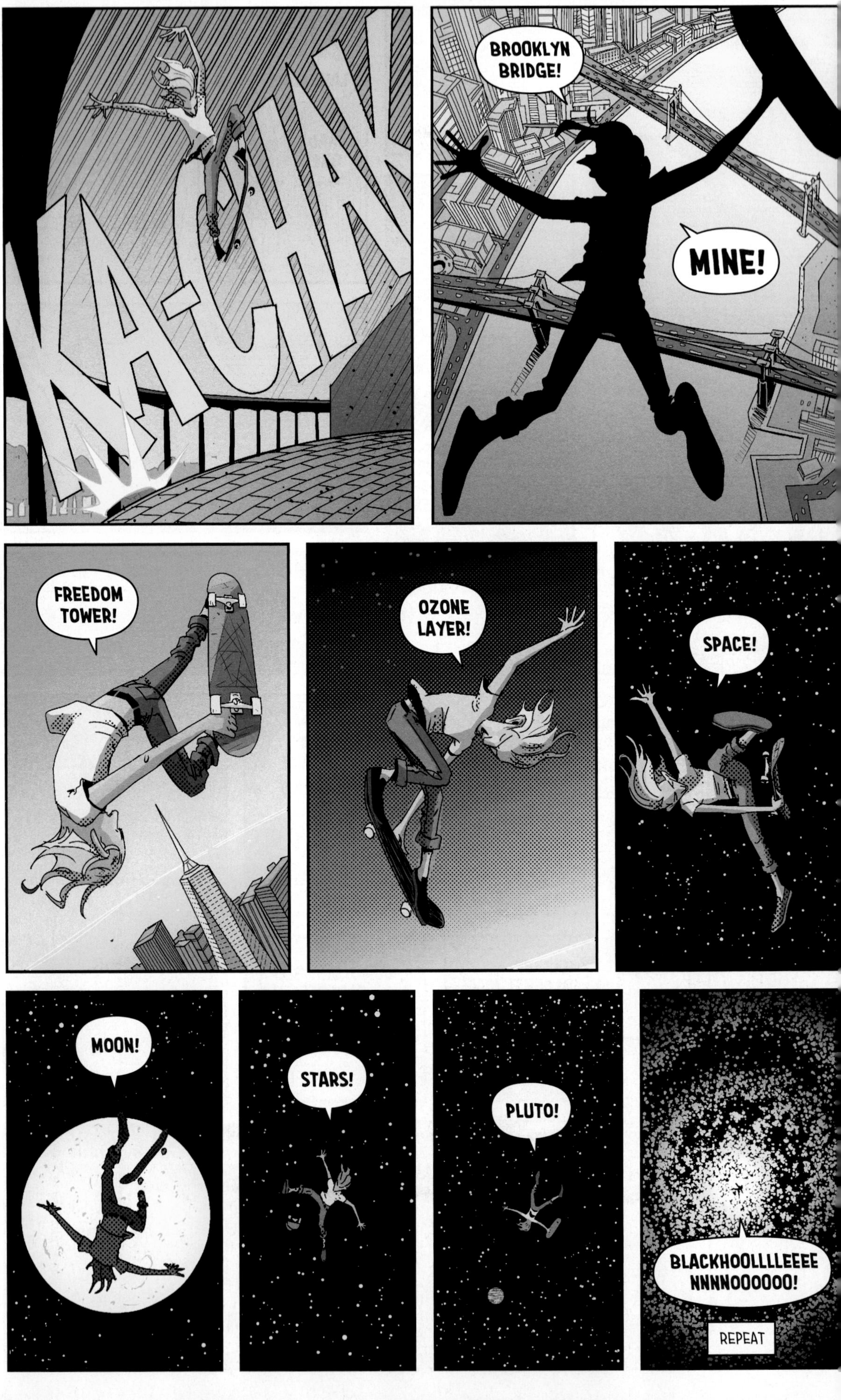
KA-CHAK
BROOKLYN BRIDGE!
MINE!
FREEDOM TOWER!
OZONE LAYER!
SPACE!
MOON!
STARS!
PLUTO!
BLACKHOOLLLLEEEE NNNNOOOOOO!
REPEAT

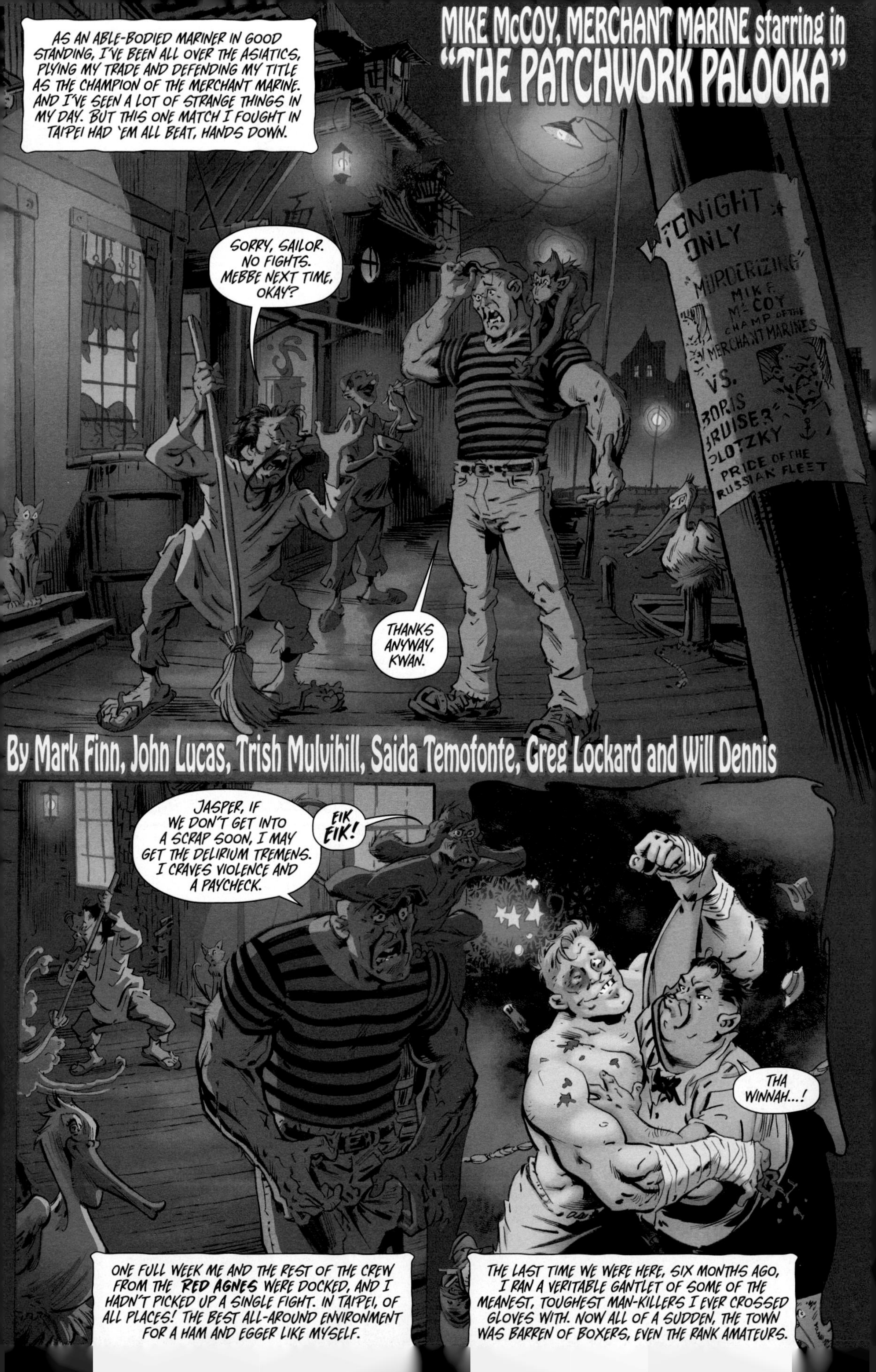
MIKE McCOY, MERCHANT MARINE starring in
"THE PATCHWORK PALOOKA"
AS AN ABLE-BODIED MARINER IN GOOD STANDING, I'VE BEEN ALL OVER THE ASIATICS, PLYING MY TRADE AND DEFENDING MY TITLE AS THE CHAMPION OF THE MERCHANT MARINE. AND I'VE SEEN A LOT OF STRANGE THINGS IN MY DAY. BUT THIS ONE MATCH I FOUGHT IN TAIPEI HAD 'EM ALL BEAT, HANDS DOWN.
TONIGHT ONLY
MURDERIZING MIKE McCOY CHAMP OF THE MERCHANT MARINES
VS.
BORIS BRUISER BLOTZKY PRIDE OF THE RUSSIAN FLEET
SORRY, SAILOR. NO FIGHTS. MEBBE NEXT TIME, OKAY?
THANKS ANYWAY, KWAN.
By Mark Finn, John Lucas, Trish Mulvihill, Saida Temofonte, Greg Lockard and Will Dennis
JASPER, IF WE DON'T GET INTO A SCRAP SOON, I MAY GET THE DELIRIUM TREMENS. I CRAVES VIOLENCE AND A PAYCHECK.
EIK EIK!
THA WINNAH...!
ONE FULL WEEK ME AND THE REST OF THE CREW FROM THE RED AGNES WERE DOCKED, AND I HADN'T PICKED UP A SINGLE FIGHT. IN TAIPEI, OF ALL PLACES! THE BEST ALL-AROUND ENVIRONMENT FOR A HAM AND EGGER LIKE MYSELF.
THE LAST TIME WE WERE HERE, SIX MONTHS AGO, I RAN A VERITABLE GANTLET OF SOME OF THE MEANEST, TOUGHEST MAN-KILLERS I EVER CROSSED GLOVES WITH. NOW ALL OF A SUDDEN, THE TOWN WAS BARREN OF BOXERS, EVEN THE RANK AMATEURS.

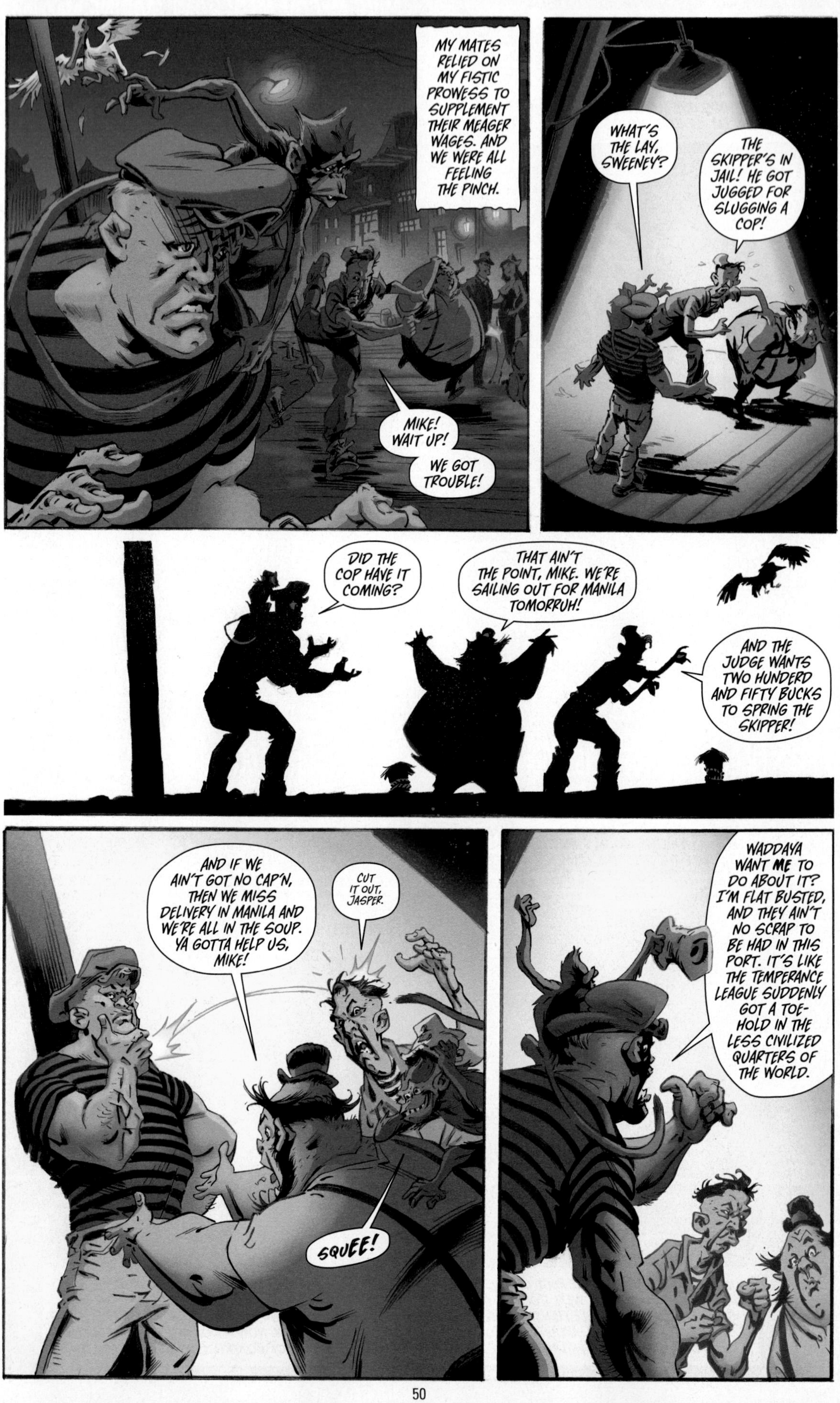

MY MATES RELIED ON MY FISTIC PROWESS TO SUPPLEMENT THEIR MEAGER WAGES. AND WE WERE ALL FEELING THE PINCH.
MIKE! WAIT UP!
WE GOT TROUBLE!
WHAT'S THE LAY, SWEENEY?
THE SKIPPER'S IN JAIL! HE GOT JUGGED FOR SLUGGING A COP!
DID THE COP HAVE IT COMING?
THAT AIN'T THE POINT, MIKE. WE'RE SAILING OUT FOR MANILA TOMORRUH!
AND THE JUDGE WANTS TWO HUNDERD AND FIFTY BUCKS TO SPRING THE SKIPPER!
AND IF WE AIN'T GOT NO CAP'N, THEN WE MISS DELIVERY IN MANILA AND WE'RE ALL IN THE SOUP. YA GOTTA HELP US, MIKE!
CUT IT OUT, JASPER.
SQUEE!
WADDAYA WANT **ME** TO DO ABOUT IT? I'M FLAT BUSTED, AND THEY AIN'T NO SCRAP TO BE HAD IN THIS PORT. IT'S LIKE THE TEMPERANCE LEAGUE SUDDENLY GOT A TOE-HOLD IN THE LESS CIVILIZED QUARTERS OF THE WORLD.

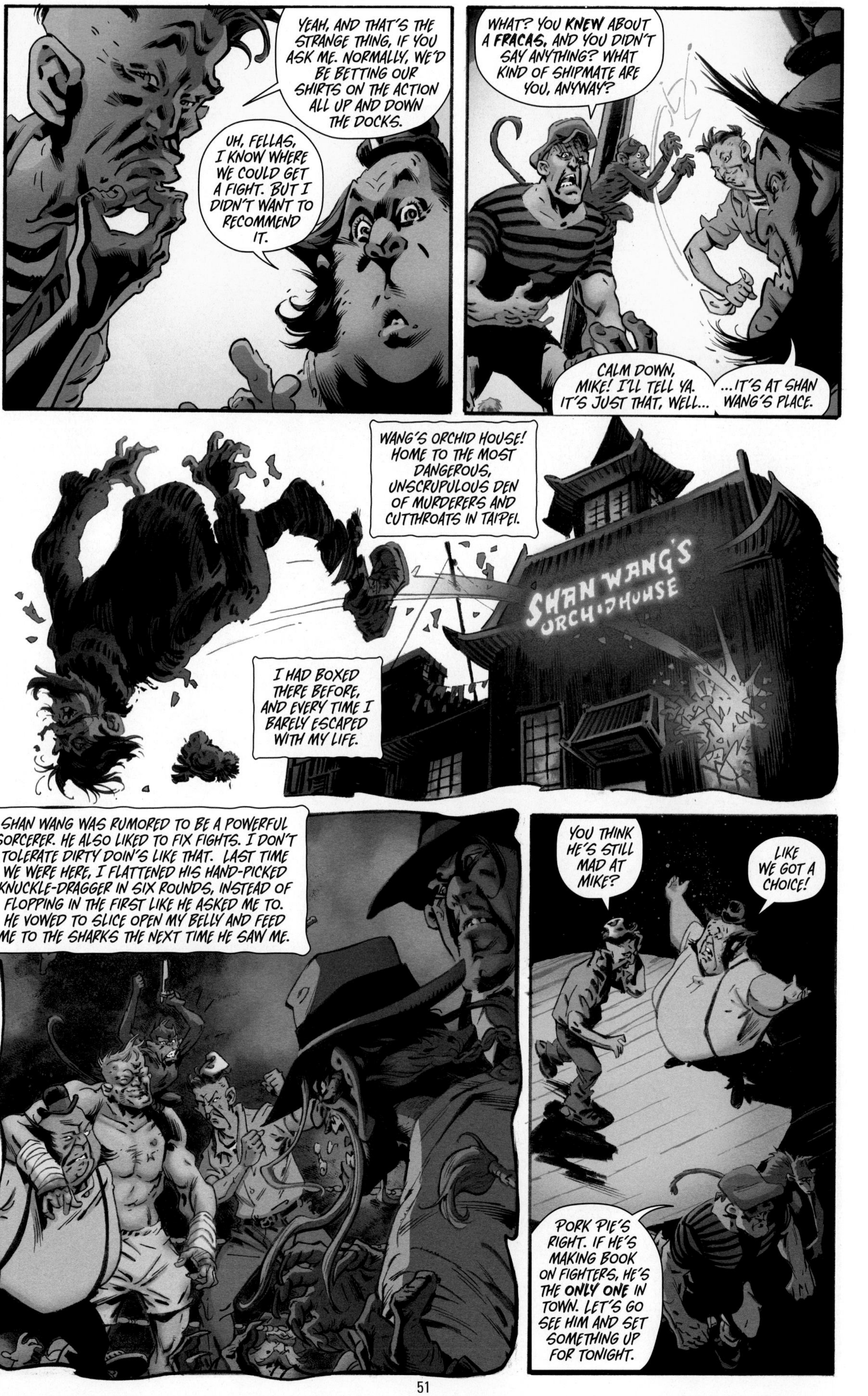
YEAH, AND THAT'S THE STRANGE THING, IF YOU ASK ME. NORMALLY, WE'D BE BETTING OUR SHIRTS ON THE ACTION ALL UP AND DOWN THE DOCKS.
UH, FELLAS, I KNOW WHERE WE COULD GET A FIGHT. BUT I DIDN'T WANT TO RECOMMEND IT.
WHAT? YOU **KNEW** ABOUT A **FRACAS**, AND YOU DIDN'T SAY ANYTHING? WHAT KIND OF SHIPMATE ARE YOU, ANYWAY?
CALM DOWN, MIKE! I'LL TELL YA. IT'S JUST THAT, WELL...
...IT'S AT SHAN WANG'S PLACE.
WANG'S ORCHID HOUSE! HOME TO THE MOST DANGEROUS, UNSCRUPULOUS DEN OF MURDERERS AND CUTTHROATS IN TAIPEI.
SHAN WANG'S ORCHID HOUSE
I HAD BOXED THERE BEFORE, AND EVERY TIME I BARELY ESCAPED WITH MY LIFE.
SHAN WANG WAS RUMORED TO BE A POWERFUL SORCERER. HE ALSO LIKED TO FIX FIGHTS. I DON'T TOLERATE DIRTY DOIN'S LIKE THAT. LAST TIME WE WERE HERE, I FLATTENED HIS HAND-PICKED KNUCKLE-DRAGGER IN SIX ROUNDS, INSTEAD OF FLOPPING IN THE FIRST LIKE HE ASKED ME TO. HE VOWED TO SLICE OPEN MY BELLY AND FEED ME TO THE SHARKS THE NEXT TIME HE SAW ME.
YOU THINK HE'S STILL MAD AT MIKE?
LIKE WE GOT A CHOICE!
PORK PIE'S RIGHT. IF HE'S MAKING BOOK ON FIGHTERS, HE'S THE **ONLY ONE** IN TOWN. LET'S GO SEE HIM AND SET SOMETHING UP FOR TONIGHT.

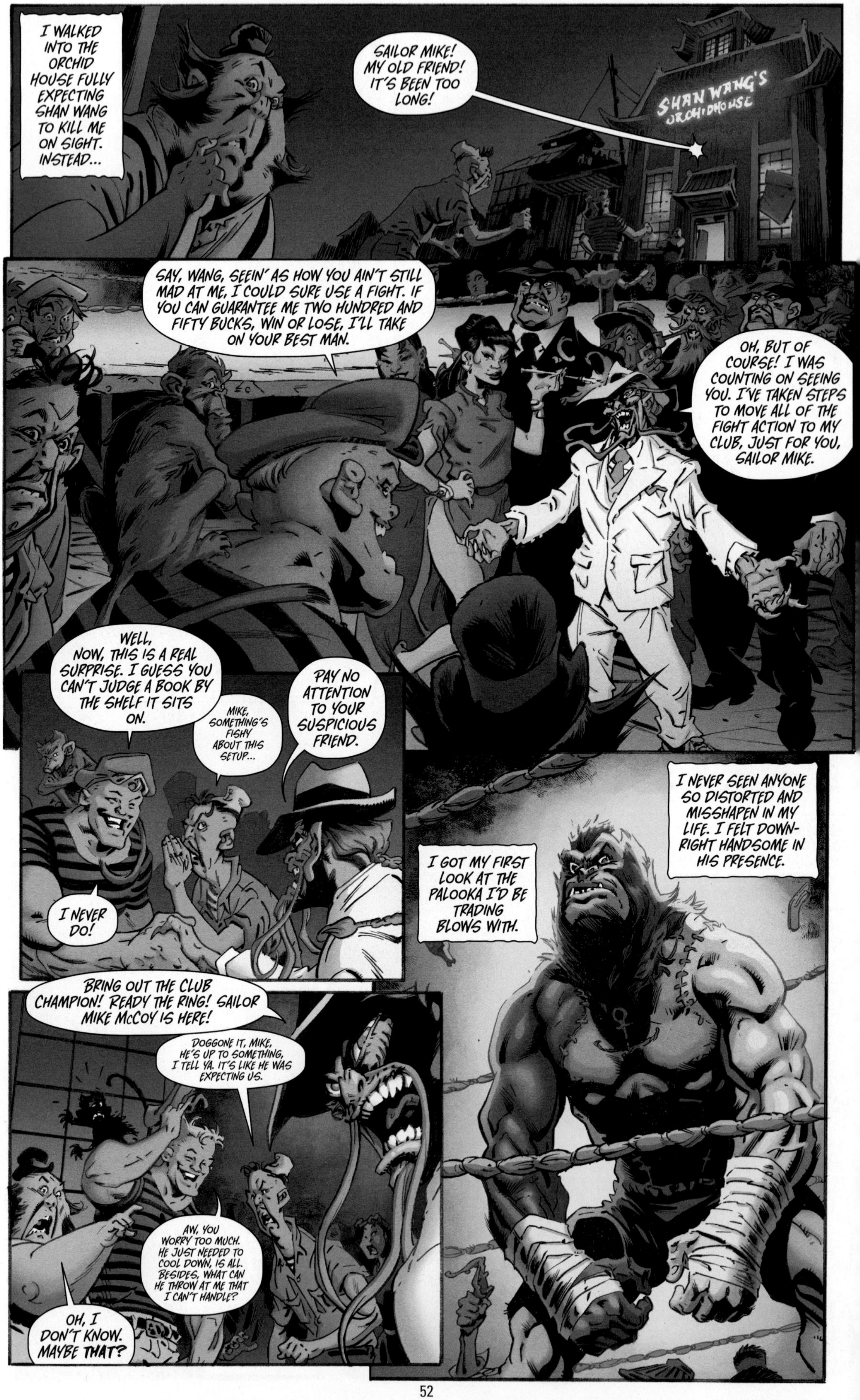
I WALKED INTO THE ORCHID HOUSE FULLY EXPECTING SHAN WANG TO KILL ME ON SIGHT. INSTEAD...
SAILOR MIKE! MY OLD FRIEND! IT'S BEEN TOO LONG!
SHAN WANG'S ORCHIDHOUSE
SAY, WANG, SEEIN' AS HOW YOU AIN'T STILL MAD AT ME, I COULD SURE USE A FIGHT. IF YOU CAN GUARANTEE ME TWO HUNDRED AND FIFTY BUCKS, WIN OR LOSE, I'LL TAKE ON YOUR BEST MAN.
OH, BUT OF COURSE! I WAS COUNTING ON SEEING YOU. I'VE TAKEN STEPS TO MOVE ALL OF THE FIGHT ACTION TO MY CLUB, JUST FOR YOU, SAILOR MIKE.
WELL, NOW, THIS IS A REAL SURPRISE. I GUESS YOU CAN'T JUDGE A BOOK BY THE SHELF IT SITS ON.
MIKE, SOMETHING'S FISHY ABOUT THIS SETUP...
PAY NO ATTENTION TO YOUR SUSPICIOUS FRIEND.
I NEVER DO!
I GOT MY FIRST LOOK AT THE PALOOKA I'D BE TRADING BLOWS WITH.
I NEVER SEEN ANYONE SO DISTORTED AND MISSHAPEN IN MY LIFE. I FELT DOWN-RIGHT HANDSOME IN HIS PRESENCE.
BRING OUT THE CLUB CHAMPION! READY THE RING! SAILOR MIKE McCOY IS HERE!
DOGGONE IT, MIKE, HE'S UP TO SOMETHING, I TELL YA. IT'S LIKE HE WAS EXPECTING US.
AW, YOU WORRY TOO MUCH. HE JUST NEEDED TO COOL DOWN, IS ALL. BESIDES, WHAT CAN HE THROW AT ME THAT I CAN'T HANDLE?
OH, I DON'T KNOW. MAYBE THAT?

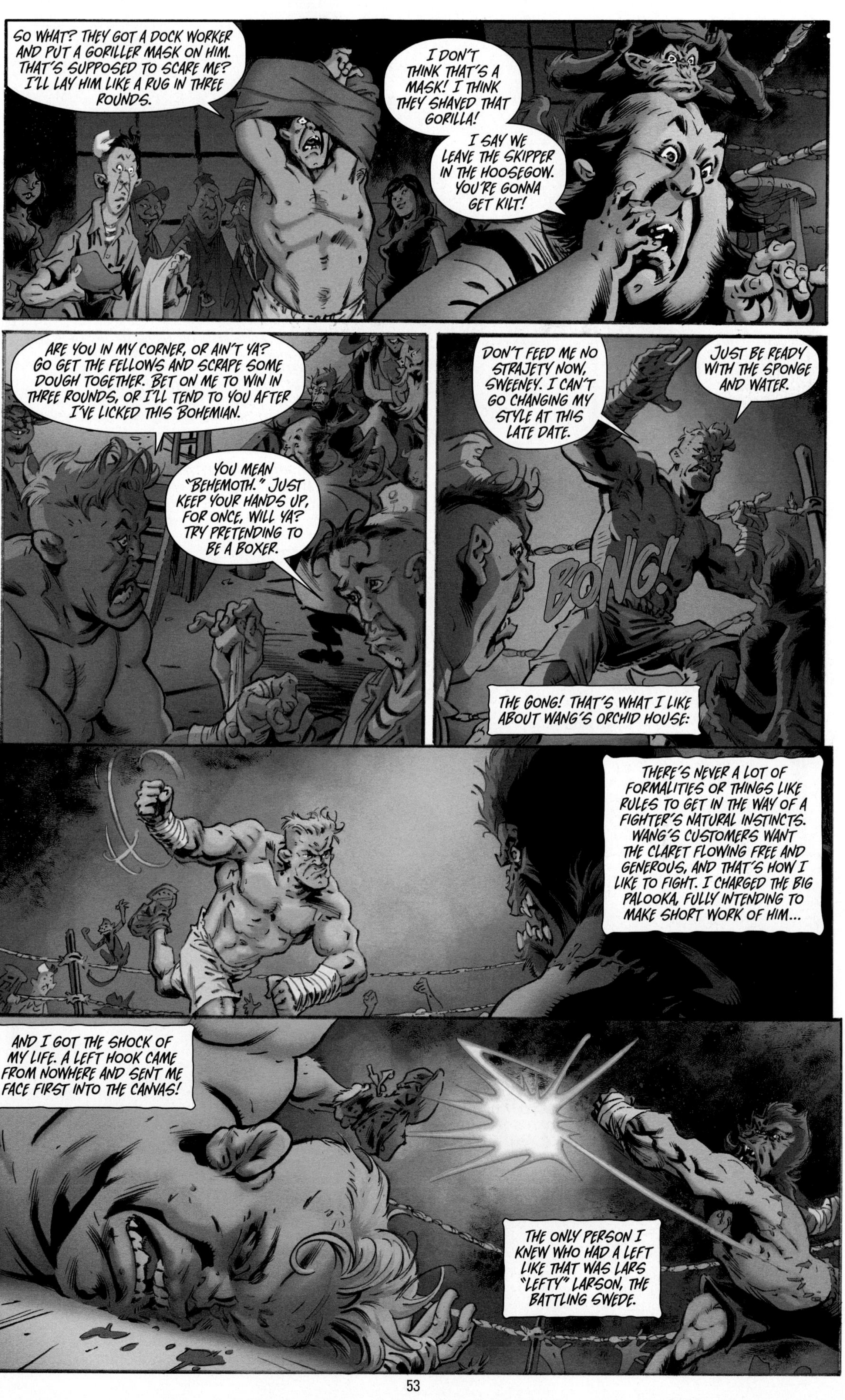
SO WHAT? THEY GOT A DOCK WORKER AND PUT A GORILLER MASK ON HIM. THAT'S SUPPOSED TO SCARE ME? I'LL LAY HIM LIKE A RUG IN THREE ROUNDS.
I DON'T THINK THAT'S A MASK! I THINK THEY SHAVED THAT GORILLA!
I SAY WE LEAVE THE SKIPPER IN THE HOOSEGOW. YOU'RE GONNA GET KILT!
ARE YOU IN MY CORNER, OR AIN'T YA? GO GET THE FELLOWS AND SCRAPE SOME DOUGH TOGETHER. BET ON ME TO WIN IN THREE ROUNDS, OR I'LL TEND TO YOU AFTER I'VE LICKED THIS BOHEMIAN.
YOU MEAN "BEHEMOTH." JUST KEEP YOUR HANDS UP, FOR ONCE, WILL YA? TRY PRETENDING TO BE A BOXER.
DON'T FEED ME NO STRAJETY NOW, SWEENEY. I CAN'T GO CHANGING MY STYLE AT THIS LATE DATE.
JUST BE READY WITH THE SPONGE AND WATER.
BONG!
THE GONG! THAT'S WHAT I LIKE ABOUT WANG'S ORCHID HOUSE:
THERE'S NEVER A LOT OF FORMALITIES OR THINGS LIKE RULES TO GET IN THE WAY OF A FIGHTER'S NATURAL INSTINCTS. WANG'S CUSTOMERS WANT THE CLARET FLOWING FREE AND GENEROUS, AND THAT'S HOW I LIKE TO FIGHT. I CHARGED THE BIG PALOOKA, FULLY INTENDING TO MAKE SHORT WORK OF HIM...
AND I GOT THE SHOCK OF MY LIFE. A LEFT HOOK CAME FROM NOWHERE AND SENT ME FACE FIRST INTO THE CANVAS!
THE ONLY PERSON I KNEW WHO HAD A LEFT LIKE THAT WAS LARS "LEFTY" LARSON, THE BATTLING SWEDE.

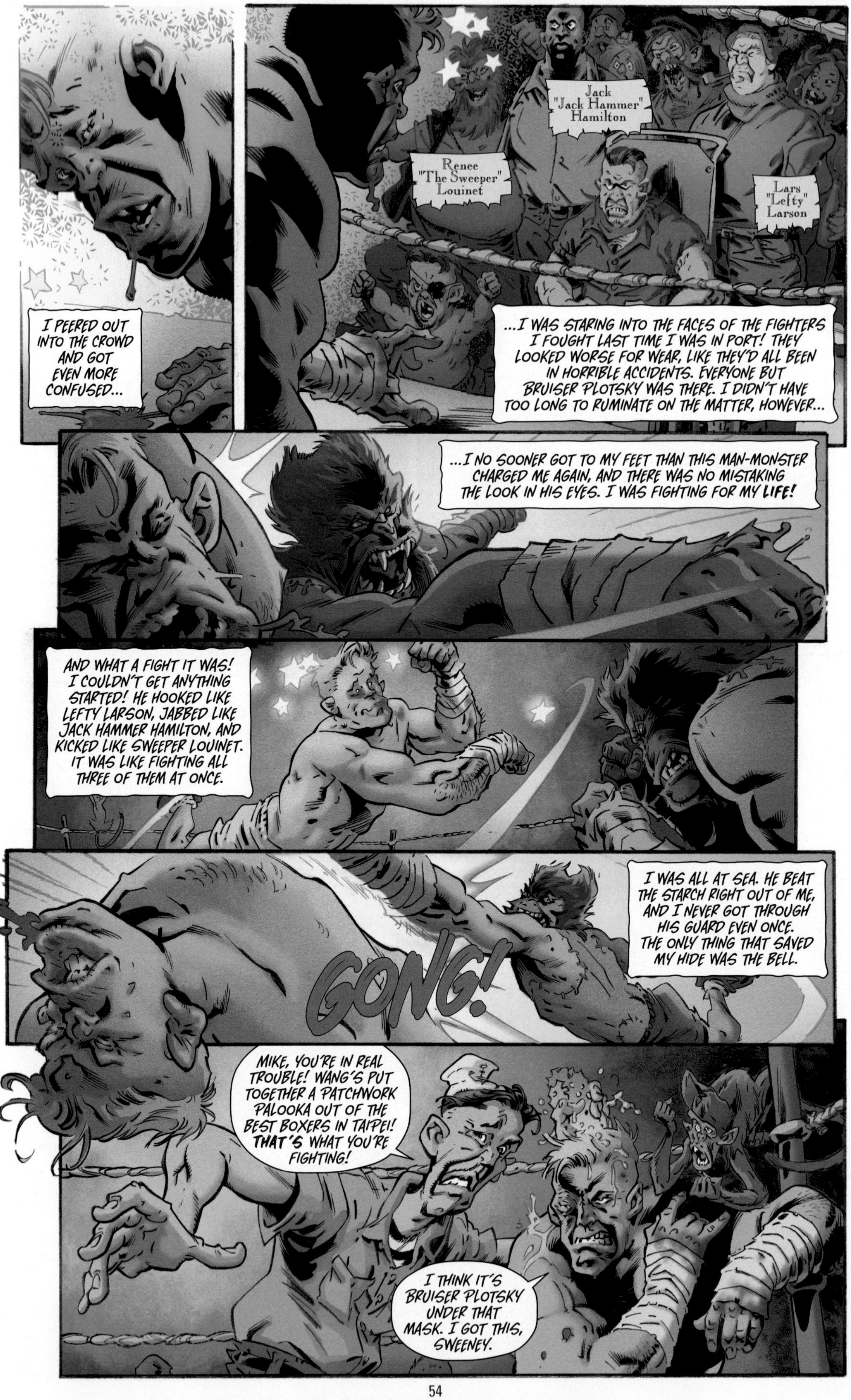
Jack "Jack Hammer" Hamilton
Renee "The Sweeper" Louinet
Lars "Lefty" Larson
I PEERED OUT INTO THE CROWD AND GOT EVEN MORE CONFUSED...
...I WAS STARING INTO THE FACES OF THE FIGHTERS I FOUGHT LAST TIME I WAS IN PORT! THEY LOOKED WORSE FOR WEAR, LIKE THEY'D ALL BEEN IN HORRIBLE ACCIDENTS. EVERYONE BUT BRUISER PLOTSKY WAS THERE. I DIDN'T HAVE TOO LONG TO RUMINATE ON THE MATTER, HOWEVER...
...I NO SOONER GOT TO MY FEET THAN THIS MAN-MONSTER CHARGED ME AGAIN, AND THERE WAS NO MISTAKING THE LOOK IN HIS EYES. I WAS FIGHTING FOR MY **LIFE!**
AND WHAT A FIGHT IT WAS! I COULDN'T GET ANYTHING STARTED! HE HOOKED LIKE LEFTY LARSON, JABBED LIKE JACK HAMMER HAMILTON, AND KICKED LIKE SWEEPER LOUINET. IT WAS LIKE FIGHTING ALL THREE OF THEM AT ONCE.
I WAS ALL AT SEA. HE BEAT THE STARCH RIGHT OUT OF ME, AND I NEVER GOT THROUGH HIS GUARD EVEN ONCE. THE ONLY THING THAT SAVED MY HIDE WAS THE BELL.
GONG!
MIKE, YOU'RE IN REAL TROUBLE! WANG'S PUT TOGETHER A PATCHWORK PALOOKA OUT OF THE BEST BOXERS IN TAIPEI! **THAT'S** WHAT YOU'RE FIGHTING!
I THINK IT'S BRUISER PLOTSKY UNDER THAT MASK. I GOT THIS, SWEENEY.

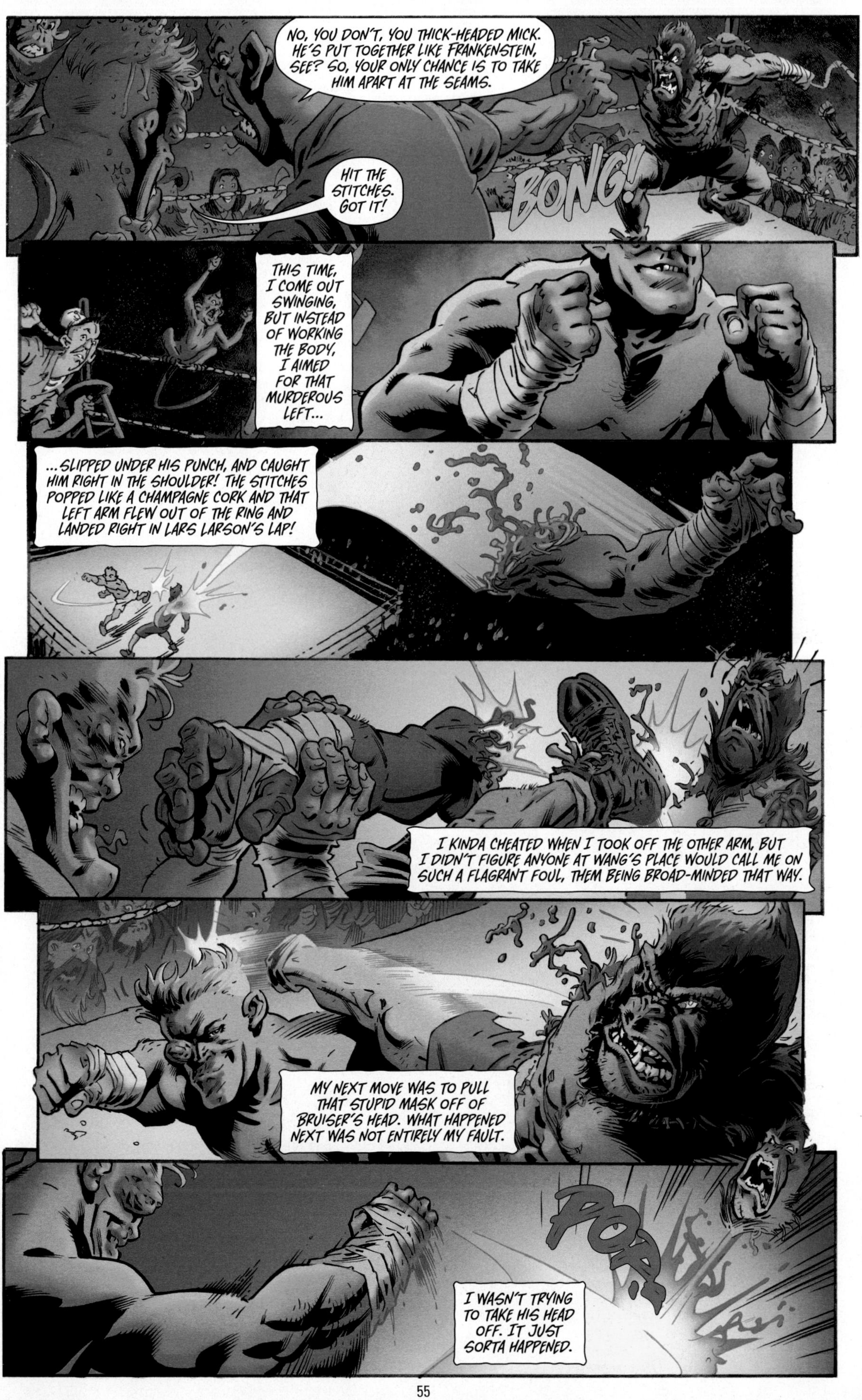
NO, YOU DON'T, YOU THICK-HEADED MICK. HE'S PUT TOGETHER LIKE FRANKENSTEIN, SEE? SO, YOUR ONLY CHANCE IS TO TAKE HIM APART AT THE SEAMS.
HIT THE STITCHES. GOT IT!
BONG!!
THIS TIME, I COME OUT SWINGING, BUT INSTEAD OF WORKING THE BODY, I AIMED FOR THAT MURDEROUS LEFT...
...SLIPPED UNDER HIS PUNCH, AND CAUGHT HIM RIGHT IN THE SHOULDER! THE STITCHES POPPED LIKE A CHAMPAGNE CORK AND THAT LEFT ARM FLEW OUT OF THE RING AND LANDED RIGHT IN LARS LARSON'S LAP!
I KINDA CHEATED WHEN I TOOK OFF THE OTHER ARM, BUT I DIDN'T FIGURE ANYONE AT WANG'S PLACE WOULD CALL ME ON SUCH A FLAGRANT FOUL, THEM BEING BROAD-MINDED THAT WAY.
MY NEXT MOVE WAS TO PULL THAT STUPID MASK OFF OF BRUISER'S HEAD. WHAT HAPPENED NEXT WAS NOT ENTIRELY MY FAULT.
POP!
I WASN'T TRYING TO TAKE HIS HEAD OFF. IT JUST SORTA HAPPENED.

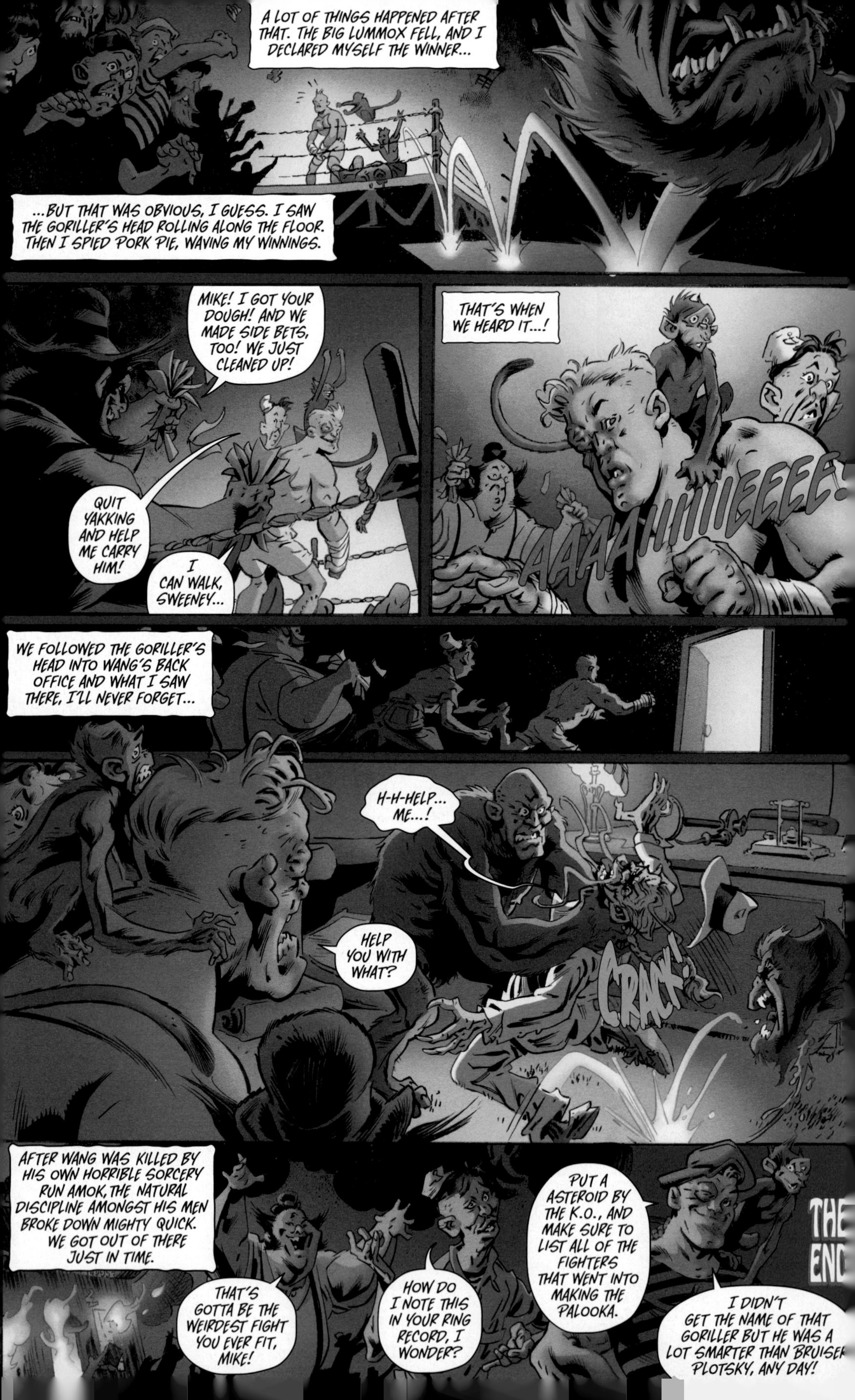
A LOT OF THINGS HAPPENED AFTER THAT. THE BIG LUMMOX FELL, AND I DECLARED MYSELF THE WINNER...
...BUT THAT WAS OBVIOUS, I GUESS. I SAW THE GORILLER'S HEAD ROLLING ALONG THE FLOOR. THEN I SPIED PORK PIE, WAVING MY WINNINGS.
MIKE! I GOT YOUR DOUGH! AND WE MADE SIDE BETS, TOO! WE JUST CLEANED UP!
QUIT YAKKING AND HELP ME CARRY HIM!
I CAN WALK, SWEENEY...
THAT'S WHEN WE HEARD IT...!
AAAAHHHHEEEEE!
WE FOLLOWED THE GORILLER'S HEAD INTO WANG'S BACK OFFICE AND WHAT I SAW THERE, I'LL NEVER FORGET...
H-H-HELP... ME...!
HELP YOU WITH WHAT?
CRACK!
AFTER WANG WAS KILLED BY HIS OWN HORRIBLE SORCERY RUN AMOK, THE NATURAL DISCIPLINE AMONGST HIS MEN BROKE DOWN MIGHTY QUICK. WE GOT OUT OF THERE JUST IN TIME.
THAT'S GOTTA BE THE WEIRDEST FIGHT YOU EVER FIT, MIKE!
HOW DO I NOTE THIS IN YOUR RING RECORD, I WONDER?
PUT A ASTEROID BY THE K.O., AND MAKE SURE TO LIST ALL OF THE FIGHTERS THAT WENT INTO MAKING THE PALOOKA.
I DIDN'T GET THE NAME OF THAT GORILLER BUT HE WAS A LOT SMARTER THAN BRUISER PLOTSKY, ANY DAY!
THE END

COSMIC BALL TRYOUTS HAPPEN ONCE IN A LIFETIME! AND SMALL-TOWN BOYS KURT AND MIKE MADE IT THROUGH EACH COMPETITIVE ROUND...BUT ONE OF THESE LIFELONG FRIENDS HAS A *SECRET*...AND, PERHAPS...

NOT ALLOWED TO PLAY BALL!

SCRIPT, PENCILS AND INKS—TIM FISH
COLORS— MICHAEL J. DIMOTTA
LETTERS— TOM NAPOLITANO
EDITS— GREG LOCKARD

I CAN'T BELIEVE IT, MIKE! COSMIC CITY *COMETS* TRYOUTS!

I KNOW! WHO EVER WOULD HAVE THOUGHT WE'D MAKE IT ALL THE WAY HERE?!?

...I'VE HEARD THAT SOUND IN YOUR VOICE BEFORE...

YOU'RE WORRIED.

STOP IT. WE'RE *BOTH* GREAT PLAYERS. JUST STAY FOCUSED ON THE *TRYOUTS*.

BUT...IF THEY FIND OUT... DUDE, THEY WOULD *NOT* BE COOL WITH IT.

GET ON THE FIELD!

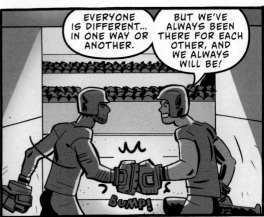

EVERYONE IS DIFFERENT... IN ONE WAY OR ANOTHER.

BUT WE'VE ALWAYS BEEN THERE FOR EACH OTHER, AND WE ALWAYS WILL BE!

BUMP!

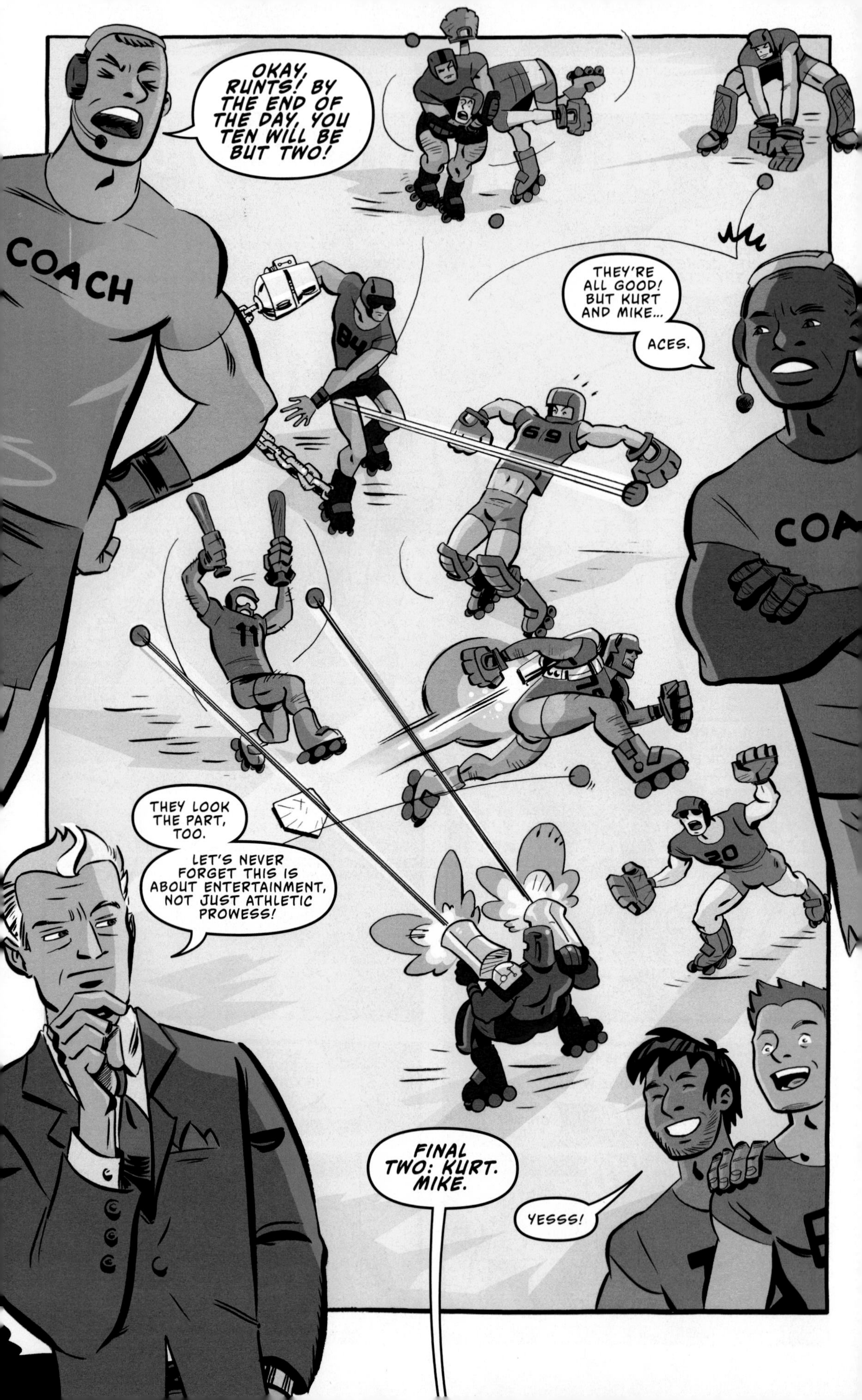
OKAY, RUNTS! BY THE END OF THE DAY, YOU TEN WILL BE BUT TWO!
THEY'RE ALL GOOD! BUT KURT AND MIKE...
ACES.
THEY LOOK THE PART, TOO.
LET'S NEVER FORGET THIS IS ABOUT ENTERTAINMENT, NOT JUST ATHLETIC PROWESS!
FINAL TWO: KURT. MIKE.
YESSS!

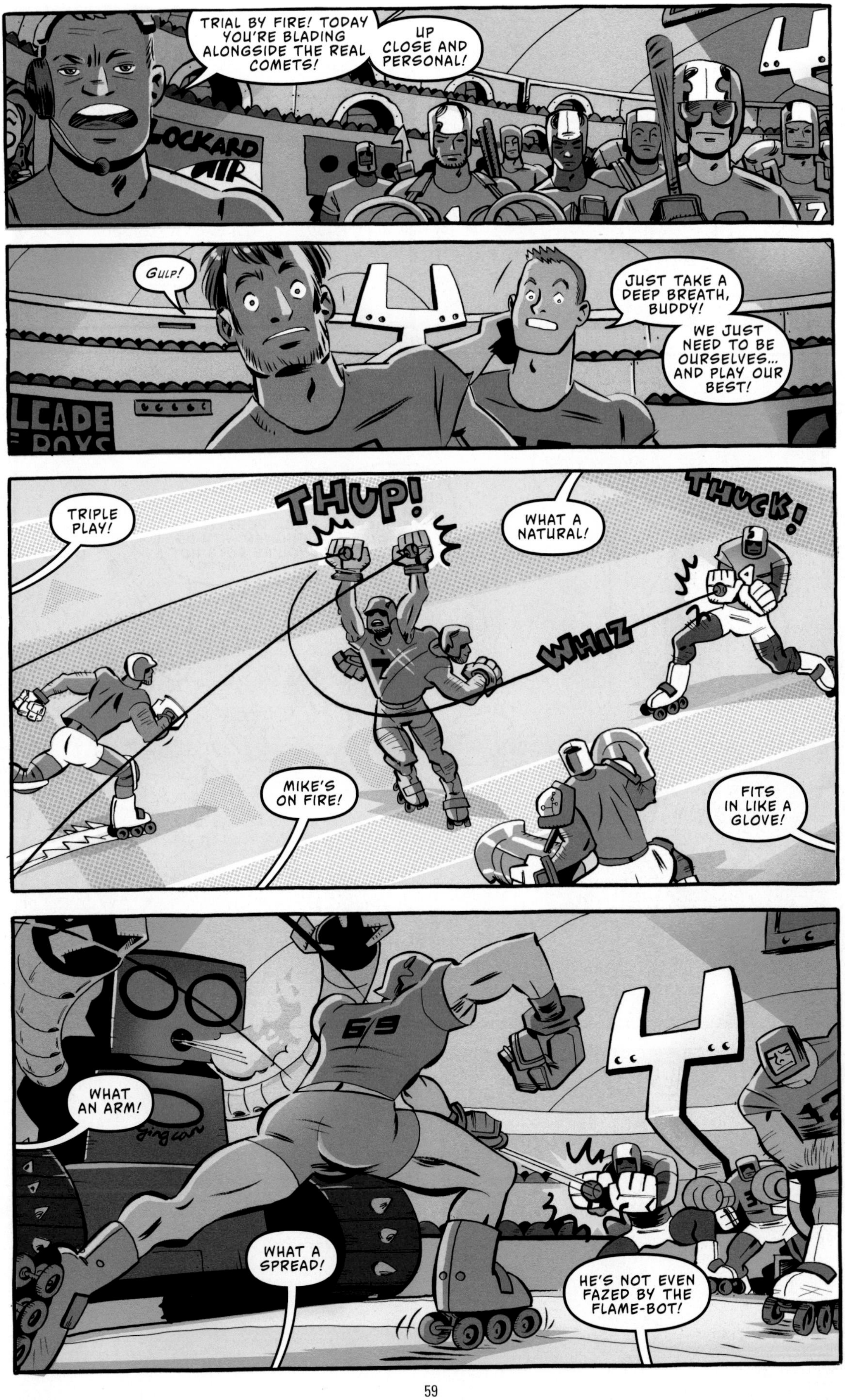
TRIAL BY FIRE! TODAY YOU'RE BLADING ALONGSIDE THE REAL COMETS!
UP CLOSE AND PERSONAL!
LOCKARD AIR
GULP!
JUST TAKE A DEEP BREATH, BUDDY!
WE JUST NEED TO BE OURSELVES... AND PLAY OUR BEST!
LCADE
TRIPLE PLAY!
THUP!
WHAT A NATURAL!
THUCK!
WHIZ
MIKE'S ON FIRE!
FITS IN LIKE A GLOVE!
WHAT AN ARM!
WHAT A SPREAD!
HE'S NOT EVEN FAZED BY THE FLAME-BOT!

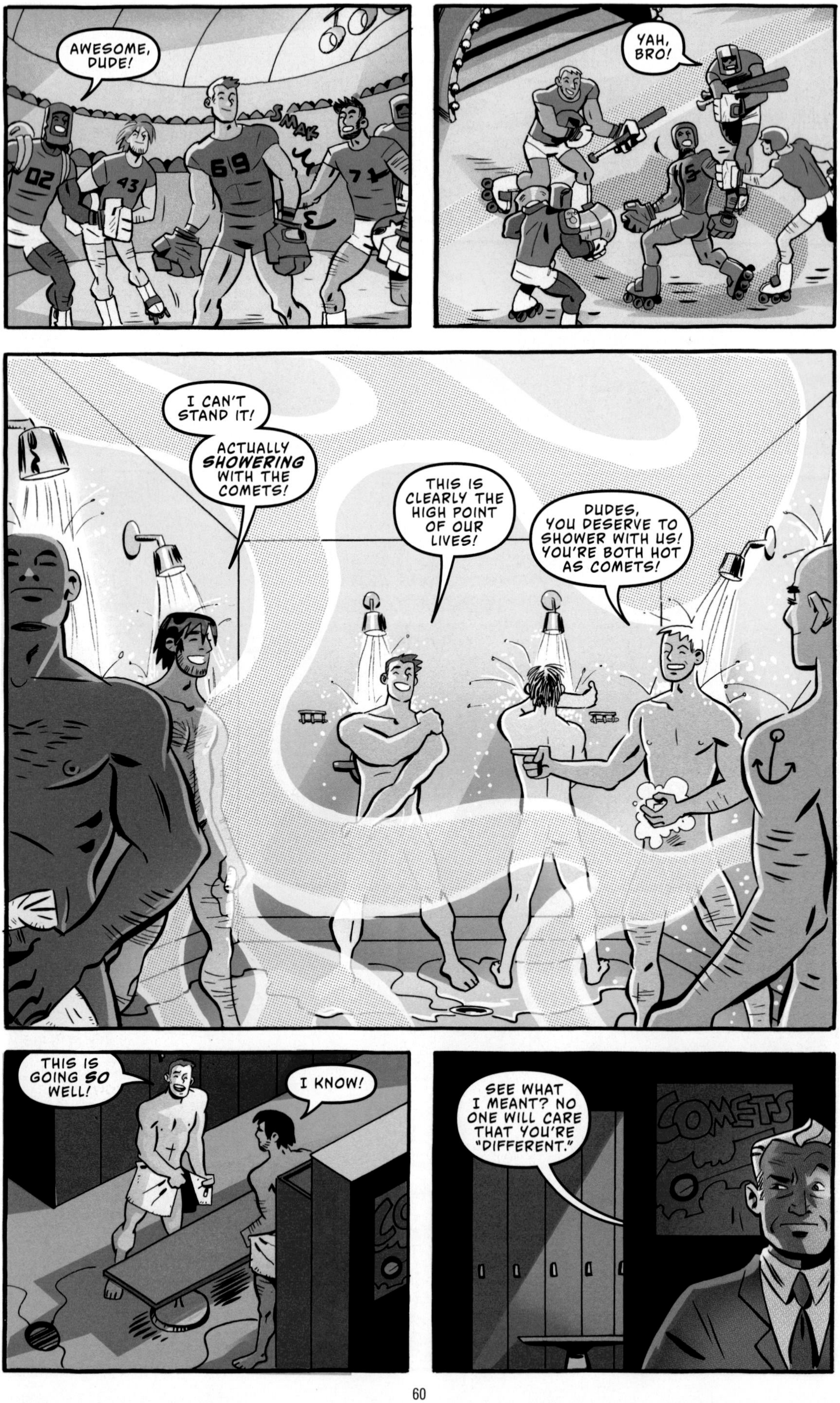
AWESOME, DUDE!
SMAK
YAH, BRO!
I CAN'T STAND IT!
ACTUALLY *SHOWERING* WITH THE COMETS!
THIS IS CLEARLY THE HIGH POINT OF OUR LIVES!
DUDES, YOU DESERVE TO SHOWER WITH US! YOU'RE BOTH HOT AS COMETS!
THIS IS GOING *SO* WELL!
I KNOW!
SEE WHAT I MEANT? NO ONE WILL CARE THAT YOU'RE "DIFFERENT."
COMETS

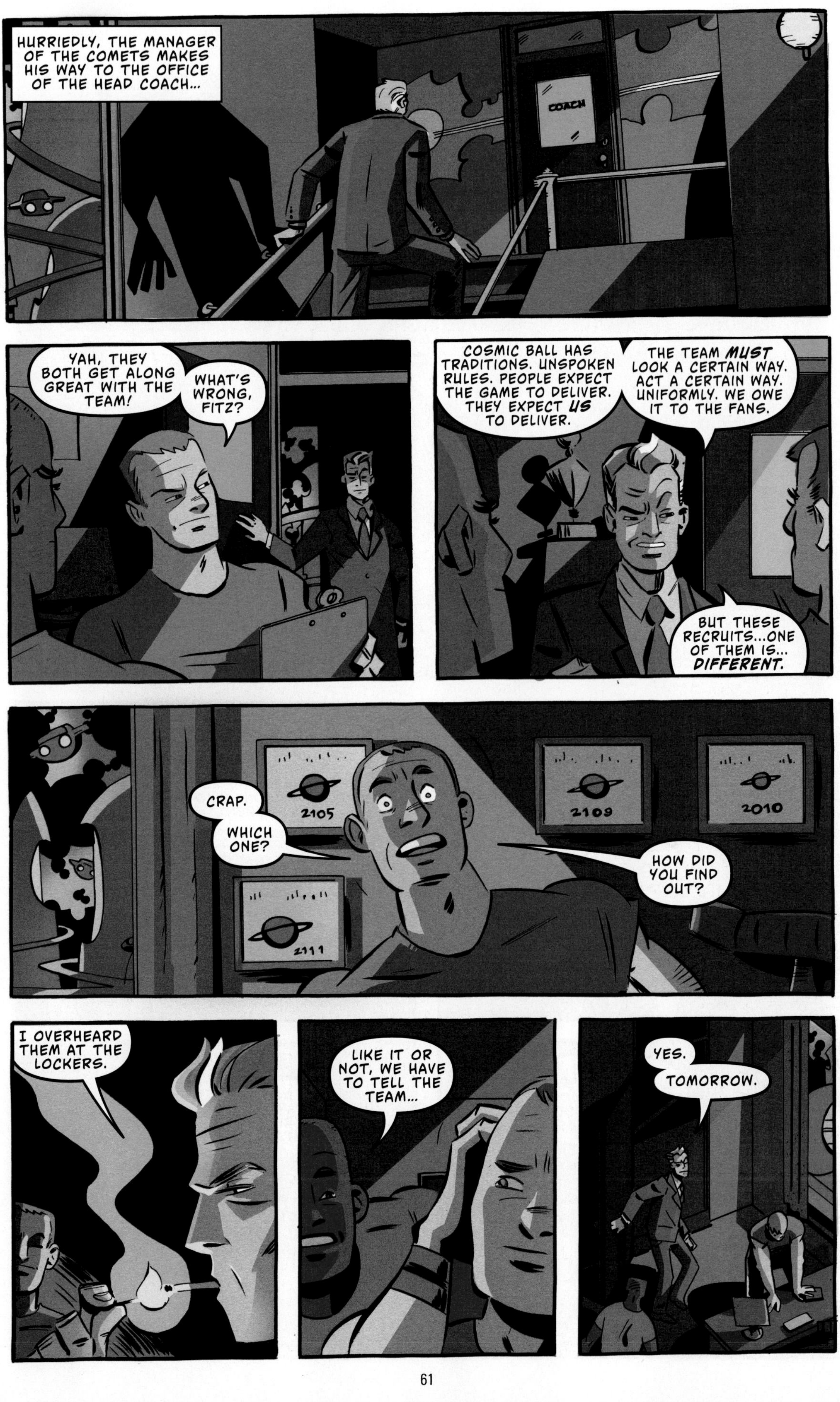
HURRIEDLY, THE MANAGER OF THE COMETS MAKES HIS WAY TO THE OFFICE OF THE HEAD COACH...
COACH
YAH, THEY BOTH GET ALONG GREAT WITH THE TEAM!
WHAT'S WRONG, FITZ?
COSMIC BALL HAS TRADITIONS. UNSPOKEN RULES. PEOPLE EXPECT THE GAME TO DELIVER. THEY EXPECT US TO DELIVER.
THE TEAM MUST LOOK A CERTAIN WAY. ACT A CERTAIN WAY. UNIFORMLY. WE OWE IT TO THE FANS.
BUT THESE RECRUITS...ONE OF THEM IS... DIFFERENT.
CRAP.
WHICH ONE?
2105
2109
2010
2111
HOW DID YOU FIND OUT?
I OVERHEARD THEM AT THE LOCKERS.
LIKE IT OR NOT, WE HAVE TO TELL THE TEAM...
YES.
TOMORROW.

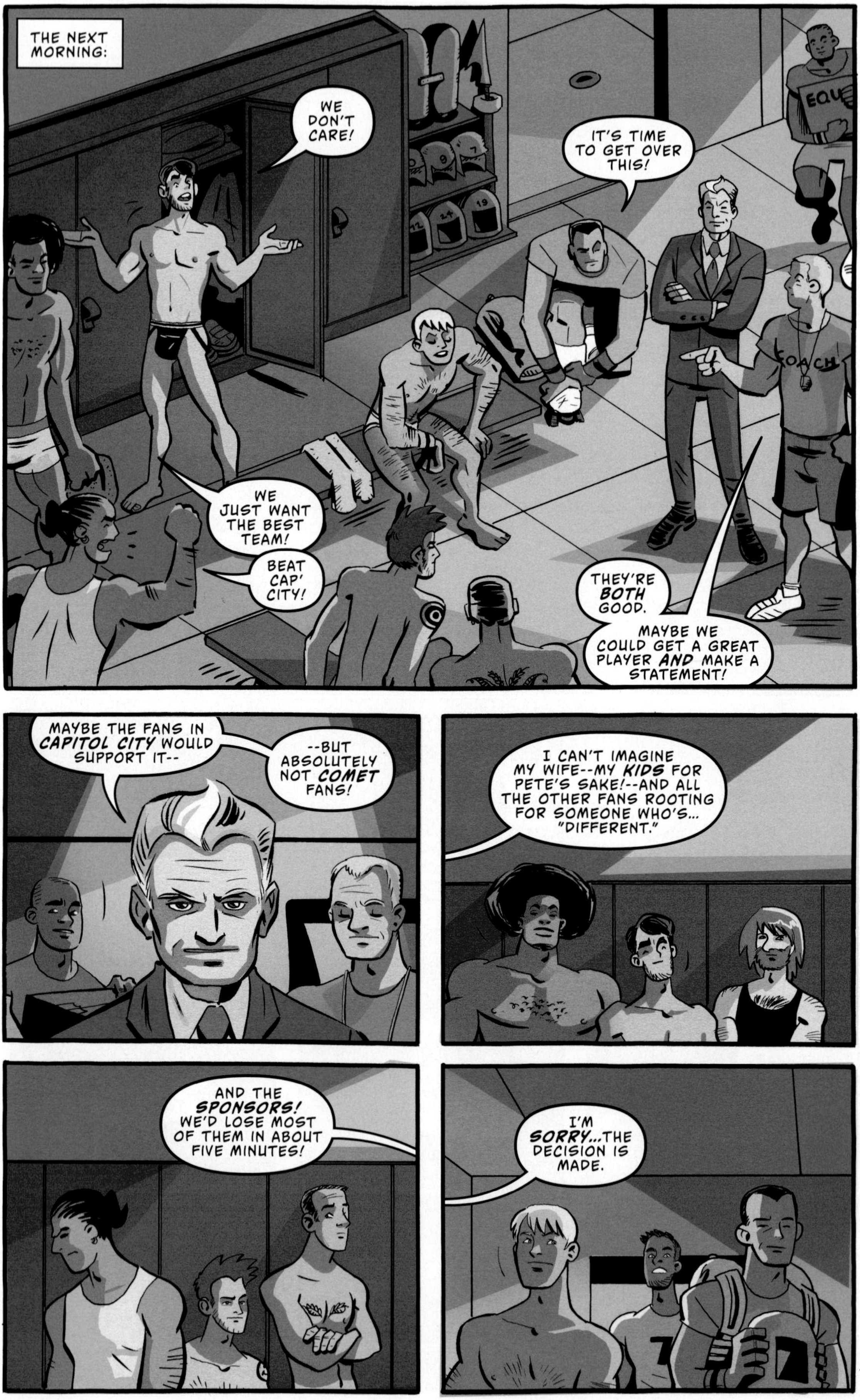
THE NEXT MORNING:
WE DON'T CARE!
IT'S TIME TO GET OVER THIS!
WE JUST WANT THE BEST TEAM!
BEAT CAP' CITY!
THEY'RE BOTH GOOD.
MAYBE WE COULD GET A GREAT PLAYER AND MAKE A STATEMENT!
MAYBE THE FANS IN CAPITOL CITY WOULD SUPPORT IT--
--BUT ABSOLUTELY NOT COMET FANS!
I CAN'T IMAGINE MY WIFE--MY KIDS FOR PETE'S SAKE!--AND ALL THE OTHER FANS ROOTING FOR SOMEONE WHO'S... "DIFFERENT."
AND THE SPONSORS! WE'D LOSE MOST OF THEM IN ABOUT FIVE MINUTES!
I'M SORRY... THE DECISION IS MADE.

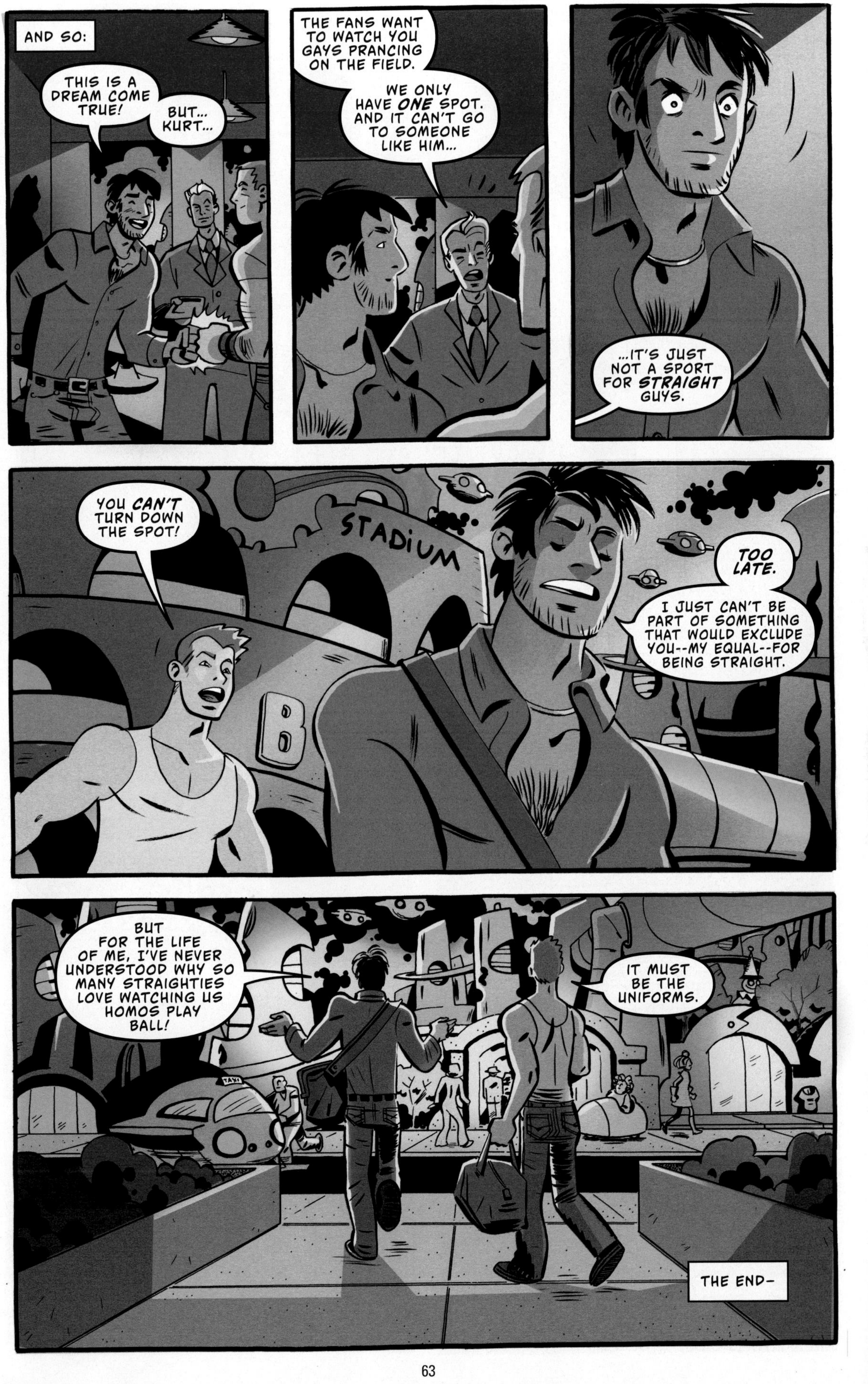
AND SO:
THIS IS A DREAM COME TRUE!
BUT... KURT...
THE FANS WANT TO WATCH YOU GAYS PRANCING ON THE FIELD.
WE ONLY HAVE ONE SPOT. AND IT CAN'T GO TO SOMEONE LIKE HIM...
...IT'S JUST NOT A SPORT FOR STRAIGHT GUYS.
YOU CAN'T TURN DOWN THE SPOT!
STADIUM
TOO LATE.
I JUST CAN'T BE PART OF SOMETHING THAT WOULD EXCLUDE YOU--MY EQUAL--FOR BEING STRAIGHT.
BUT FOR THE LIFE OF ME, I'VE NEVER UNDERSTOOD WHY SO MANY STRAIGHTIES LOVE WATCHING US HOMOS PLAY BALL!
IT MUST BE THE UNIFORMS.
TAXI
THE END-

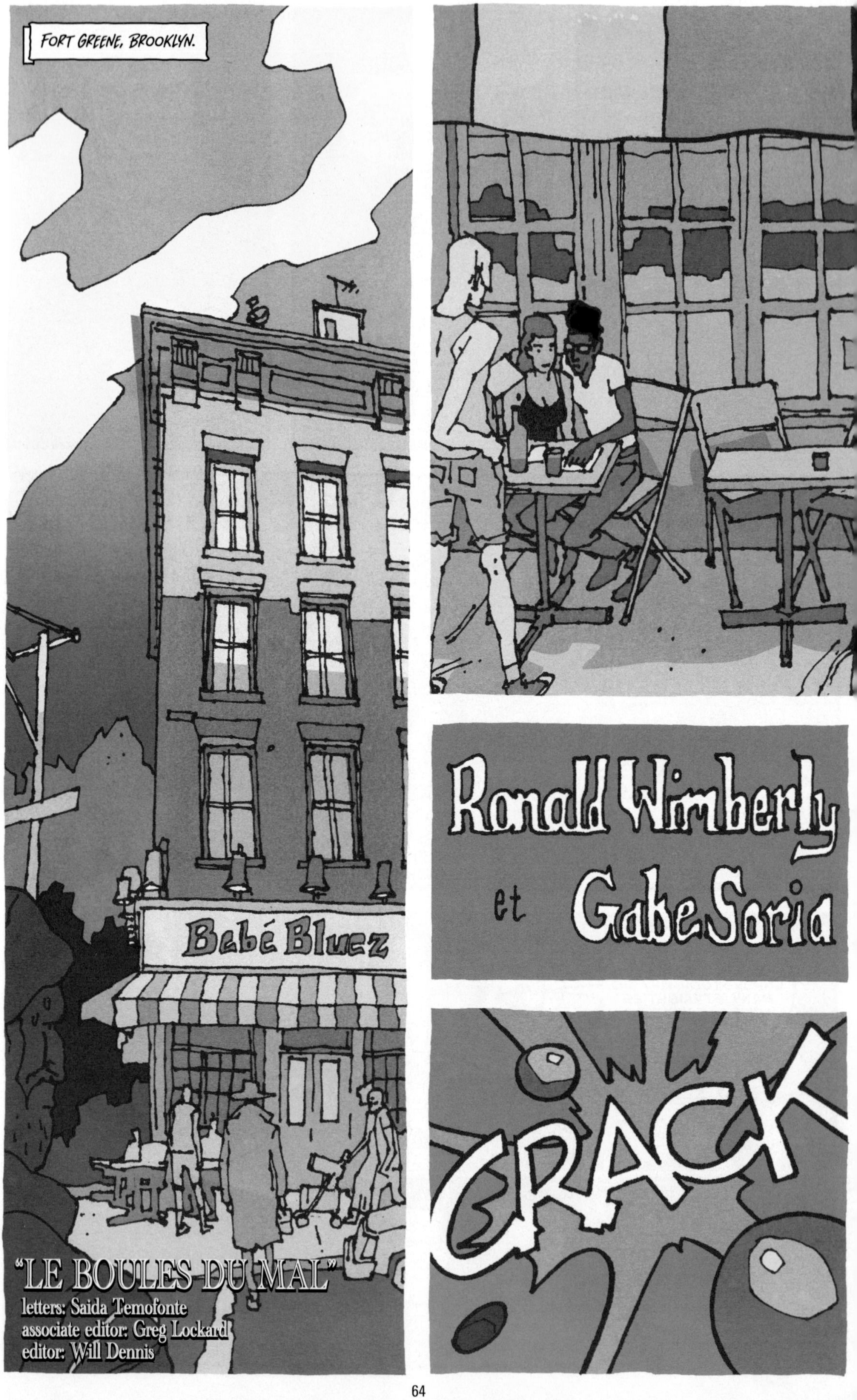
FORT GREENE, BROOKLYN.
Bebé Bluez
"LE BOULES DU MAL"
letters: Saida Temofonte
associate editor: Greg Lockard
editor: Will Dennis
Ronald Wimberly
et
Gabe Soria
CRACK

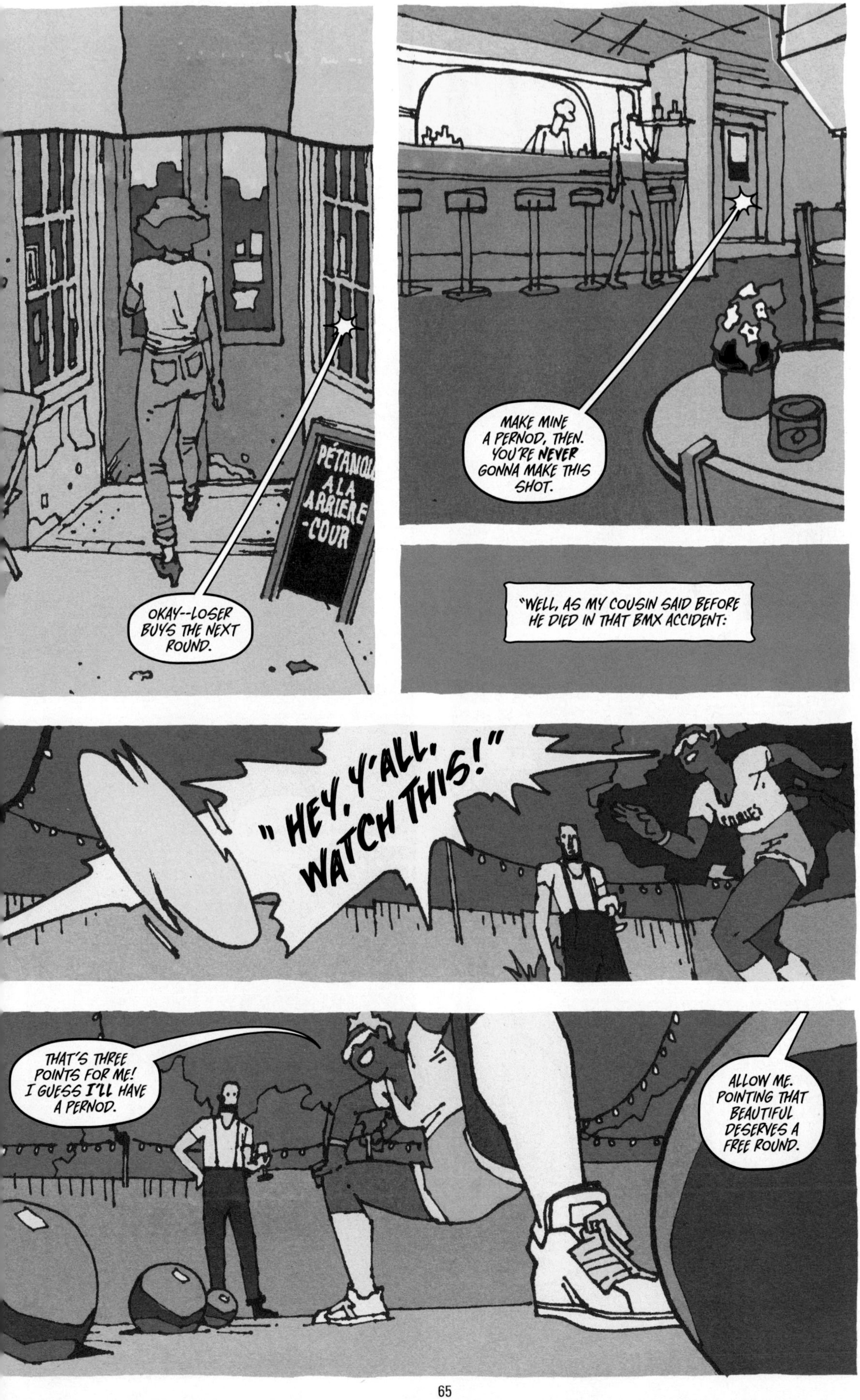
PÉTANQUE A LA ARRIERE -COUR
OKAY--LOSER BUYS THE NEXT ROUND.
MAKE MINE A PERNOD, THEN. YOU'RE **NEVER** GONNA MAKE THIS SHOT.
"WELL, AS MY COUSIN SAID BEFORE HE DIED IN THAT BMX ACCIDENT:
"HEY, Y'ALL, WATCH THIS!"
THAT'S THREE POINTS FOR ME! I GUESS **I'LL** HAVE A PERNOD.
ALLOW ME. POINTING THAT BEAUTIFUL DESERVES A FREE ROUND.

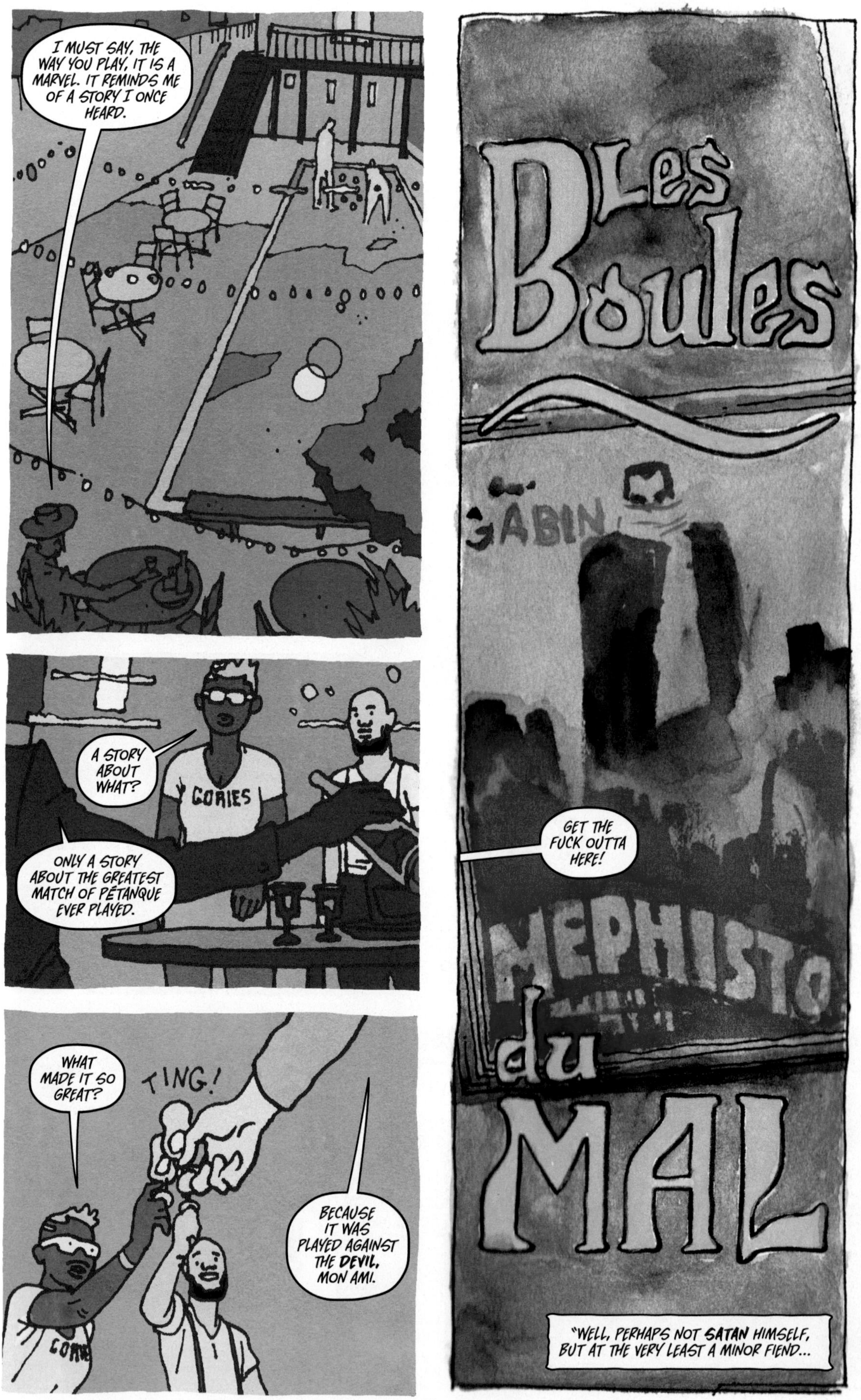
I MUST SAY, THE WAY YOU PLAY, IT IS A MARVEL. IT REMINDS ME OF A STORY I ONCE HEARD.
A STORY ABOUT WHAT?
GORIES
ONLY A STORY ABOUT THE GREATEST MATCH OF PÉTANQUE EVER PLAYED.
WHAT MADE IT SO GREAT?
TING!
BECAUSE IT WAS PLAYED AGAINST THE **DEVIL**, MON AMI.
GORIES
Les Boules
GABIN
GET THE FUCK OUTTA HERE!
MEPHISTO
du MAL
"WELL, PERHAPS NOT **SATAN** HIMSELF, BUT AT THE VERY LEAST A MINOR FIEND...

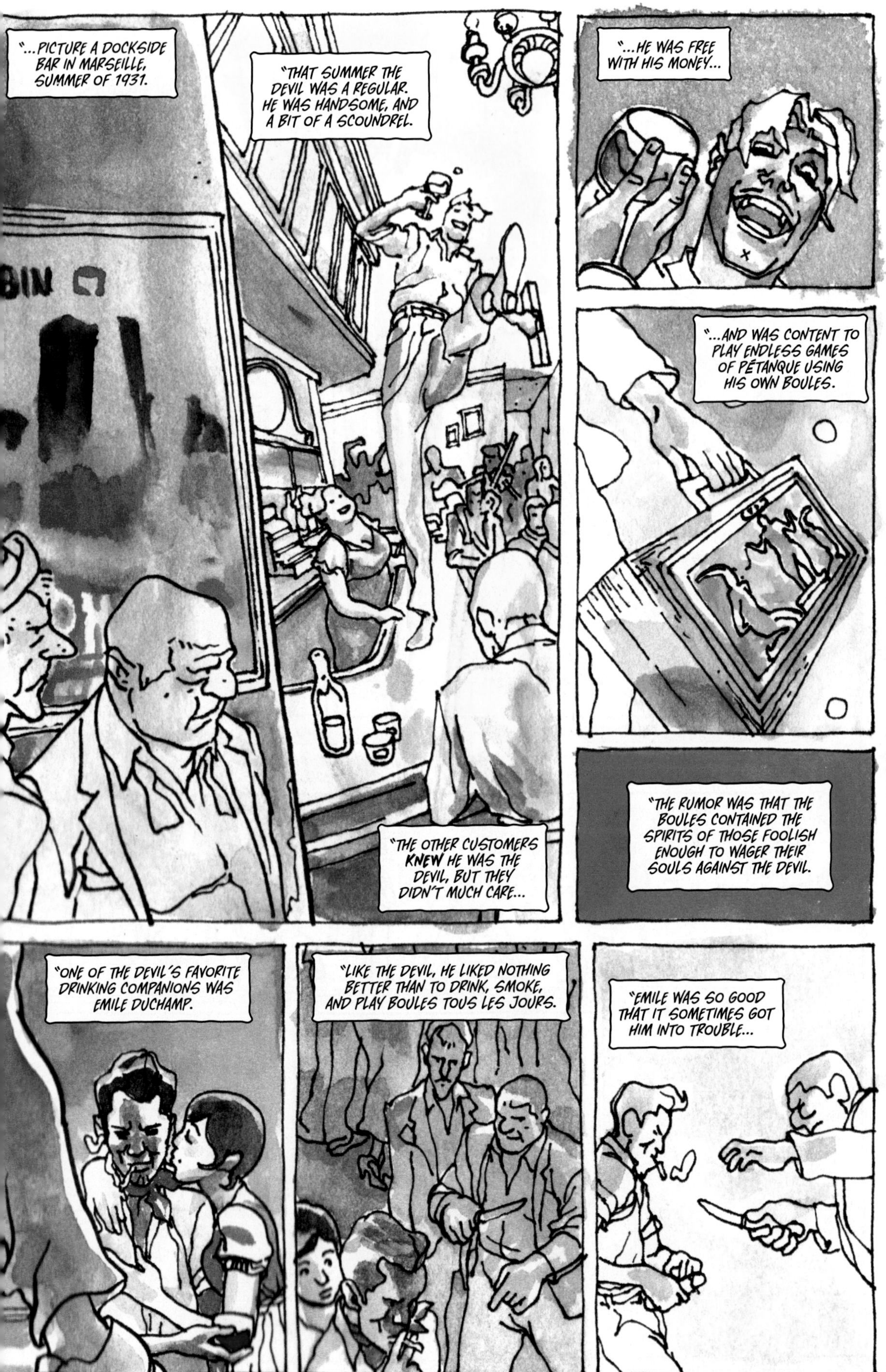
"...PICTURE A DOCKSIDE BAR IN MARSEILLE, SUMMER OF 1931.
"THAT SUMMER THE DEVIL WAS A REGULAR. HE WAS HANDSOME, AND A BIT OF A SCOUNDREL.
"THE OTHER CUSTOMERS **KNEW** HE WAS THE DEVIL, BUT THEY DIDN'T MUCH CARE...
"...HE WAS FREE WITH HIS MONEY...
"...AND WAS CONTENT TO PLAY ENDLESS GAMES OF PÉTANQUE USING HIS OWN BOULES.
"THE RUMOR WAS THAT THE BOULES CONTAINED THE SPIRITS OF THOSE FOOLISH ENOUGH TO WAGER THEIR SOULS AGAINST THE DEVIL.
"ONE OF THE DEVIL'S FAVORITE DRINKING COMPANIONS WAS EMILE DUCHAMP.
"LIKE THE DEVIL, HE LIKED NOTHING BETTER THAN TO DRINK, SMOKE, AND PLAY BOULES TOUS LES JOURS.
"EMILE WAS SO GOOD THAT IT SOMETIMES GOT HIM INTO TROUBLE...

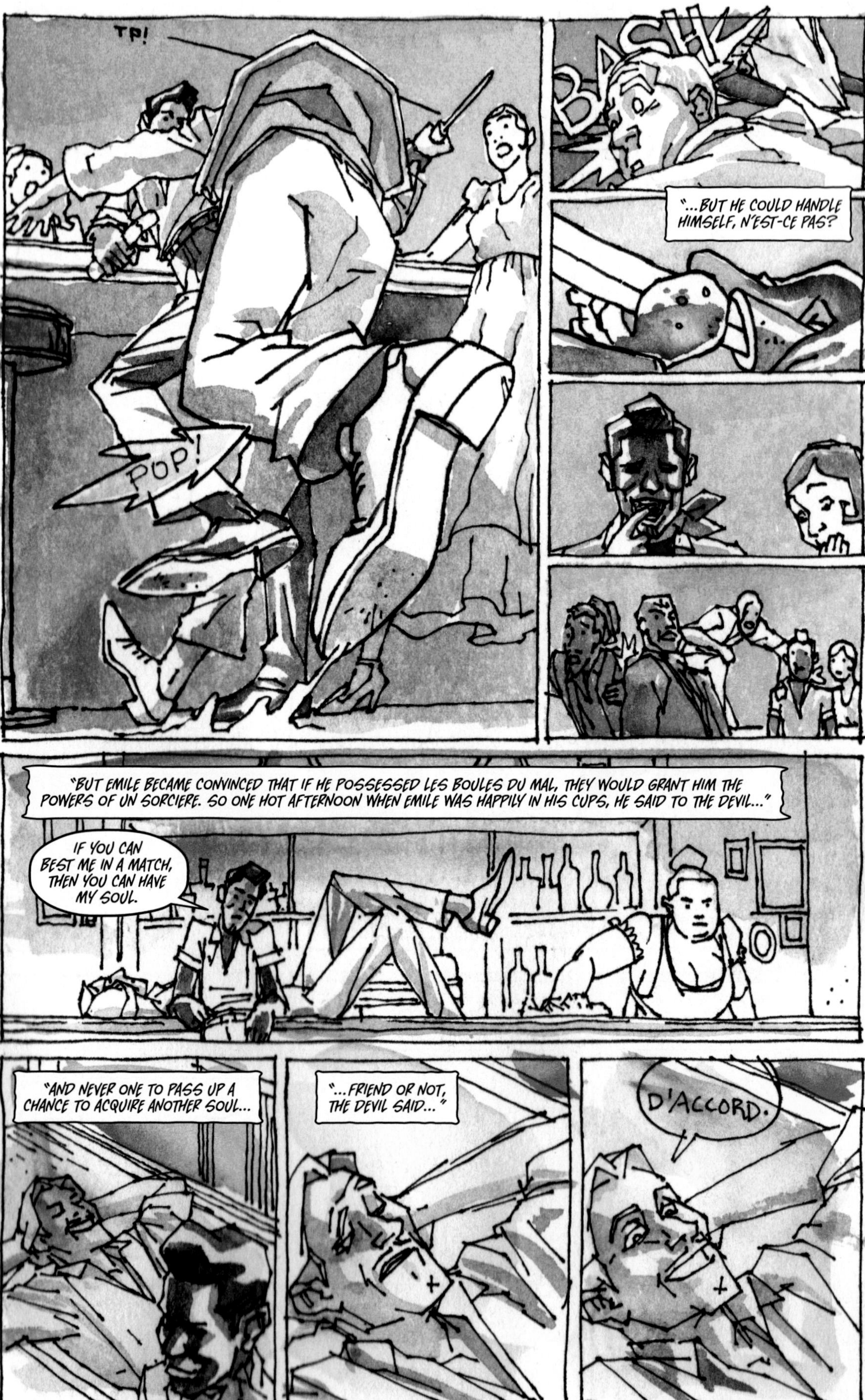
TP!
BASH
"...BUT HE COULD HANDLE HIMSELF, N'EST-CE PAS?
POP!
"BUT EMILE BECAME CONVINCED THAT IF HE POSSESSED LES BOULES DU MAL, THEY WOULD GRANT HIM THE POWERS OF UN SORCIERE. SO ONE HOT AFTERNOON WHEN EMILE WAS HAPPILY IN HIS CUPS, HE SAID TO THE DEVIL..."
IF YOU CAN BEST ME IN A MATCH, THEN YOU CAN HAVE MY SOUL.
"AND NEVER ONE TO PASS UP A CHANCE TO ACQUIRE ANOTHER SOUL...
"...FRIEND OR NOT, THE DEVIL SAID..."
D'ACCORD.

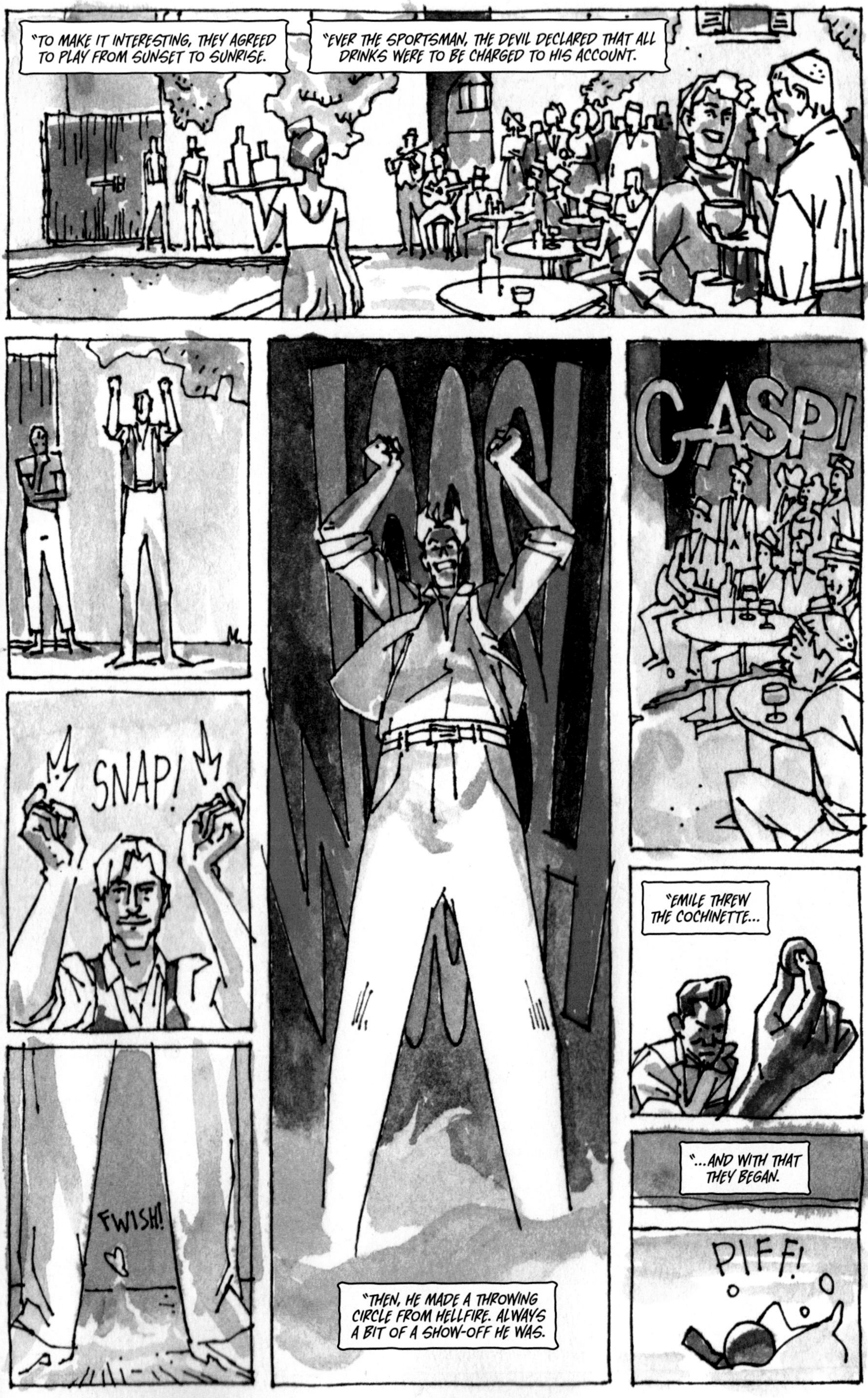
"TO MAKE IT INTERESTING, THEY AGREED TO PLAY FROM SUNSET TO SUNRISE.
"EVER THE SPORTSMAN, THE DEVIL DECLARED THAT ALL DRINKS WERE TO BE CHARGED TO HIS ACCOUNT.
SNAP!
FWISH!
"THEN, HE MADE A THROWING CIRCLE FROM HELLFIRE. ALWAYS A BIT OF A SHOW-OFF HE WAS.
GASPI
"EMILE THREW THE COCHINETTE...
"...AND WITH THAT THEY BEGAN.
PIFF!

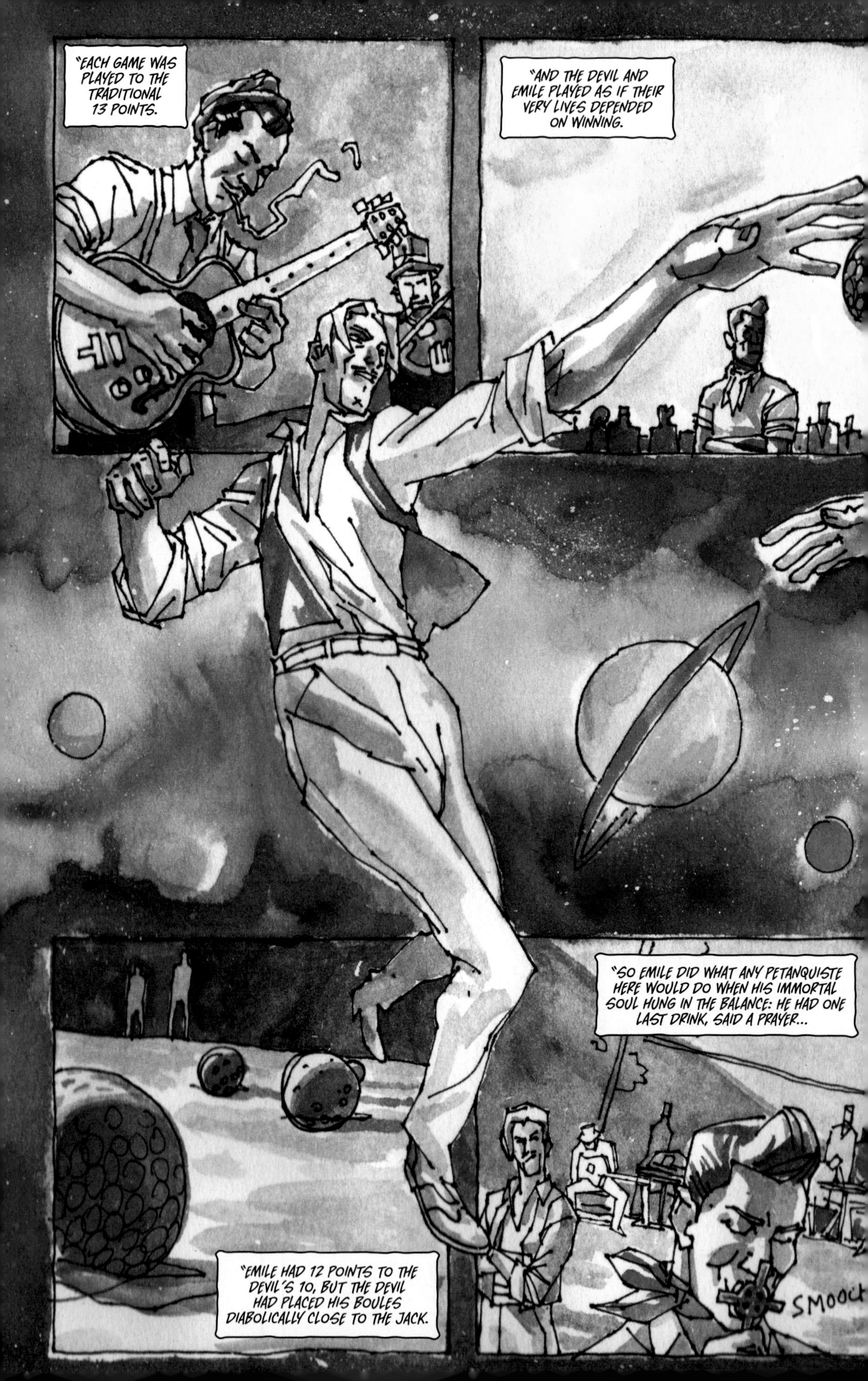
"EACH GAME WAS PLAYED TO THE TRADITIONAL 13 POINTS.
"AND THE DEVIL AND EMILE PLAYED AS IF THEIR VERY LIVES DEPENDED ON WINNING.
"EMILE HAD 12 POINTS TO THE DEVIL'S 10, BUT THE DEVIL HAD PLACED HIS BOULES DIABOLICALLY CLOSE TO THE JACK.
"SO EMILE DID WHAT ANY PETANQUISTE HERE WOULD DO WHEN HIS IMMORTAL SOUL HUNG IN THE BALANCE: HE HAD ONE LAST DRINK, SAID A PRAYER...
SMOOCH

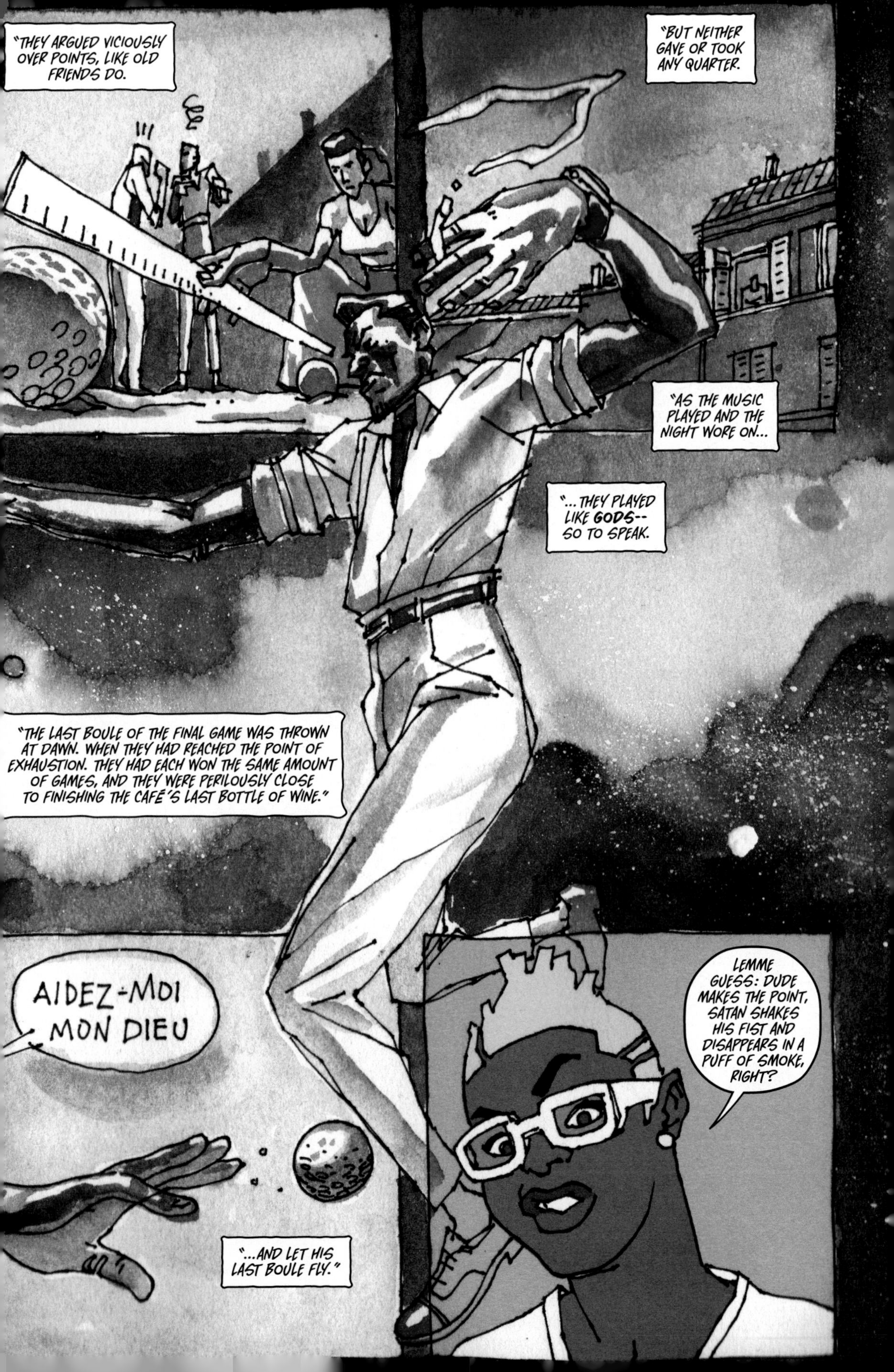
"THEY ARGUED VICIOUSLY OVER POINTS, LIKE OLD FRIENDS DO.
"BUT NEITHER GAVE OR TOOK ANY QUARTER.
"AS THE MUSIC PLAYED AND THE NIGHT WORE ON...
"...THEY PLAYED LIKE **GODS**-- SO TO SPEAK.
"THE LAST BOULE OF THE FINAL GAME WAS THROWN AT DAWN. WHEN THEY HAD REACHED THE POINT OF EXHAUSTION. THEY HAD EACH WON THE SAME AMOUNT OF GAMES, AND THEY WERE PERILOUSLY CLOSE TO FINISHING THE CAFÉ'S LAST BOTTLE OF WINE."
AIDEZ-MOI MON DIEU
"...AND LET HIS LAST BOULE FLY."
LEMME GUESS: DUDE MAKES THE POINT, SATAN SHAKES HIS FIST AND DISAPPEARS IN A PUFF OF SMOKE, RIGHT?

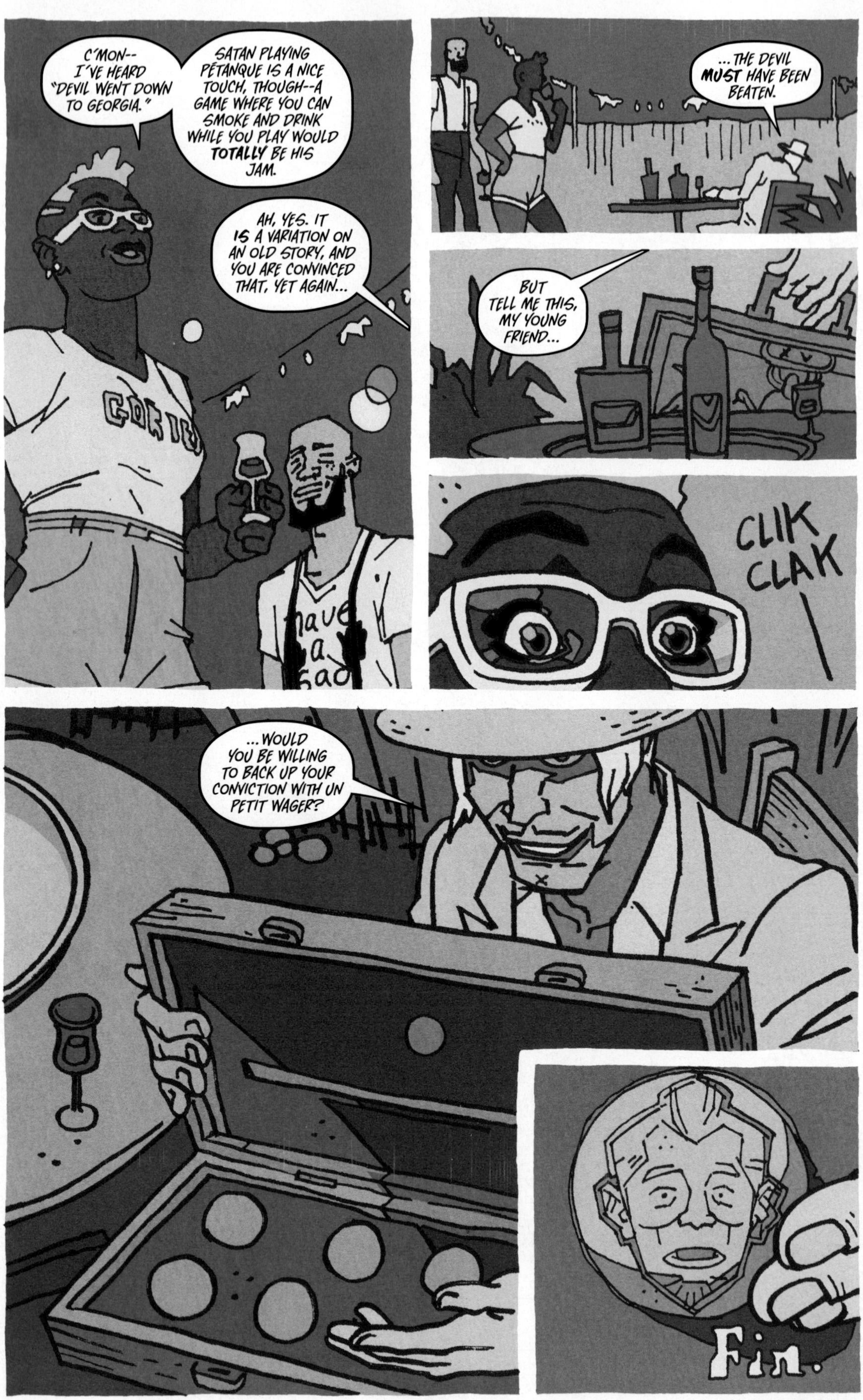
C'MON-- I'VE HEARD "DEVIL WENT DOWN TO GEORGIA."
SATAN PLAYING PÉTANQUE IS A NICE TOUCH, THOUGH--A GAME WHERE YOU CAN SMOKE AND DRINK WHILE YOU PLAY WOULD TOTALLY BE HIS JAM.
AH, YES. IT IS A VARIATION ON AN OLD STORY, AND YOU ARE CONVINCED THAT, YET AGAIN...
...THE DEVIL MUST HAVE BEEN BEATEN.
BUT TELL ME THIS, MY YOUNG FRIEND...
CLIK CLAK
...WOULD YOU BE WILLING TO BACK UP YOUR CONVICTION WITH UN PETIT WAGER?
Fin.

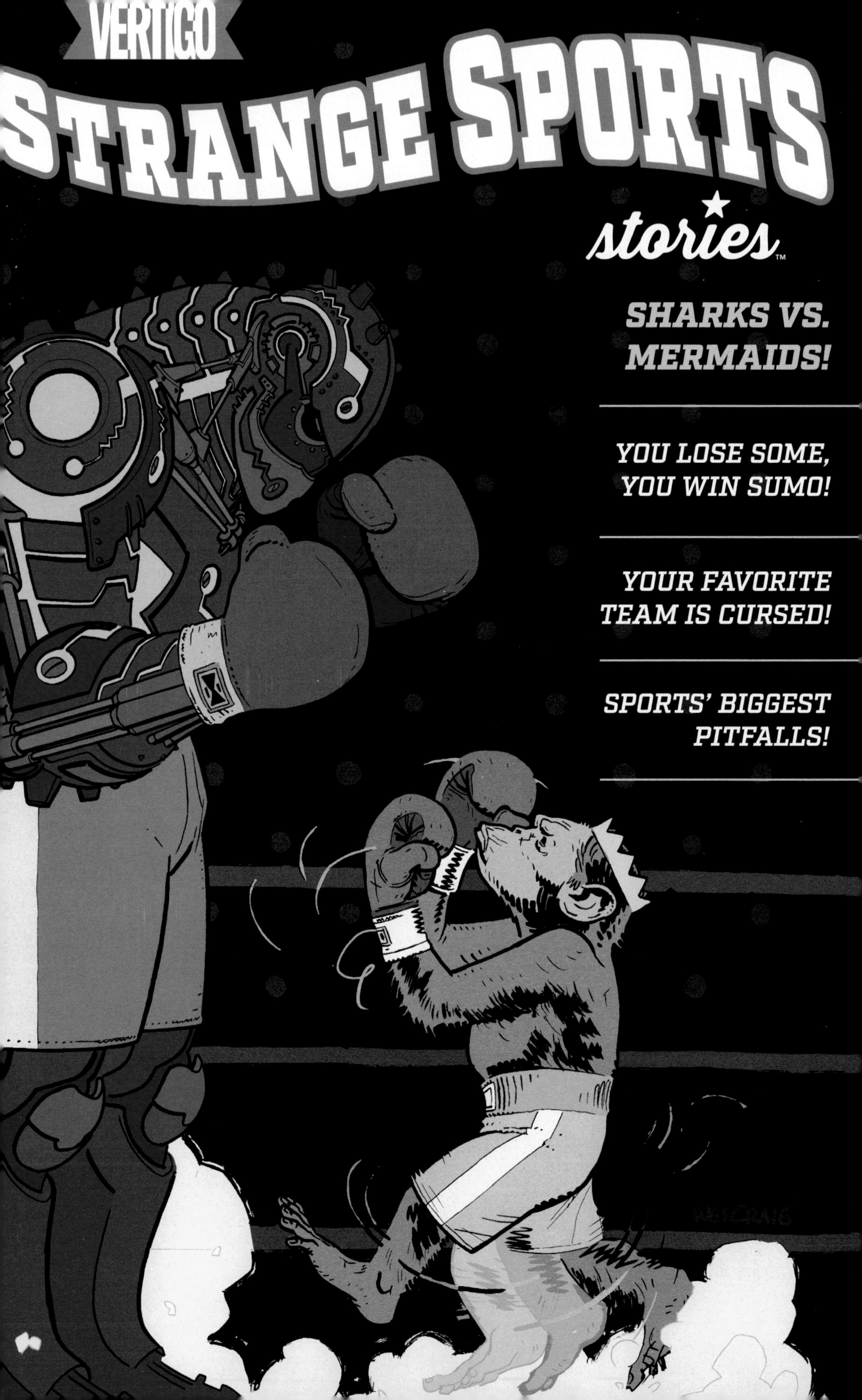
VERTIGO
STRANGE SPORTS
stories™
SHARKS VS. MERMAIDS!
YOU LOSE SOME, YOU WIN SUMO!
YOUR FAVORITE TEAM IS CURSED!
SPORTS' BIGGEST PITFALLS!

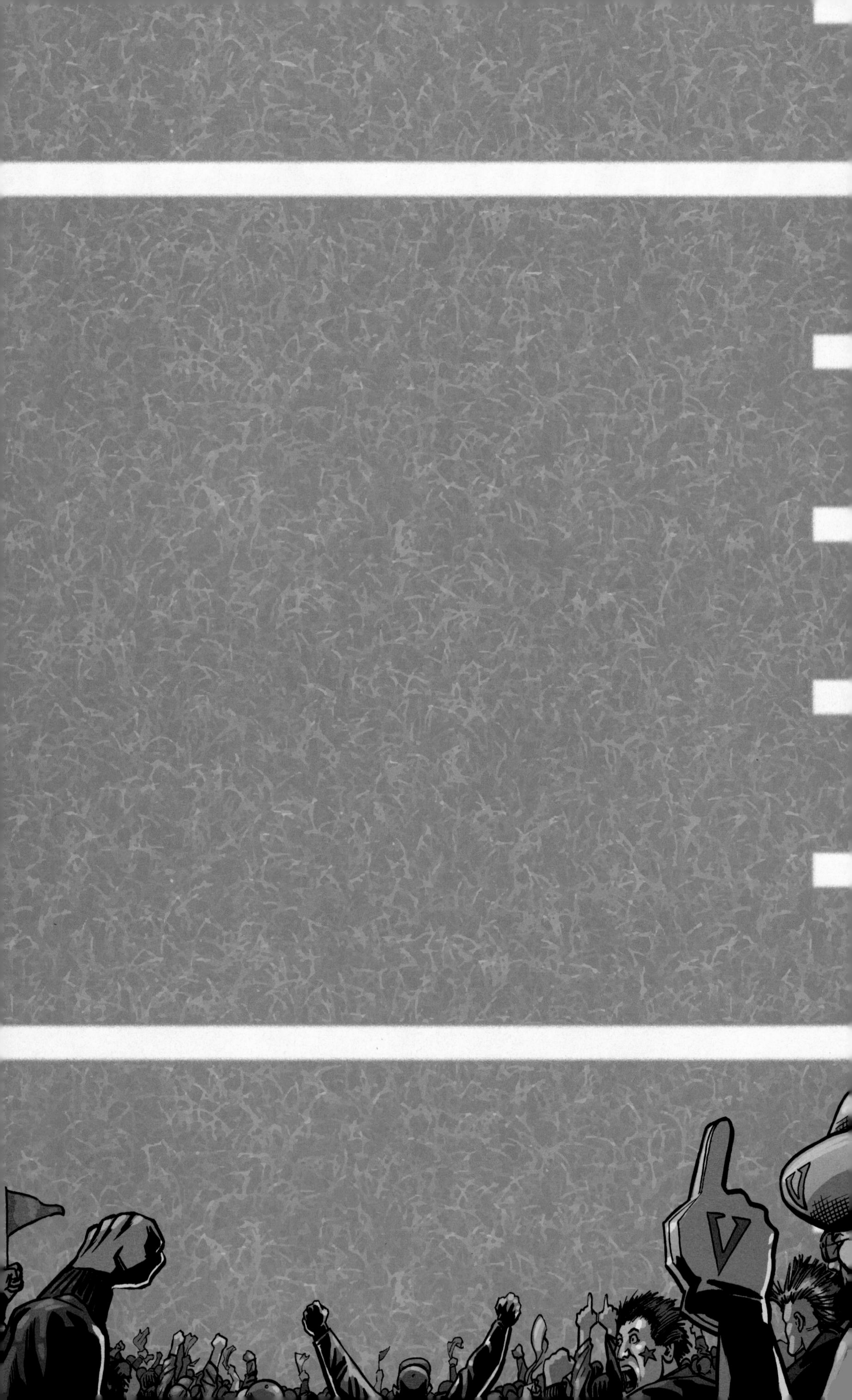

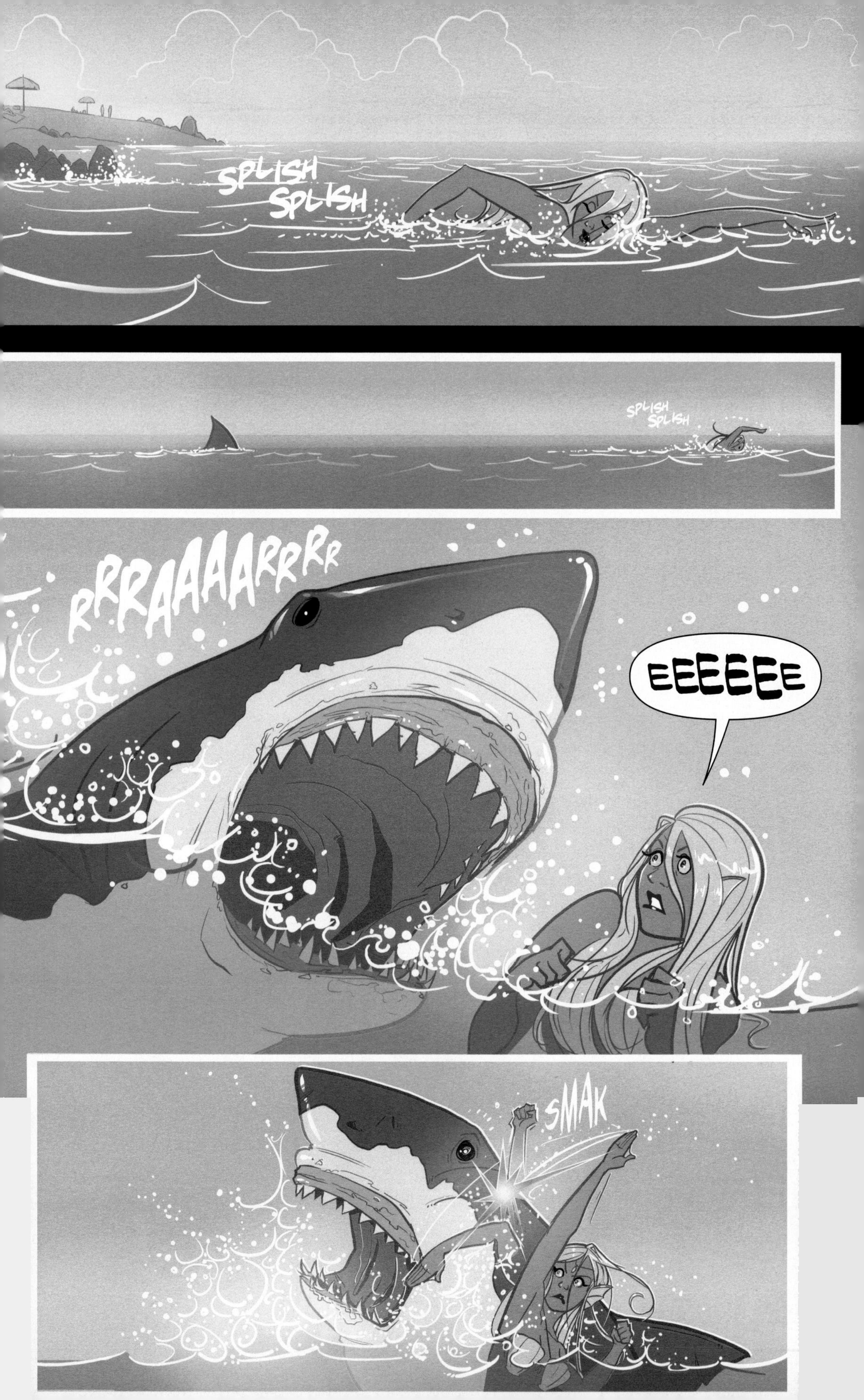
SPLISH
SPLISH
SPLISH
SPLISH
RRRAAAARRRR
EEEEEE
SMAK

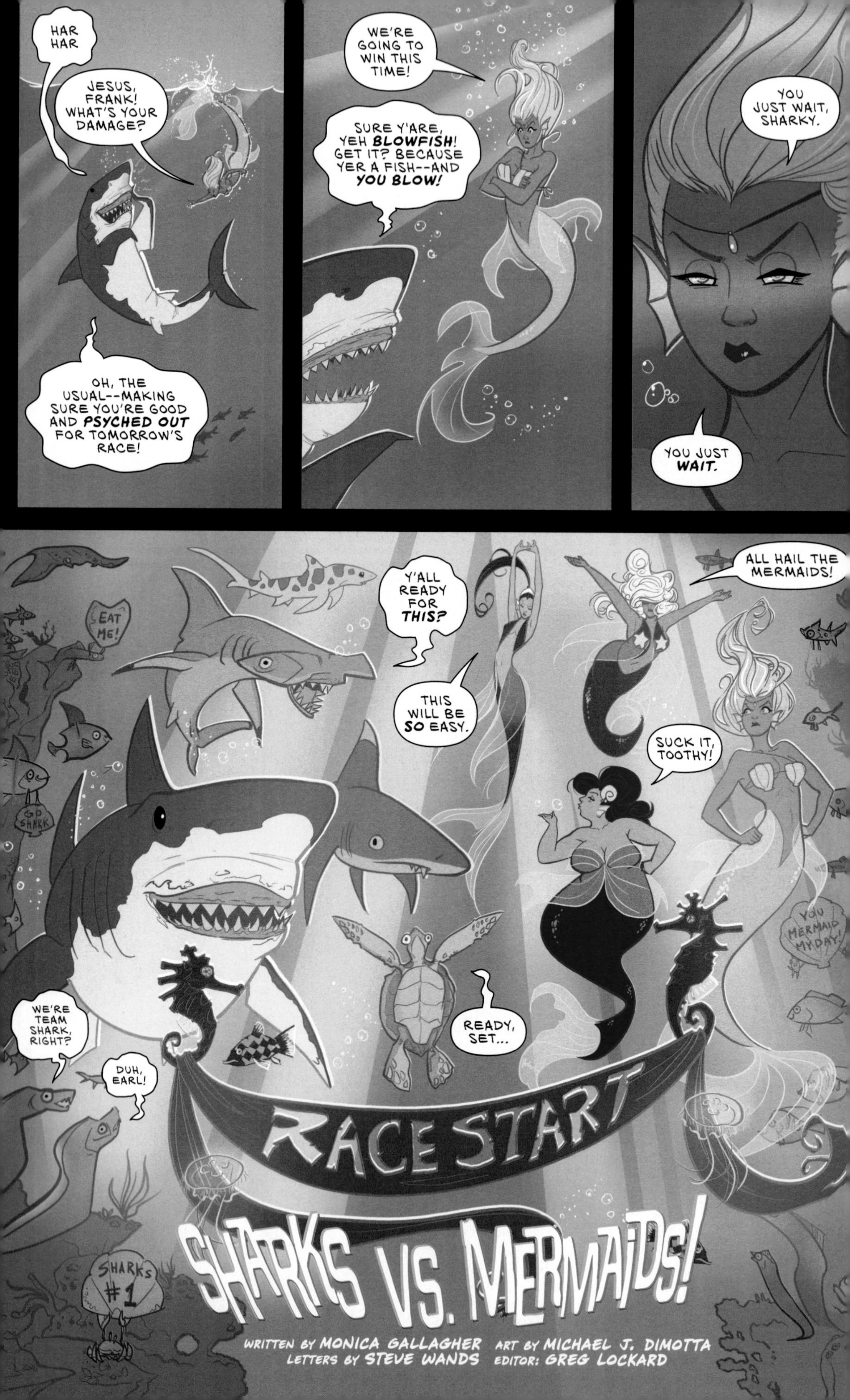
HAR HAR
JESUS, FRANK! WHAT'S YOUR DAMAGE?
OH, THE USUAL--MAKING SURE YOU'RE GOOD AND **PSYCHED OUT** FOR TOMORROW'S RACE!
WE'RE GOING TO WIN THIS TIME!
SURE Y'ARE, YEH **BLOWFISH**! GET IT? BECAUSE YER A FISH--AND **YOU BLOW!**
YOU JUST WAIT, SHARKY.
YOU JUST **WAIT.**
EAT ME!
GO SHARK
Y'ALL READY FOR **THIS?**
THIS WILL BE **SO** EASY.
ALL HAIL THE MERMAIDS!
SUCK IT, TOOTHY!
YOU MERMAID MY DAY!
WE'RE TEAM SHARK, RIGHT?
DUH, EARL!
READY, SET...
RACE START
SHARKS #1
SHARKS VS. MERMAIDS!
WRITTEN BY MONICA GALLAGHER ART BY MICHAEL J. DIMOTTA
LETTERS BY STEVE WANDS EDITOR: GREG LOCKARD

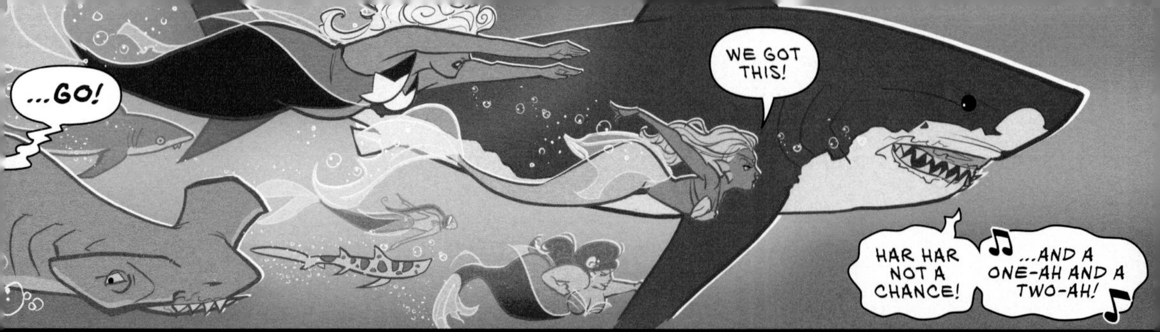
...GO!
WE GOT THIS!
HAR HAR NOT A CHANCE!
...AND A ONE-AH AND A TWO-AH!

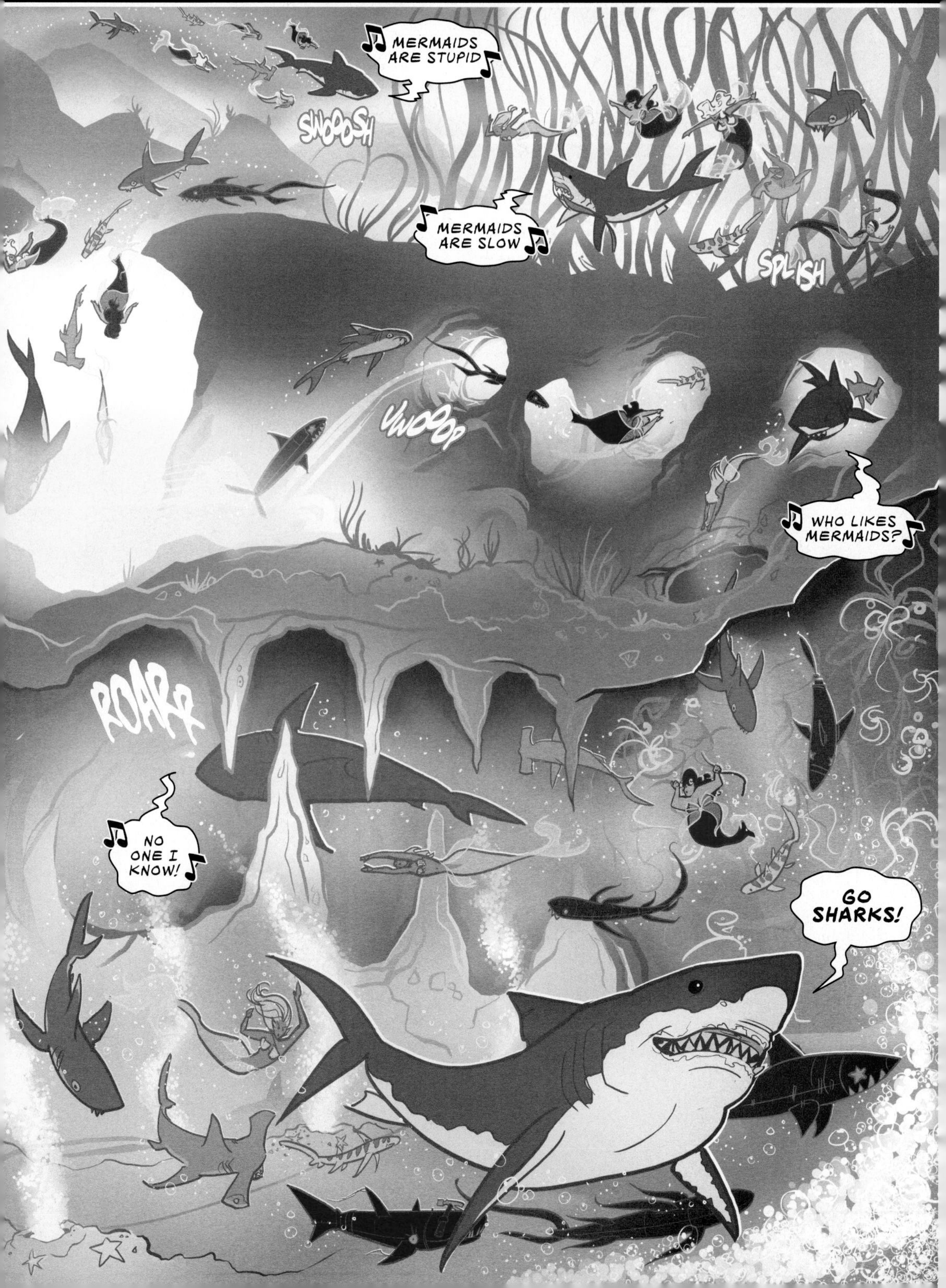
MERMAIDS ARE STUPID
SWOOOSH
MERMAIDS ARE SLOW
SPLISH
WHOOOP
WHO LIKES MERMAIDS?
ROARR
NO ONE I KNOW!
GO SHARKS!

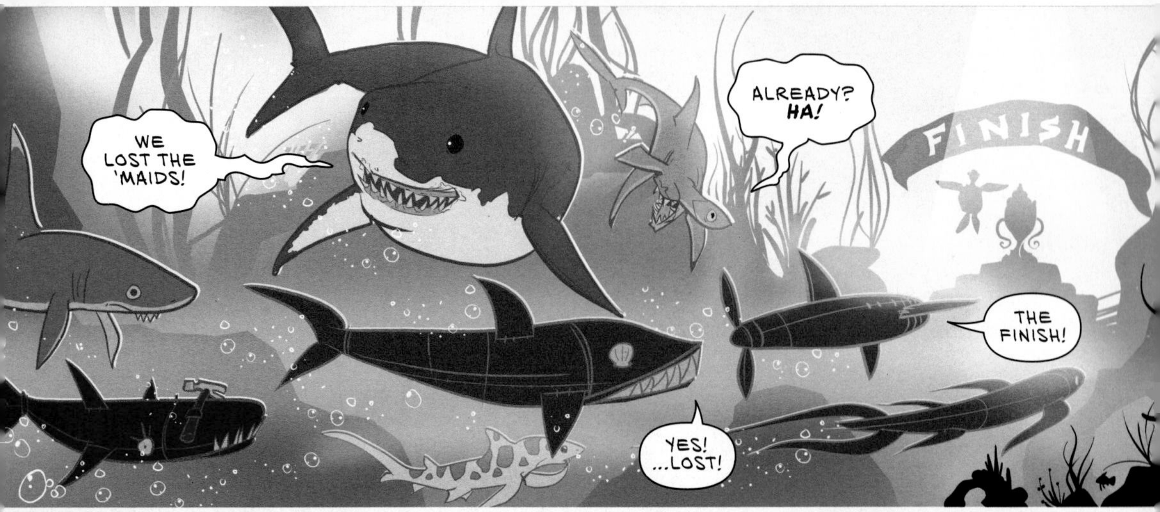
FINISH
WE LOST THE 'MAIDS!
ALREADY? HA!
THE FINISH!
YES! ...LOST!

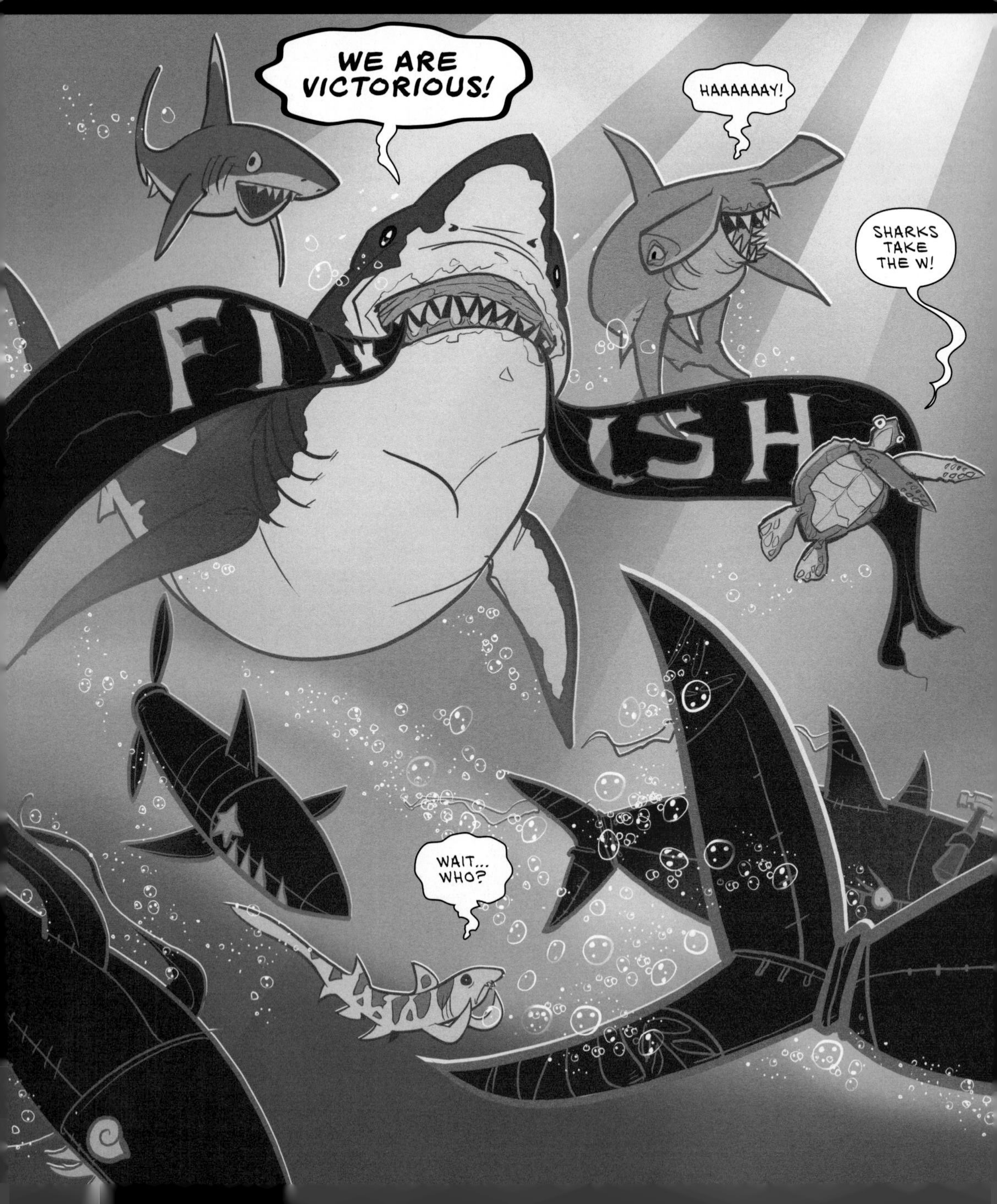
WE ARE VICTORIOUS!
HAAAAAAY!
SHARKS TAKE THE W!
FI ISH
WAIT... WHO?

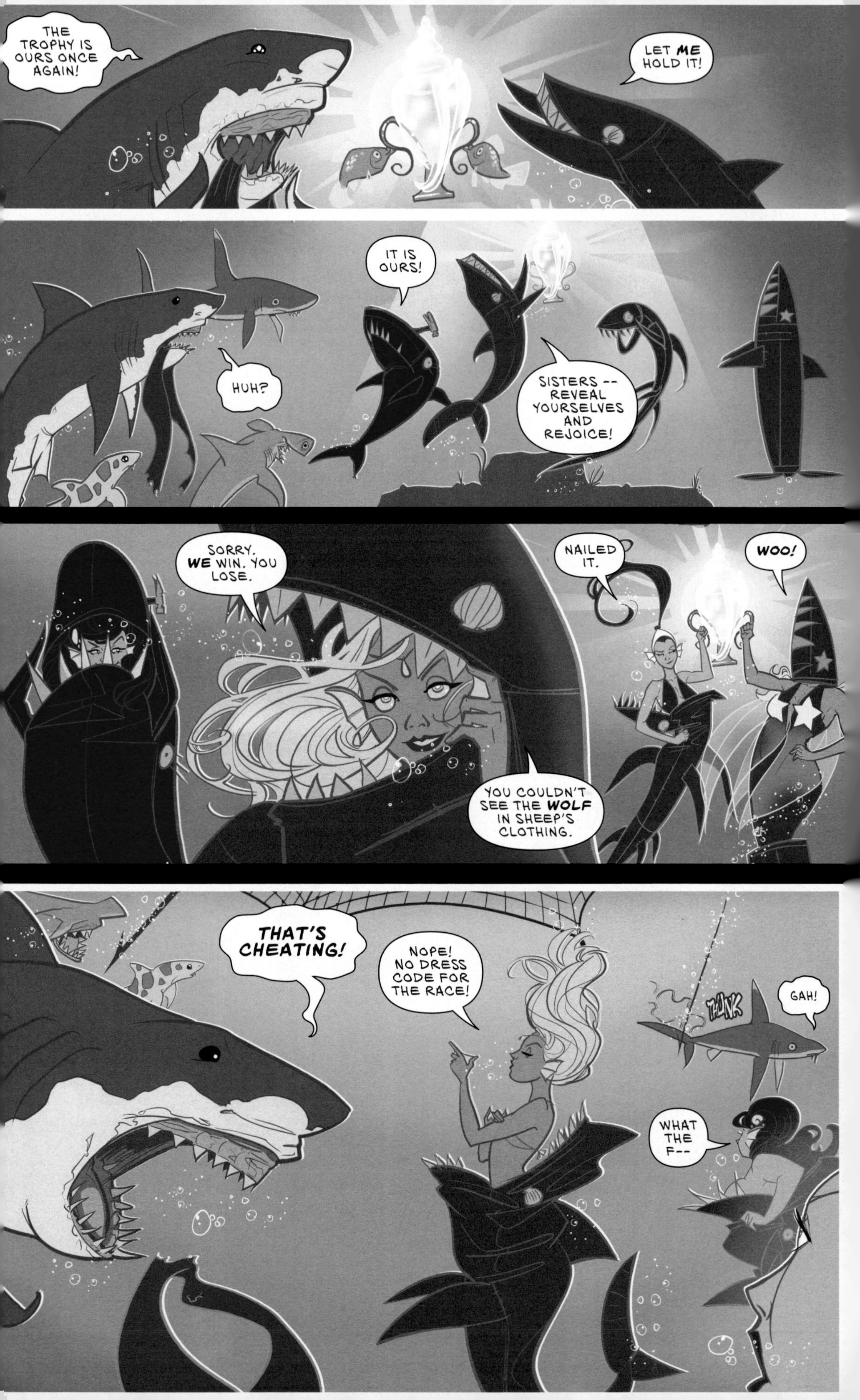
THE TROPHY IS OURS ONCE AGAIN!
LET ME HOLD IT!
IT IS OURS!
HUH?
SISTERS -- REVEAL YOURSELVES AND REJOICE!
SORRY. WE WIN. YOU LOSE.
NAILED IT.
WOO!
YOU COULDN'T SEE THE WOLF IN SHEEP'S CLOTHING.
THAT'S CHEATING!
NOPE! NO DRESS CODE FOR THE RACE!
THUNK
GAH!
WHAT THE F--

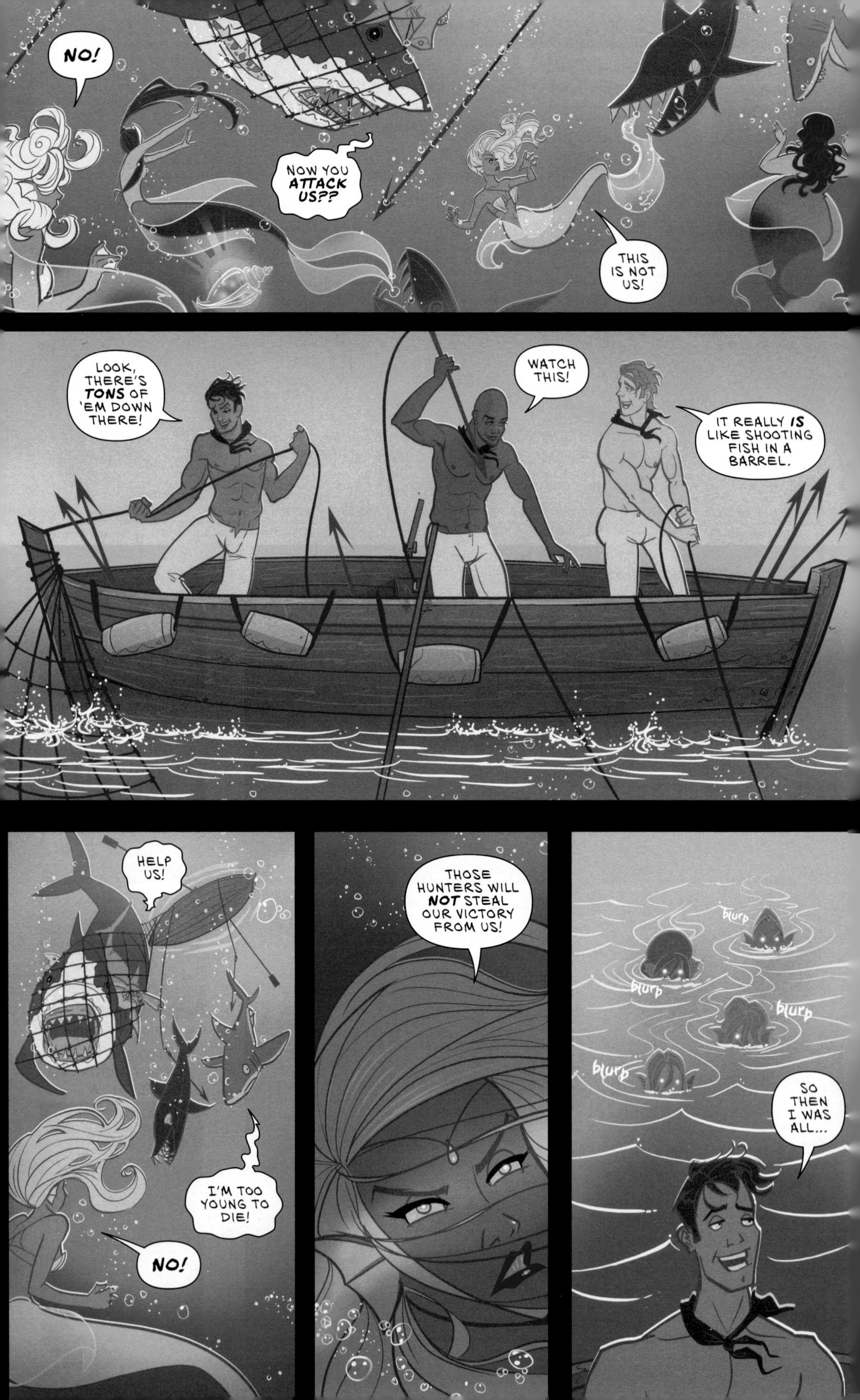
NO!
NOW YOU ATTACK US??
THIS IS NOT US!
LOOK, THERE'S TONS OF 'EM DOWN THERE!
WATCH THIS!
IT REALLY IS LIKE SHOOTING FISH IN A BARREL.
HELP US!
I'M TOO YOUNG TO DIE!
NO!
THOSE HUNTERS WILL NOT STEAL OUR VICTORY FROM US!
blurp
blurp
blurp
blurp
SO THEN I WAS ALL...

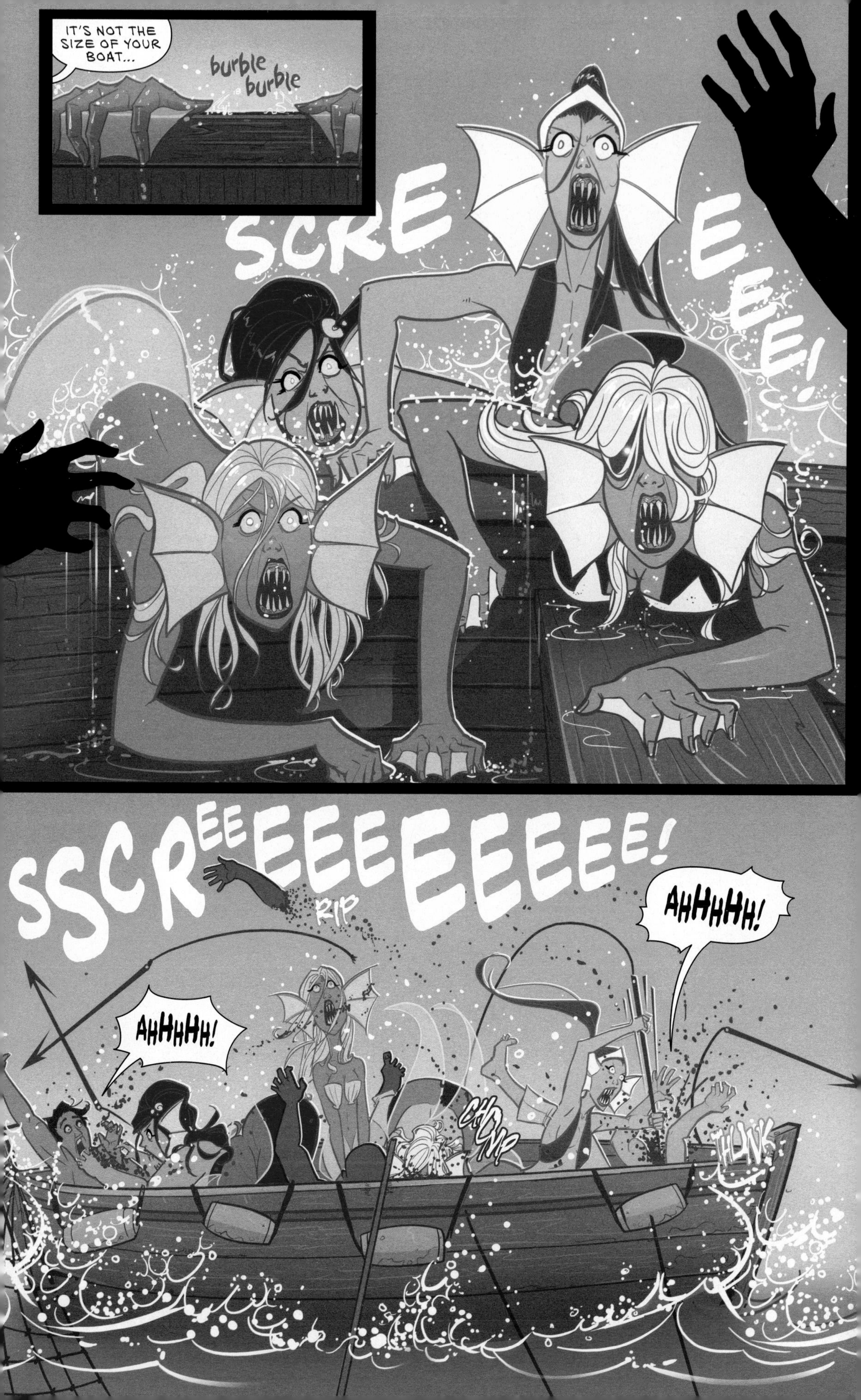
IT'S NOT THE SIZE OF YOUR BOAT...
burble burble
SCREEEE!
SSCREEEEEEEEEE!
RIP
AHHHHH!
AHHHHH!
CHOMP
THUNK

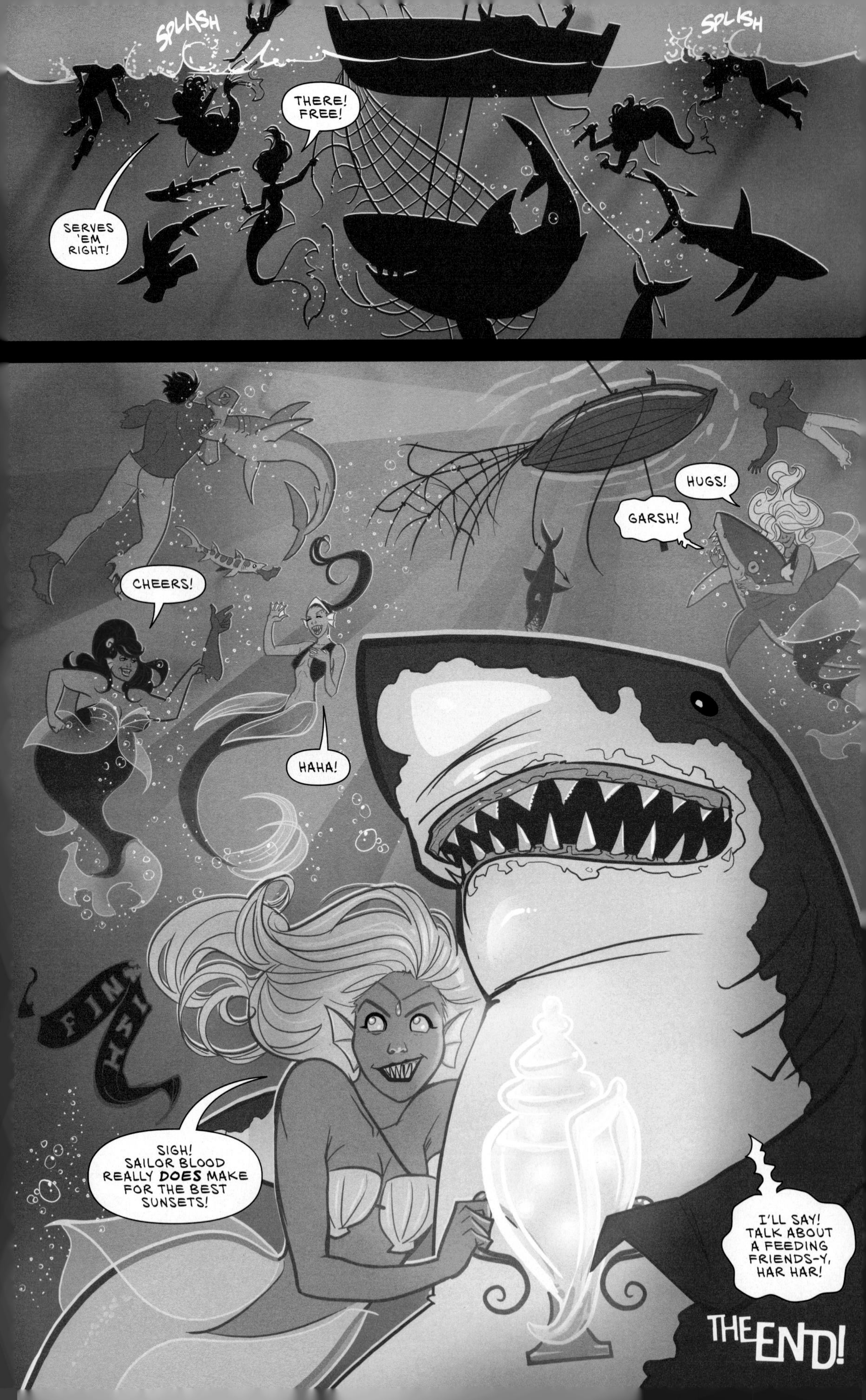
SPLASH
THERE! FREE!
SERVES 'EM RIGHT!
SPLISH
CHEERS!
HAHA!
HUGS!
GARSH!
SIGH! SAILOR BLOOD REALLY **DOES** MAKE FOR THE BEST SUNSETS!
I'LL SAY! TALK ABOUT A FEEDING FRIENDS-Y, HAR HAR!
THE END!

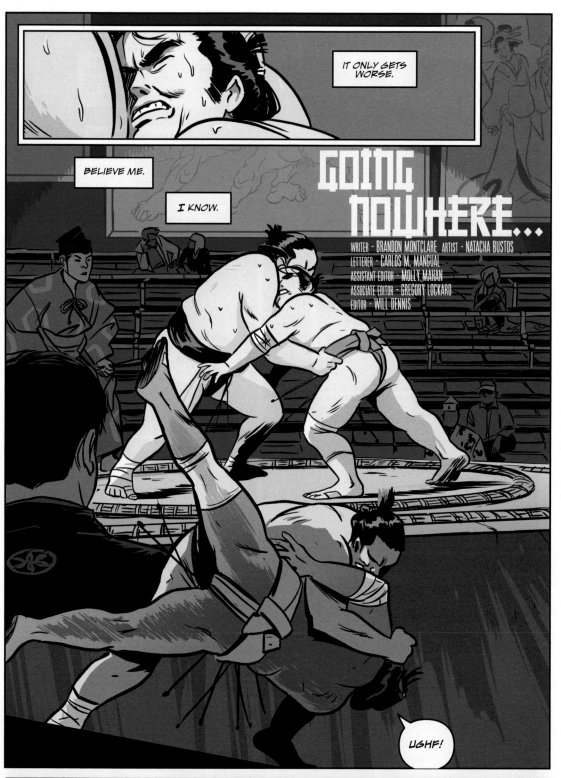

IT ONLY GETS WORSE.

BELIEVE ME.

I KNOW.

GOING NOWHERE...

WRITER · BRANDON MONTCLARE ARTIST · NATACHA BUSTOS
LETTERER · CARLOS M. MANGUAL
ASSISTANT EDITOR · MOLLY MAHAN
ASSOCIATE EDITOR · GREGORY LOCKARD
EDITOR · WILL DENNIS

UGHF!

THE BODY CAN HIT ROCK BOTTOM...

...BUT THE SPIRIT...

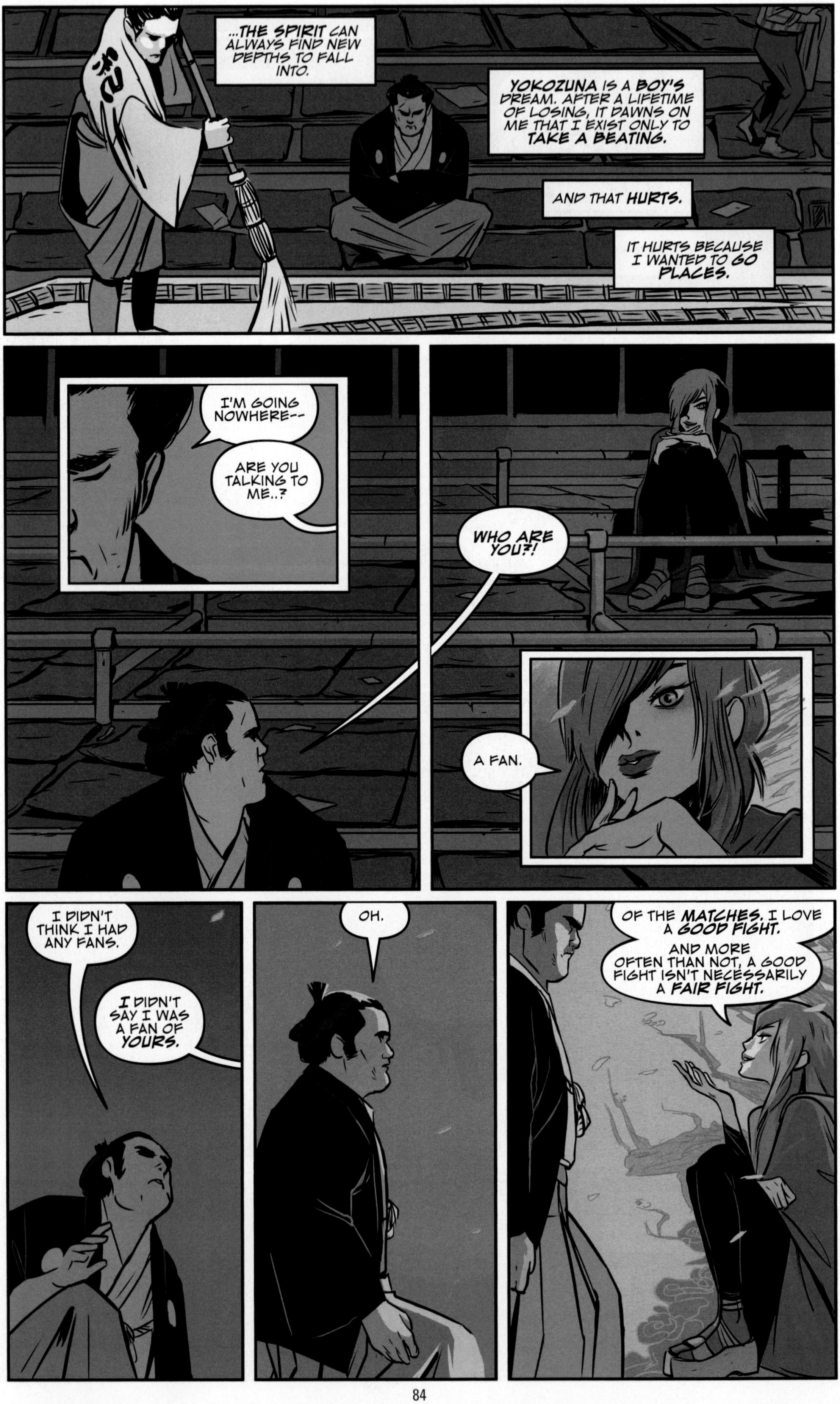
...THE SPIRIT CAN ALWAYS FIND NEW DEPTHS TO FALL INTO.
YOKOZUNA IS A BOY'S DREAM. AFTER A LIFETIME OF LOSING, IT DAWNS ON ME THAT I EXIST ONLY TO TAKE A BEATING.
AND THAT HURTS.
IT HURTS BECAUSE I WANTED TO GO PLACES.
I'M GOING NOWHERE--
ARE YOU TALKING TO ME..?
WHO ARE YOU?!
A FAN.
I DIDN'T THINK I HAD ANY FANS.
I DIDN'T SAY I WAS A FAN OF YOURS.
OH.
OF THE MATCHES. I LOVE A GOOD FIGHT.
AND MORE OFTEN THAN NOT, A GOOD FIGHT ISN'T NECESSARILY A FAIR FIGHT.

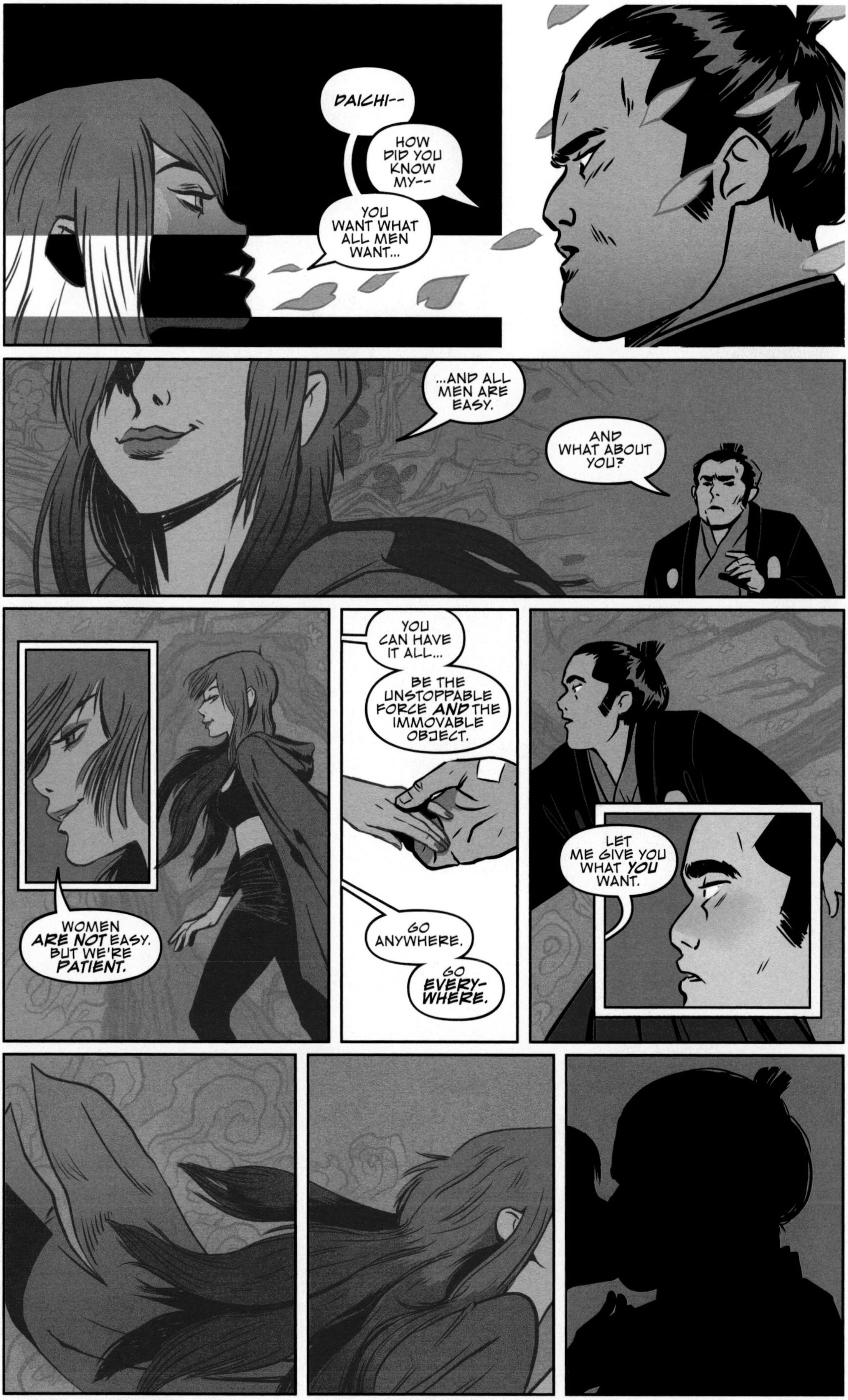

DAICHI--
HOW DID YOU KNOW MY--
YOU WANT WHAT ALL MEN WANT...
...AND ALL MEN ARE EASY.
AND WHAT ABOUT YOU?
WOMEN ARE NOT EASY. BUT WE'RE PATIENT.
YOU CAN HAVE IT ALL...
BE THE UNSTOPPABLE FORCE AND THE IMMOVABLE OBJECT.
GO ANYWHERE.
GO EVERYWHERE.
LET ME GIVE YOU WHAT YOU WANT.

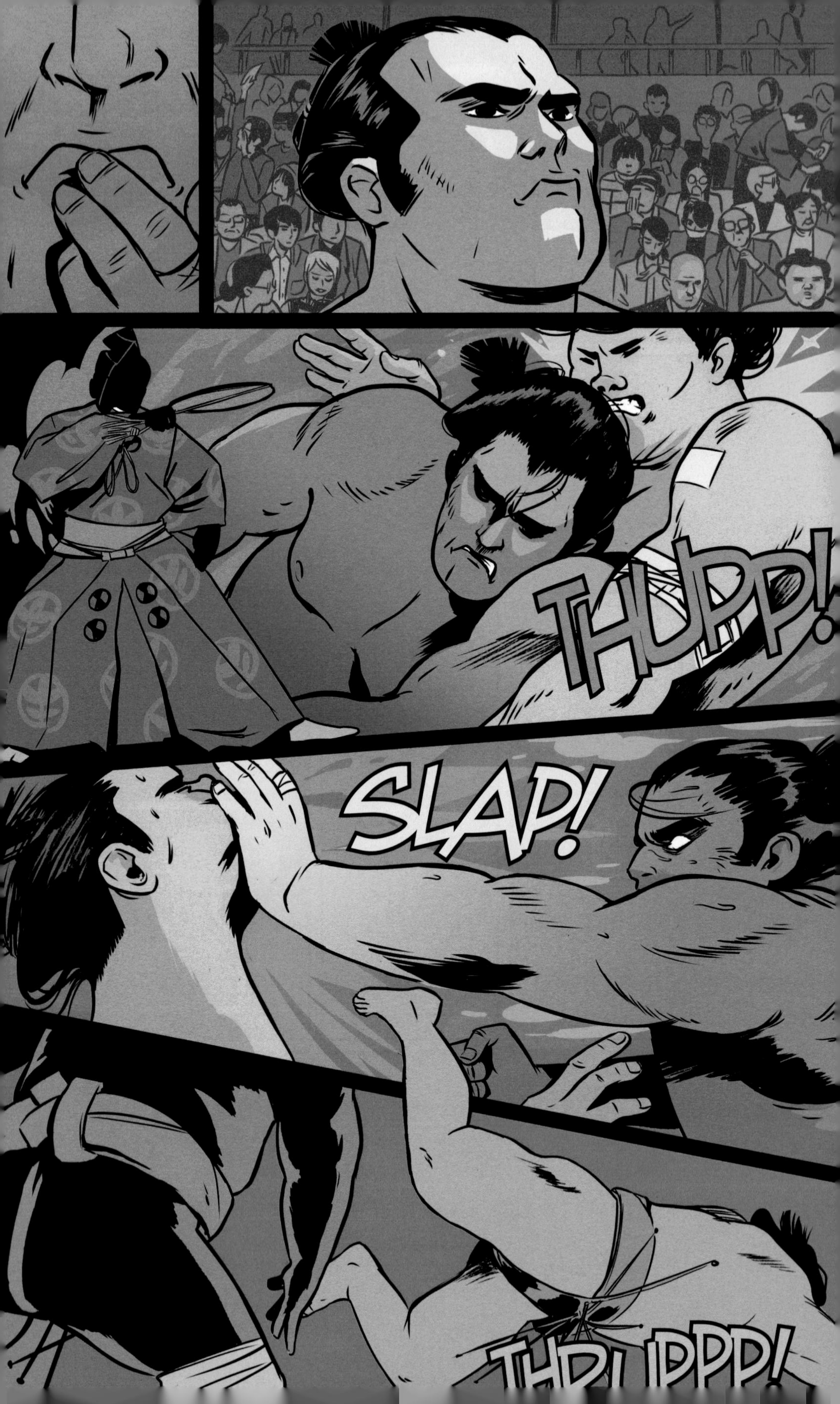
THUPP!
SLAP!
THRUPPP!

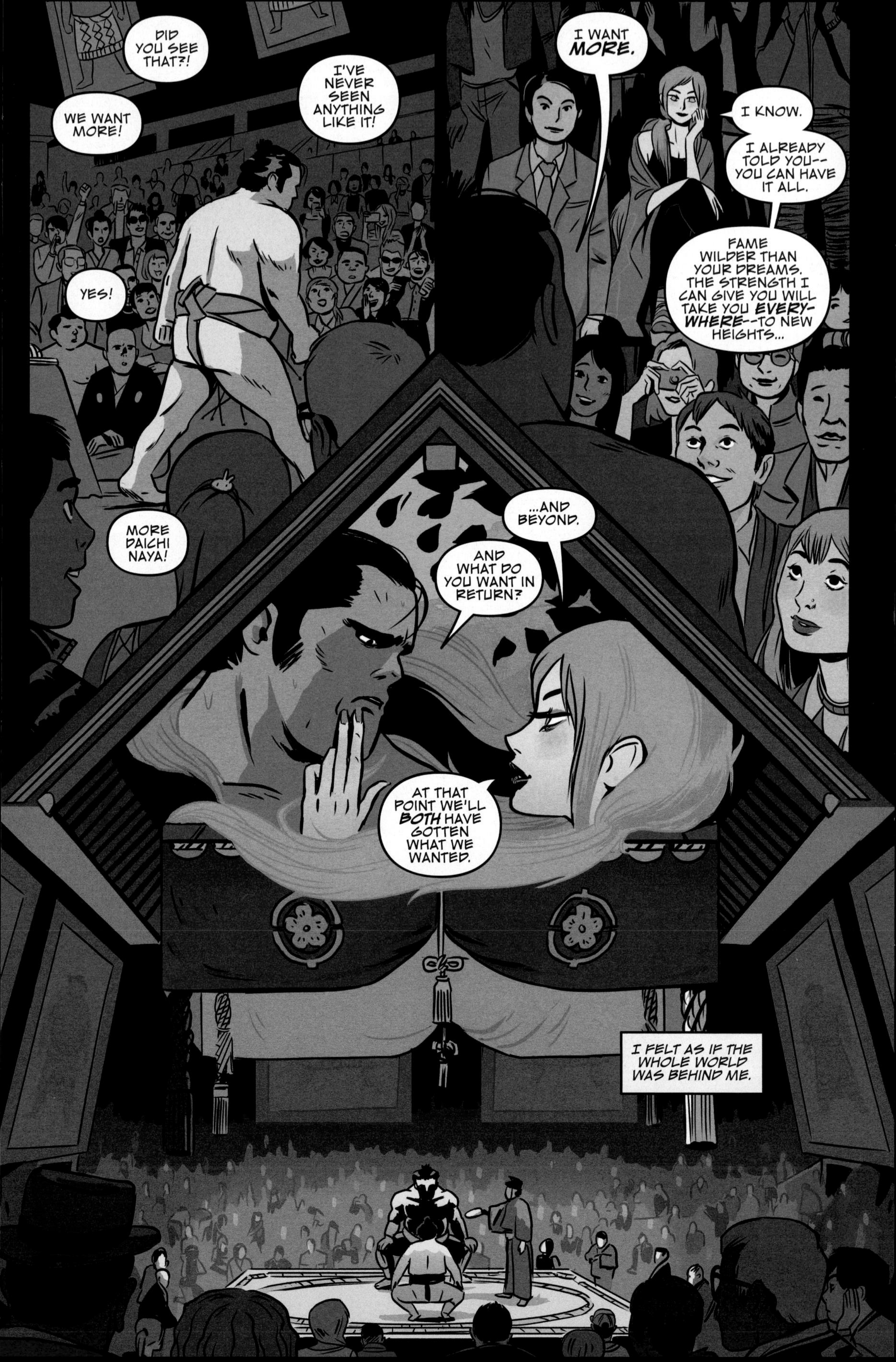
DID YOU SEE THAT?!
WE WANT MORE!
I'VE NEVER SEEN ANYTHING LIKE IT!
YES!
MORE DAICHI NAYA!
I WANT MORE.
I KNOW.
I ALREADY TOLD YOU-- YOU CAN HAVE IT ALL.
FAME WILDER THAN YOUR DREAMS. THE STRENGTH I CAN GIVE YOU WILL TAKE YOU EVERY-WHERE--TO NEW HEIGHTS...
...AND BEYOND.
AND WHAT DO YOU WANT IN RETURN?
AT THAT POINT WE'LL BOTH HAVE GOTTEN WHAT WE WANTED.
I FELT AS IF THE WHOLE WORLD WAS BEHIND ME.

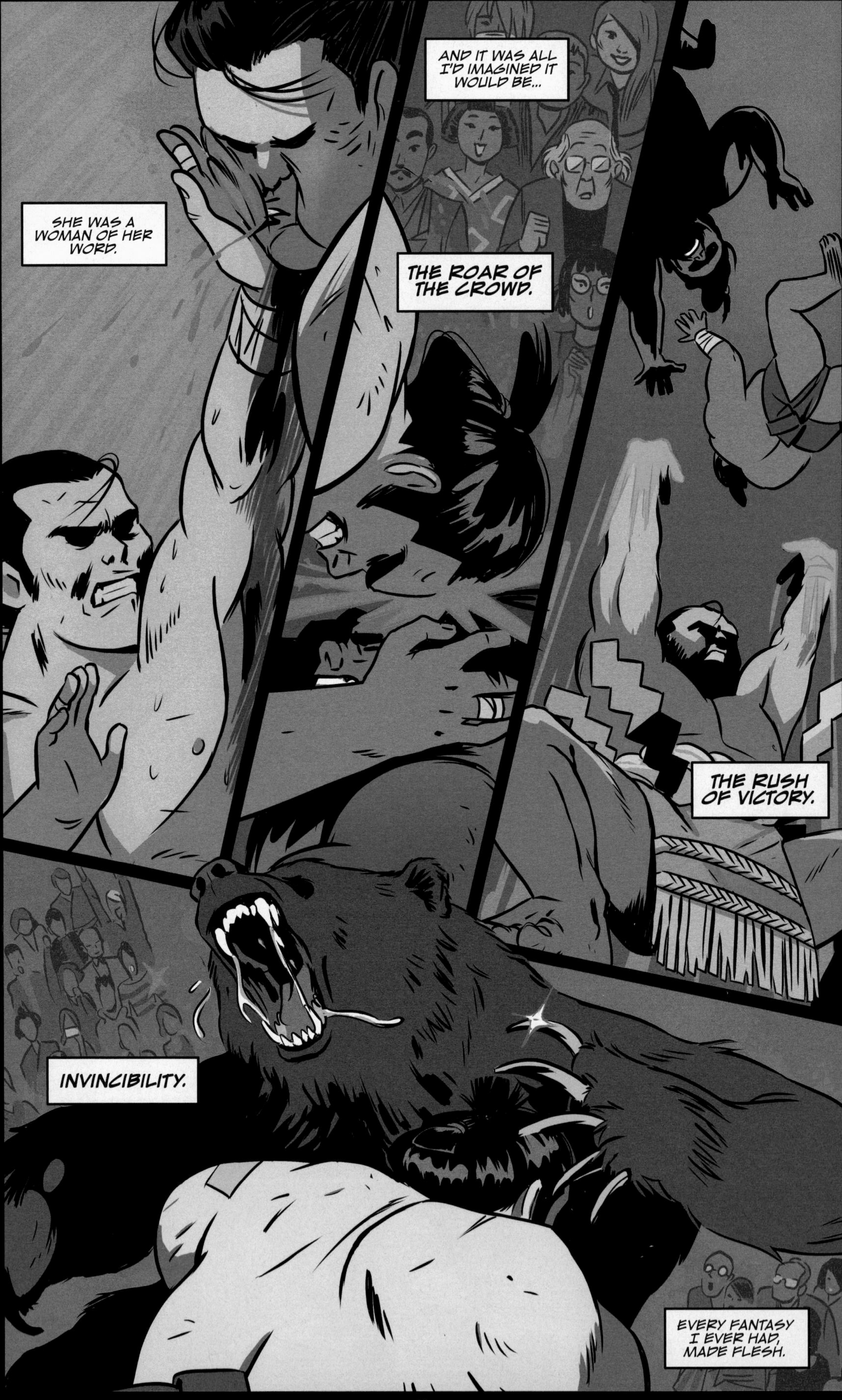
SHE WAS A WOMAN OF HER WORD.
AND IT WAS ALL I'D IMAGINED IT WOULD BE...
THE ROAR OF THE CROWD.
THE RUSH OF VICTORY.
INVINCIBILITY.
EVERY FANTASY I EVER HAD, MADE FLESH.

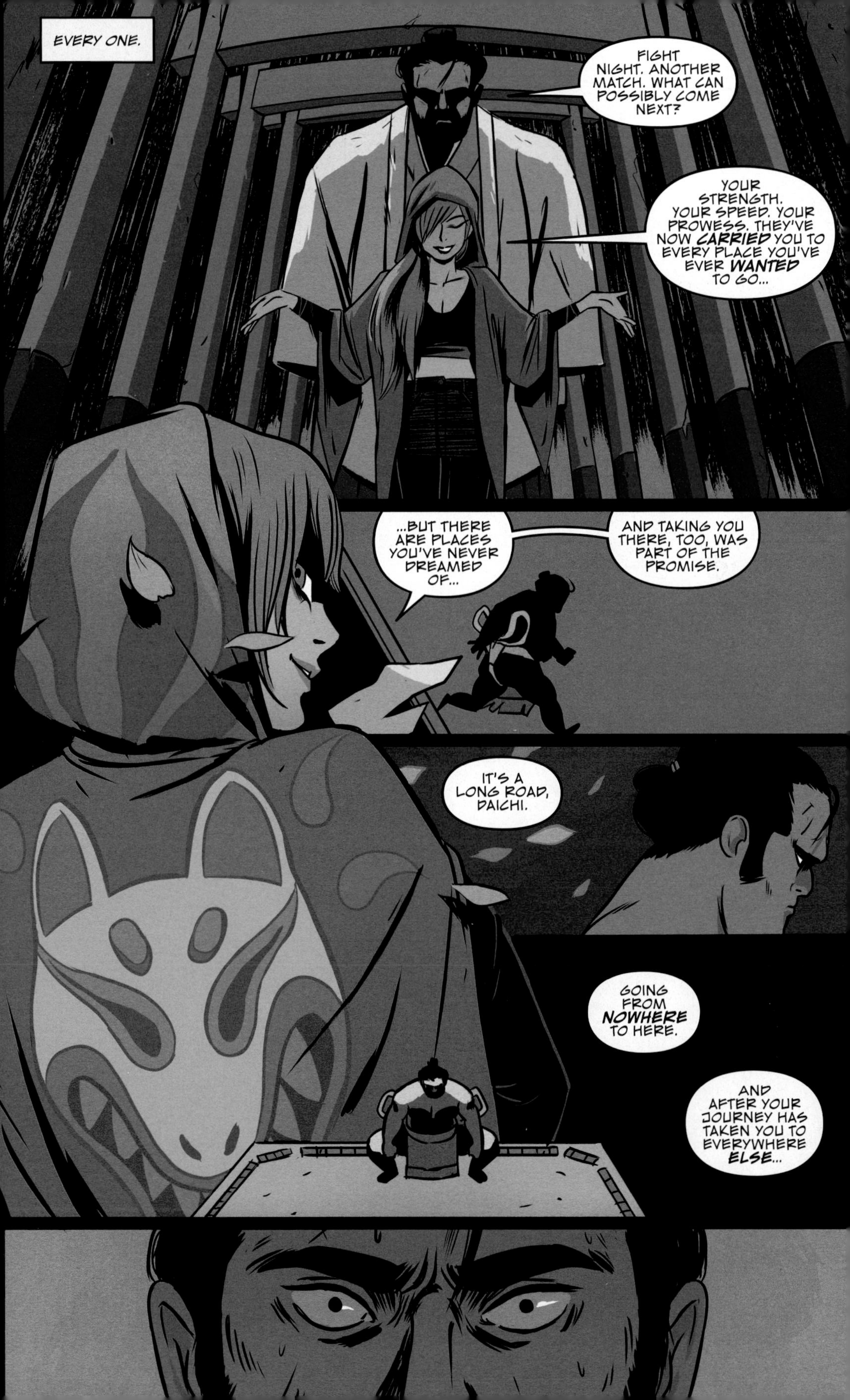
EVERY ONE.
FIGHT NIGHT. ANOTHER MATCH. WHAT CAN POSSIBLY COME NEXT?
YOUR STRENGTH. YOUR SPEED. YOUR PROWESS. THEY'VE NOW CARRIED YOU TO EVERY PLACE YOU'VE EVER WANTED TO GO...
...BUT THERE ARE PLACES YOU'VE NEVER DREAMED OF...
AND TAKING YOU THERE, TOO, WAS PART OF THE PROMISE.
IT'S A LONG ROAD, DAICHI.
GOING FROM NOWHERE TO HERE.
AND AFTER YOUR JOURNEY HAS TAKEN YOU TO EVERYWHERE ELSE...

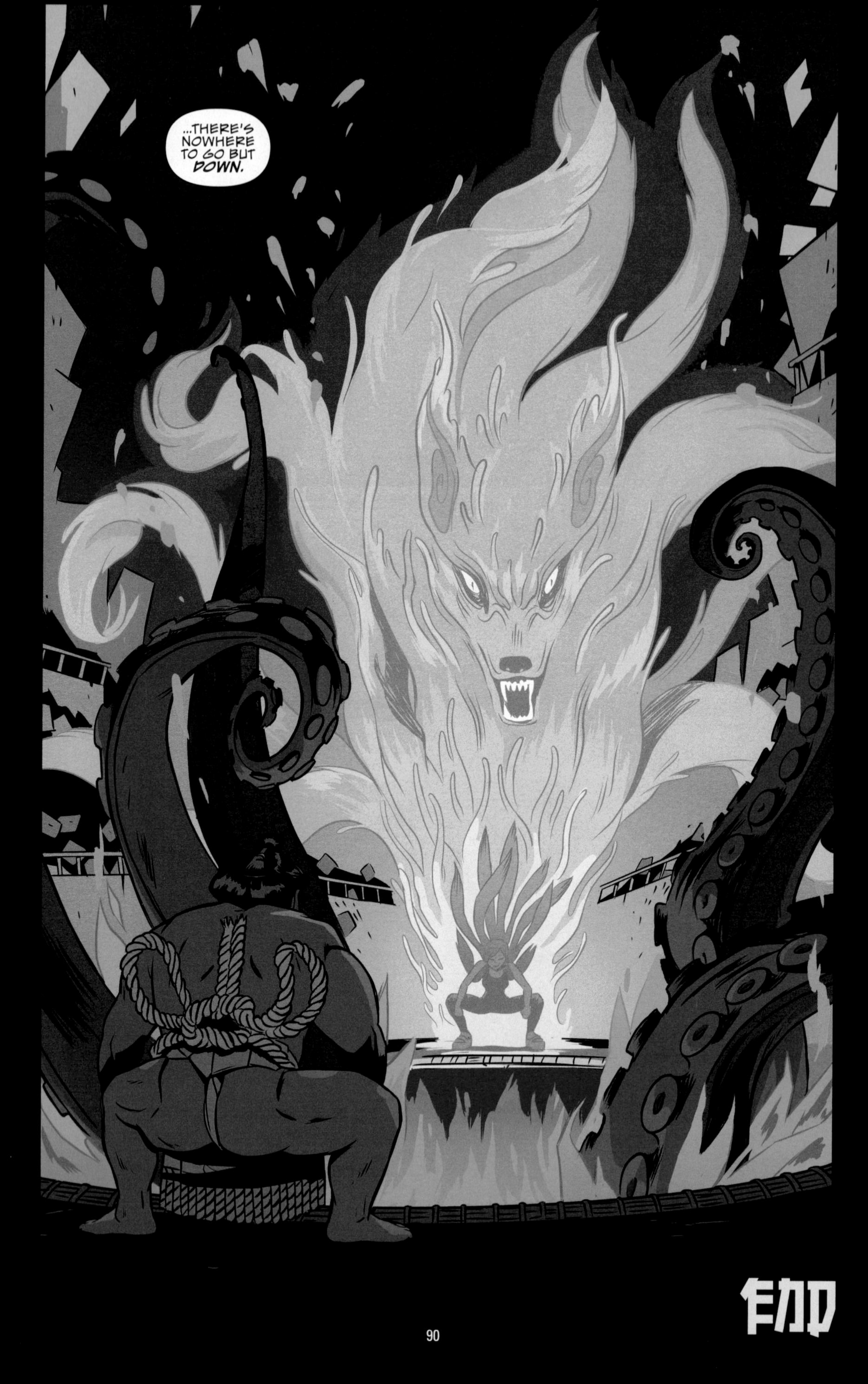
...THERE'S NOWHERE TO GO BUT DOWN.
END

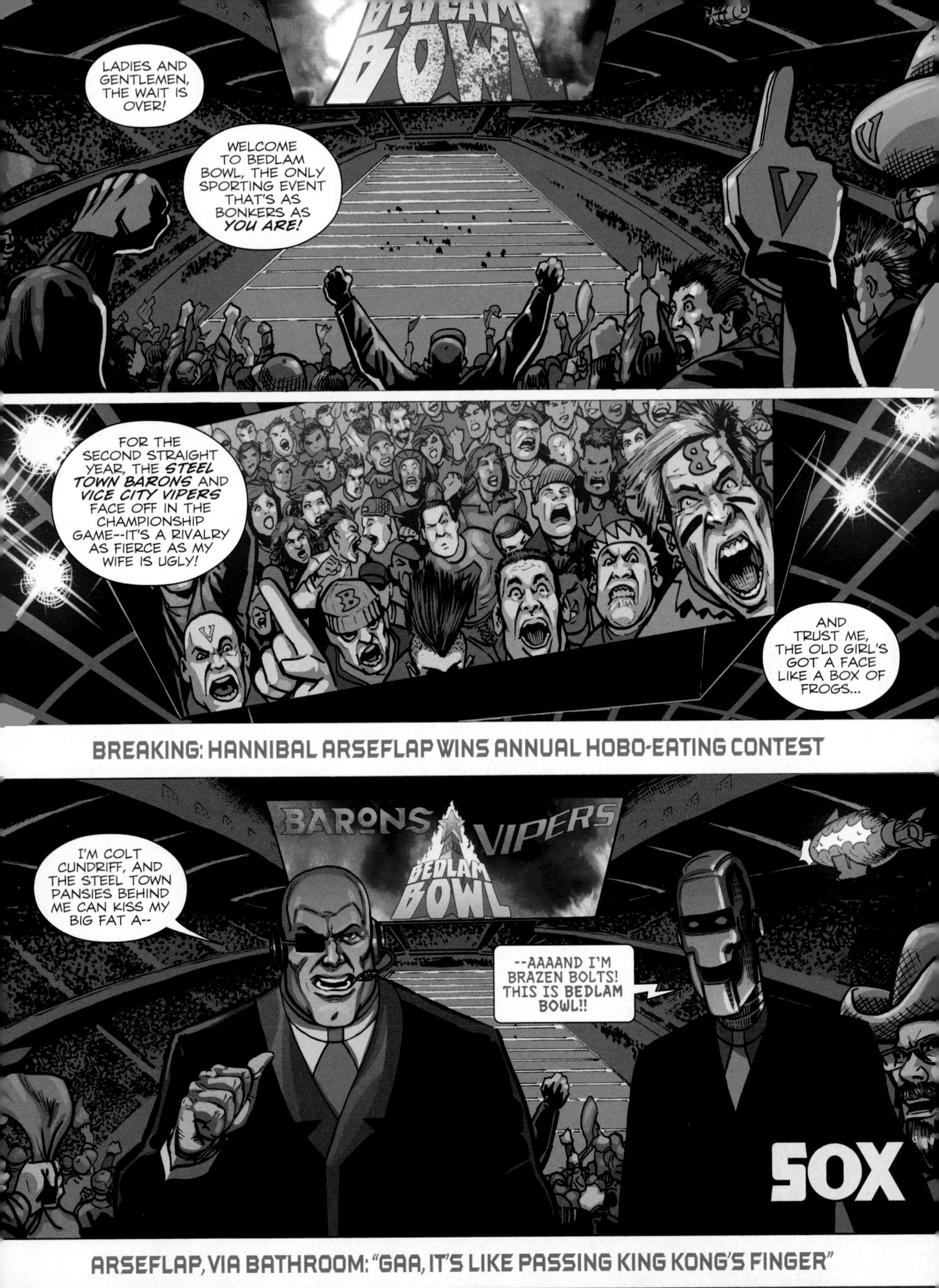
BEDLAM BOWL
LADIES AND GENTLEMEN, THE WAIT IS OVER!
WELCOME TO BEDLAM BOWL, THE ONLY SPORTING EVENT THAT'S AS BONKERS AS *YOU ARE!*
FOR THE SECOND STRAIGHT YEAR, THE ***STEEL TOWN BARONS*** AND ***VICE CITY VIPERS*** FACE OFF IN THE CHAMPIONSHIP GAME--IT'S A RIVALRY AS FIERCE AS MY WIFE IS UGLY!
AND TRUST ME, THE OLD GIRL'S GOT A FACE LIKE A BOX OF FROGS...
BREAKING: HANNIBAL ARSEFLAP WINS ANNUAL HOBO-EATING CONTEST
BARONS VIPERS
BEDLAM BOWL
I'M COLT CUNDRIFF, AND THE STEEL TOWN PANSIES BEHIND ME CAN KISS MY BIG FAT A--
--AAAAND I'M BRAZEN BOLTS! THIS IS BEDLAM BOWL!!
SOX
ARSEFLAP, VIA BATHROOM: "GAA, IT'S LIKE PASSING KING KONG'S FINGER"

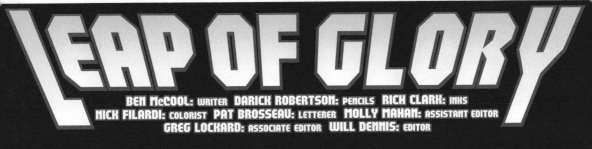

LEAP OF GLORY

BEN McCOOL: WRITER DARICK ROBERTSON: PENCILS RICH CLARK: INKS
NICK FILARDI: COLORIST PAT BROSSEAU: LETTERER MOLLY MAHAN: ASSISTANT EDITOR
GREG LOCKARD: ASSOCIATE EDITOR WILL DENNIS: EDITOR

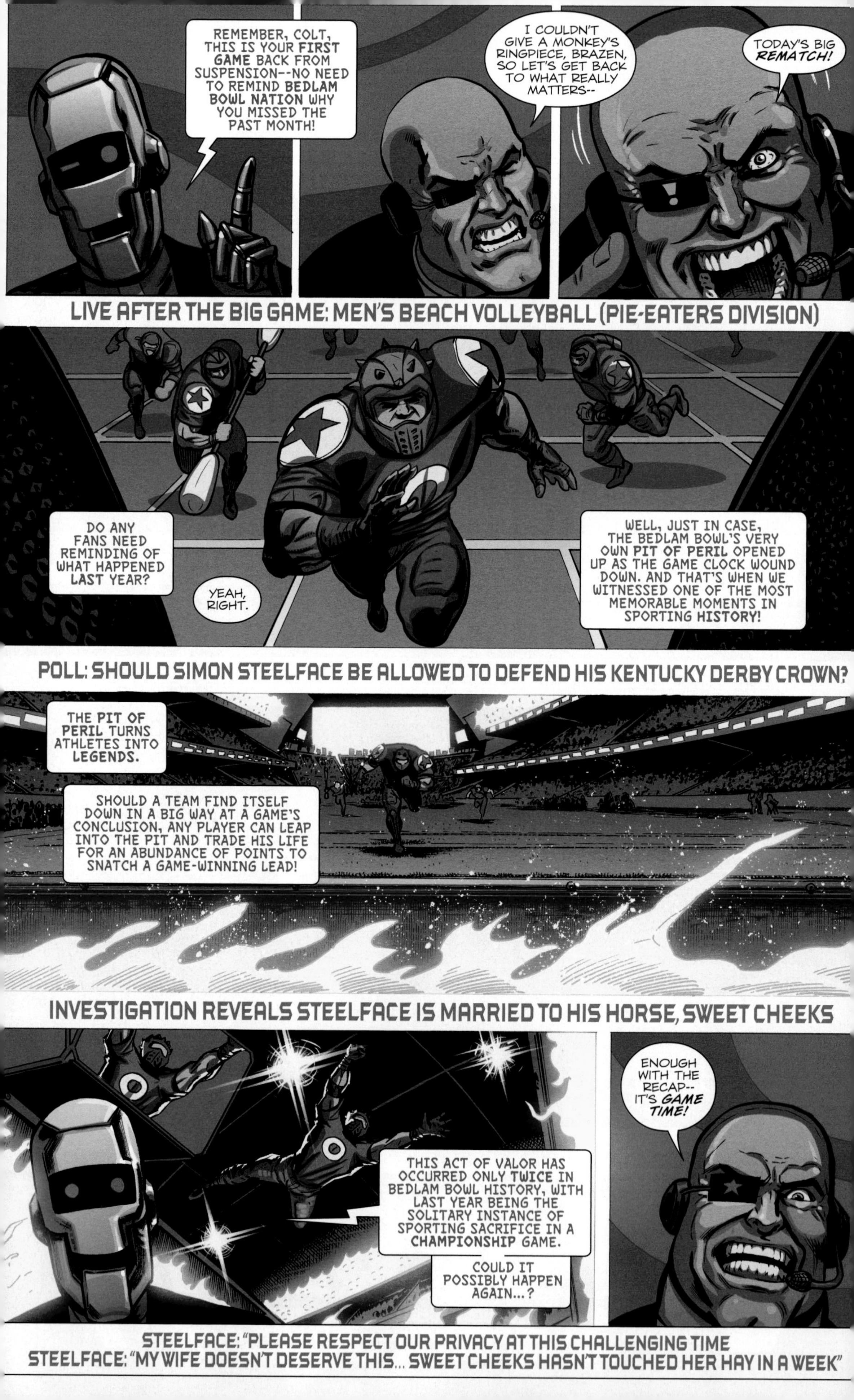
REMEMBER, COLT, THIS IS YOUR FIRST GAME BACK FROM SUSPENSION--NO NEED TO REMIND BEDLAM BOWL NATION WHY YOU MISSED THE PAST MONTH!
I COULDN'T GIVE A MONKEY'S RINGPIECE, BRAZEN, SO LET'S GET BACK TO WHAT REALLY MATTERS--
TODAY'S BIG REMATCH!
LIVE AFTER THE BIG GAME: MEN'S BEACH VOLLEYBALL (PIE-EATERS DIVISION)
DO ANY FANS NEED REMINDING OF WHAT HAPPENED LAST YEAR?
YEAH, RIGHT.
WELL, JUST IN CASE, THE BEDLAM BOWL'S VERY OWN PIT OF PERIL OPENED UP AS THE GAME CLOCK WOUND DOWN. AND THAT'S WHEN WE WITNESSED ONE OF THE MOST MEMORABLE MOMENTS IN SPORTING HISTORY!
POLL: SHOULD SIMON STEELFACE BE ALLOWED TO DEFEND HIS KENTUCKY DERBY CROWN?
THE PIT OF PERIL TURNS ATHLETES INTO LEGENDS.
SHOULD A TEAM FIND ITSELF DOWN IN A BIG WAY AT A GAME'S CONCLUSION, ANY PLAYER CAN LEAP INTO THE PIT AND TRADE HIS LIFE FOR AN ABUNDANCE OF POINTS TO SNATCH A GAME-WINNING LEAD!
INVESTIGATION REVEALS STEELFACE IS MARRIED TO HIS HORSE, SWEET CHEEKS
THIS ACT OF VALOR HAS OCCURRED ONLY TWICE IN BEDLAM BOWL HISTORY, WITH LAST YEAR BEING THE SOLITARY INSTANCE OF SPORTING SACRIFICE IN A CHAMPIONSHIP GAME.
COULD IT POSSIBLY HAPPEN AGAIN...?
ENOUGH WITH THE RECAP-- IT'S GAME TIME!
STEELFACE: "PLEASE RESPECT OUR PRIVACY AT THIS CHALLENGING TIME
STEELFACE: "MY WIFE DOESN'T DESERVE THIS... SWEET CHEEKS HASN'T TOUCHED HER HAY IN A WEEK"

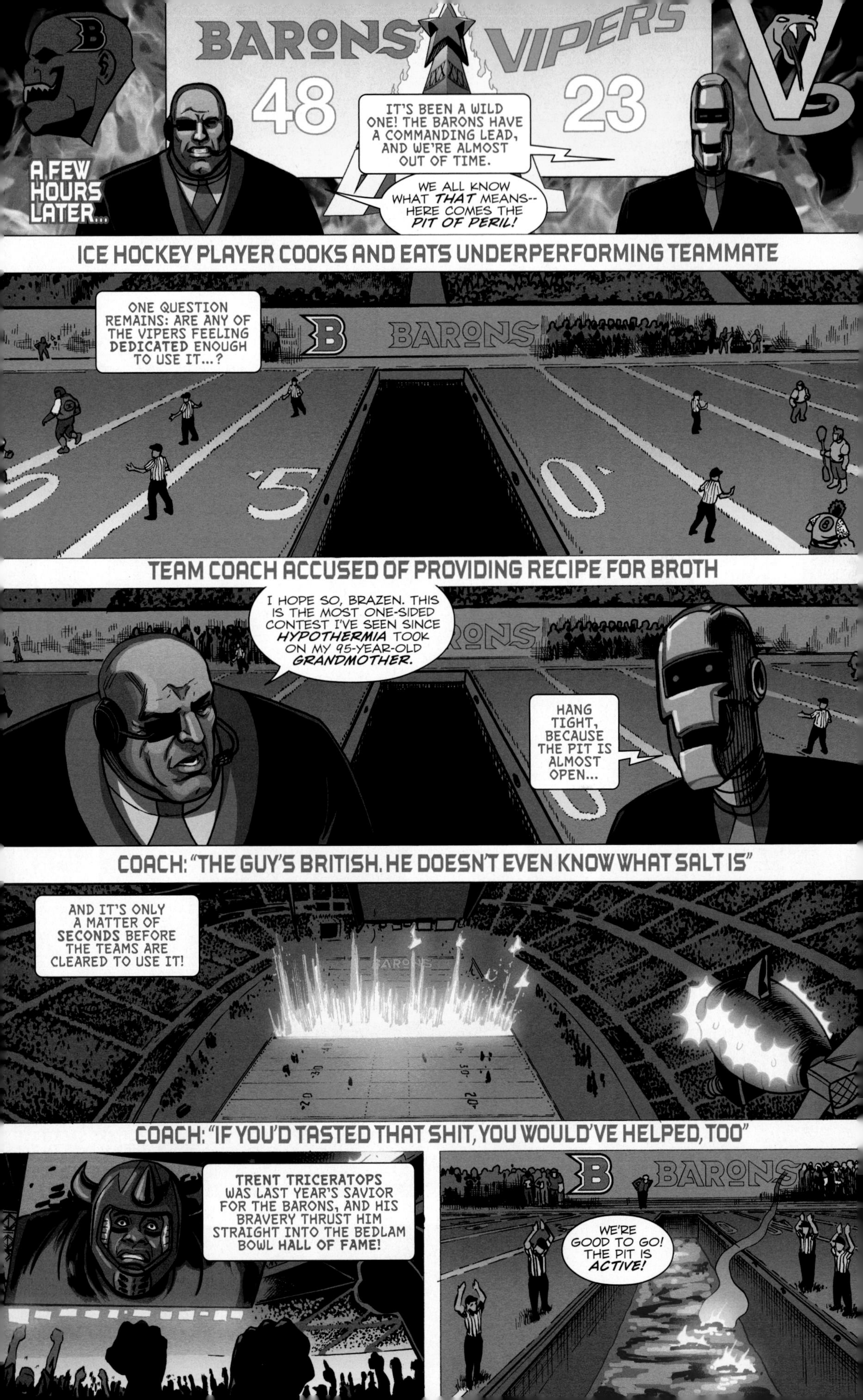
BARONS
VIPERS
48
23
A FEW HOURS LATER...
IT'S BEEN A WILD ONE! THE BARONS HAVE A COMMANDING LEAD, AND WE'RE ALMOST OUT OF TIME.
WE ALL KNOW WHAT THAT MEANS-- HERE COMES THE PIT OF PERIL!
ICE HOCKEY PLAYER COOKS AND EATS UNDERPERFORMING TEAMMATE
ONE QUESTION REMAINS: ARE ANY OF THE VIPERS FEELING DEDICATED ENOUGH TO USE IT...?
BARONS
TEAM COACH ACCUSED OF PROVIDING RECIPE FOR BROTH
I HOPE SO, BRAZEN. THIS IS THE MOST ONE-SIDED CONTEST I'VE SEEN SINCE HYPOTHERMIA TOOK ON MY 95-YEAR-OLD GRANDMOTHER.
HANG TIGHT, BECAUSE THE PIT IS ALMOST OPEN...
COACH: "THE GUY'S BRITISH. HE DOESN'T EVEN KNOW WHAT SALT IS"
AND IT'S ONLY A MATTER OF SECONDS BEFORE THE TEAMS ARE CLEARED TO USE IT!
COACH: "IF YOU'D TASTED THAT SHIT, YOU WOULD'VE HELPED, TOO"
TRENT TRICERATOPS WAS LAST YEAR'S SAVIOR FOR THE BARONS, AND HIS BRAVERY THRUST HIM STRAIGHT INTO THE BEDLAM BOWL HALL OF FAME!
BARONS
WE'RE GOOD TO GO! THE PIT IS ACTIVE!

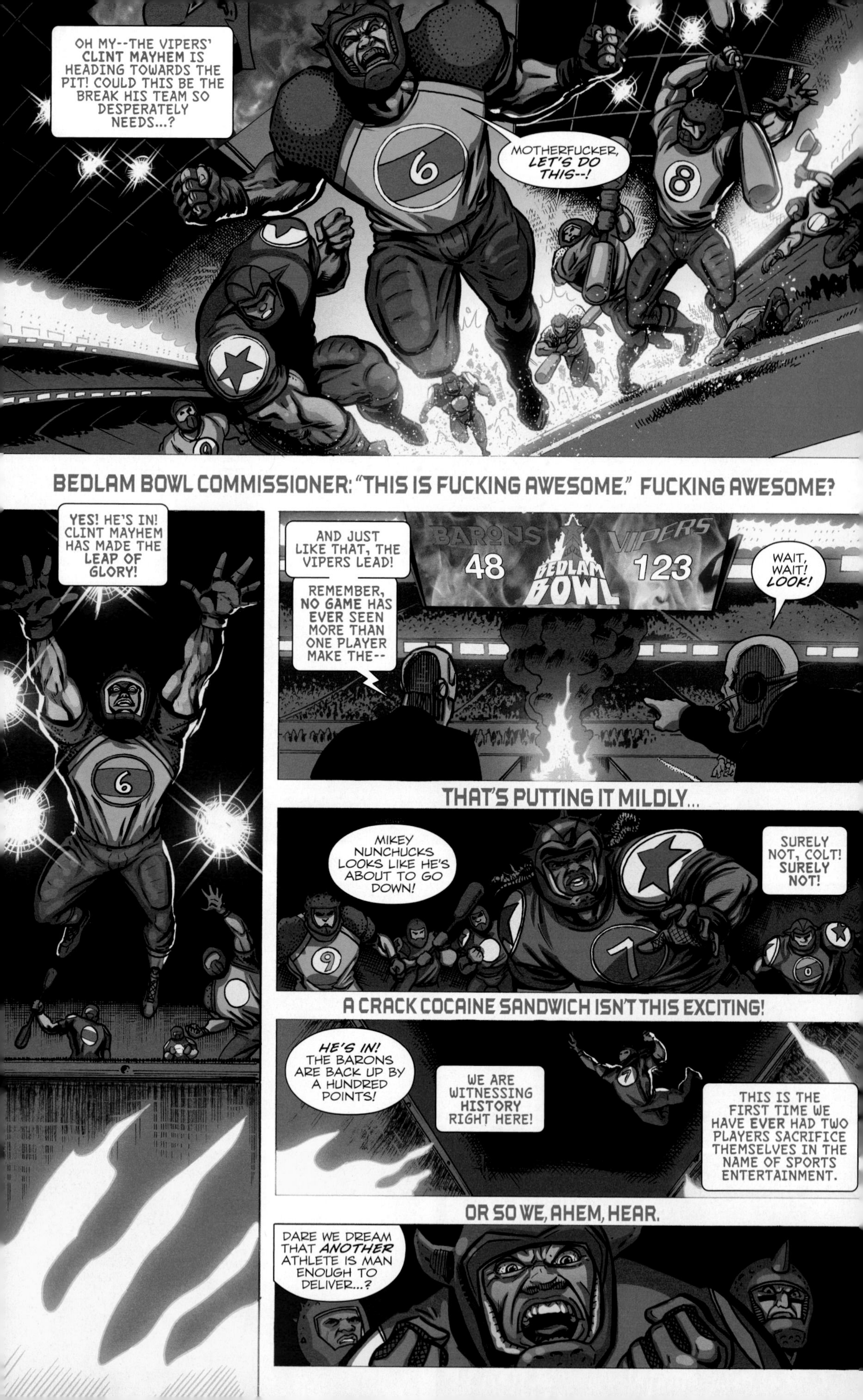

OH MY--THE VIPERS' CLINT MAYHEM IS HEADING TOWARDS THE PIT! COULD THIS BE THE BREAK HIS TEAM SO DESPERATELY NEEDS...?
MOTHERFUCKER, LET'S DO THIS--!
BEDLAM BOWL COMMISSIONER: "THIS IS FUCKING AWESOME." FUCKING AWESOME?
YES! HE'S IN! CLINT MAYHEM HAS MADE THE LEAP OF GLORY!
AND JUST LIKE THAT, THE VIPERS LEAD!
BARONS 48 BEDLAM BOWL VIPERS 123
REMEMBER, NO GAME HAS EVER SEEN MORE THAN ONE PLAYER MAKE THE--
WAIT, WAIT! LOOK!
THAT'S PUTTING IT MILDLY...
MIKEY NUNCHUCKS LOOKS LIKE HE'S ABOUT TO GO DOWN!
SURELY NOT, COLT! SURELY NOT!
A CRACK COCAINE SANDWICH ISN'T THIS EXCITING!
HE'S IN! THE BARONS ARE BACK UP BY A HUNDRED POINTS!
WE ARE WITNESSING HISTORY RIGHT HERE!
THIS IS THE FIRST TIME WE HAVE EVER HAD TWO PLAYERS SACRIFICE THEMSELVES IN THE NAME OF SPORTS ENTERTAINMENT.
OR SO WE, AHEM, HEAR.
DARE WE DREAM THAT ANOTHER ATHLETE IS MAN ENOUGH TO DELIVER...?

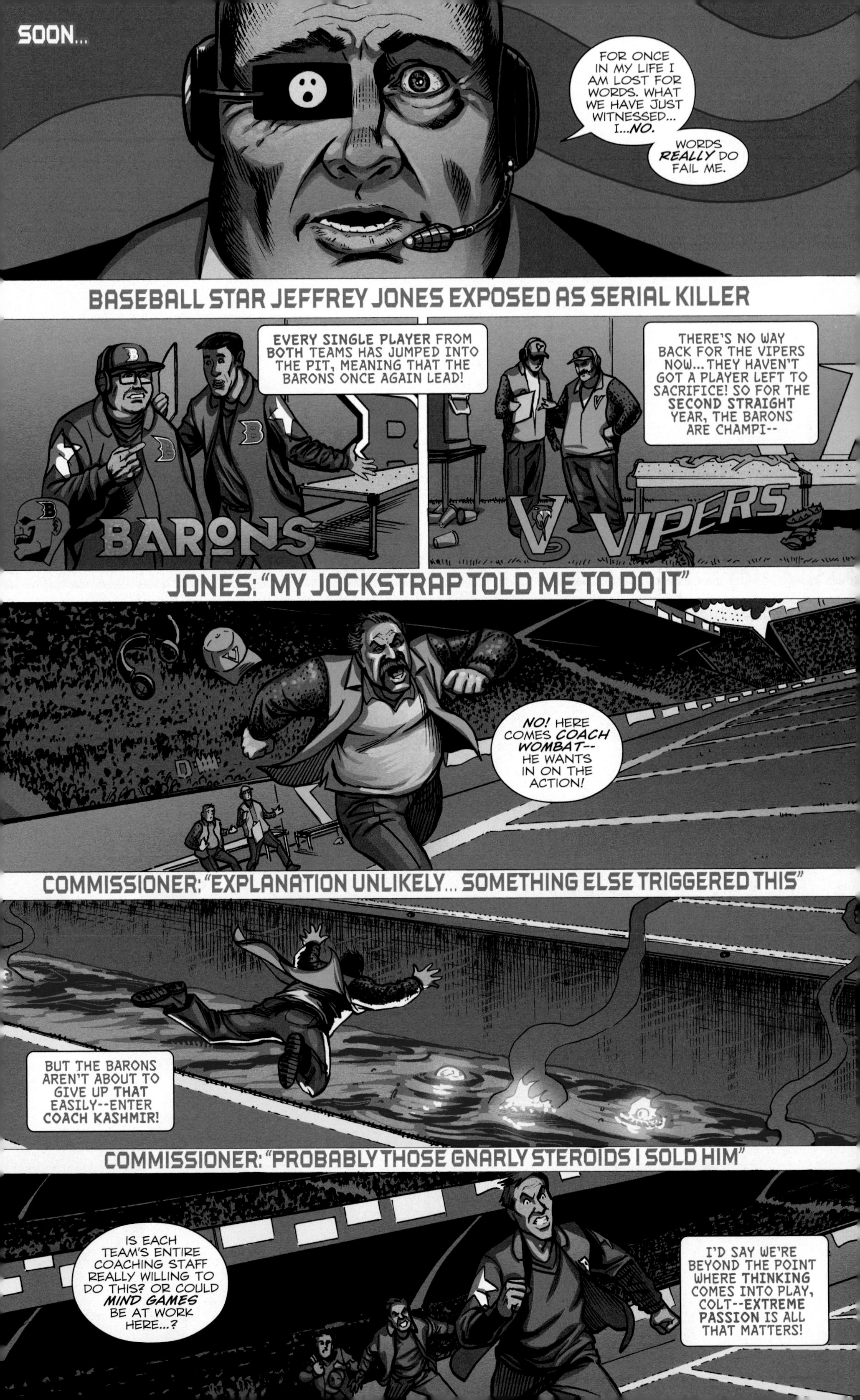
SOON...
FOR ONCE IN MY LIFE I AM LOST FOR WORDS. WHAT WE HAVE JUST WITNESSED... I...NO.
WORDS REALLY DO FAIL ME.
BASEBALL STAR JEFFREY JONES EXPOSED AS SERIAL KILLER
EVERY SINGLE PLAYER FROM BOTH TEAMS HAS JUMPED INTO THE PIT, MEANING THAT THE BARONS ONCE AGAIN LEAD!
BARONS
THERE'S NO WAY BACK FOR THE VIPERS NOW...THEY HAVEN'T GOT A PLAYER LEFT TO SACRIFICE! SO FOR THE SECOND STRAIGHT YEAR, THE BARONS ARE CHAMPI--
VIPERS
JONES: "MY JOCKSTRAP TOLD ME TO DO IT"
NO! HERE COMES COACH WOMBAT-- HE WANTS IN ON THE ACTION!
COMMISSIONER: "EXPLANATION UNLIKELY... SOMETHING ELSE TRIGGERED THIS"
BUT THE BARONS AREN'T ABOUT TO GIVE UP THAT EASILY--ENTER COACH KASHMIR!
COMMISSIONER: "PROBABLY THOSE GNARLY STEROIDS I SOLD HIM"
IS EACH TEAM'S ENTIRE COACHING STAFF REALLY WILLING TO DO THIS? OR COULD MIND GAMES BE AT WORK HERE...?
I'D SAY WE'RE BEYOND THE POINT WHERE THINKING COMES INTO PLAY, COLT--EXTREME PASSION IS ALL THAT MATTERS!

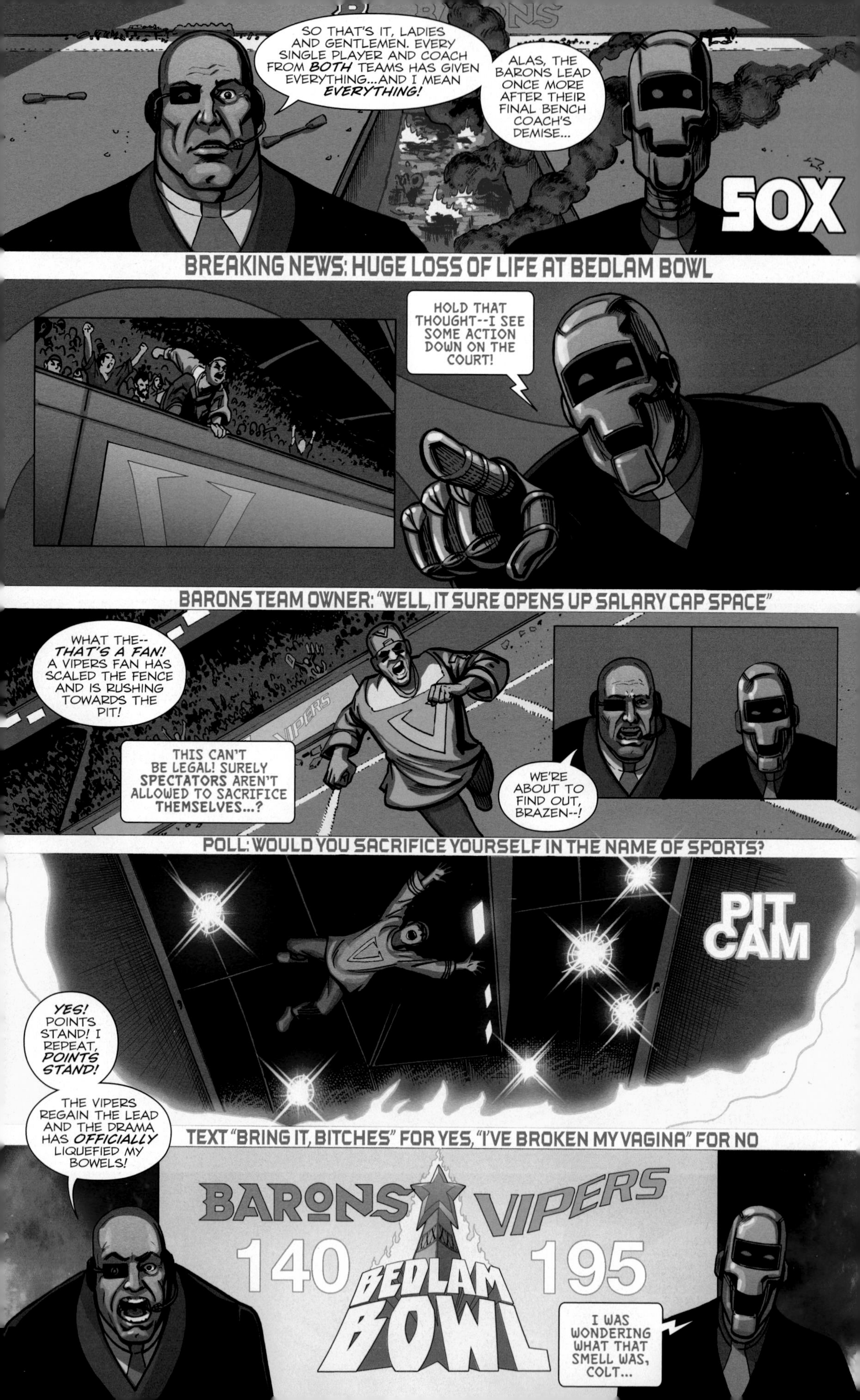
SO THAT'S IT, LADIES AND GENTLEMEN. EVERY SINGLE PLAYER AND COACH FROM BOTH TEAMS HAS GIVEN EVERYTHING...AND I MEAN EVERYTHING!
ALAS, THE BARONS LEAD ONCE MORE AFTER THEIR FINAL BENCH COACH'S DEMISE...
SOX
BREAKING NEWS: HUGE LOSS OF LIFE AT BEDLAM BOWL
HOLD THAT THOUGHT--I SEE SOME ACTION DOWN ON THE COURT!
BARONS TEAM OWNER: "WELL, IT SURE OPENS UP SALARY CAP SPACE"
WHAT THE-- THAT'S A FAN! A VIPERS FAN HAS SCALED THE FENCE AND IS RUSHING TOWARDS THE PIT!
VIPERS
THIS CAN'T BE LEGAL! SURELY SPECTATORS AREN'T ALLOWED TO SACRIFICE THEMSELVES...?
WE'RE ABOUT TO FIND OUT, BRAZEN--!
POLL: WOULD YOU SACRIFICE YOURSELF IN THE NAME OF SPORTS?
PIT CAM
YES! POINTS STAND! I REPEAT, POINTS STAND!
THE VIPERS REGAIN THE LEAD AND THE DRAMA HAS OFFICIALLY LIQUEFIED MY BOWELS!
TEXT "BRING IT, BITCHES" FOR YES, "I'VE BROKEN MY VAGINA" FOR NO
BARONS VIPERS
140 195
BEDLAM BOWL
I WAS WONDERING WHAT THAT SMELL WAS, COLT...

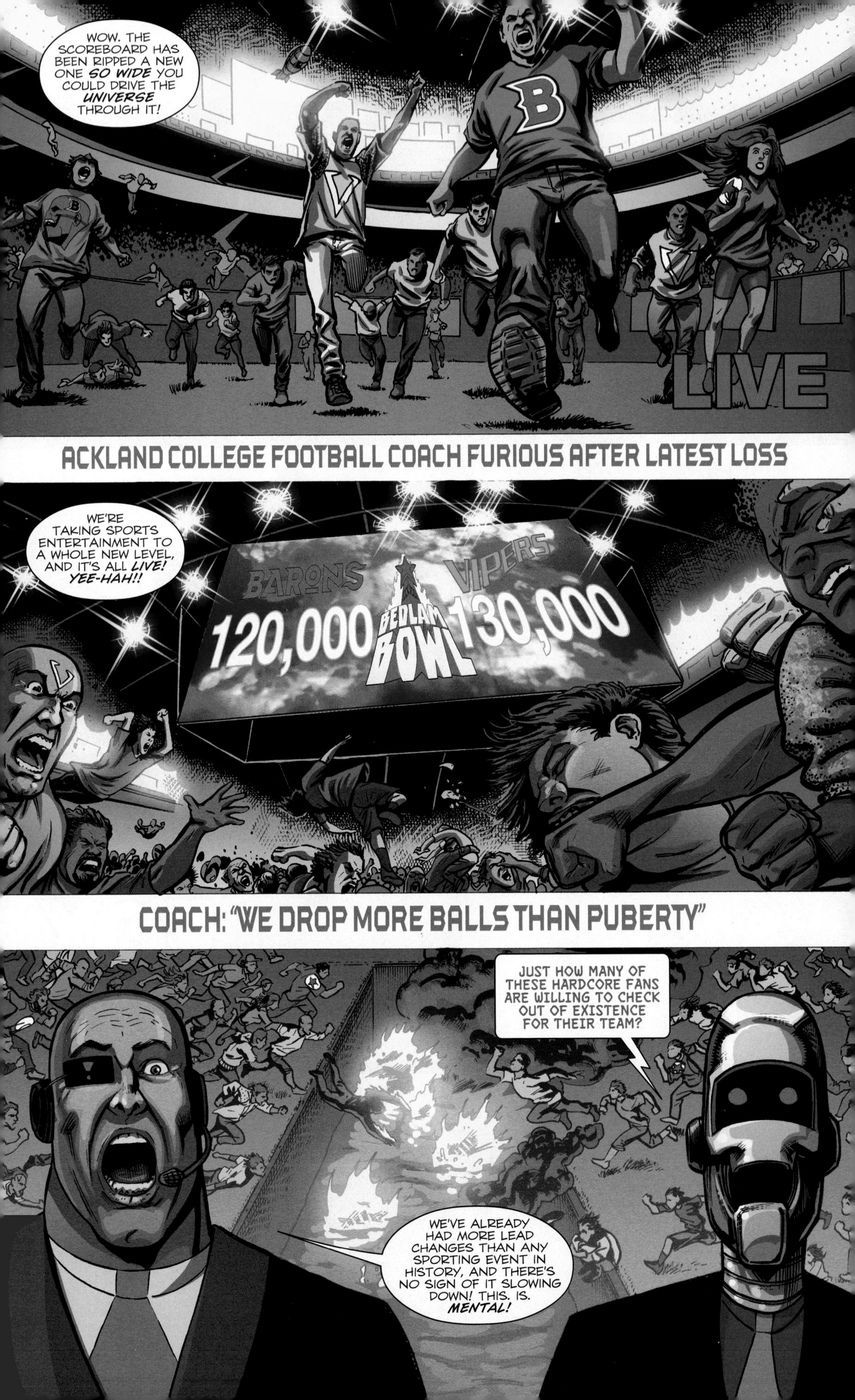
WOW. THE SCOREBOARD HAS BEEN RIPPED A NEW ONE SO WIDE YOU COULD DRIVE THE UNIVERSE THROUGH IT!
LIVE
ACKLAND COLLEGE FOOTBALL COACH FURIOUS AFTER LATEST LOSS
WE'RE TAKING SPORTS ENTERTAINMENT TO A WHOLE NEW LEVEL, AND IT'S ALL LIVE! YEE-HAH!!
BARONS
VIPERS
120,000
BEDLAM BOWL
130,000
COACH: "WE DROP MORE BALLS THAN PUBERTY"
JUST HOW MANY OF THESE HARDCORE FANS ARE WILLING TO CHECK OUT OF EXISTENCE FOR THEIR TEAM?
WE'VE ALREADY HAD MORE LEAD CHANGES THAN ANY SPORTING EVENT IN HISTORY, AND THERE'S NO SIGN OF IT SLOWING DOWN! THIS. IS. MENTAL!

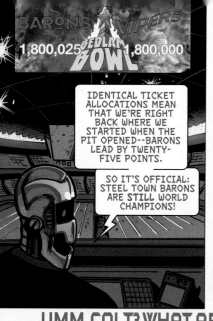

BAR♦NS ★ VIPERS
BEDLAM BOWL
1,800,025 | 1,800,000

IDENTICAL TICKET ALLOCATIONS MEAN THAT WE'RE RIGHT BACK WHERE WE STARTED WHEN THE PIT OPENED--BARONS LEAD BY TWENTY-FIVE POINTS.

SO IT'S OFFICIAL: STEEL TOWN BARONS ARE STILL WORLD CHAMPIONS!

NOT SO FAST, BRAZEN.

WAIT, WHAT? COLT, C'MON! YOU CAN'T DO THIS!

YOUR TEAM BIAS HAS ALREADY SEEN YOU SUSPENDED--SURELY YOU CAN'T FOLLOW THAT BY THROWING AWAY YOUR LIFE!

ONLY ONE THING MATTERS IN SPORTS: *WINNING.*

UMM, COLT? WHAT ARE YOU DOING...?

THERE'S AN ANNOUNCER ON THE COURT!

I THOUGHT IT WAS ALL OVER--

SOX

FUCK IT. WE WERE GONNA HAVE HIM KILLED ANYWAY

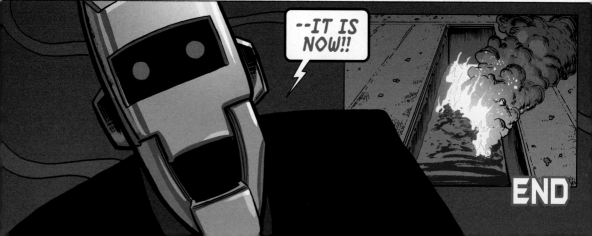

--IT IS NOW!!

END

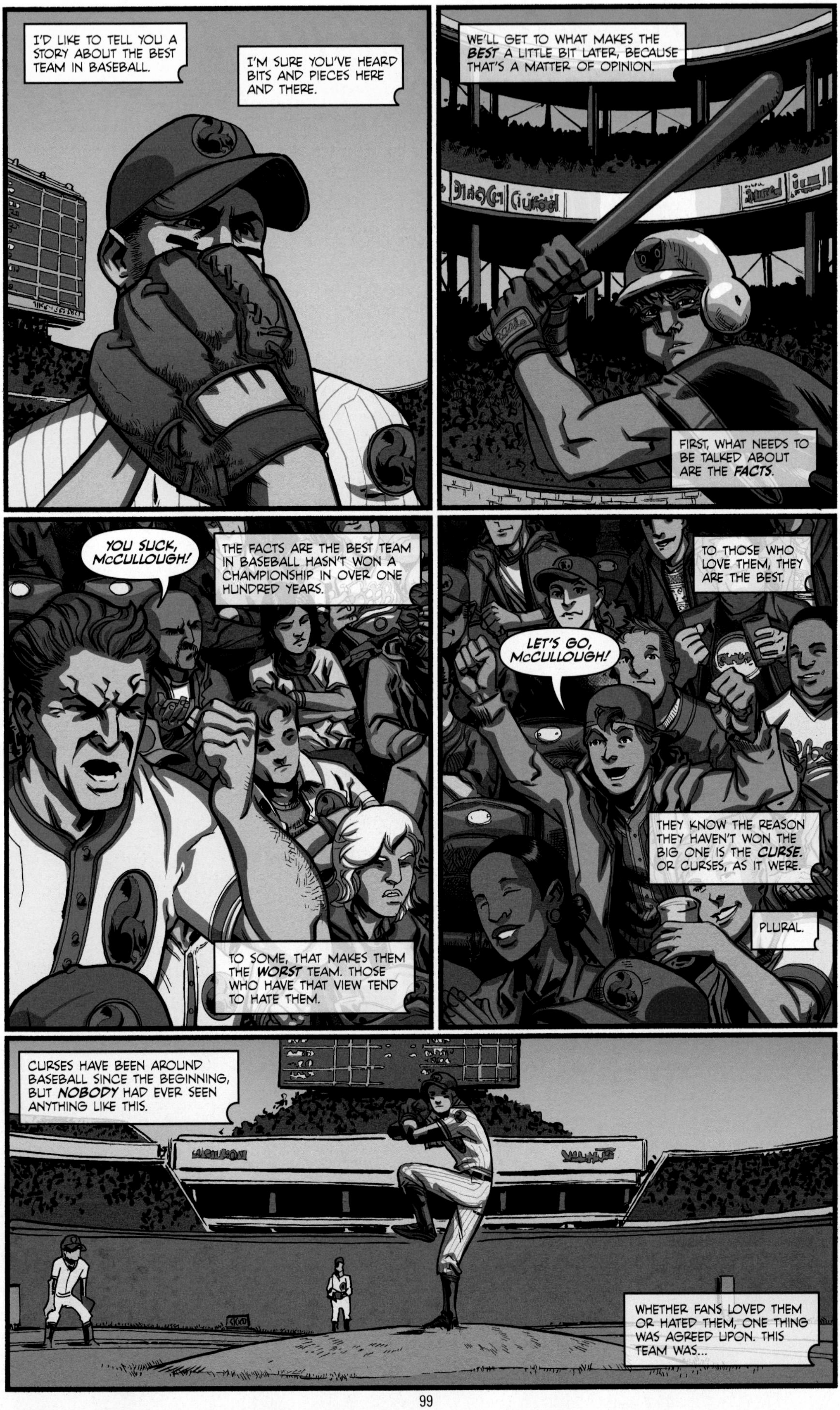
I'D LIKE TO TELL YOU A STORY ABOUT THE BEST TEAM IN BASEBALL.
I'M SURE YOU'VE HEARD BITS AND PIECES HERE AND THERE.
WE'LL GET TO WHAT MAKES THE BEST A LITTLE BIT LATER, BECAUSE THAT'S A MATTER OF OPINION.
FIRST, WHAT NEEDS TO BE TALKED ABOUT ARE THE FACTS.
YOU SUCK, McCULLOUGH!
THE FACTS ARE THE BEST TEAM IN BASEBALL HASN'T WON A CHAMPIONSHIP IN OVER ONE HUNDRED YEARS.
TO SOME, THAT MAKES THEM THE WORST TEAM. THOSE WHO HAVE THAT VIEW TEND TO HATE THEM.
TO THOSE WHO LOVE THEM, THEY ARE THE BEST.
LET'S GO, McCULLOUGH!
THEY KNOW THE REASON THEY HAVEN'T WON THE BIG ONE IS THE CURSE. OR CURSES, AS IT WERE.
PLURAL.
CURSES HAVE BEEN AROUND BASEBALL SINCE THE BEGINNING, BUT NOBODY HAD EVER SEEN ANYTHING LIKE THIS.
WHETHER FANS LOVED THEM OR HATED THEM, ONE THING WAS AGREED UPON. THIS TEAM WAS...

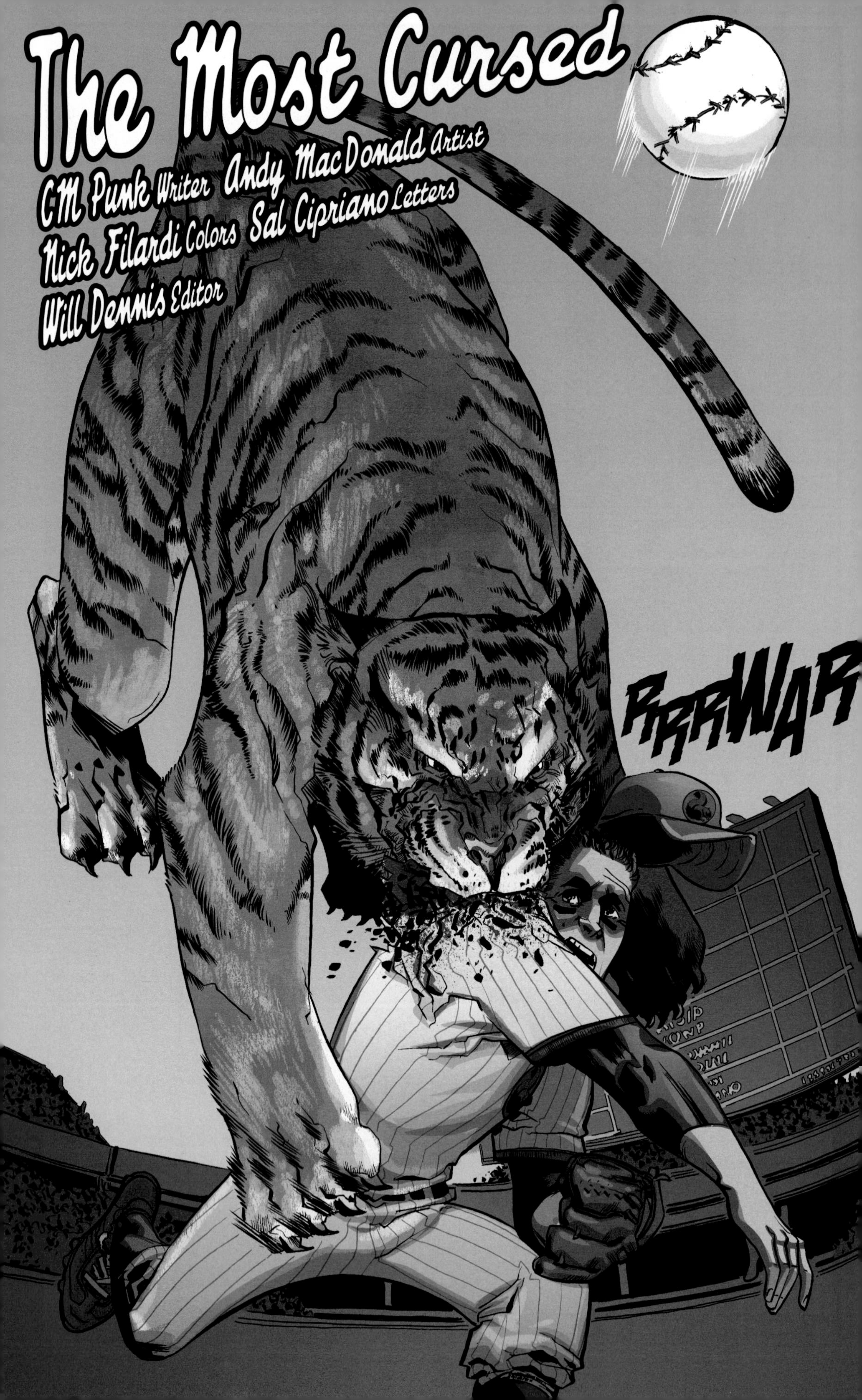

The Most Cursed
CM Punk Writer Andy MacDonald Artist
Nick Filardi Colors Sal Cipriano Letters
Will Dennis Editor
RRRWAR

THAT DAY SURE WAS STRANGE. McCULLOUGH WAS SUPPOSED TO WIN THE TEAM A DIVISION TITLE, NOT LOSE HIS ARM.

IT WAS THE CURSE. BUT *WHICH* ONE?

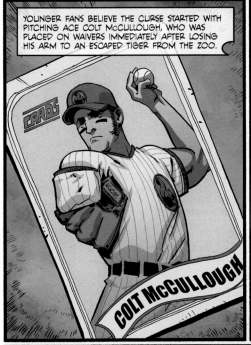

YOUNGER FANS BELIEVE THE CURSE STARTED WITH PITCHING ACE COLT McCULLOUGH, WHO WAS PLACED ON WAIVERS IMMEDIATELY AFTER LOSING HIS ARM TO AN ESCAPED TIGER FROM THE ZOO.

COLT McCULLOUGH

FURIOUS ABOUT BEING LET GO, HE REPORTEDLY CURSED THE TEAM. IN THE OFF SEASON HE TAUGHT HIMSELF TO THROW WITH HIS LEFT ARM AND *SWEPT* HIS FORMER TEAM IN THE WORLD SERIES THE NEXT YEAR.

HIS NEW TEAM? THE *TIGERS.*

THERE'RE THE PEOPLE WHO SAY IT'S THE GROUND THAT'S CURSED, NOT THE TEAM.

GET OFF MY LAWN!

AFTER ALL, THE PARK WAS BUILT ON TOP OF A SACRED INDIAN BURIAL GROUND.

THEN THERE ARE SOME WHO SAY THE TEAM ITSELF WAS CURSED BY AN OLD MAN WHO WAS *DENIED* ENTRY TO THE PARK. HE WAS TRYING TO GET IN WITH HIS PET *GOAT.*

THIS, OF COURSE, IS THE MOST FAR-FETCHED STORY. WHO WOULD BELIEVE THAT?!

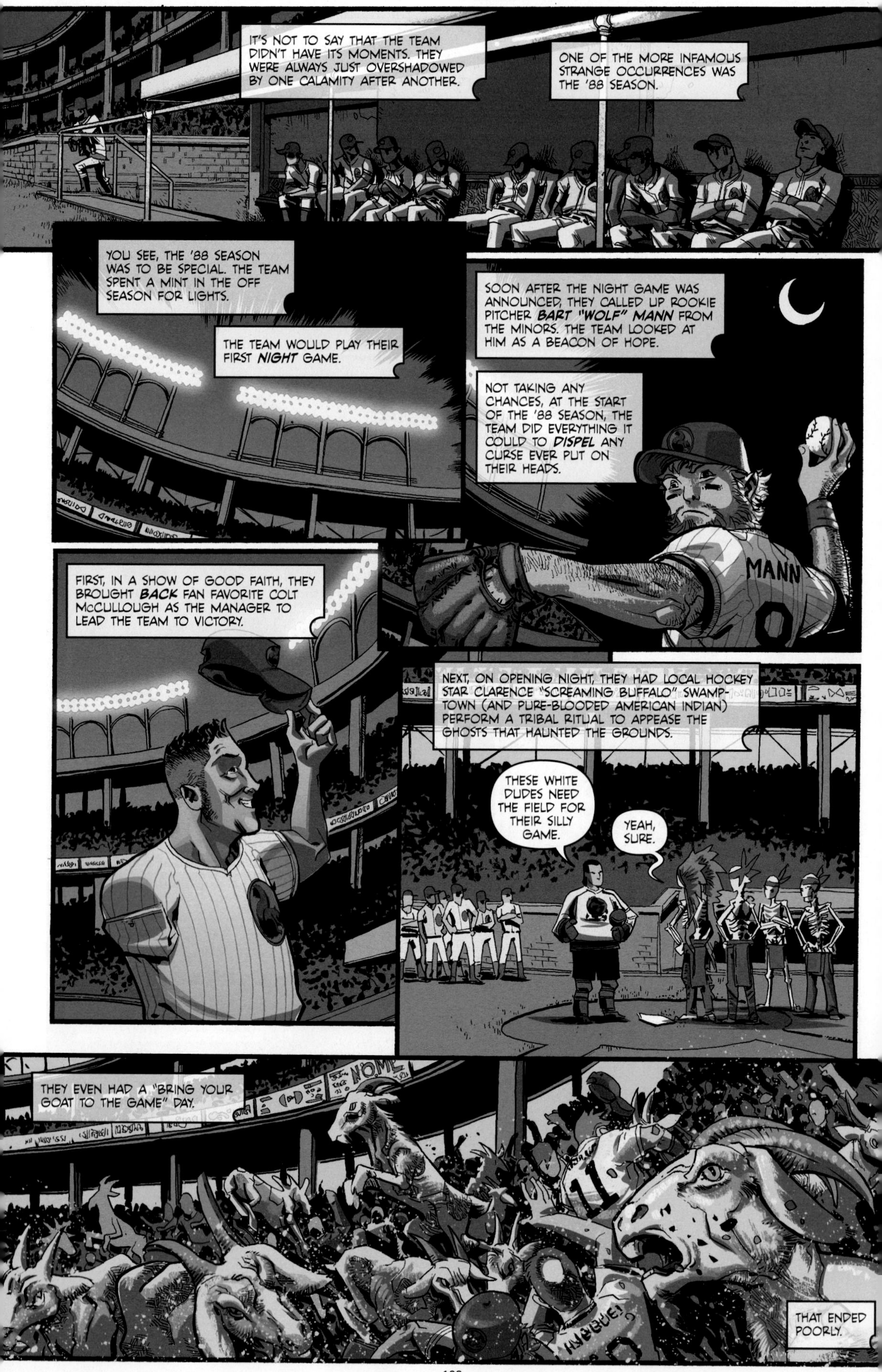
IT'S NOT TO SAY THAT THE TEAM DIDN'T HAVE ITS MOMENTS. THEY WERE ALWAYS JUST OVERSHADOWED BY ONE CALAMITY AFTER ANOTHER.
ONE OF THE MORE INFAMOUS STRANGE OCCURRENCES WAS THE '88 SEASON.
YOU SEE, THE '88 SEASON WAS TO BE SPECIAL. THE TEAM SPENT A MINT IN THE OFF SEASON FOR LIGHTS.
THE TEAM WOULD PLAY THEIR FIRST NIGHT GAME.
SOON AFTER THE NIGHT GAME WAS ANNOUNCED, THEY CALLED UP ROOKIE PITCHER BART "WOLF" MANN FROM THE MINORS. THE TEAM LOOKED AT HIM AS A BEACON OF HOPE.
NOT TAKING ANY CHANCES, AT THE START OF THE '88 SEASON, THE TEAM DID EVERYTHING IT COULD TO DISPEL ANY CURSE EVER PUT ON THEIR HEADS.
MANN
FIRST, IN A SHOW OF GOOD FAITH, THEY BROUGHT BACK FAN FAVORITE COLT McCULLOUGH AS THE MANAGER TO LEAD THE TEAM TO VICTORY.
NEXT, ON OPENING NIGHT, THEY HAD LOCAL HOCKEY STAR CLARENCE "SCREAMING BUFFALO" SWAMP-TOWN (AND PURE-BLOODED AMERICAN INDIAN) PERFORM A TRIBAL RITUAL TO APPEASE THE GHOSTS THAT HAUNTED THE GROUNDS.
THESE WHITE DUDES NEED THE FIELD FOR THEIR SILLY GAME.
YEAH, SURE.
THEY EVEN HAD A "BRING YOUR GOAT TO THE GAME" DAY.
THAT ENDED POORLY.

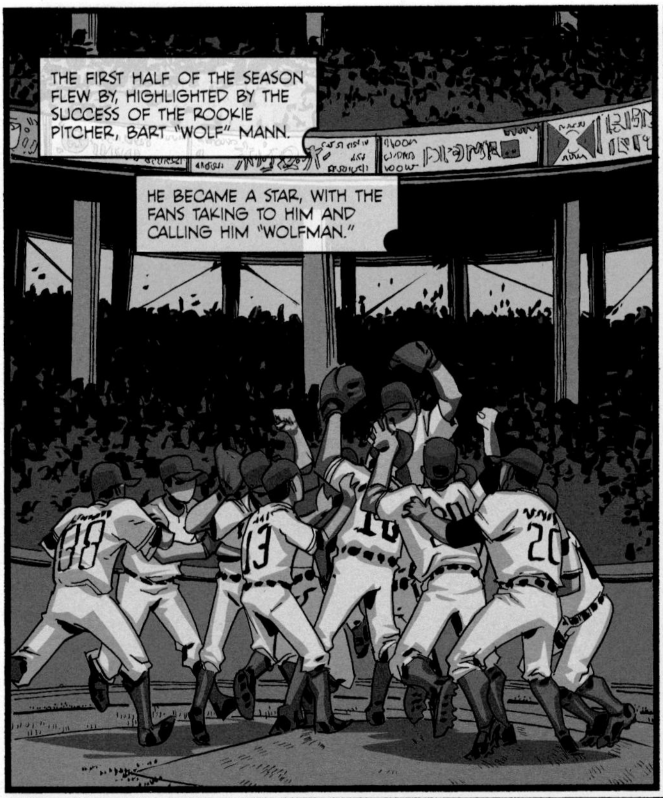
THE FIRST HALF OF THE SEASON FLEW BY, HIGHLIGHTED BY THE SUCCESS OF THE ROOKIE PITCHER, BART "WOLF" MANN.
HE BECAME A STAR, WITH THE FANS TAKING TO HIM AND CALLING HIM "WOLFMAN."

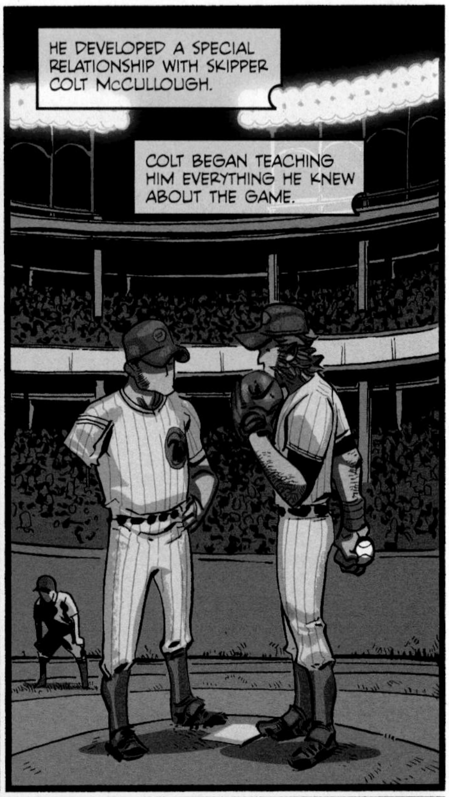
HE DEVELOPED A SPECIAL RELATIONSHIP WITH SKIPPER COLT McCULLOUGH.
COLT BEGAN TEACHING HIM EVERYTHING HE KNEW ABOUT THE GAME.

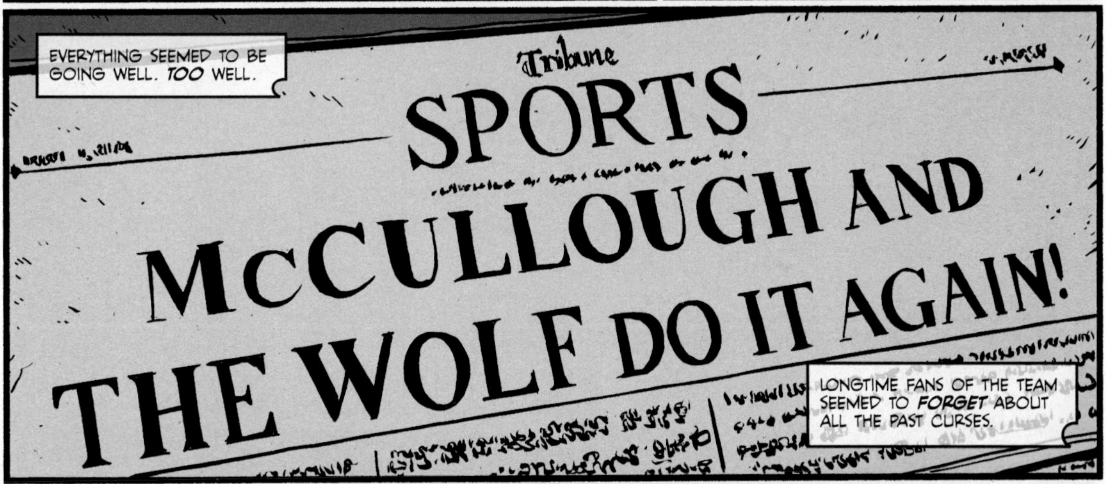
EVERYTHING SEEMED TO BE GOING WELL. *TOO* WELL.
Tribune
SPORTS
McCULLOUGH AND THE WOLF DO IT AGAIN!
LONGTIME FANS OF THE TEAM SEEMED TO *FORGET* ABOUT ALL THE PAST CURSES.

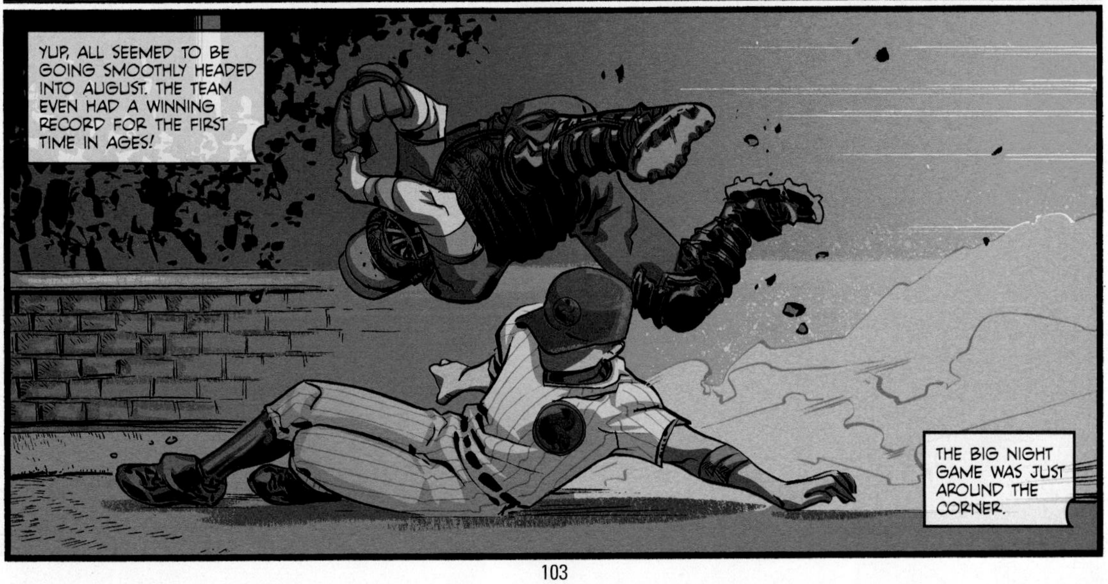
YUP, ALL SEEMED TO BE GOING SMOOTHLY HEADED INTO AUGUST. THE TEAM EVEN HAD A WINNING RECORD FOR THE FIRST TIME IN AGES!
THE BIG NIGHT GAME WAS JUST AROUND THE CORNER.

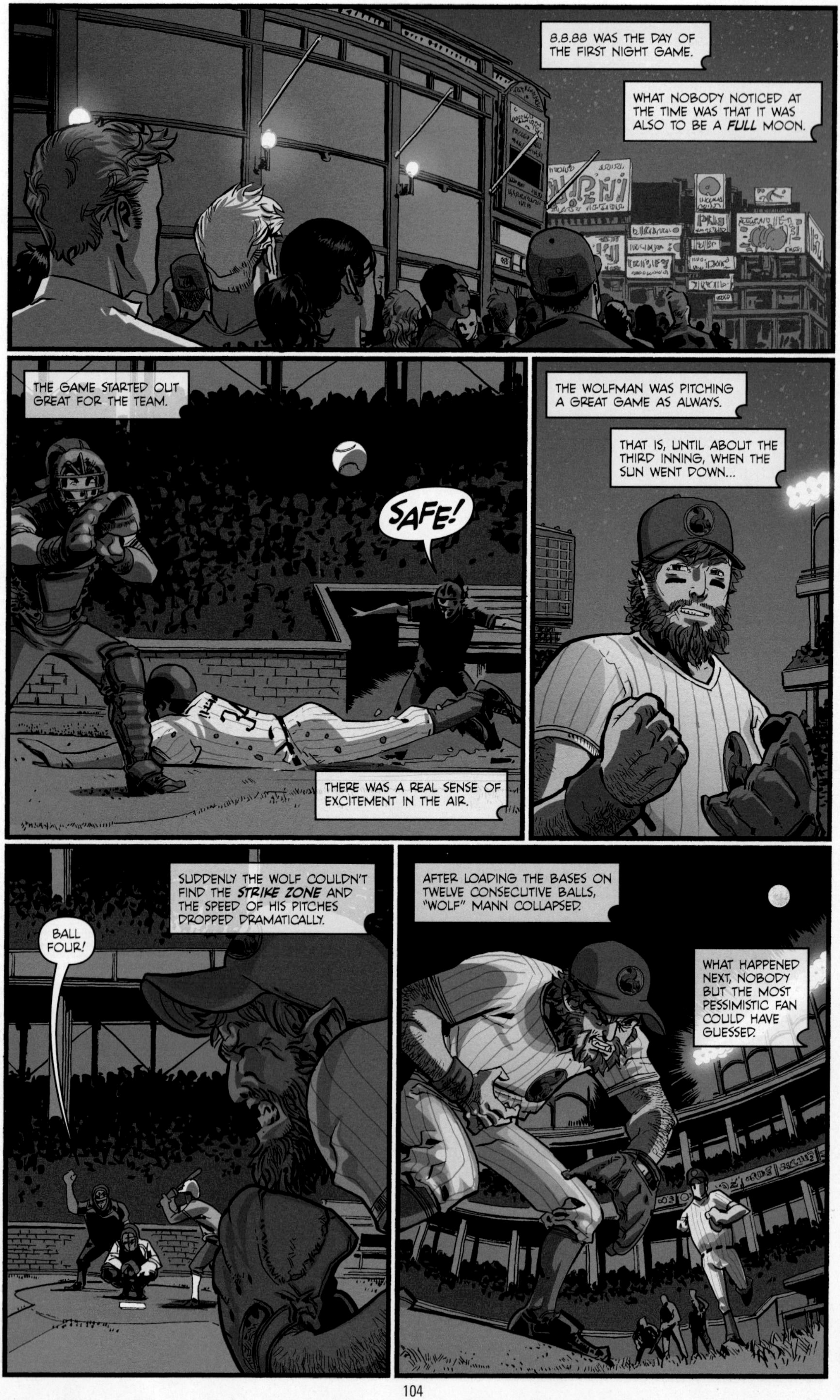

8.8.88 WAS THE DAY OF THE FIRST NIGHT GAME.
WHAT NOBODY NOTICED AT THE TIME WAS THAT IT WAS ALSO TO BE A FULL MOON.
THE GAME STARTED OUT GREAT FOR THE TEAM.
SAFE!
THERE WAS A REAL SENSE OF EXCITEMENT IN THE AIR.
THE WOLFMAN WAS PITCHING A GREAT GAME AS ALWAYS.
THAT IS, UNTIL ABOUT THE THIRD INNING, WHEN THE SUN WENT DOWN...
SUDDENLY THE WOLF COULDN'T FIND THE STRIKE ZONE AND THE SPEED OF HIS PITCHES DROPPED DRAMATICALLY.
BALL FOUR!
AFTER LOADING THE BASES ON TWELVE CONSECUTIVE BALLS, "WOLF" MANN COLLAPSED.
WHAT HAPPENED NEXT, NOBODY BUT THE MOST PESSIMISTIC FAN COULD HAVE GUESSED.

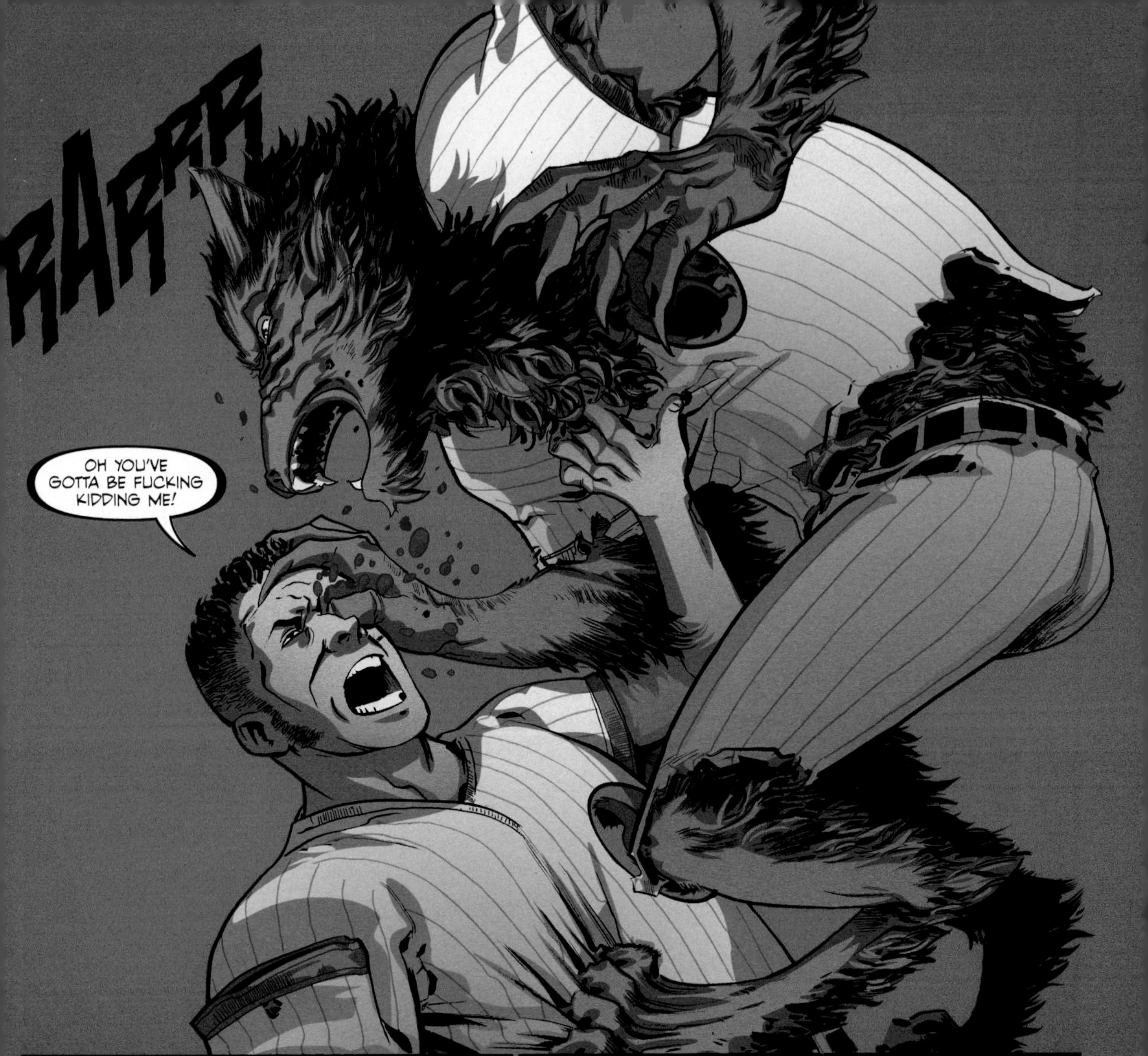
RARRR
OH YOU'VE GOTTA BE FUCKING KIDDING ME!

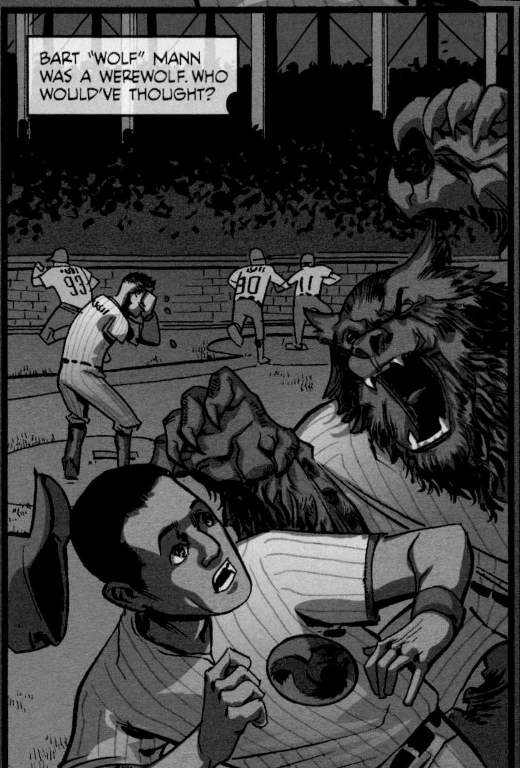
BART "WOLF" MANN WAS A WEREWOLF. WHO WOULD'VE THOUGHT?

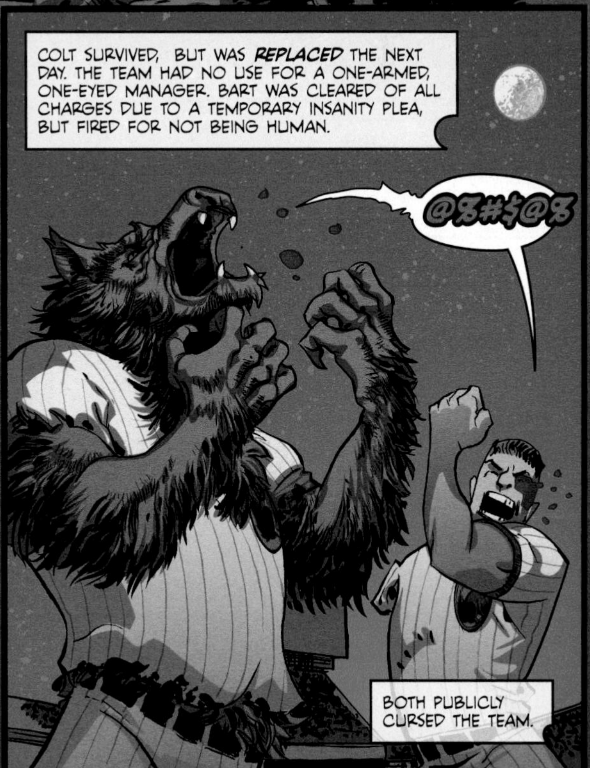
COLT SURVIVED, BUT WAS ***REPLACED*** THE NEXT DAY. THE TEAM HAD NO USE FOR A ONE-ARMED, ONE-EYED MANAGER. BART WAS CLEARED OF ALL CHARGES DUE TO A TEMPORARY INSANITY PLEA, BUT FIRED FOR NOT BEING HUMAN.
@%#$@%
BOTH PUBLICLY CURSED THE TEAM.

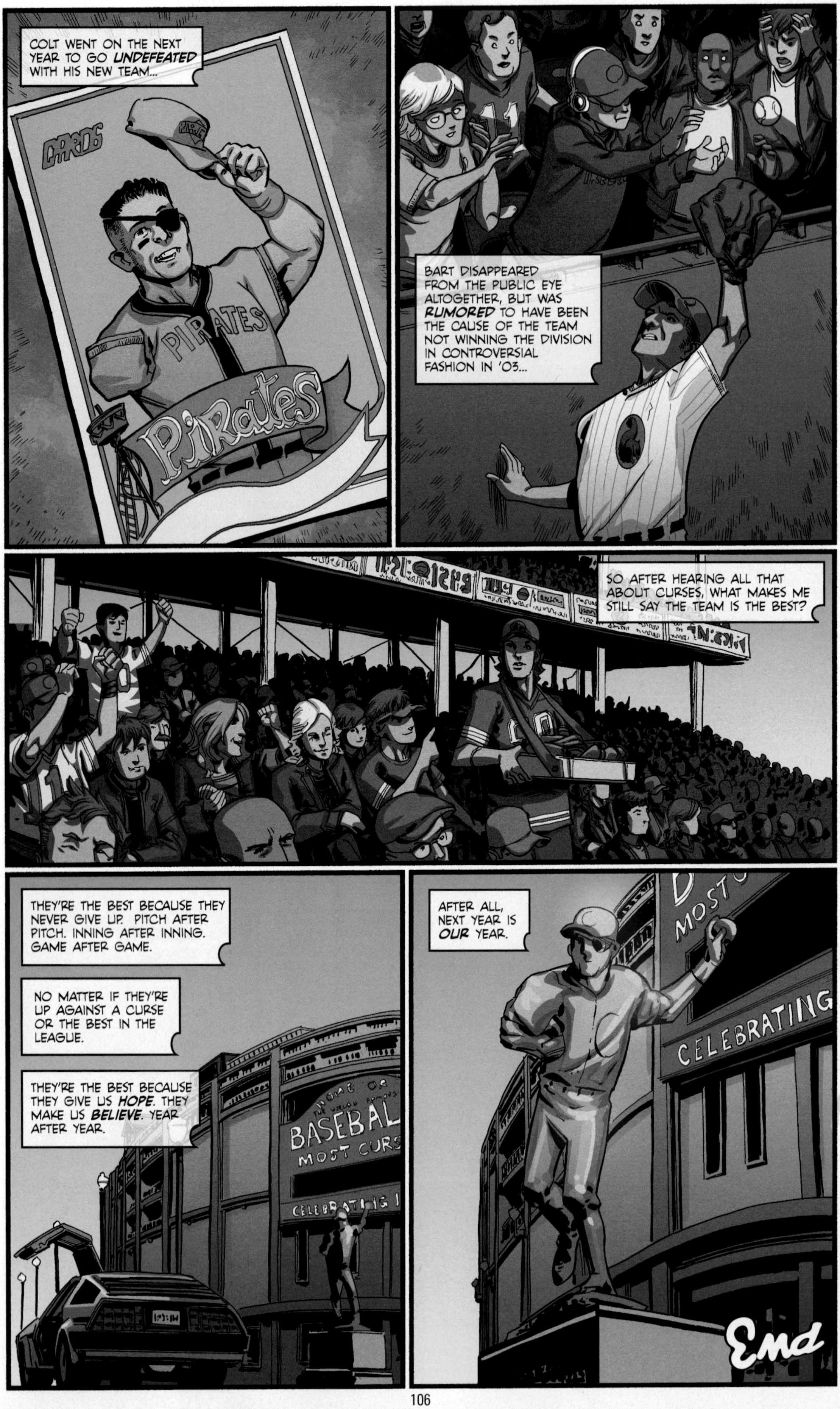
COLT WENT ON THE NEXT YEAR TO GO **UNDEFEATED** WITH HIS NEW TEAM...
CARDS
PIRATES
Pirates
BART DISAPPEARED FROM THE PUBLIC EYE ALTOGETHER, BUT WAS **RUMORED** TO HAVE BEEN THE CAUSE OF THE TEAM NOT WINNING THE DIVISION IN CONTROVERSIAL FASHION IN '03...
SO AFTER HEARING ALL THAT ABOUT CURSES, WHAT MAKES ME STILL SAY THE TEAM IS THE BEST?
THEY'RE THE BEST BECAUSE THEY NEVER GIVE UP. PITCH AFTER PITCH. INNING AFTER INNING. GAME AFTER GAME.
NO MATTER IF THEY'RE UP AGAINST A CURSE OR THE BEST IN THE LEAGUE.
THEY'RE THE BEST BECAUSE THEY GIVE US **HOPE**. THEY MAKE US **BELIEVE**. YEAR AFTER YEAR.
BASEBAL
MOST CURS
CELEBRATING
AFTER ALL, NEXT YEAR IS **OUR** YEAR.
MOST
CELEBRATING
End

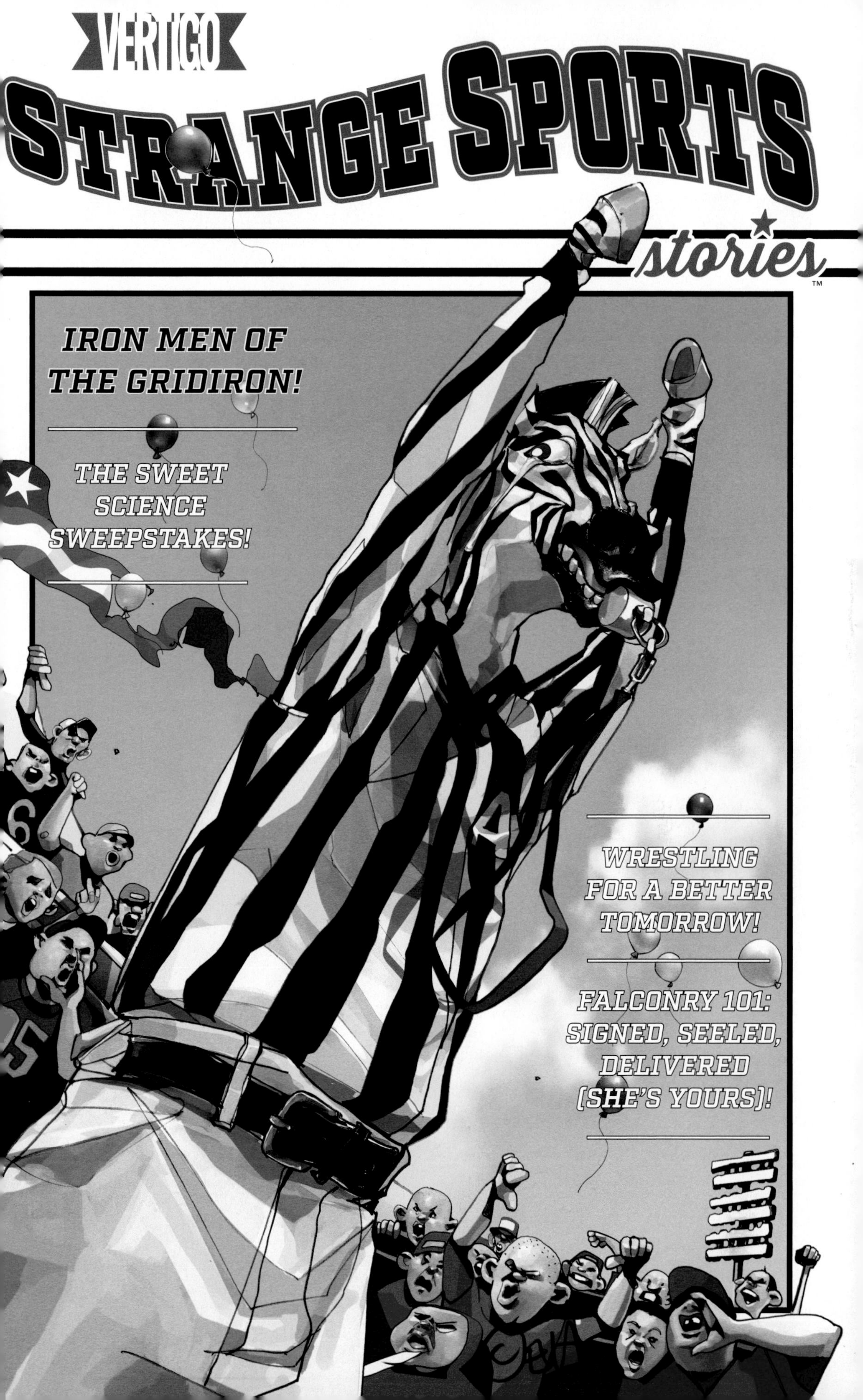
VERTIGO
STRANGE SPORTS stories™
IRON MEN OF THE GRIDIRON!
THE SWEET SCIENCE SWEEPSTAKES!
WRESTLING FOR A BETTER TOMORROW!
FALCONRY 101: SIGNED, SEELED, DELIVERED (SHE'S YOURS)!

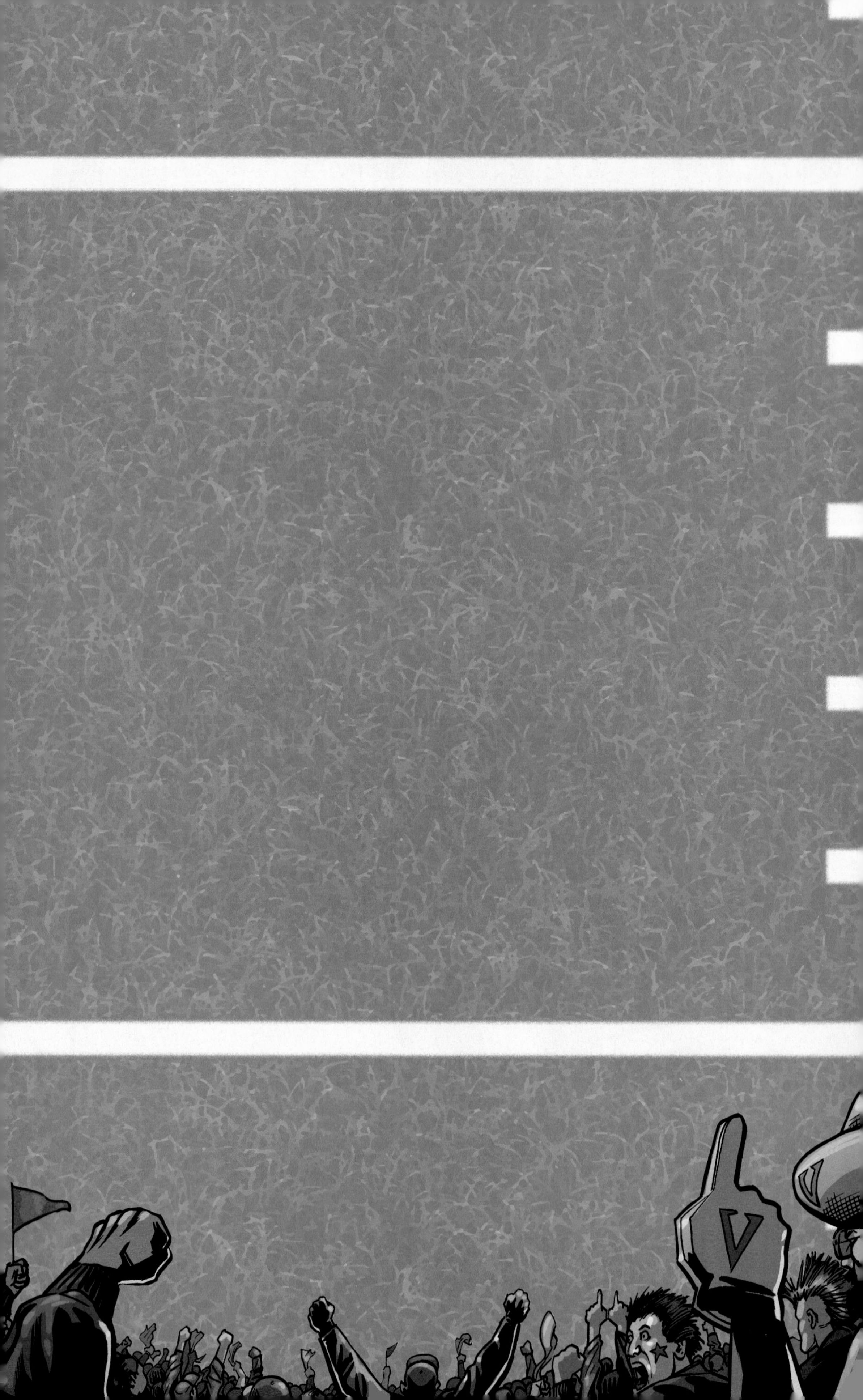

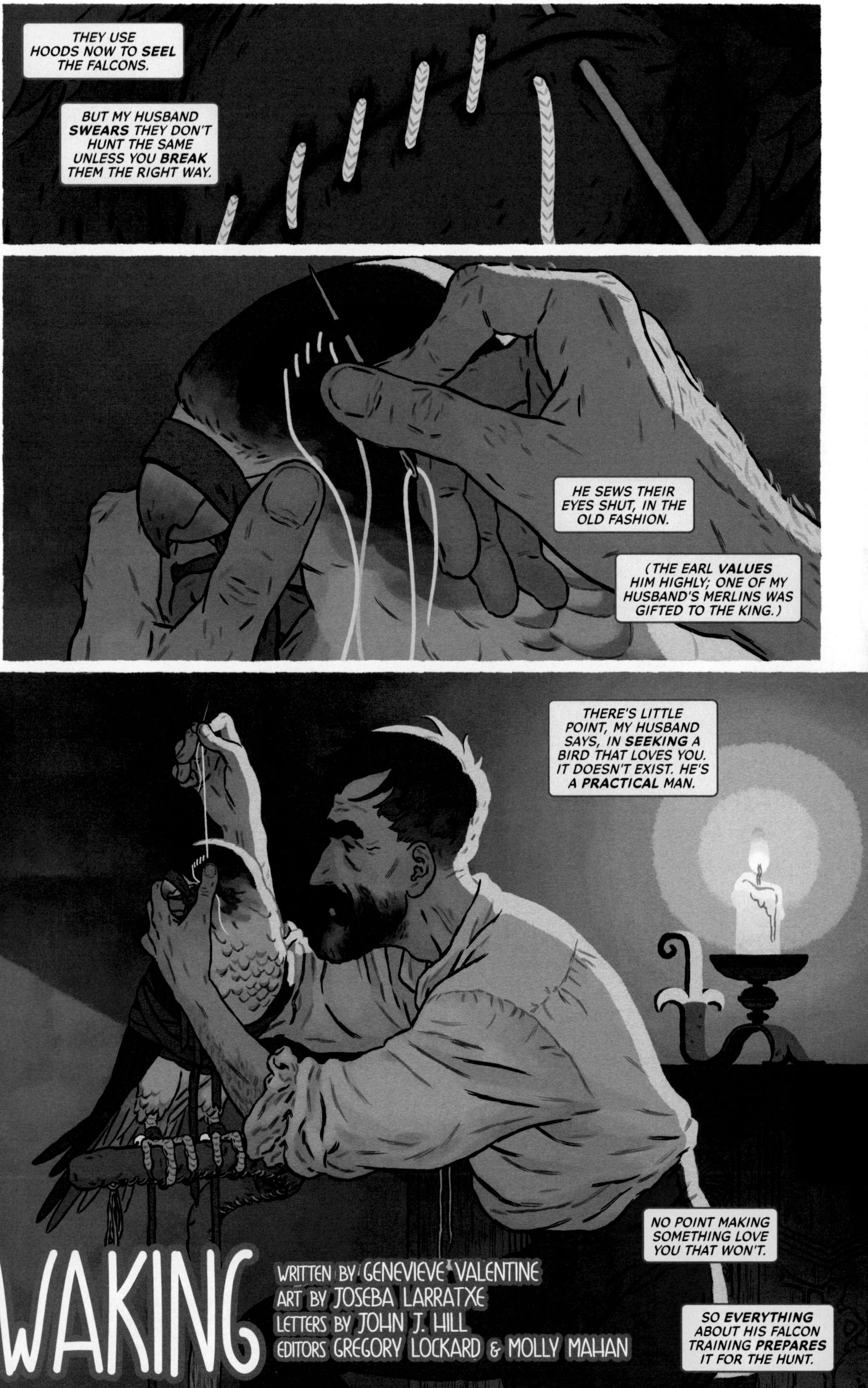
THEY USE HOODS NOW TO SEEL THE FALCONS.
BUT MY HUSBAND SWEARS THEY DON'T HUNT THE SAME UNLESS YOU BREAK THEM THE RIGHT WAY.
HE SEWS THEIR EYES SHUT, IN THE OLD FASHION.
(THE EARL VALUES HIM HIGHLY; ONE OF MY HUSBAND'S MERLINS WAS GIFTED TO THE KING.)
THERE'S LITTLE POINT, MY HUSBAND SAYS, IN SEEKING A BIRD THAT LOVES YOU. IT DOESN'T EXIST. HE'S A PRACTICAL MAN.
WAKING
WRITTEN BY GENEVIEVE VALENTINE
ART BY JOSEBA LARRATXE
LETTERS BY JOHN J. HILL
EDITORS GREGORY LOCKARD & MOLLY MAHAN
NO POINT MAKING SOMETHING LOVE YOU THAT WON'T.
SO EVERYTHING ABOUT HIS FALCON TRAINING PREPARES IT FOR THE HUNT.

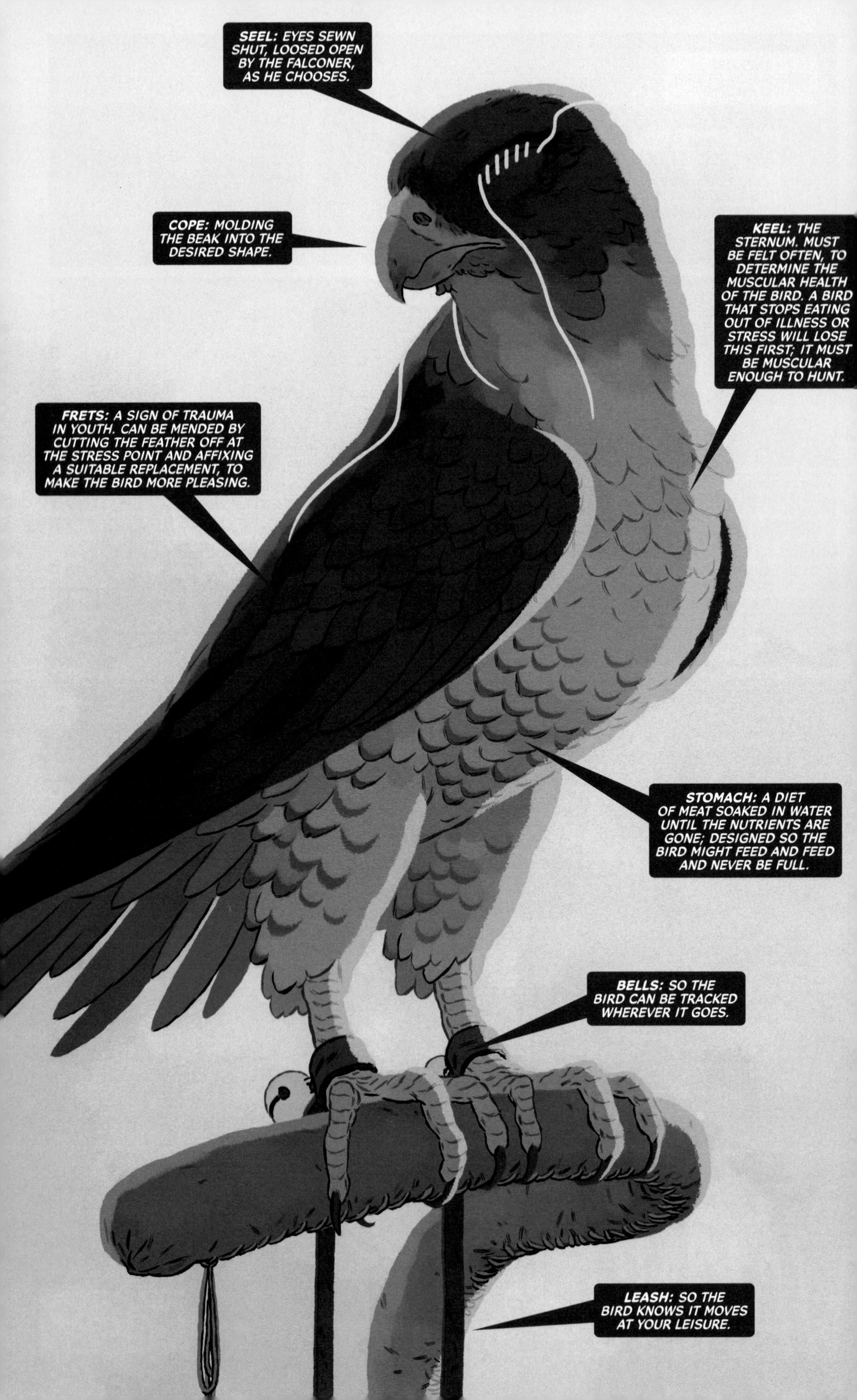
SEEL: EYES SEWN SHUT, LOOSED OPEN BY THE FALCONER, AS HE CHOOSES.
COPE: MOLDING THE BEAK INTO THE DESIRED SHAPE.
KEEL: THE STERNUM. MUST BE FELT OFTEN, TO DETERMINE THE MUSCULAR HEALTH OF THE BIRD. A BIRD THAT STOPS EATING OUT OF ILLNESS OR STRESS WILL LOSE THIS FIRST; IT MUST BE MUSCULAR ENOUGH TO HUNT.
FRETS: A SIGN OF TRAUMA IN YOUTH. CAN BE MENDED BY CUTTING THE FEATHER OFF AT THE STRESS POINT AND AFFIXING A SUITABLE REPLACEMENT, TO MAKE THE BIRD MORE PLEASING.
STOMACH: A DIET OF MEAT SOAKED IN WATER UNTIL THE NUTRIENTS ARE GONE; DESIGNED SO THE BIRD MIGHT FEED AND FEED AND NEVER BE FULL.
BELLS: SO THE BIRD CAN BE TRACKED WHEREVER IT GOES.
LEASH: SO THE BIRD KNOWS IT MOVES AT YOUR LEISURE.

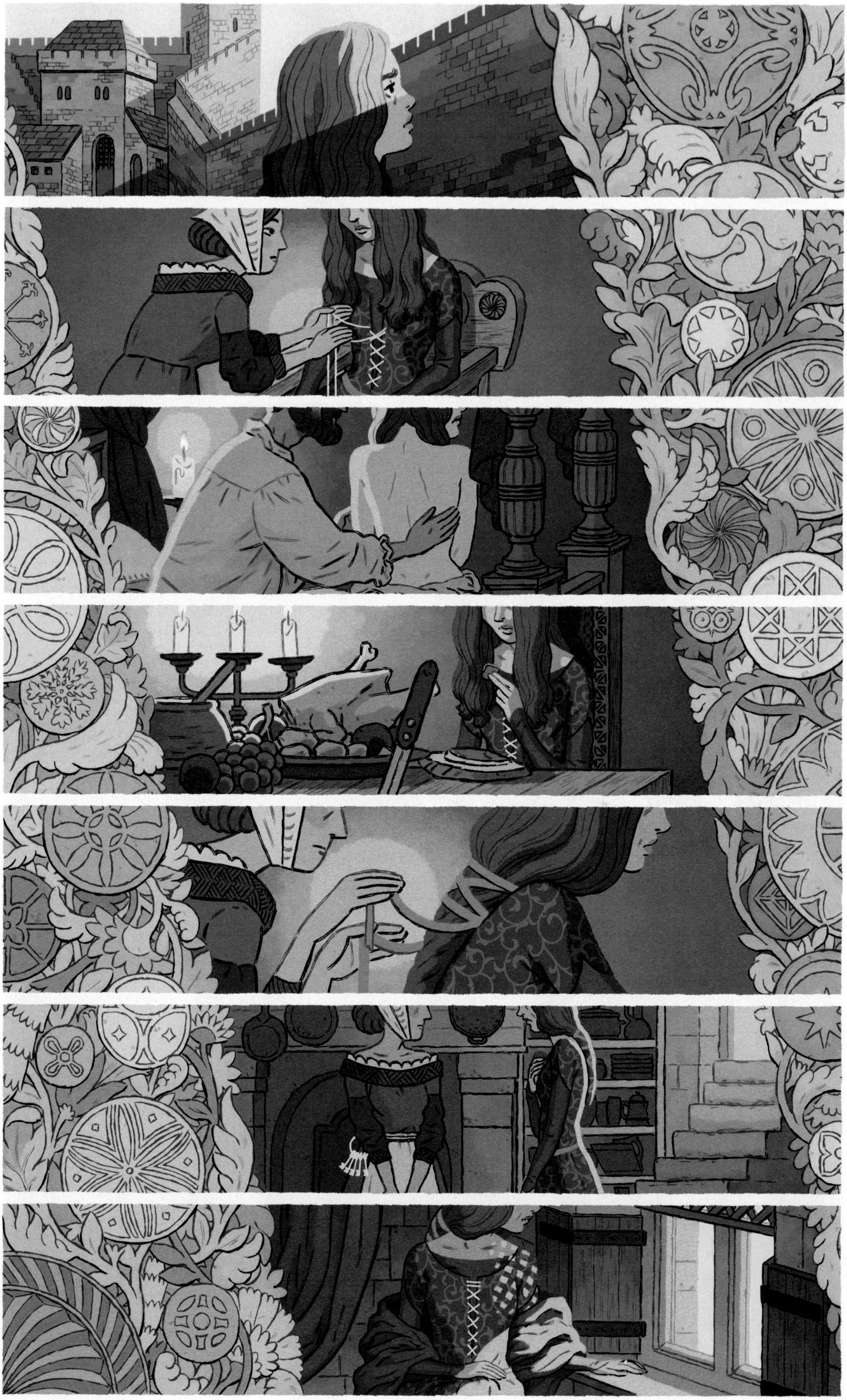

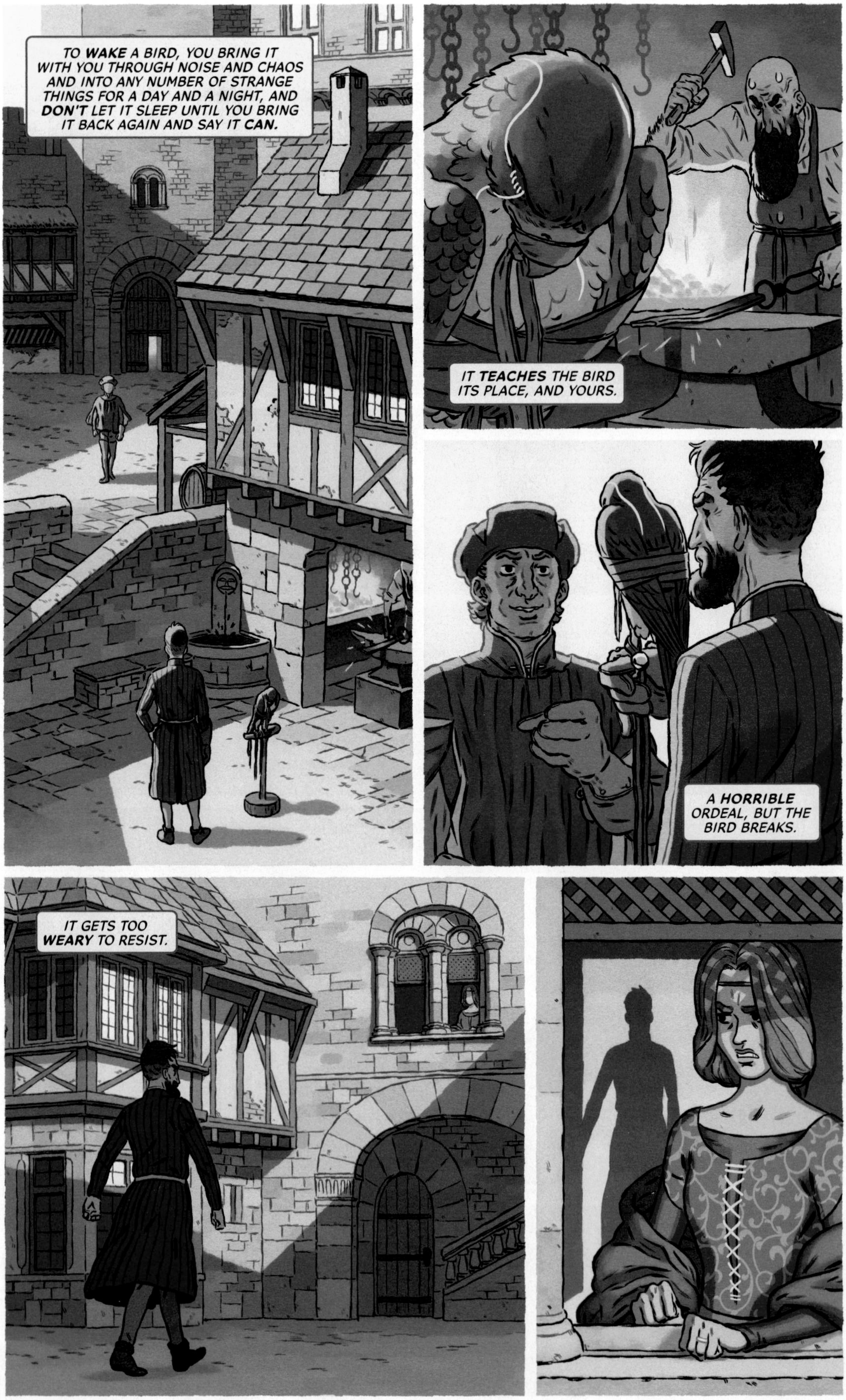
TO **WAKE** A BIRD, YOU BRING IT WITH YOU THROUGH NOISE AND CHAOS AND INTO ANY NUMBER OF STRANGE THINGS FOR A DAY AND A NIGHT, AND **DON'T** LET IT SLEEP UNTIL YOU BRING IT BACK AGAIN AND SAY IT **CAN.**
IT **TEACHES** THE BIRD ITS PLACE, AND YOURS.
A **HORRIBLE** ORDEAL, BUT THE BIRD BREAKS.
IT GETS TOO **WEARY** TO RESIST.

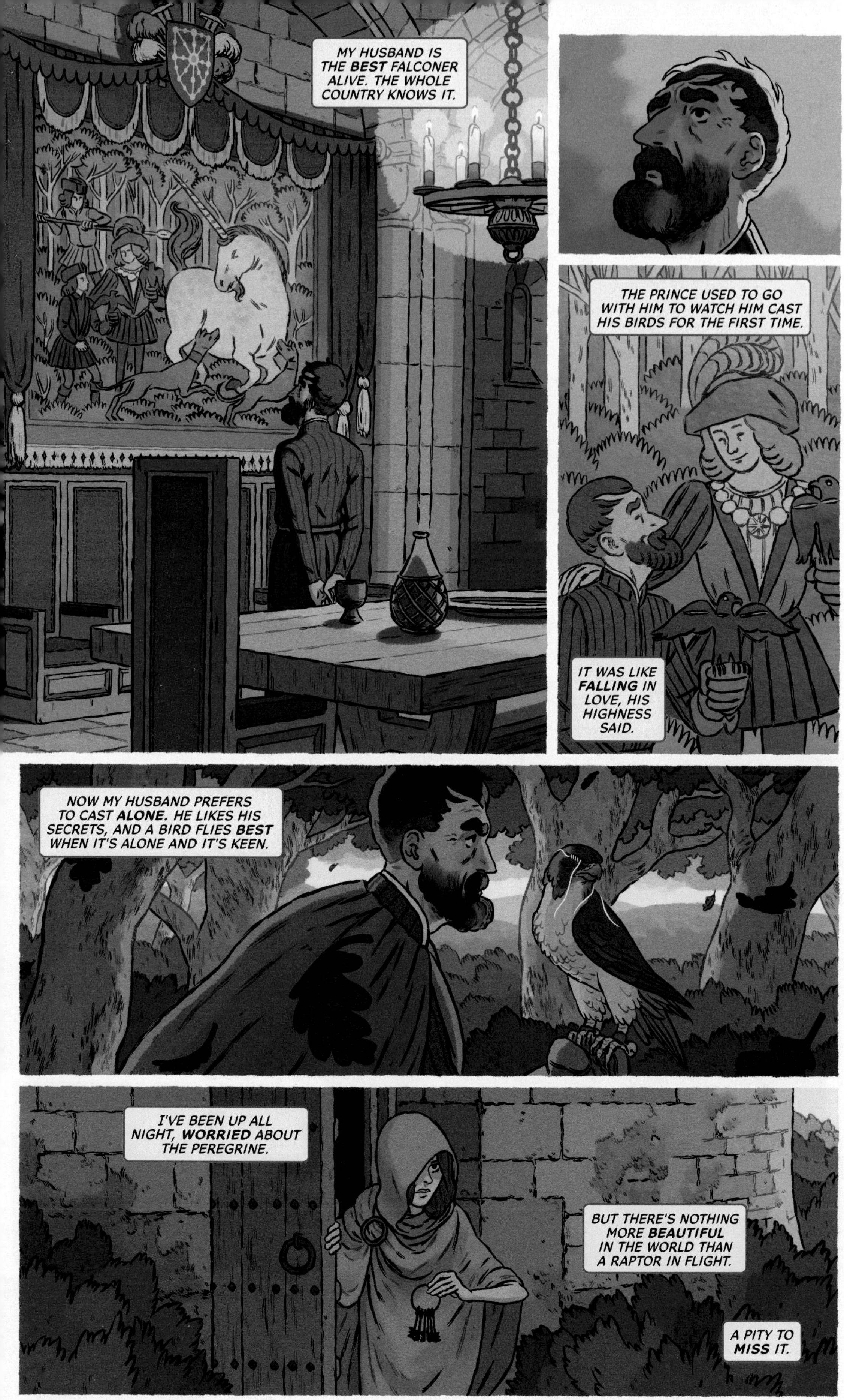
MY HUSBAND IS THE **BEST** FALCONER ALIVE. THE WHOLE COUNTRY KNOWS IT.
THE PRINCE USED TO GO WITH HIM TO WATCH HIM CAST HIS BIRDS FOR THE FIRST TIME.
IT WAS LIKE **FALLING** IN LOVE, HIS HIGHNESS SAID.
NOW MY HUSBAND PREFERS TO CAST **ALONE.** HE LIKES HIS SECRETS, AND A BIRD FLIES **BEST** WHEN IT'S ALONE AND IT'S KEEN.
I'VE BEEN UP ALL NIGHT, **WORRIED** ABOUT THE PEREGRINE.
BUT THERE'S NOTHING MORE **BEAUTIFUL** IN THE WORLD THAN A RAPTOR IN FLIGHT.
A PITY TO **MISS** IT.

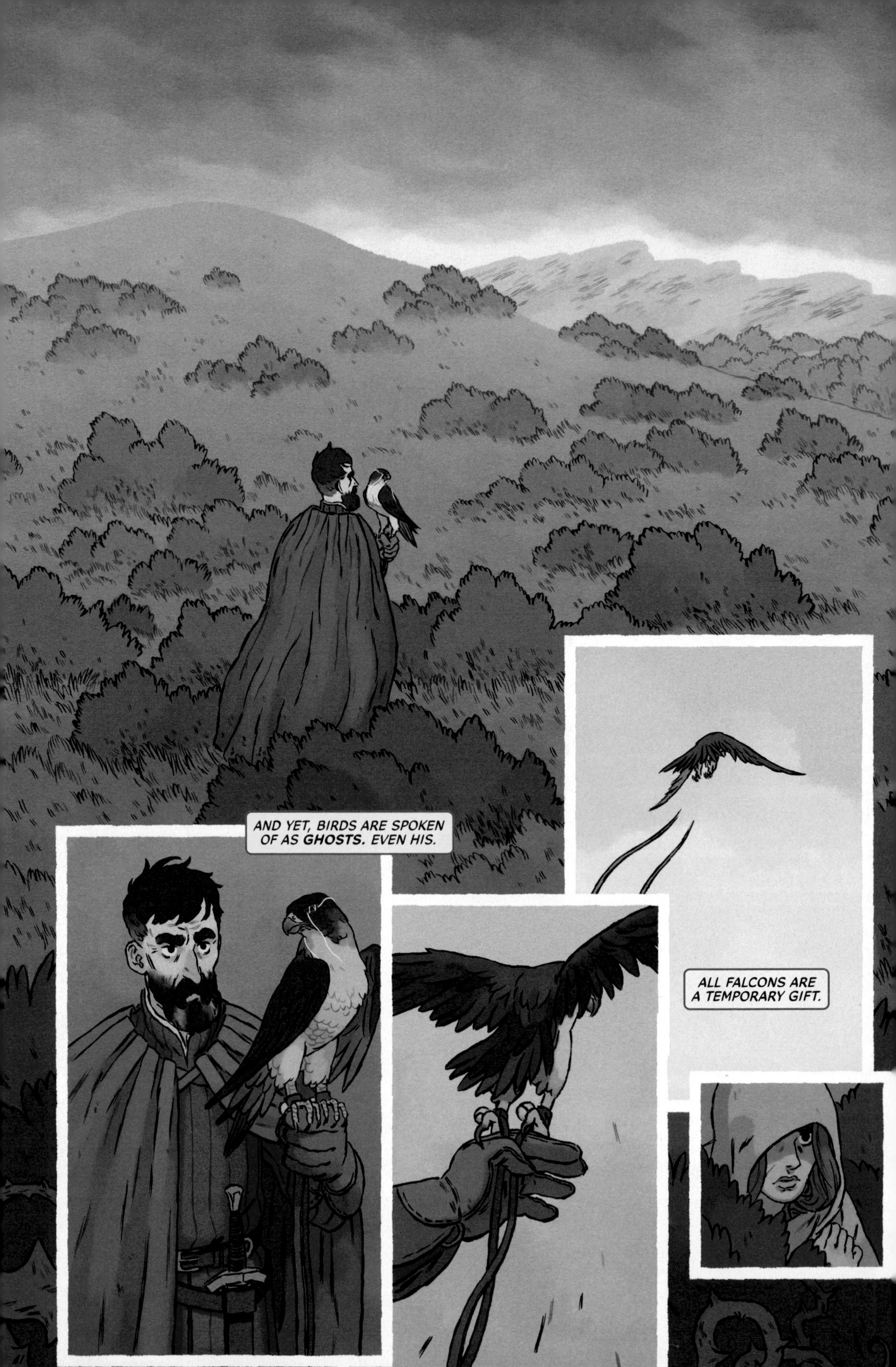
AND YET, BIRDS ARE SPOKEN OF AS **GHOSTS.** EVEN HIS.
ALL FALCONS ARE A TEMPORARY GIFT.

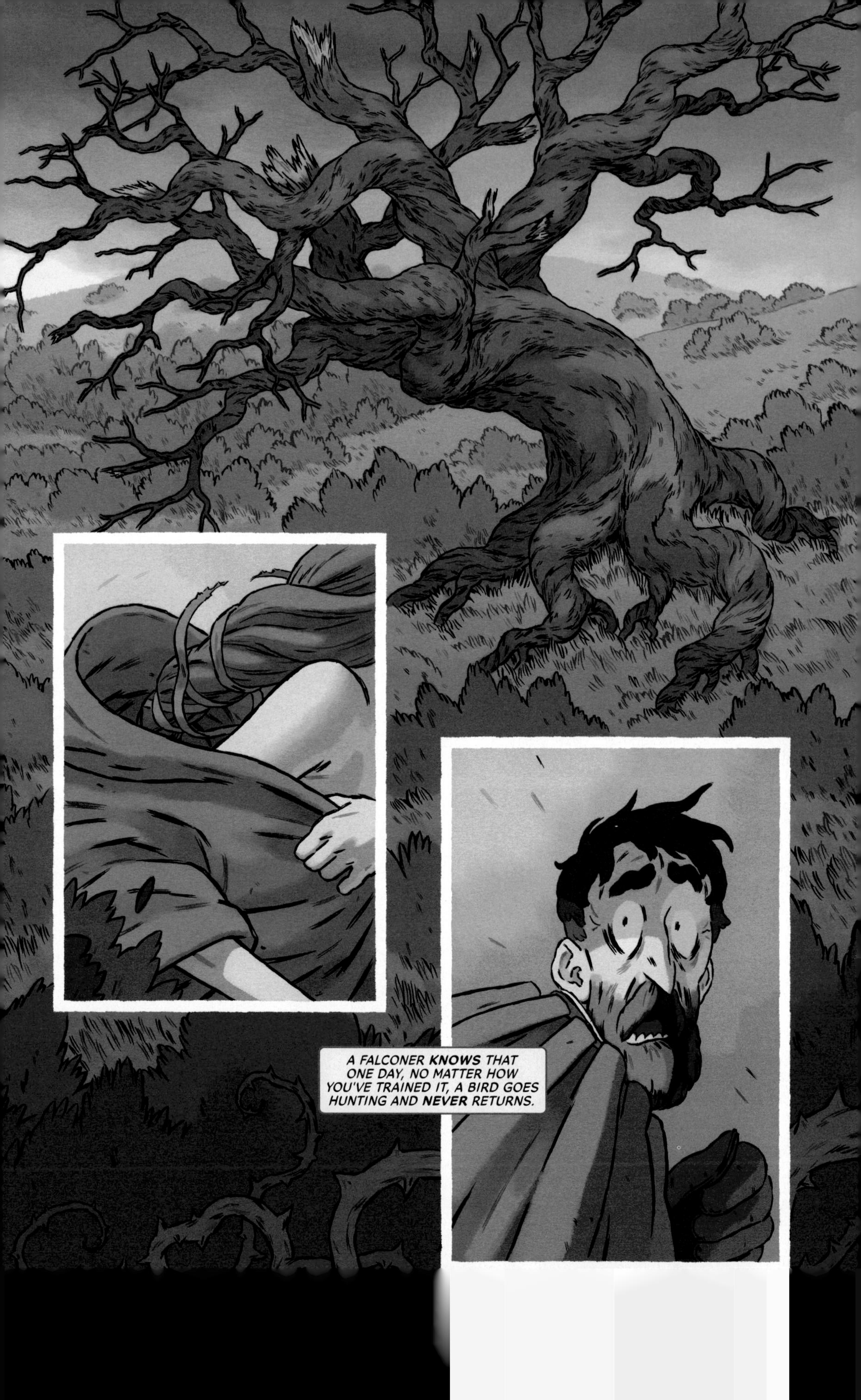
A FALCONER **KNOWS** THAT ONE DAY, NO MATTER HOW YOU'VE TRAINED IT, A BIRD GOES HUNTING AND **NEVER** RETURNS.

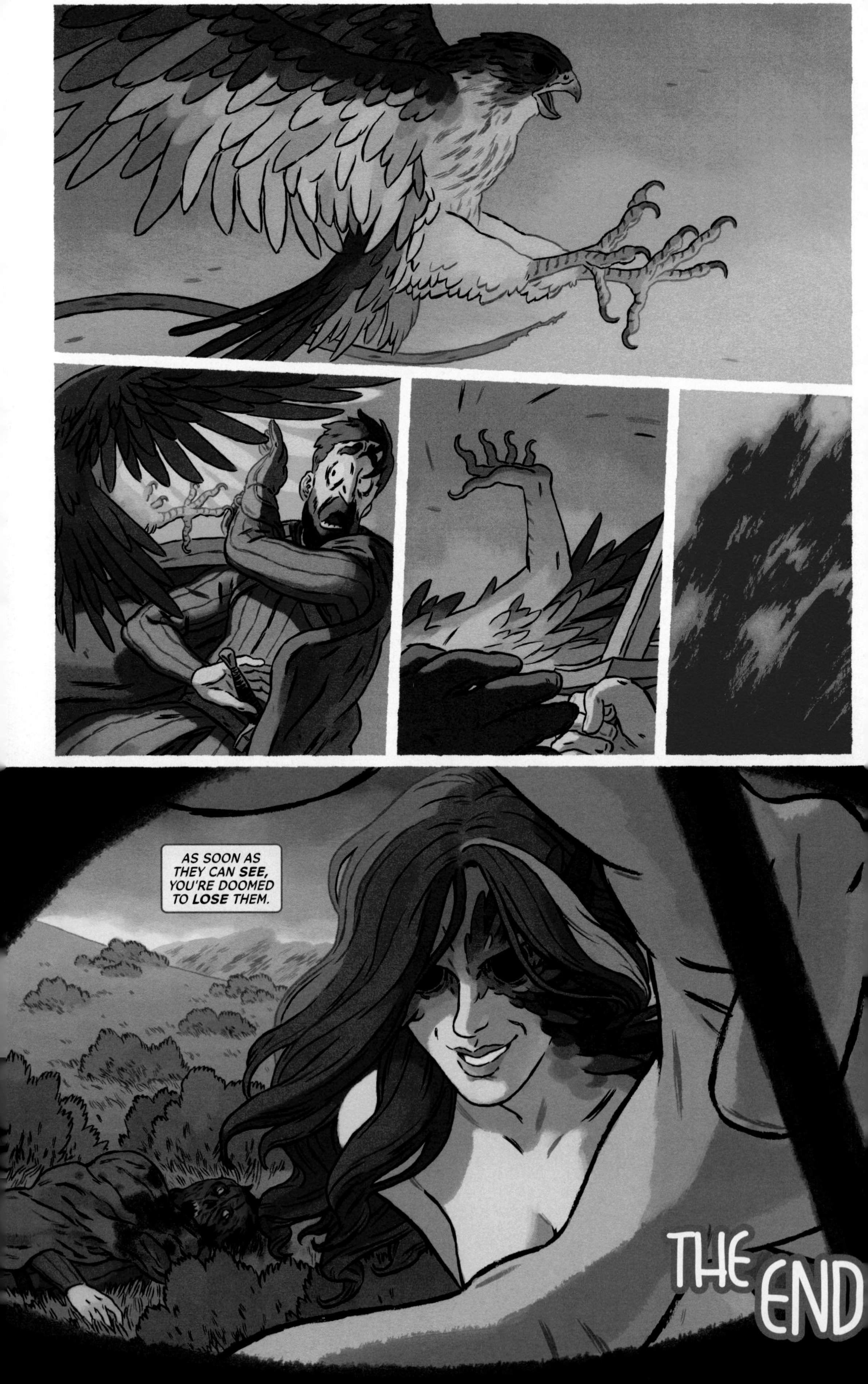
AS SOON AS THEY CAN **SEE**, YOU'RE DOOMED TO **LOSE** THEM.
THE END

Lottery

Written by BRIAN BUCCELLATO
Pencils and Inks by MEGAN LEVENS
Colors by GIULIA BRUSCO
Letters by COREY BREEN
MOLLY MAHAN Editor

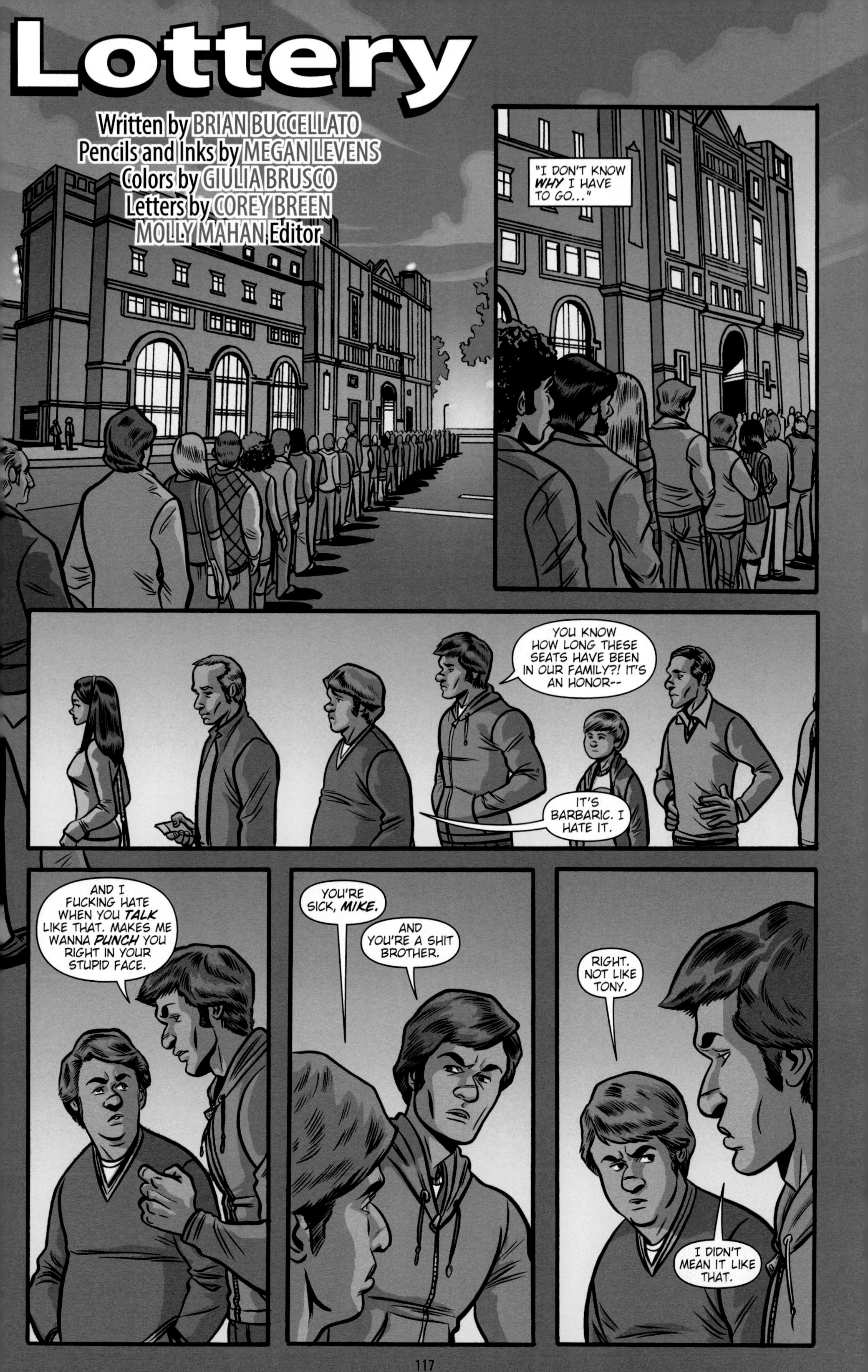
"I DON'T KNOW *WHY* I HAVE TO GO..."
YOU KNOW HOW LONG THESE SEATS HAVE BEEN IN OUR FAMILY?! IT'S AN HONOR--
IT'S BARBARIC. I HATE IT.
AND I FUCKING HATE WHEN YOU *TALK* LIKE THAT. MAKES ME WANNA *PUNCH* YOU RIGHT IN YOUR STUPID FACE.
YOU'RE SICK, *MIKE.*
AND YOU'RE A SHIT BROTHER.
RIGHT. NOT LIKE TONY.
I DIDN'T MEAN IT LIKE THAT.

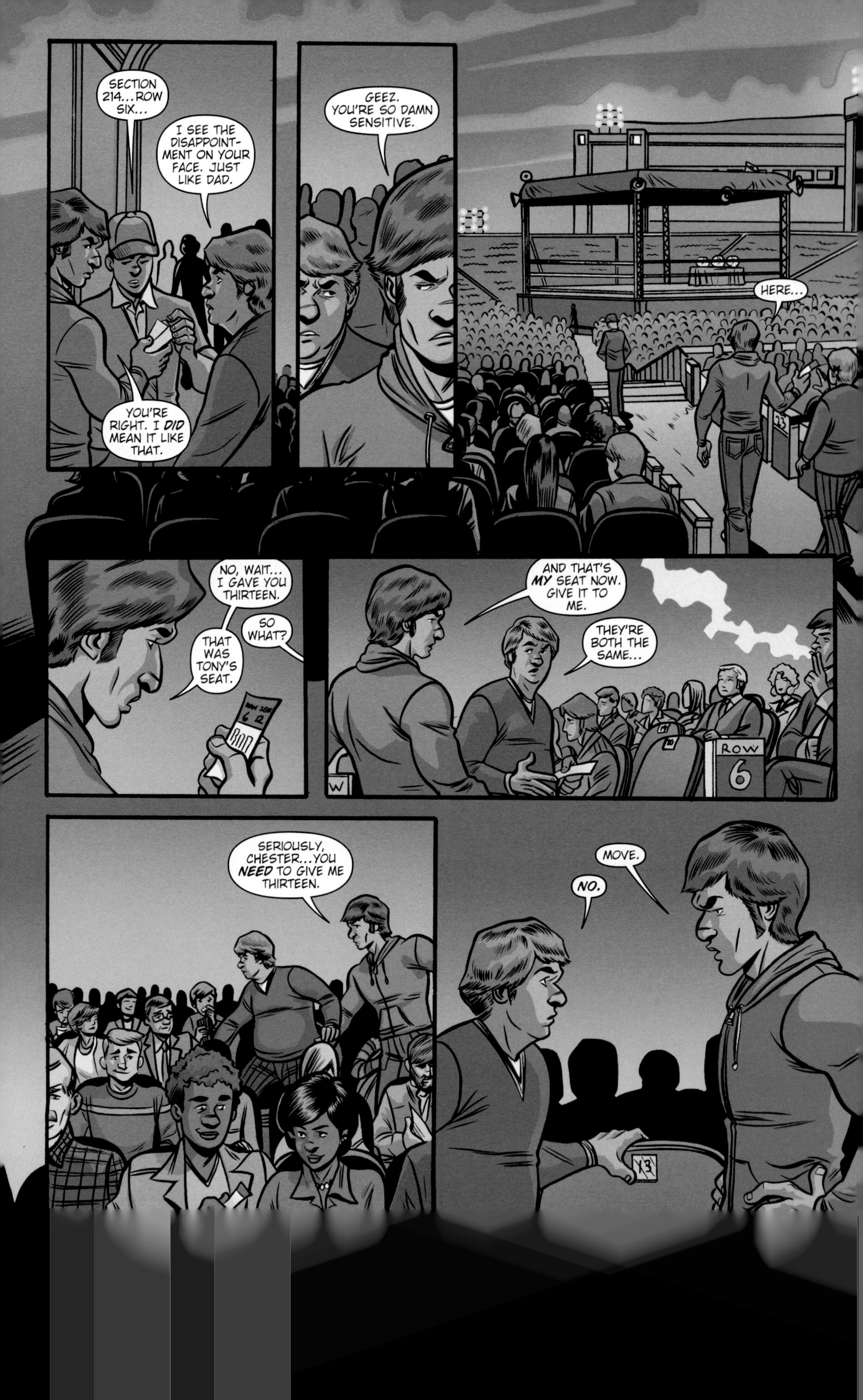
SECTION 214...ROW SIX...
I SEE THE DISAPPOINTMENT ON YOUR FACE. JUST LIKE DAD.
YOU'RE RIGHT. I DID MEAN IT LIKE THAT.
GEEZ. YOU'RE SO DAMN SENSITIVE.
HERE...
ROW 6
NO, WAIT... I GAVE YOU THIRTEEN.
THAT WAS TONY'S SEAT.
SO WHAT?
AND THAT'S MY SEAT NOW. GIVE IT TO ME.
THEY'RE BOTH THE SAME...
ROW 6
SERIOUSLY, CHESTER...YOU NEED TO GIVE ME THIRTEEN.
MOVE.
NO.

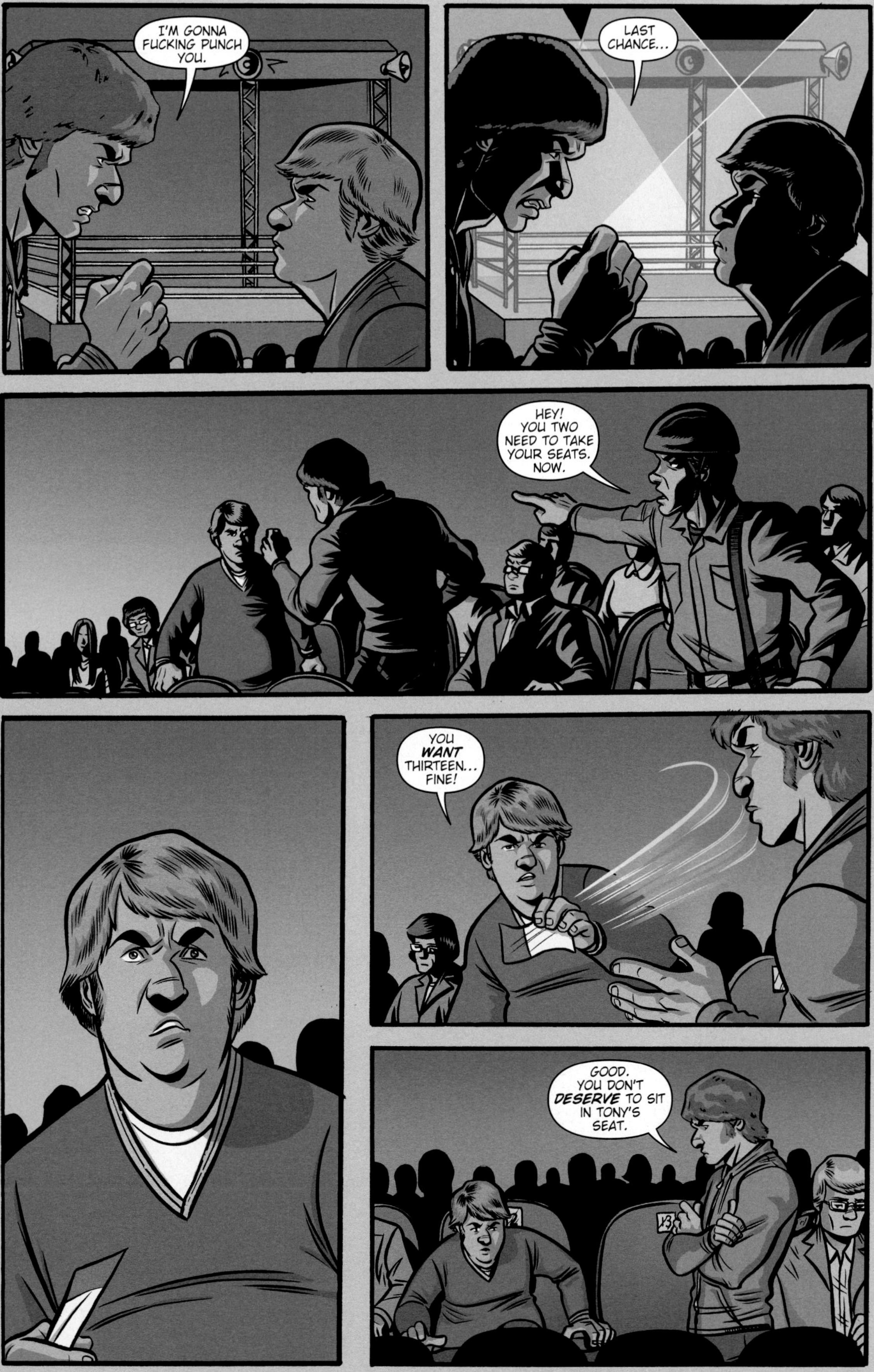
I'M GONNA FUCKING PUNCH YOU.
LAST CHANCE...
HEY! YOU TWO NEED TO TAKE YOUR SEATS. NOW.
YOU *WANT* THIRTEEN... FINE!
GOOD. YOU DON'T *DESERVE* TO SIT IN TONY'S SEAT.

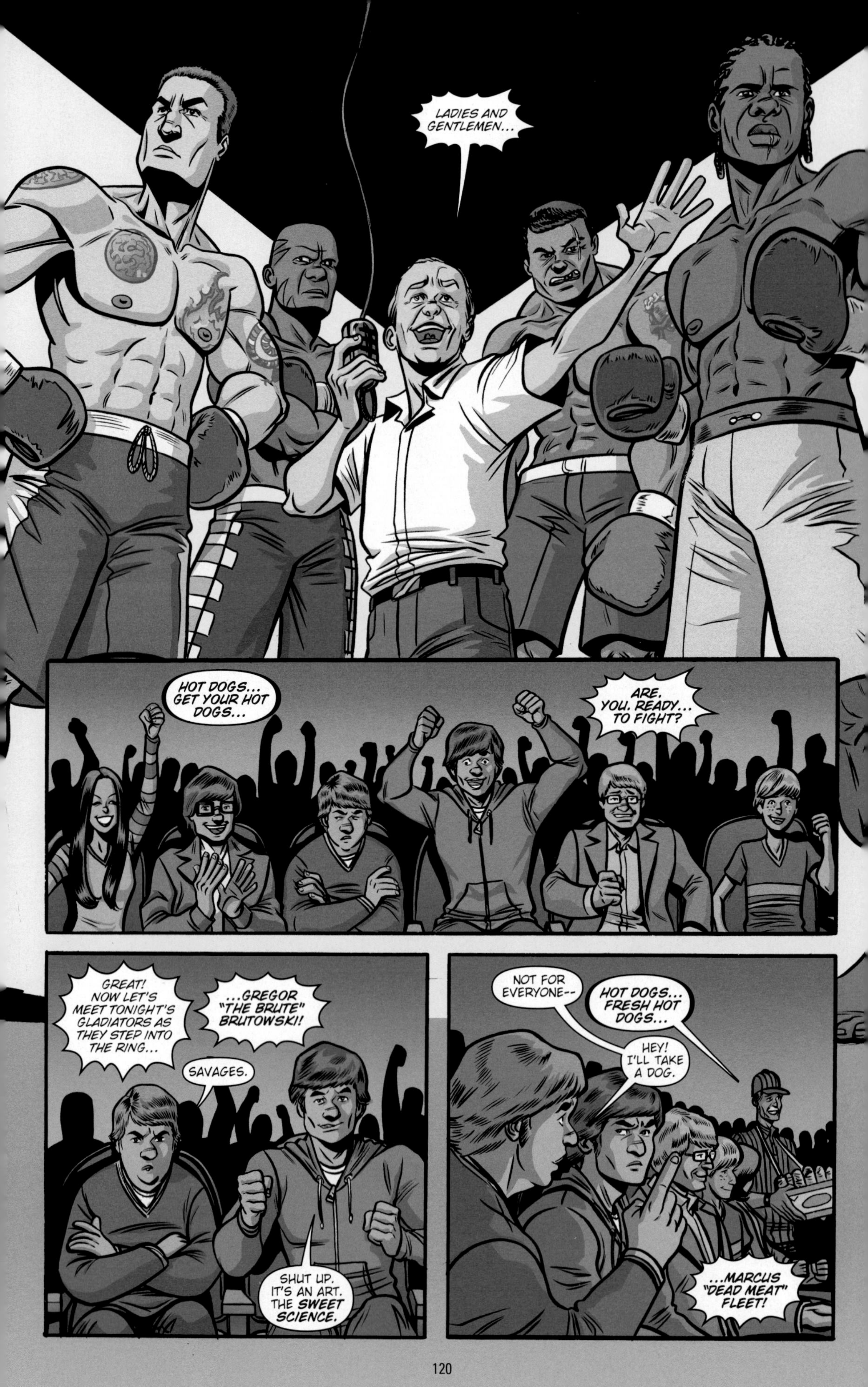
LADIES AND GENTLEMEN...
HOT DOGS... GET YOUR HOT DOGS...
ARE. YOU. READY... TO FIGHT?
GREAT! NOW LET'S MEET TONIGHT'S GLADIATORS AS THEY STEP INTO THE RING...
...GREGOR "THE BRUTE" BRUTOWSKI!
SAVAGES.
SHUT UP. IT'S AN ART. THE SWEET SCIENCE.
NOT FOR EVERYONE--
HOT DOGS... FRESH HOT DOGS...
HEY! I'LL TAKE A DOG.
...MARCUS "DEAD MEAT" FLEET!

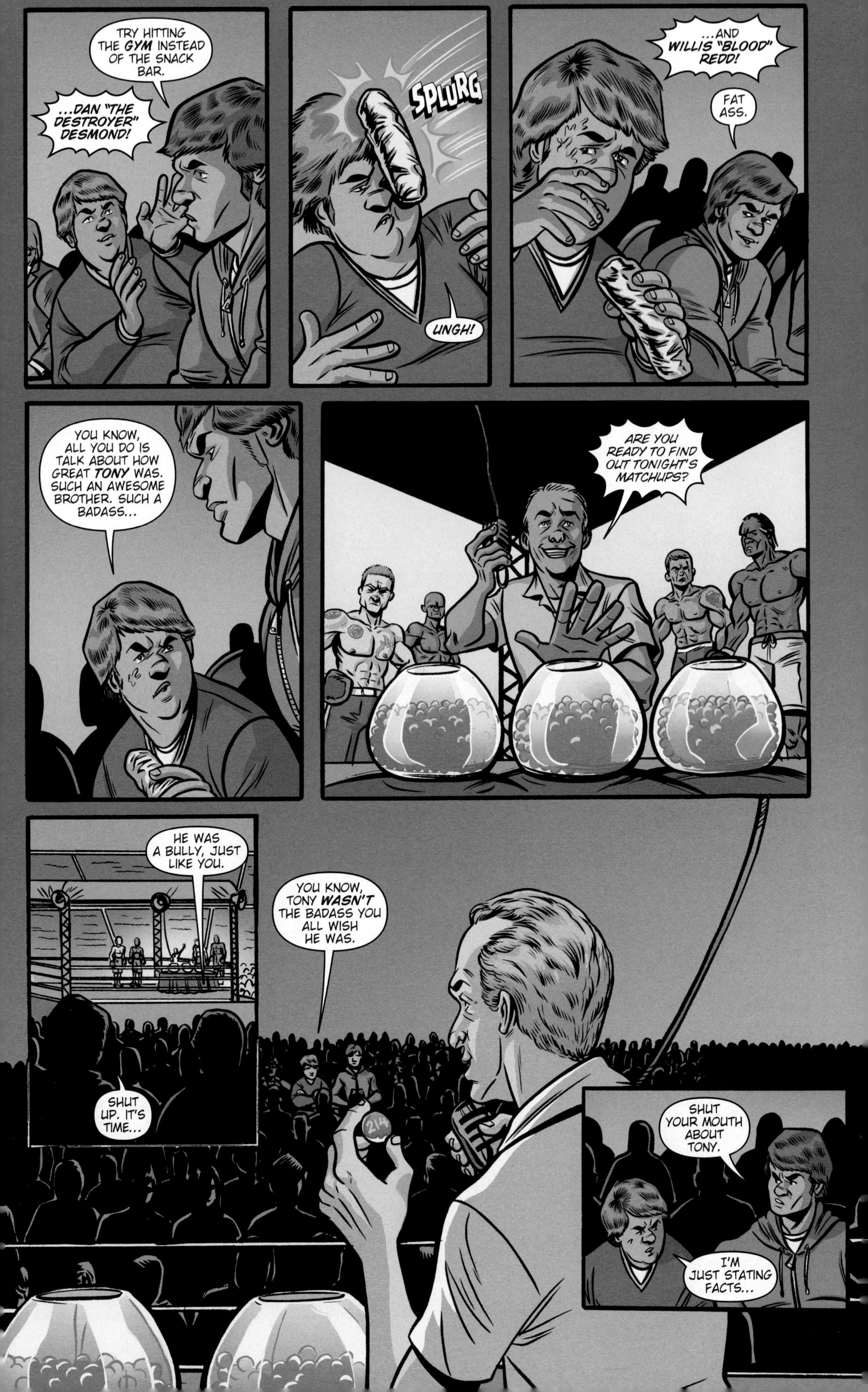
...DAN "THE DESTROYER" DESMOND!
TRY HITTING THE GYM INSTEAD OF THE SNACK BAR.
SPLURG
UNGH!
...AND WILLIS "BLOOD" REDD!
FAT ASS.
YOU KNOW, ALL YOU DO IS TALK ABOUT HOW GREAT TONY WAS. SUCH AN AWESOME BROTHER. SUCH A BADASS...
ARE YOU READY TO FIND OUT TONIGHT'S MATCHUPS?
HE WAS A BULLY, JUST LIKE YOU.
SHUT UP. IT'S TIME...
YOU KNOW, TONY WASN'T THE BADASS YOU ALL WISH HE WAS.
SHUT YOUR MOUTH ABOUT TONY.
I'M JUST STATING FACTS...

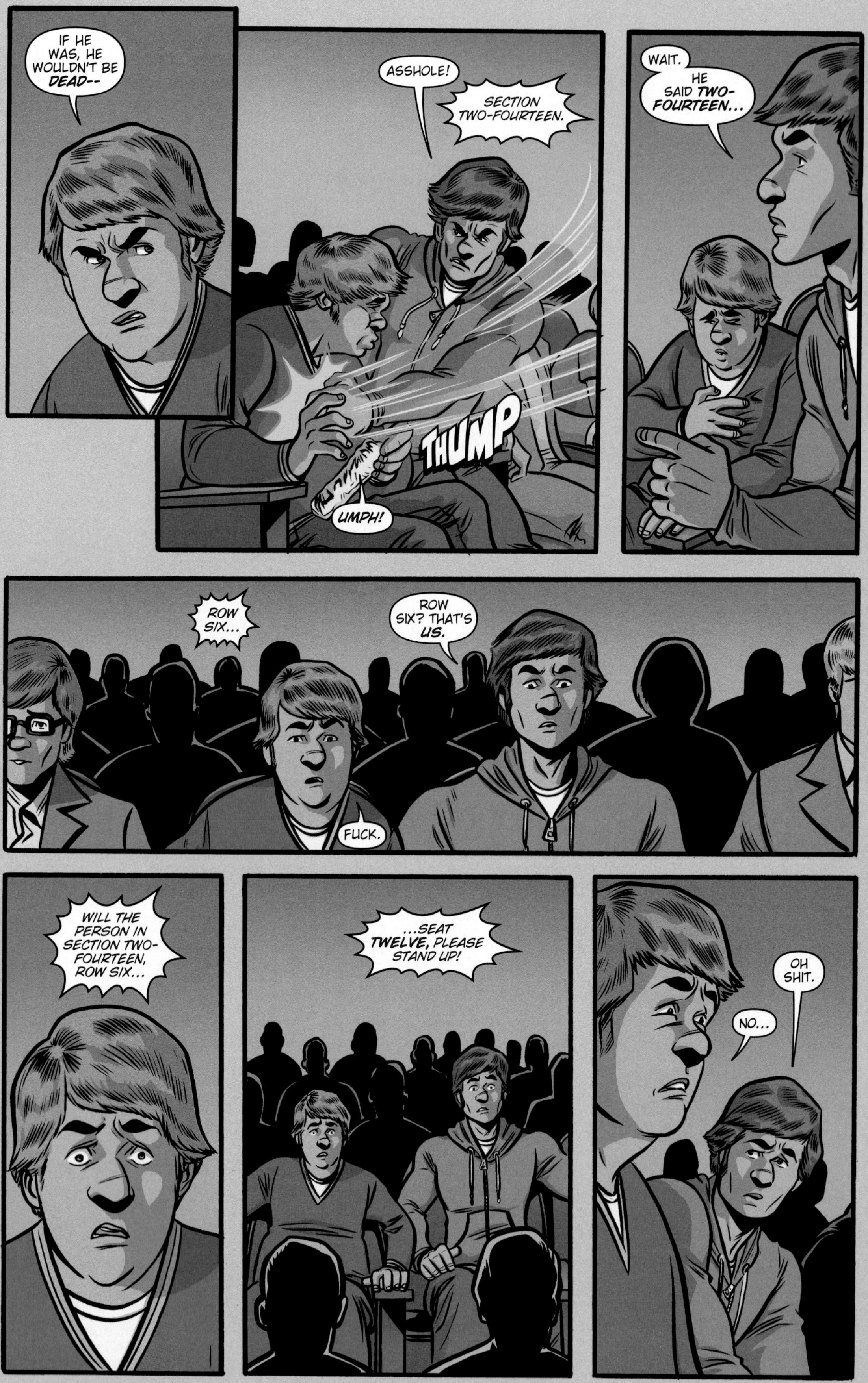
IF HE WAS, HE WOULDN'T BE DEAD--
ASSHOLE!
SECTION TWO-FOURTEEN.
THUMP
UMPH!
WAIT.
HE SAID TWO-FOURTEEN...
ROW SIX...
ROW SIX? THAT'S US.
FUCK.
WILL THE PERSON IN SECTION TWO-FOURTEEN, ROW SIX...
...SEAT TWELVE, PLEASE STAND UP!
OH SHIT.
NO...

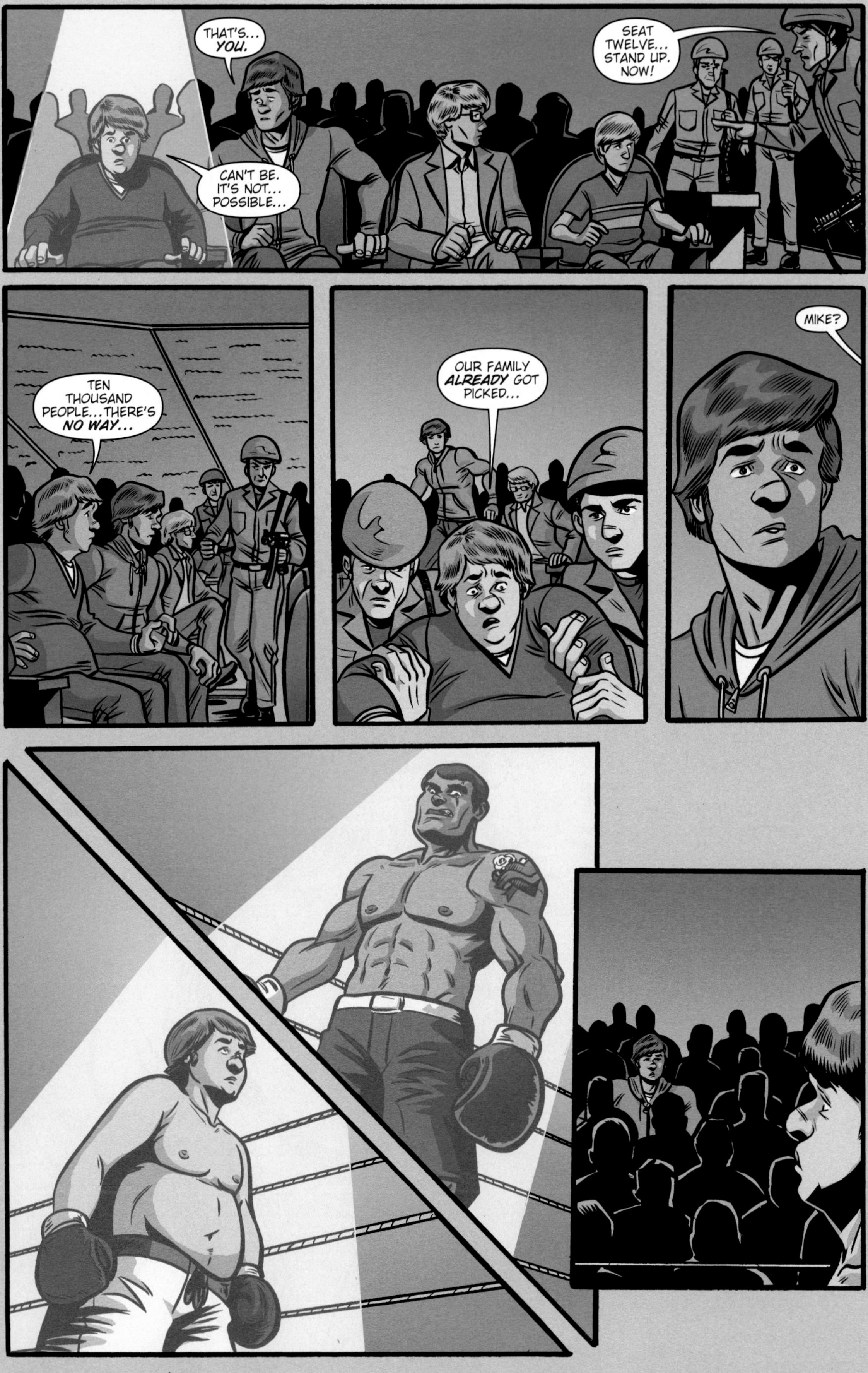
THAT'S... YOU.
SEAT TWELVE... STAND UP. NOW!
CAN'T BE. IT'S NOT... POSSIBLE...
TEN THOUSAND PEOPLE...THERE'S NO WAY...
OUR FAMILY ALREADY GOT PICKED...
MIKE?

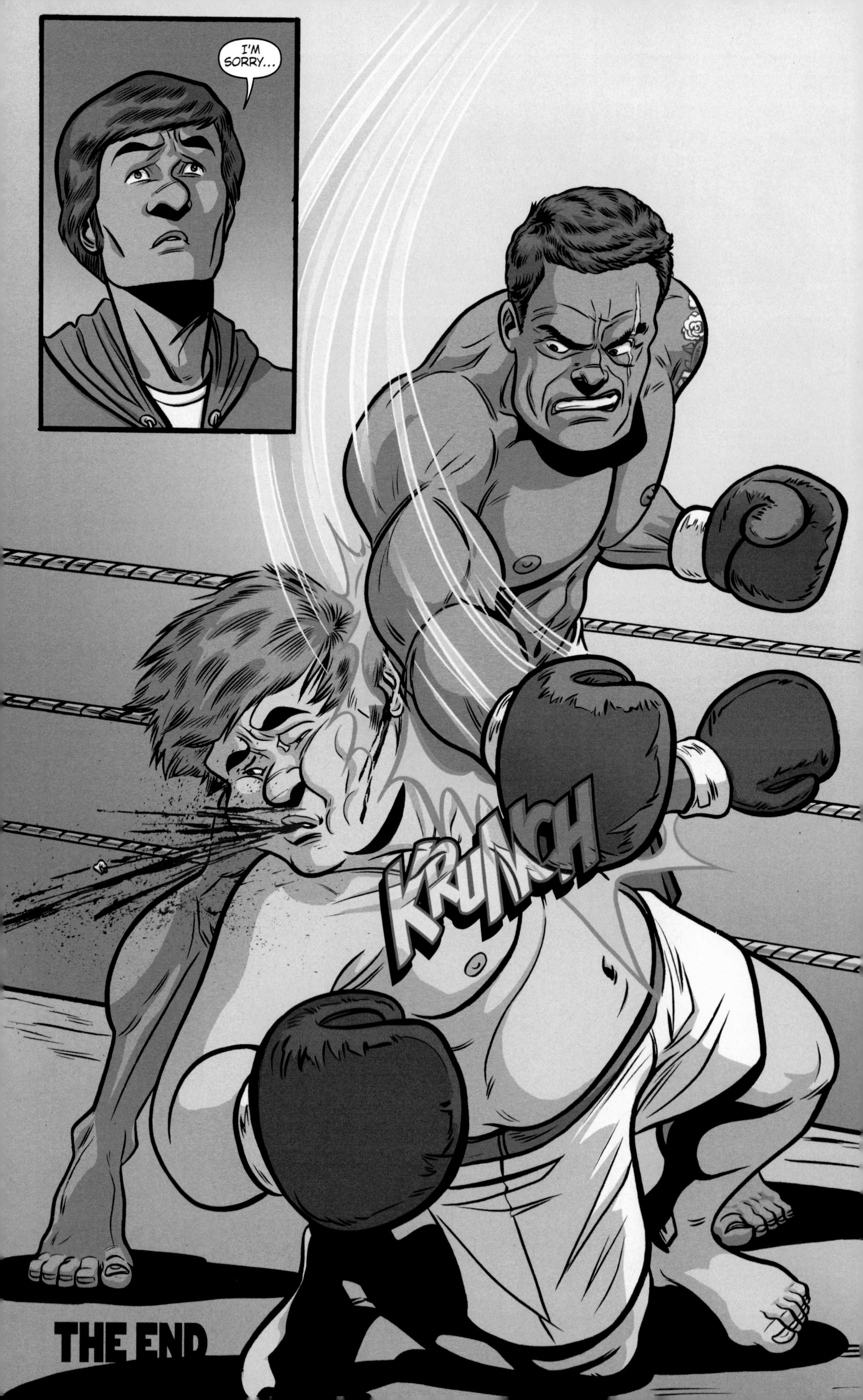
I'M SORRY...
KRUNCH
THE END

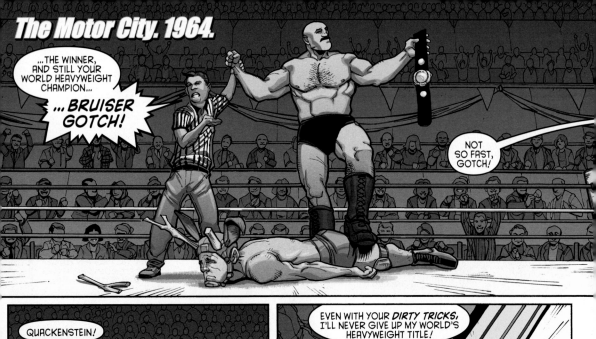

The Motor City. 1964.

...THE WINNER, AND STILL YOUR WORLD HEAVYWEIGHT CHAMPION...

...*BRUISER GOTCH!*

NOT SO FAST, GOTCH!

QUACKENSTEIN!

THAT'S *DOCTOR* QUACKENSTEIN!

YOU BESTED MY *JACKALOPE,* BUT I'M NOT THROUGH WITH YOU YET!

EVEN WITH YOUR *DIRTY TRICKS,* I'LL NEVER GIVE UP MY WORLD'S HEAVYWEIGHT TITLE!

NO? BUT WHAT IF YOU AREN'T *HERE* TO DEFEND IT?!

WHERE WOULD I GO? *DETROIT'S* THE GREATEST CITY ON GOD'S GREEN EARTH!

NOT *WHERE,* YOU HYPERTROPHIC BUFFOON...

...BUT *WHEN!*

FZZZZAK!

QUACKENSTEIN USED HIS *PROFANE* SCIENCE TO CAST THE MIGHTY BRUISER GOTCH INTO THE *TIMESTREAM!*

CONDEMNED TO WANDER THROUGH THE AGES, HONOR-BOUND TO RIGHT WRONGS AND *POWERBOMB* INTO *OBLIVION* THOSE WHO WOULD OPPOSE HIM. HE WAS...

...THE TIME-GRAPPLER!

writer: AUBREY SITTERSON
pencils: MAX DUNBAR
inks: ANDE PARKS
colors: NICK FILARDI
letters: WES ABBOTT
edits: MOLLY MAHAN

JUMPING JOE SAVOLDI!

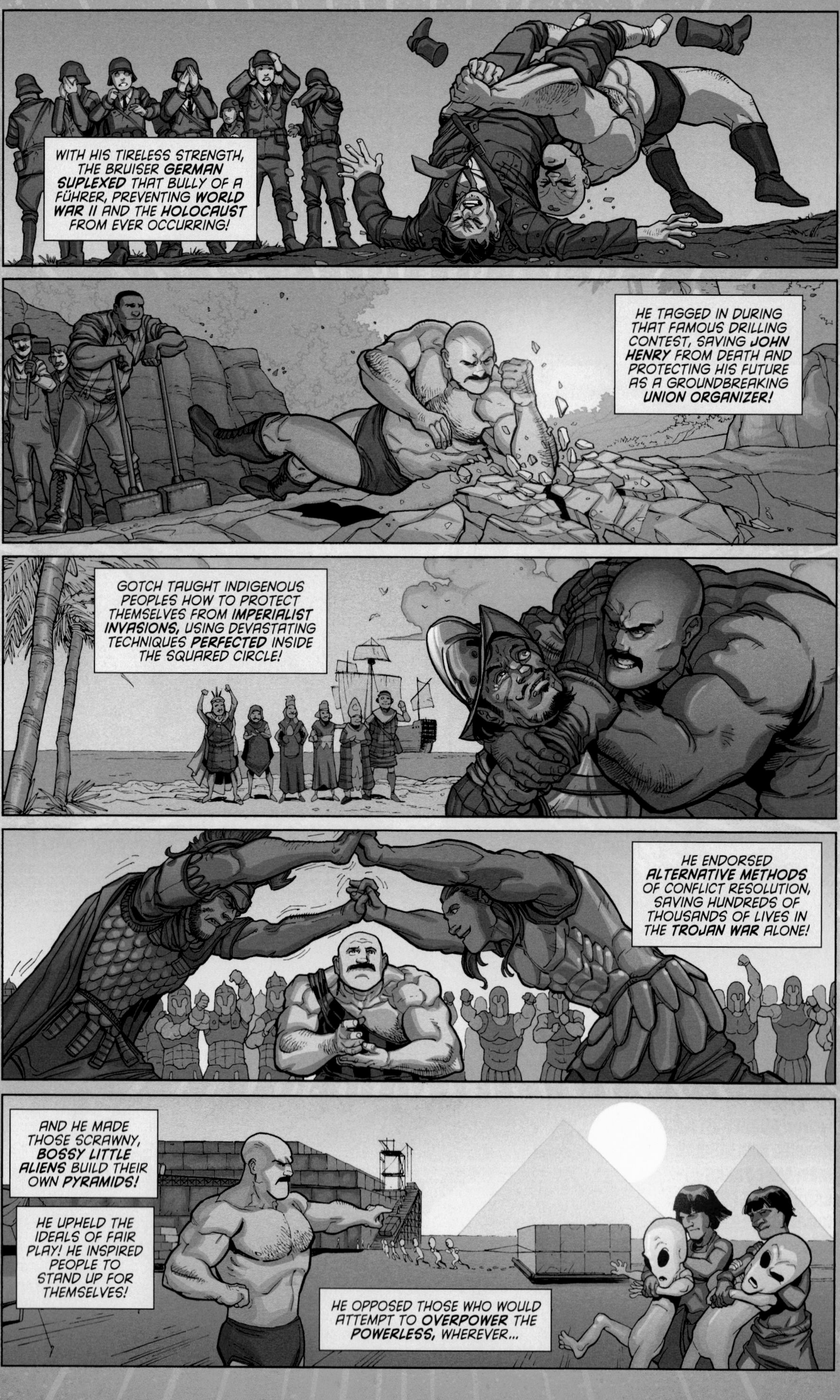

WITH HIS TIRELESS STRENGTH, THE BRUISER **GERMAN SUPLEXED** THAT BULLY OF A FÜHRER, PREVENTING **WORLD WAR II** AND THE **HOLOCAUST** FROM EVER OCCURRING!
HE TAGGED IN DURING THAT FAMOUS DRILLING CONTEST, SAVING **JOHN HENRY** FROM DEATH AND PROTECTING HIS FUTURE AS A GROUNDBREAKING **UNION ORGANIZER!**
GOTCH TAUGHT INDIGENOUS PEOPLES HOW TO PROTECT THEMSELVES FROM **IMPERIALIST INVASIONS,** USING DEVASTATING TECHNIQUES **PERFECTED** INSIDE THE SQUARED CIRCLE!
HE ENDORSED **ALTERNATIVE METHODS** OF CONFLICT RESOLUTION, SAVING HUNDREDS OF THOUSANDS OF LIVES IN THE **TROJAN WAR** ALONE!
AND HE MADE THOSE SCRAWNY, **BOSSY LITTLE ALIENS** BUILD THEIR OWN **PYRAMIDS!**
HE UPHELD THE IDEALS OF FAIR PLAY! HE INSPIRED PEOPLE TO STAND UP FOR THEMSELVES!
HE OPPOSED THOSE WHO WOULD ATTEMPT TO **OVERPOWER** THE **POWERLESS,** WHEREVER...

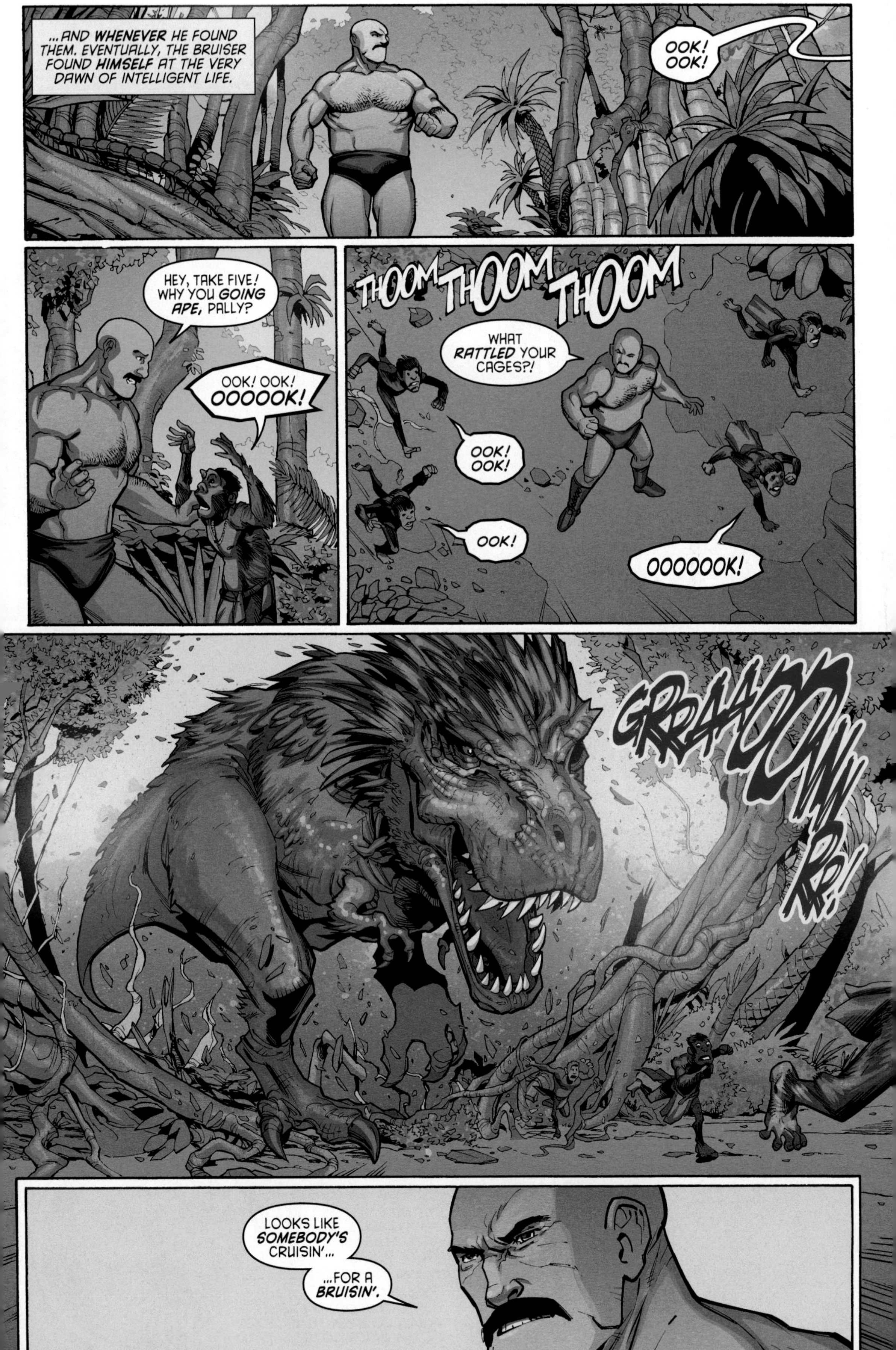
...AND WHENEVER HE FOUND THEM. EVENTUALLY, THE BRUISER FOUND HIMSELF AT THE VERY DAWN OF INTELLIGENT LIFE.
OOK! OOK!
HEY, TAKE FIVE! WHY YOU GOING APE, PALLY?
OOK! OOK! OOOOOK!
THOOM THOOM THOOM
WHAT RATTLED YOUR CAGES?!
OOK! OOK!
OOK!
OOOOOOK!
GRRAAOOWWRR!
LOOKS LIKE SOMEBODY'S CRUISIN'...
...FOR A BRUISIN'.

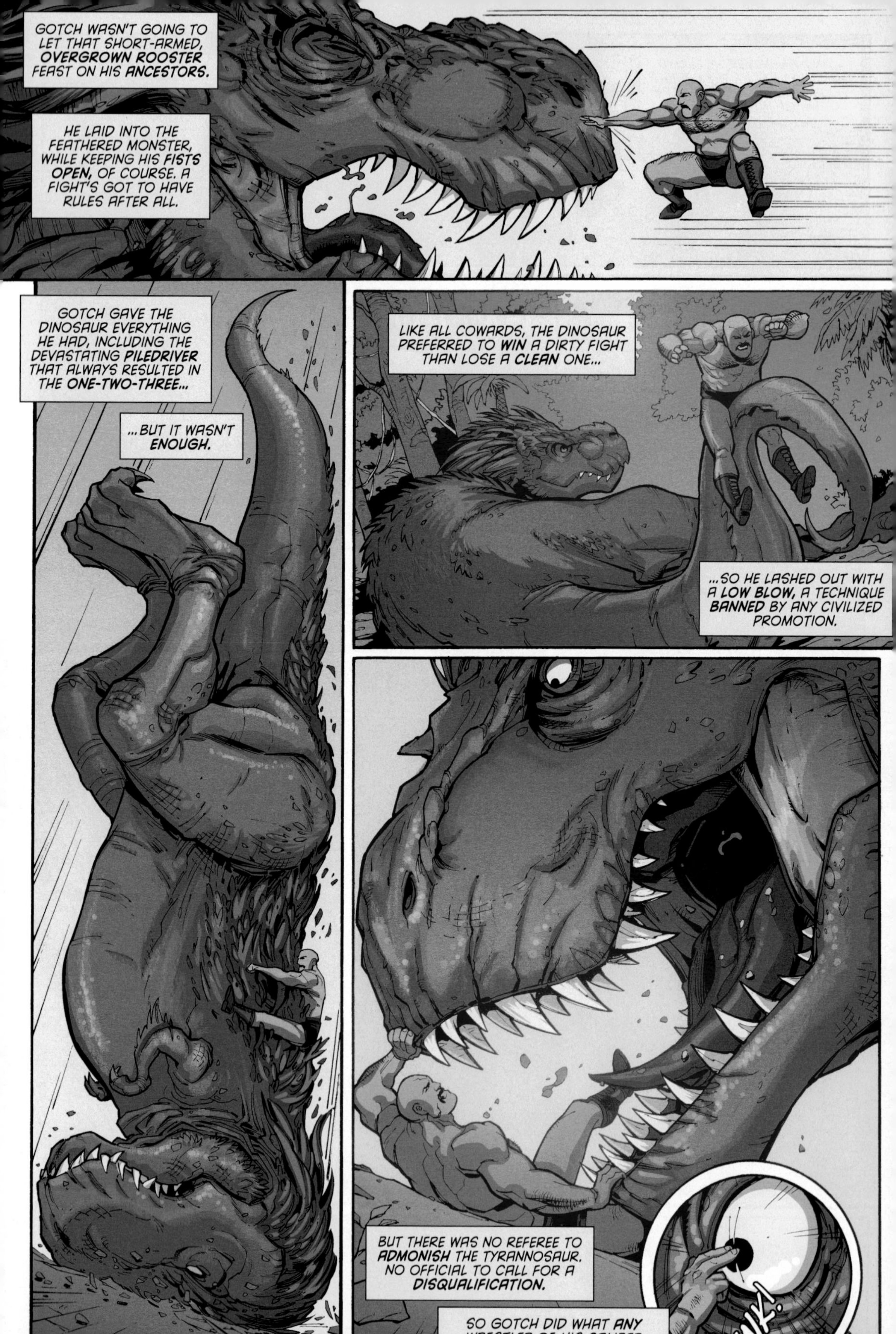
GOTCH WASN'T GOING TO LET THAT SHORT-ARMED, OVERGROWN ROOSTER FEAST ON HIS ANCESTORS.
HE LAID INTO THE FEATHERED MONSTER, WHILE KEEPING HIS FISTS OPEN, OF COURSE. A FIGHT'S GOT TO HAVE RULES AFTER ALL.
GOTCH GAVE THE DINOSAUR EVERYTHING HE HAD, INCLUDING THE DEVASTATING PILEDRIVER THAT ALWAYS RESULTED IN THE ONE-TWO-THREE...
...BUT IT WASN'T ENOUGH.
LIKE ALL COWARDS, THE DINOSAUR PREFERRED TO WIN A DIRTY FIGHT THAN LOSE A CLEAN ONE...
...SO HE LASHED OUT WITH A LOW BLOW, A TECHNIQUE BANNED BY ANY CIVILIZED PROMOTION.
BUT THERE WAS NO REFEREE TO ADMONISH THE TYRANNOSAUR. NO OFFICIAL TO CALL FOR A DISQUALIFICATION.
SO GOTCH DID WHAT ANY WRESTLER OF HIS CALIBER WOULD DO WHEN CONFRONTED WITH AN INCORRIGIBLE CHEAT...
POINK!

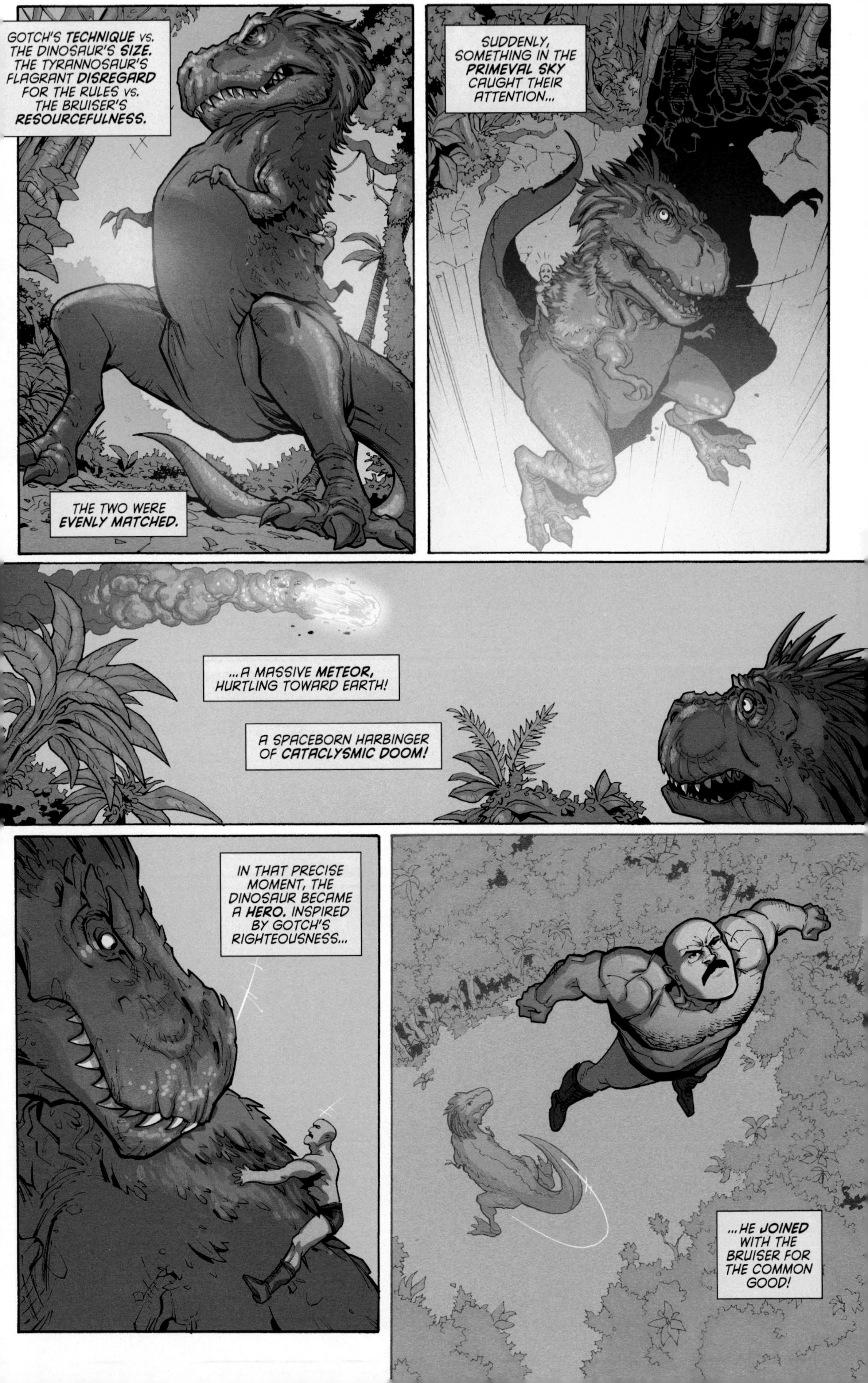
GOTCH'S TECHNIQUE VS. THE DINOSAUR'S SIZE. THE TYRANNOSAUR'S FLAGRANT DISREGARD FOR THE RULES VS. THE BRUISER'S RESOURCEFULNESS.
THE TWO WERE EVENLY MATCHED.
SUDDENLY, SOMETHING IN THE PRIMEVAL SKY CAUGHT THEIR ATTENTION...
...A MASSIVE METEOR, HURTLING TOWARD EARTH!
A SPACEBORN HARBINGER OF CATACLYSMIC DOOM!
IN THAT PRECISE MOMENT, THE DINOSAUR BECAME A HERO. INSPIRED BY GOTCH'S RIGHTEOUSNESS...
...HE JOINED WITH THE BRUISER FOR THE COMMON GOOD!

KRAKKA-BARAKKA-BA-DOOOOM!

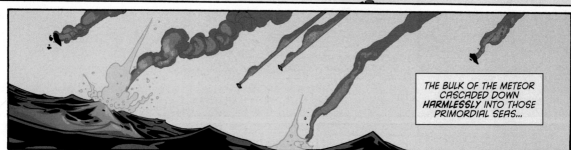

THE BULK OF THE METEOR CASCADED DOWN *HARMLESSLY* INTO THOSE PRIMORDIAL SEAS...

...WHILE WHAT MADE IT TO LAND WAS *QUICKLY* EXTINGUISHED.

THOOM

THOOM

THOOM

TUMP TUMP TUMP

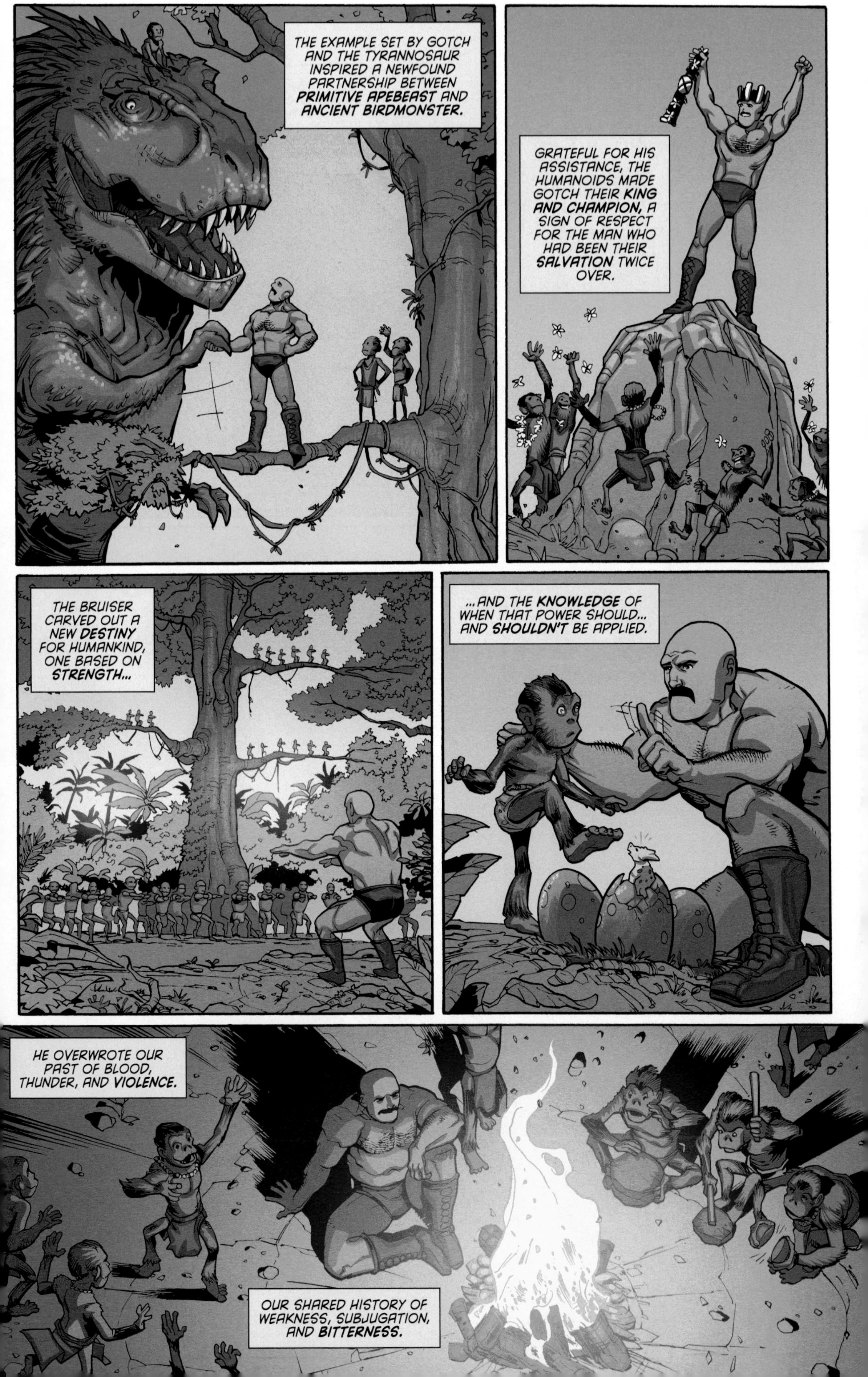
THE EXAMPLE SET BY GOTCH AND THE TYRANNOSAUR INSPIRED A NEWFOUND PARTNERSHIP BETWEEN **PRIMITIVE APEBEAST** AND **ANCIENT BIRDMONSTER.**
GRATEFUL FOR HIS ASSISTANCE, THE HUMANOIDS MADE GOTCH THEIR **KING AND CHAMPION,** A SIGN OF RESPECT FOR THE MAN WHO HAD BEEN THEIR **SALVATION** TWICE OVER.
THE BRUISER CARVED OUT A NEW **DESTINY** FOR HUMANKIND, ONE BASED ON **STRENGTH...**
...AND THE **KNOWLEDGE** OF WHEN THAT POWER SHOULD... AND **SHOULDN'T** BE APPLIED.
HE OVERWROTE OUR PAST OF BLOOD, THUNDER, AND **VIOLENCE.**
OUR SHARED HISTORY OF WEAKNESS, SUBJUGATION, AND **BITTERNESS.**

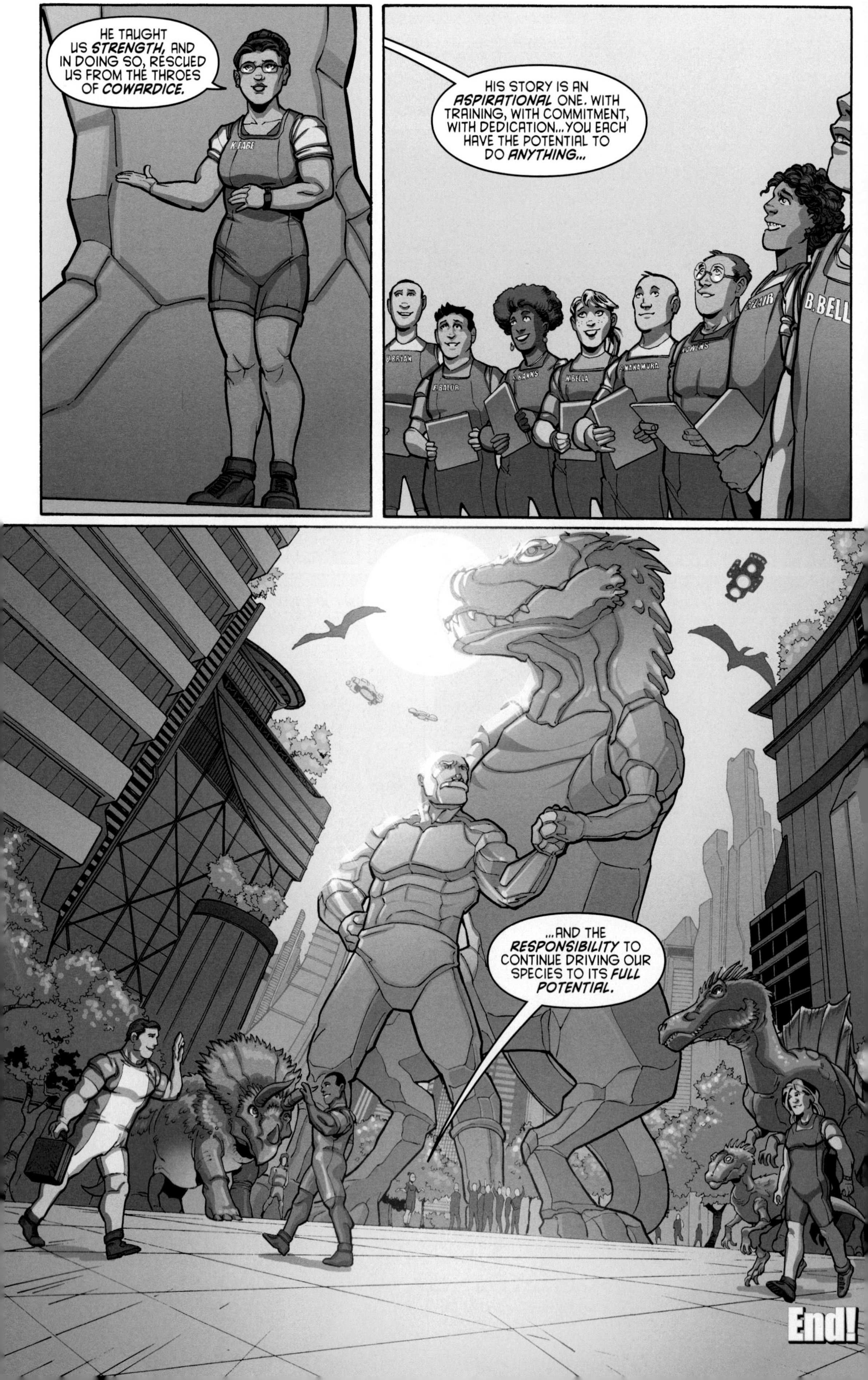
HE TAUGHT US STRENGTH, AND IN DOING SO, RESCUED US FROM THE THROES OF COWARDICE.
HIS STORY IS AN ASPIRATIONAL ONE. WITH TRAINING, WITH COMMITMENT, WITH DEDICATION...YOU EACH HAVE THE POTENTIAL TO DO ANYTHING...
...AND THE RESPONSIBILITY TO CONTINUE DRIVING OUR SPECIES TO ITS FULL POTENTIAL.
End!

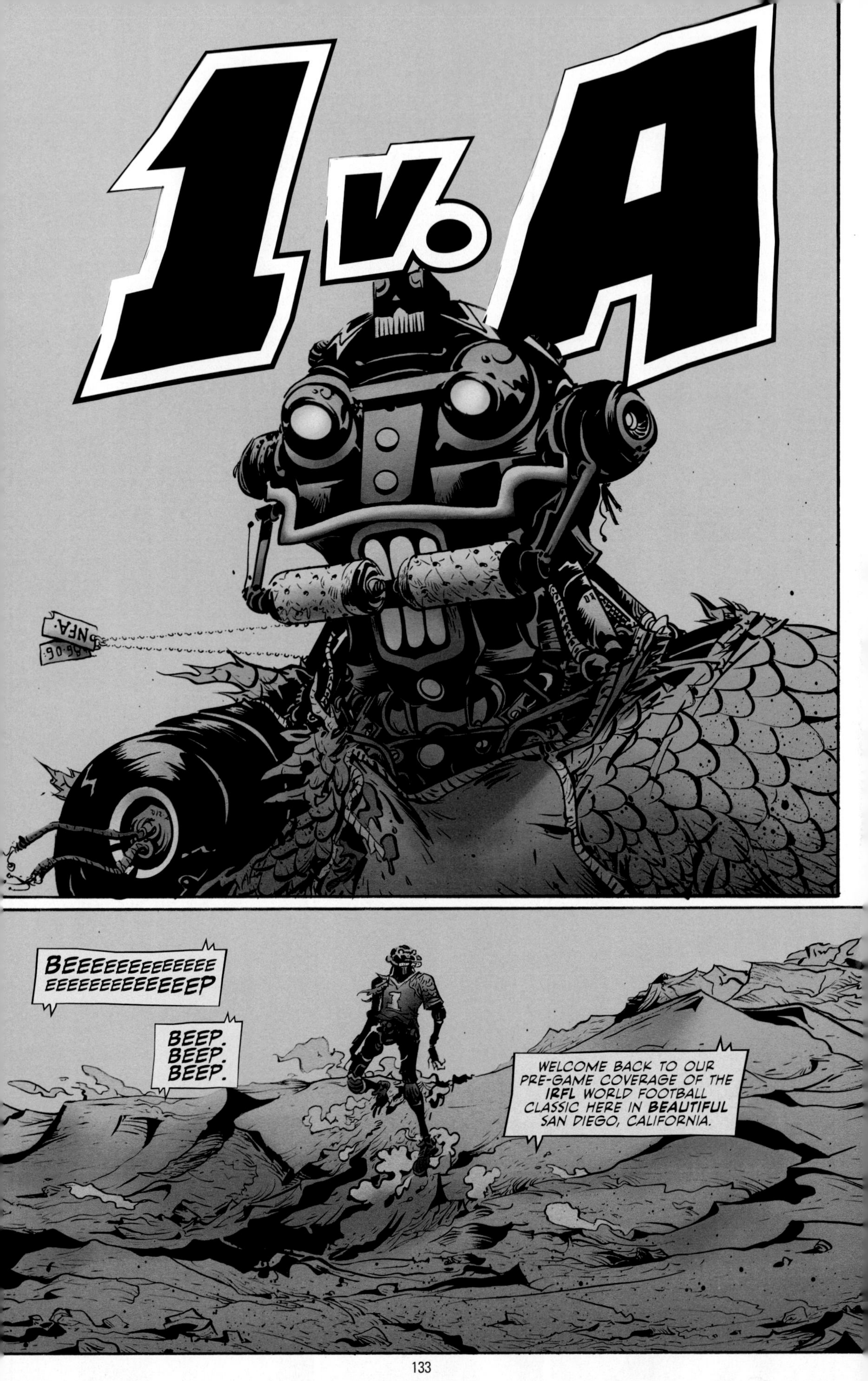
1 v. A
BEEEEEEEEEEEEE EEEEEEEEEEEEEP
BEEP. BEEP. BEEP.
WELCOME BACK TO OUR PRE-GAME COVERAGE OF THE IRFL WORLD FOOTBALL CLASSIC HERE IN BEAUTIFUL SAN DIEGO, CALIFORNIA.

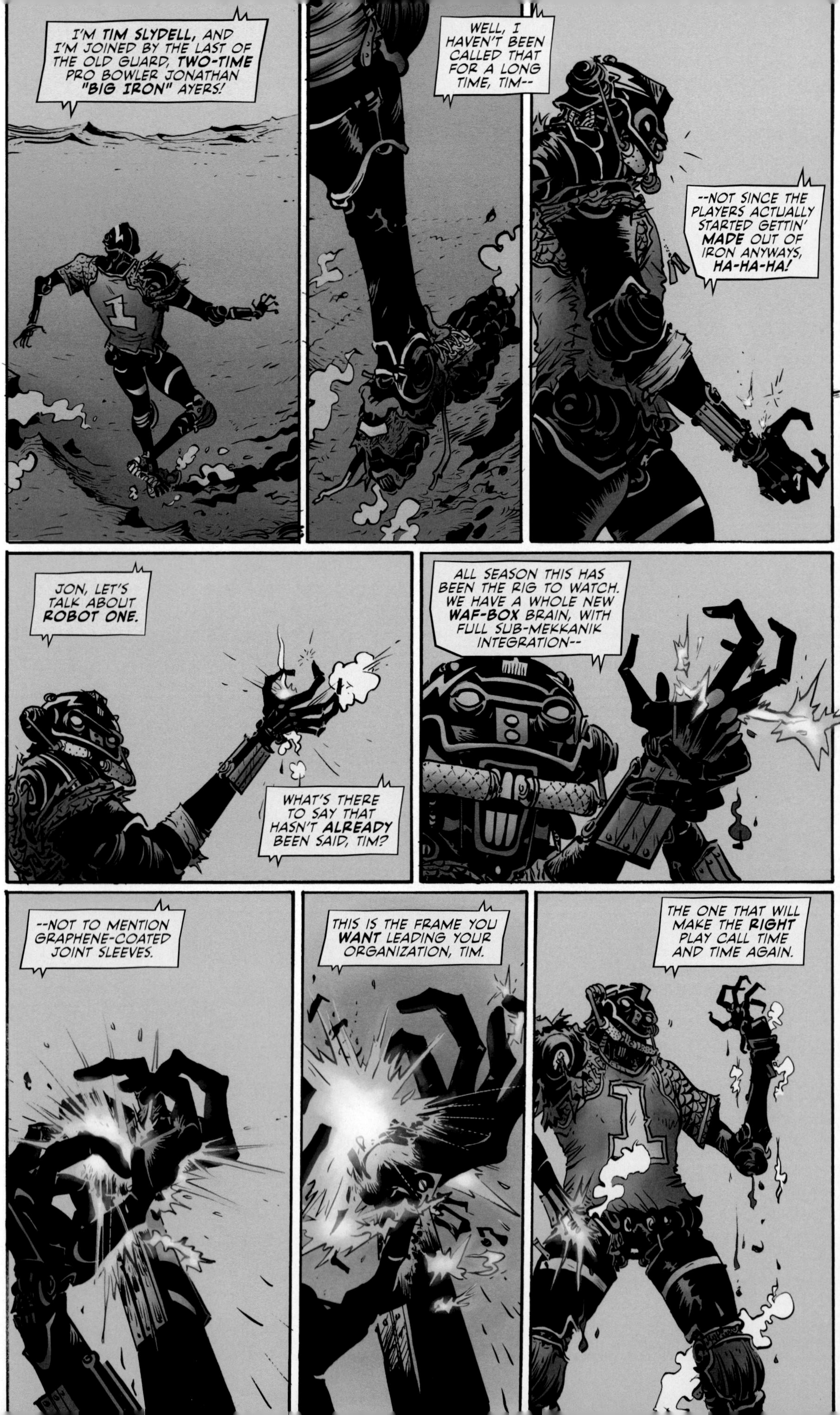
I'M TIM SLYDELL, AND I'M JOINED BY THE LAST OF THE OLD GUARD, TWO-TIME PRO BOWLER JONATHAN "BIG IRON" AYERS!
WELL, I HAVEN'T BEEN CALLED THAT FOR A LONG TIME, TIM--
--NOT SINCE THE PLAYERS ACTUALLY STARTED GETTIN' MADE OUT OF IRON ANYWAYS, HA-HA-HA!
JON, LET'S TALK ABOUT ROBOT ONE.
WHAT'S THERE TO SAY THAT HASN'T ALREADY BEEN SAID, TIM?
ALL SEASON THIS HAS BEEN THE RIG TO WATCH. WE HAVE A WHOLE NEW WAF-BOX BRAIN, WITH FULL SUB-MEKKANIK INTEGRATION--
--NOT TO MENTION GRAPHENE-COATED JOINT SLEEVES.
THIS IS THE FRAME YOU WANT LEADING YOUR ORGANIZATION, TIM.
THE ONE THAT WILL MAKE THE RIGHT PLAY CALL TIME AND TIME AGAIN.

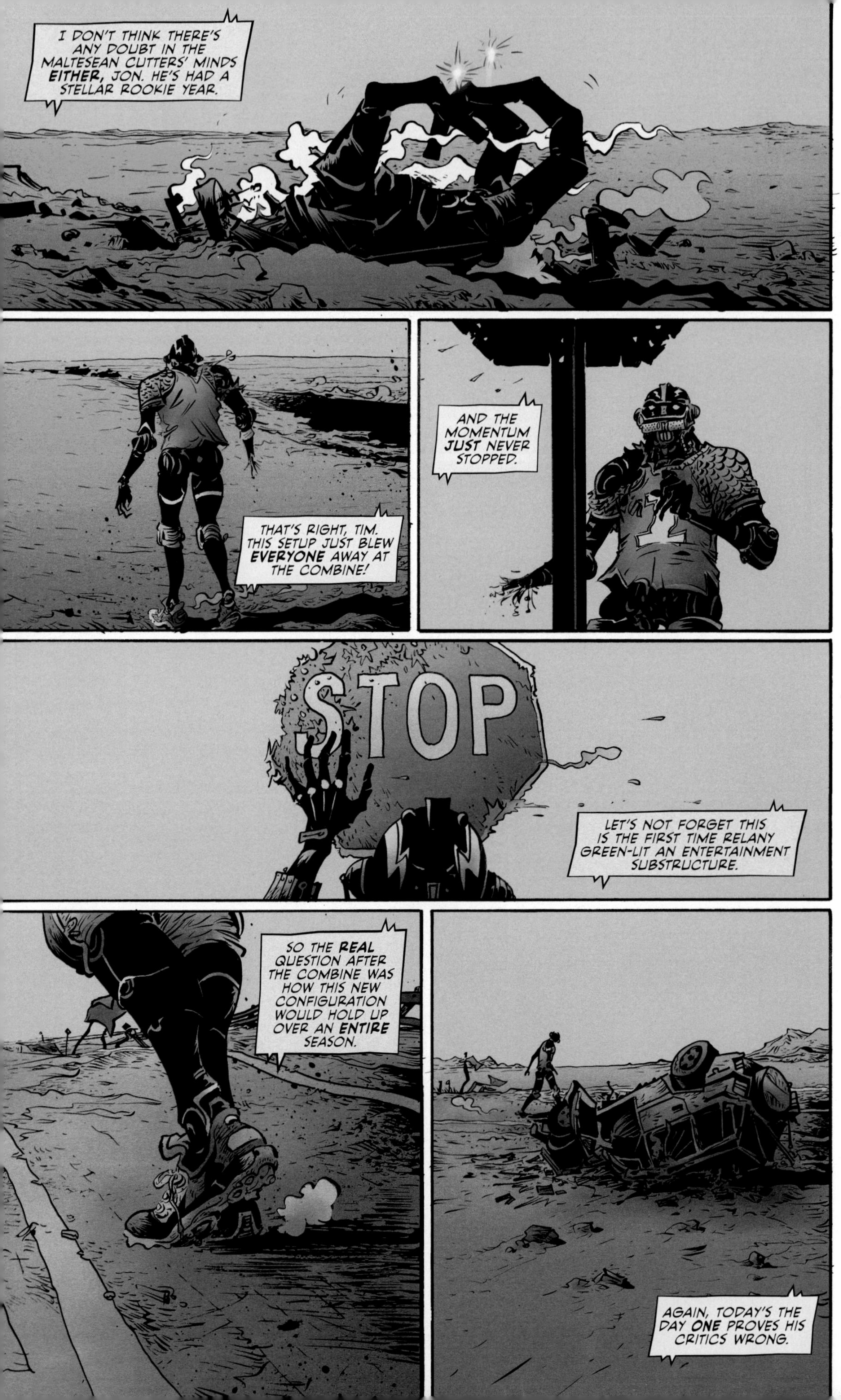
I DON'T THINK THERE'S ANY DOUBT IN THE MALTESEAN CUTTERS' MINDS EITHER, JON. HE'S HAD A STELLAR ROOKIE YEAR.
THAT'S RIGHT, TIM. THIS SETUP JUST BLEW EVERYONE AWAY AT THE COMBINE!
AND THE MOMENTUM JUST NEVER STOPPED.
STOP
LET'S NOT FORGET THIS IS THE FIRST TIME RELANY GREEN-LIT AN ENTERTAINMENT SUBSTRUCTURE.
SO THE REAL QUESTION AFTER THE COMBINE WAS HOW THIS NEW CONFIGURATION WOULD HOLD UP OVER AN ENTIRE SEASON.
AGAIN, TODAY'S THE DAY ONE PROVES HIS CRITICS WRONG.

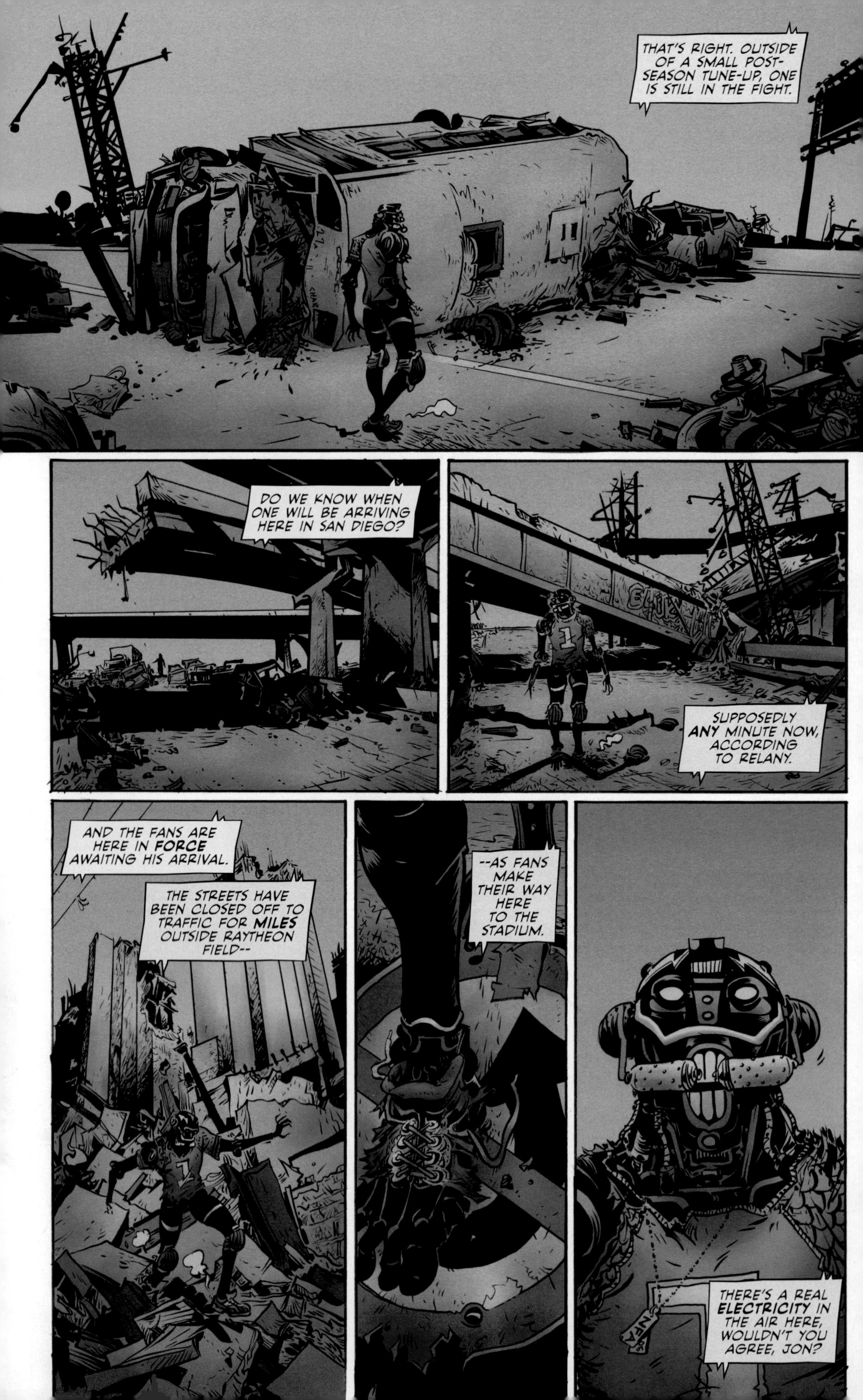
THAT'S RIGHT. OUTSIDE OF A SMALL POST-SEASON TUNE-UP, ONE IS STILL IN THE FIGHT.
DO WE KNOW WHEN ONE WILL BE ARRIVING HERE IN SAN DIEGO?
SUPPOSEDLY ANY MINUTE NOW, ACCORDING TO RELANY.
AND THE FANS ARE HERE IN FORCE AWAITING HIS ARRIVAL.
THE STREETS HAVE BEEN CLOSED OFF TO TRAFFIC FOR MILES OUTSIDE RAYTHEON FIELD--
--AS FANS MAKE THEIR WAY HERE TO THE STADIUM.
THERE'S A REAL ELECTRICITY IN THE AIR HERE, WOULDN'T YOU AGREE, JON?

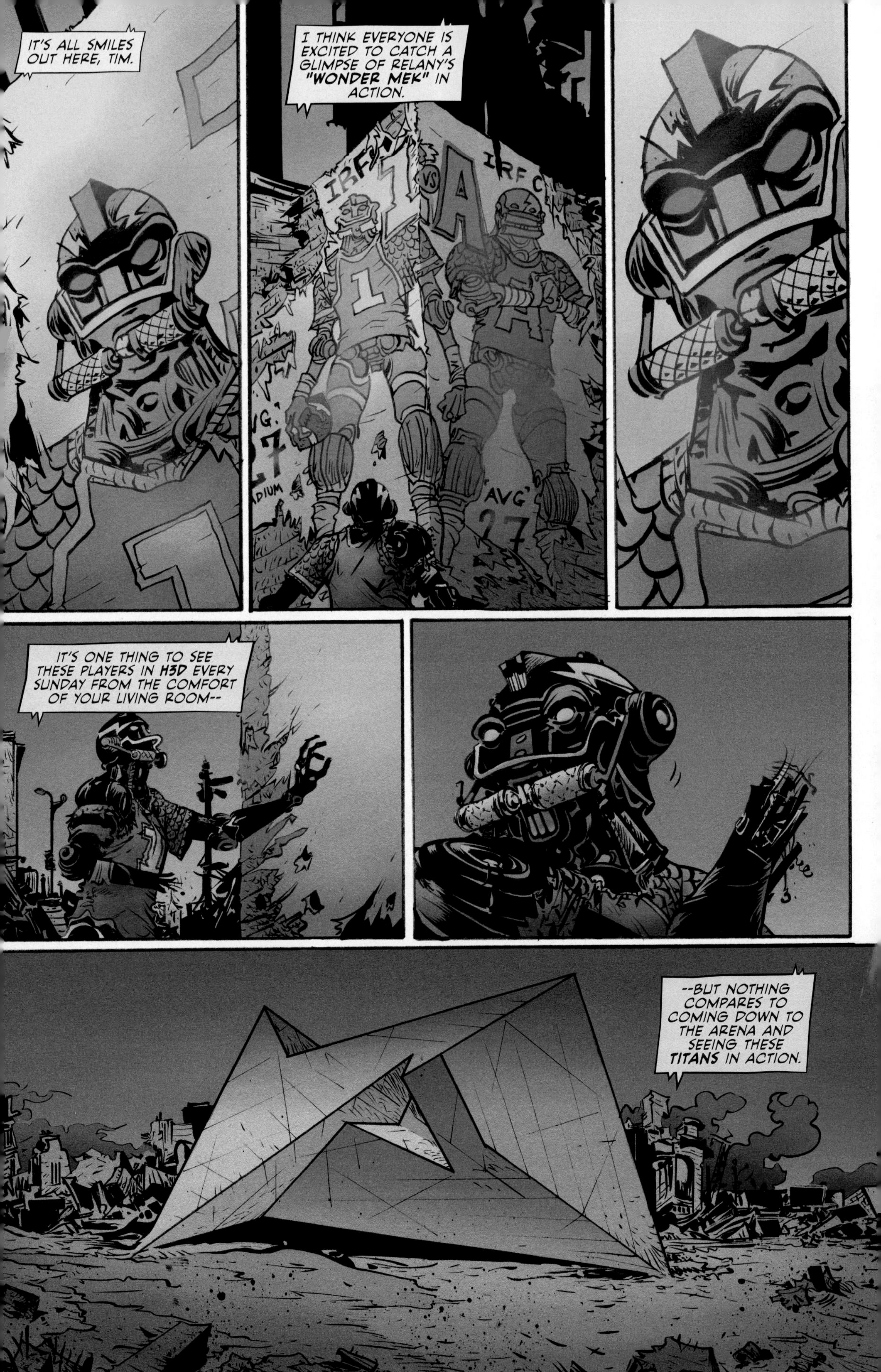
IT'S ALL SMILES OUT HERE, TIM.
I THINK EVERYONE IS EXCITED TO CATCH A GLIMPSE OF RELANY'S "WONDER MEK" IN ACTION.
IRF
VS
A
IRF C
1
AVG'
27
AVG'
27
IT'S ONE THING TO SEE THESE PLAYERS IN H3D EVERY SUNDAY FROM THE COMFORT OF YOUR LIVING ROOM--
--BUT NOTHING COMPARES TO COMING DOWN TO THE ARENA AND SEEING THESE TITANS IN ACTION.

SPEAKING OF TITANS--

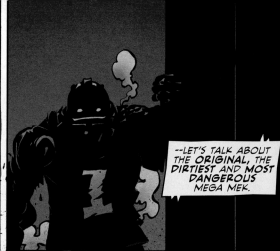

--LET'S TALK ABOUT THE ORIGINAL, THE DIRTIEST AND MOST DANGEROUS MEGA MEK.

HE'S BEEN A PART OF THE SETAUKET WHALERS' PROGRAM SINCE THE BEGINNING.

OF COURSE, WE ARE TALKING ABOUT ROBOT A.

IRFL LEADER IN MOST GAMES PLAYED, MOST PASSES INTERCEPTED, AND MOST IMPORTANTLY HERE--

--CAREER LEADER IN QUARTERBACK SACKS.

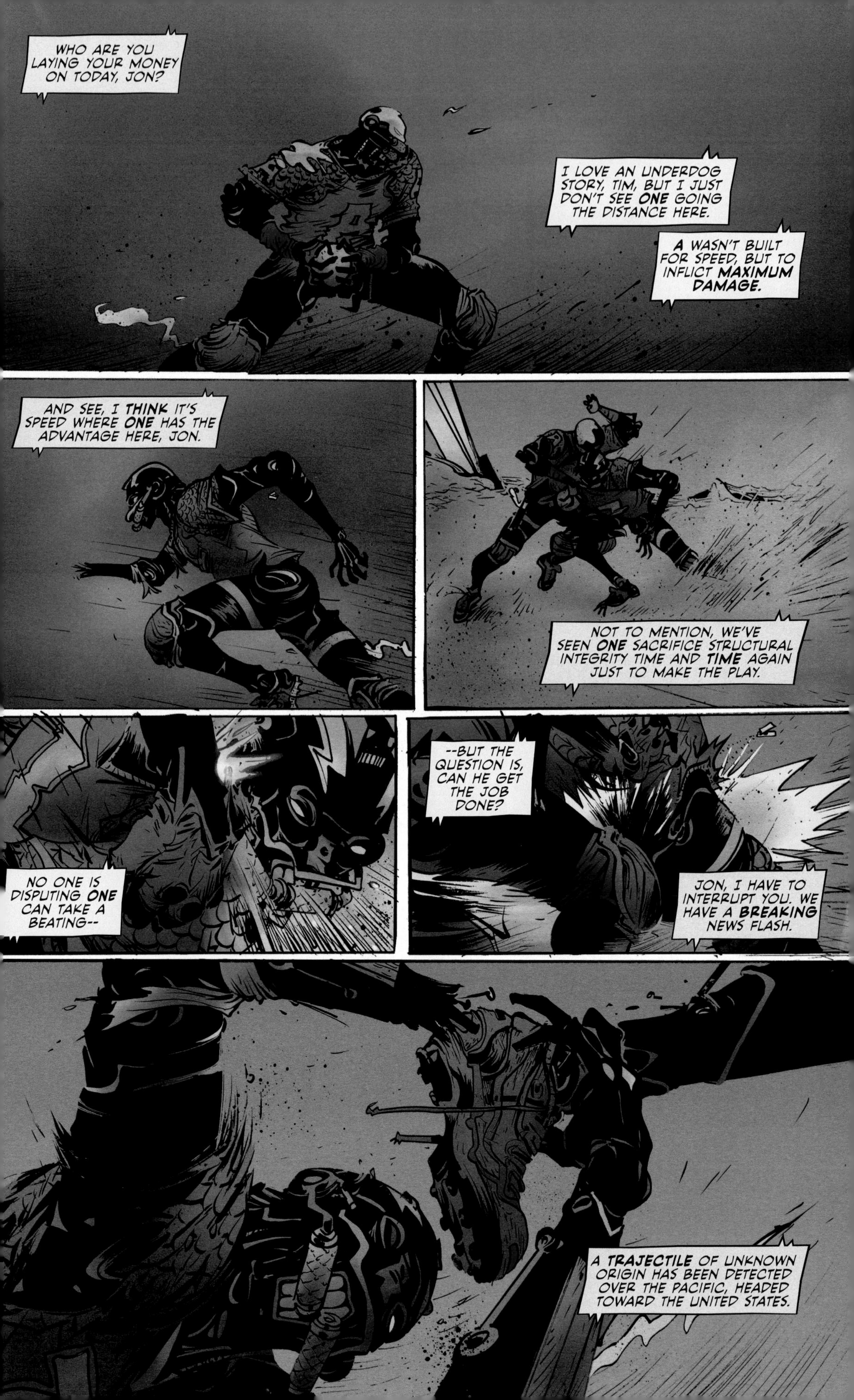
WHO ARE YOU LAYING YOUR MONEY ON TODAY, JON?
I LOVE AN UNDERDOG STORY, TIM, BUT I JUST DON'T SEE ONE GOING THE DISTANCE HERE.
A WASN'T BUILT FOR SPEED, BUT TO INFLICT MAXIMUM DAMAGE.
AND SEE, I THINK IT'S SPEED WHERE ONE HAS THE ADVANTAGE HERE, JON.
NOT TO MENTION, WE'VE SEEN ONE SACRIFICE STRUCTURAL INTEGRITY TIME AND TIME AGAIN JUST TO MAKE THE PLAY.
NO ONE IS DISPUTING ONE CAN TAKE A BEATING--
--BUT THE QUESTION IS, CAN HE GET THE JOB DONE?
JON, I HAVE TO INTERRUPT YOU. WE HAVE A BREAKING NEWS FLASH.
A TRAJECTILE OF UNKNOWN ORIGIN HAS BEEN DETECTED OVER THE PACIFIC, HEADED TOWARD THE UNITED STATES.

CITIZENS ARE URGED TO SEEK SHELTER **IMMEDIATELY.**

AGAIN, FOR THOSE OF YOU JUST JOINING US, THERE IS A TRAJECTILE INBOUND--

TIM, DID YOU SEE **THAT?** I JUST SAW A FLASH OF LIGHT. DID ANYONE ELSE JUST SEE **THAT?** IT WAS OVER TOWARDS THE NOR--

BEEP.

BEEP.

BEEP.

BEEEEEEEEEEEEE EEEEEEEEEEEEEP

THE FOLLOWING MESSAGE IS TRANSMITTED AT THE REQUEST OF THE NORTH AMERICAN SPACE COMMAND. TWO TRAJECTILES HAVE BEEN LAUNCHED WITHIN THE PAST 15 MINUTES. ONE HAS TERMINATED OUTSIDE THE CITY OF SAN DIEGO.

THE FOLLOWING MESSAGE...

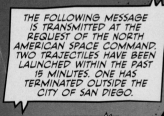

KRS *SHHT*

BEEP-BEEP-BEEP.

WRITTEN BY **PAUL POPE** & **CHRIS HUNT** ART BY **PAUL POPE** COLORS BY **SHAY PLUMMER** LETTERS BY **TOM NAPOLITANO** EDITED BY **JAMIE S. RICH** & **MOLLY MAHAN**

PLUMMER.HUNT.POPE -5-2015

VERTIGO

"FABLES is an excellent series in the tradition of SANDMAN, one that rewards careful attention and loyalty."
—PUBLISHERS WEEKLY

"[A] wonderfully twisted concept...features fairy tale characters banished to the noirish world of present-day New York."
—WASHINGTON POST

"Great fun." —BOOKLIST

READ THE ENTIRE SERIES!

FABLES VOL. 2: ANIMAL FARM

FABLES VOL. 3: STORYBOOK LOVE

FABLES VOL. 4: MARCH OF THE WOODEN SOLDIERS

FABLES VOL. 5: THE MEAN SEASONS

FABLES VOL. 6: HOMELANDS

FABLES VOL. 7: ARABIAN NIGHTS (AND DAYS)

FABLES VOL. 8: WOLVES

FABLES VOL. 9: SONS OF EMPIRE

FABLES VOL. 10: THE GOOD PRINCE

FABLES VOL. 11: WAR AND PIECES

FABLES VOL. 12: THE DARK AGES

FABLES VOL. 13: THE GREAT FABLES CROSS-OVER

FABLES VOL. 14: WITCHES

FABLES VOL. 15: ROSE RED

FABLES VOL. 16: SUPER TEAM

FABLES VOL. 17: INHERIT THE WIND

FABLES VOL. 18: CUBS IN TOYLAND

FABLES VOL. 19: SNOW WHITE

FABLES: 1001 NIGHTS OF SNOWFALL

FABLES: WEREWOLVES OF THE HEARTLAND

PETER & MAX: A FABLES NOVEL

THE FABLES ENCYCLOPEDIA

BILL WILLINGHAM

FABLES VOL. 1: LEGENDS IN EXILE

THE #1 NEW YORK TIMES BEST-SELLING SERIES
FABLES
Legends in Exile
"A top-notch fantasy comic that is on a par with SANDMAN." — Variety
DIRECTOR
BULLFINCH STREET
Bill Willingham
Lan Medina
Steve Leialoha
Craig Hamilton
VERTIGO

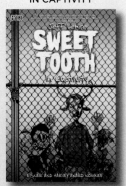
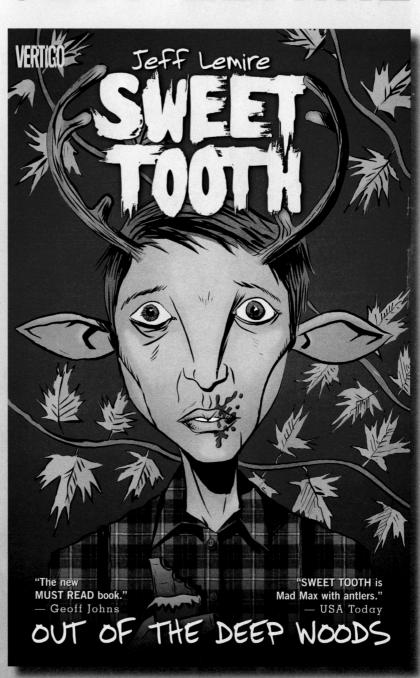

VERTIGO

FROM THE WRITER OF *ANIMAL MAN*
JAMIE DELANO
with JOHN RIDGWAY, ALFREDO ALCALA and others

JOHN CONSTANTINE, HELLBLAZER VOL. 2: THE DEVIL YOU KNOW

with DAVID LLOYD, MARK BUCKINGHAM and others

JOHN CONSTANTINE, HELLBLAZER VOL. 3: THE FEAR MACHINE

with MARK BUCKINGHAM, RICHARD PIERS RAYNER and others

JOHN CONSTANTINE, HELLBLAZER VOL. 4: THE FAMILY MAN

with GRANT MORRISON, NEIL GAIMAN and others

JOHN CONSTANTINE

HELLBLAZER

ORIGINAL SINS

VERTIGO

Jamie Delano John Ridgway
Alfredo Alcala Rick Veitch Tom Mandrake